MAR

OCT – 8 2008

A QUIET
ADJUSTMENT

Also by
Benjamin Markovits

The Syme Papers

Fathers and Daughters

Imposture

BENJAMIN MARKOVITS

—

A Quiet Adjustment

A Novel

W. W. NORTON & COMPANY

NEW YORK LONDON

For information about permission to reproduce
selections from this book, write to Permissions,
W. W. Norton & Company, Inc.,
500 Fifth Avenue, New York, NY 10110

For information about special discounts for bulk
purchases, please contact W. W. Norton Special Sales at
specialsales@wwnorton.com or 800-233-4830

Manufacturing by Courier Westford
Book design by Barbara M. Bachman
Production manager: Devon Zahn

LIBRARY OF CONGRESS
CATALOGING-IN-PUBLICATION DATA

Markovits, Benjamin.
A quiet adjustment : a novel / Benjamin Markovits.
—1st American ed.
p. cm.
ISBN 978-0-393-06700-2
1. Byron, Anne Isabella Milbanke Byron, Baroness,
1792–1860—Fiction. 2. Byron, George Gordon Byron,
Baron, 1788–1824—Fiction.
3. Leigh, Augusta, 1784–1851—Fiction. 4. Triangles
(Interpersonal relations)—Fiction. I. Title.
PS3613.A7543Q54 2008
813'.6—dc22   2008001292

W. W. Norton & Company, Inc.
500 Fifth Avenue, New York, N.Y. 10110
www.wwnorton.com

W. W. Norton & Company Ltd.
Castle House, 75/76 Wells Street, London W1T 3QT

1 2 3 4 5 6 7 8 9 0

For Stephanie

A QUIET

ADJUSTMENT

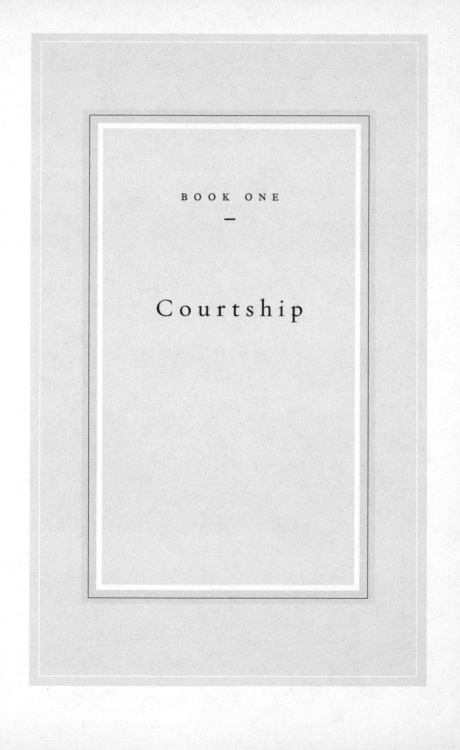

BOOK ONE

—

Courtship

Chapter One

—

SHE HAD BEEN EXPECTING an invitation—Lady Caroline had mentioned it to her—but when it came, Annabella wasted much of her morning over it in pleasant indecision. There were days to be filled; one must occupy them somehow. The bedroom she'd been given overlooked a bricked-in lawn (the red and green refreshingly contrasting); and she returned to it after breakfast and set the card on the mantelpiece, which was otherwise rather bare. Annabella had been taught to be frugal, and she had little talent for those embroideries by which women ornament not only their persons and surroundings but the passage of time itself. It was March, a bright cold day, and the ashy remains of her night's fire gave off a surprising sullen heat, for which she was not ungrateful. Guests at a house often retire to their rooms to think—Annabella justified her reclusion. But she was honest enough to admit that introspection is the crutch of the shy; it is what they get by on.

The card bore the stamp of the Melbournes': the crest of a lion with a hart peering out of its mouth. Its eye, large and bright, expressed either fear or impishness. The invitation itself had a kind of bullying brevity, which left little scope for demurral.

. . .

LADY CAROLINE INVITES YOU TO A WALTZING PARTY
AFTER BREAKFAST AT MELBOURNE HOUSE.
SHE PROMISES PROFESSIONAL INSTRUCTION.

The pressure of that promise made Annabella smile: how very like Caroline; one must always enjoy oneself on her terms. A time and a date were given. The question was, should she go? It was the kind of choice that involved Annabella's deepest intuitions, her sense of propriety. And since she enjoyed the exercise of it and trusted her own judgement, she could treat with complacence any decision arrived at. These periods of reflection offered her an excuse to con-sider the world through her sharpest lens.

She rang a bell and called for tea. There was the gossip to be weighed; Annabella was not such a blue that she considered it beneath her to indulge a little her human curiosity. Lady Caroline's affair with Lord Byron had begun to be talked about. The lovers were growing careless of appearances. Caroline, at first, had stolen to Lord Byron's rooms in various disguises; but these had in the course of their relations become not so much perfunctorily adopted as worn for a kind of show, whose purpose was very far from concealment. A page's outfit (that was the story) would, Annabella supposed, rather bring out than obscure the modesty of Caroline's feminine charms. What an odd mix of ease and restless-ness she was. Her name misrepresented her: Caroline was careless, she never cared. Lord Byron might be credited with greater discre-tion; but then, the gallantry of his role forbade too public a chas-tisement. He kept up an *air* of indifference to propriety, and Annabella was worldly enough to concede that it was just that indifference which was so improper. She must decide whether to give (this was the phrase she used from the comfort of her easy chair) 'the sanction of her attendance' to Lady Caroline—to Lord

Byron himself for that matter, a much more exciting proposition. She had never met the young poet before; it was just possible he would be there.

Annabella was nineteen years old. She reminded herself, smiling, that not nearly so much depended on her choice as she supposed—a reflection that hardly helped her to a decision. Her life never seemed to change, yet she was always being pushed into making choices: a sort of paradox that she was happy, for once, to reduce to simpler terms. She didn't want to be thought a prude, but she did not want to be thought the opposite of prudish, either. A knock at the door announced the arrival of refreshments. Tea was served in a little Sèvres pot too hot to touch; a plate of crumpets was set beside it. The only thing to spoil her pleasant appetite and spirits was the thought of getting butter on her fingers.

In the end, the presence of Lady Melbourne decided her. The party was to be held at her house. Lady Melbourne was not only Caroline's mother-in-law but also Annabella's aunt. There could be nothing improper in fulfilling the duty of a niece. Annabella, not for the first time that year, took comfort from the cushioning she had received in London from family connections: from aunts and godmothers and such. She was looked out for, but she was given her lease, too, and the length of it, really, was very much up to her. Besides, it was only a question of waltzing after breakfast. It was not a ball, or anything like one. Yes, she would go; and she was perfectly willing to admit that the chance of meeting Lord Byron had played a part in her decision—not that she ever blindly followed the fashions. Annabella had as yet refused to read *Childe Harold*, his 'remarkable poem', which had come out two months before to an acclaim excited as much by curiosity as admiration. Still, she was determined, if his *acquaintance* came her way, not to refuse *that*. She tested the tea against her lips; it was almost cool enough to drink. Among other things, she reasoned (warming her hands on the cup), a sense of her own deserts compelled her to accept the friendship of notable men. She little doubted her ability to 'live up to it', just as she trusted to her wit the acquisition of new words. Her powers of expression, she had every faith, were equal to the largest vocabulary.

The morning of the party, another fine, clear March day with a bloom of chill upon it, inevitably arrived. Annabella decided to walk from Cumberland Place. She was staying for the season at Gosford House—it seemed that half the people she knew in London had their houses named after them. The Gosfords were friends of Annabella's parents, who were expected shortly from their country home in Yorkshire. The final push to her decision had been the consciousness of their arrival. She wanted to enjoy her freedom from them; she wanted to greet them with the news of an experience. The walk took her no more than ten minutes; still, she turned gratefully from the current of Piccadilly into the quieter approach of Melbourne House. Miss Elphinstone, famously shy and beautiful, was on the steps before her. Annabella recognized her from behind. She was wearing a bright green dress, which gave to her tall and delicate figure the appearance of the sylvan. It mortified Annabella that Miss Elphinstone stopped short, with a happy smile, at the sound of her footstep; that they entered the house together. Her own modest stature, pleasant round face, and respectable dimity gown could not help looking poorer for the contrast.

The party was almost complete when the pair of them entered, arm in arm. A glance at Lady Caroline gave Annabella her first real misgiving of impropriety: not so much for anything the woman did or said as for what she might be supposed capable of feeling. Perhaps Caroline *did* care—too much, in fact. She was standing in the middle of the room, talking to a small bald-headed man with improbably long arms. Musicians scraped themselves into tune. The bones of Caroline's narrow figure were largely hidden in the fall of her dress, which hung straight down from her shoulders to her knees. There seemed to be nothing along the way to give it a shape, an absence that distinctly gestured at what was missing. She looked like a boy, almost; her movements had the freedom of a boy's. The man, who was wearing a gold waistcoat, took her by the elbow and hand and began to adjust the angle between them. But Caroline was hardly attending. She stared across the room over his shoulder to where a young couple stood, awkwardly attempting the intimate decorous embrace required by the dance. Rather handsome they looked, too. He had the kind of eloquent formal beauty that gives an illusion of its owner's good taste; she, a little softer, weaker—deviations from perfection all on the side of gentleness. Caroline winced at the sight of them. Her boyish pretty face was too quick in its expressions to carry much weight, but what Annabella saw in it was unhappiness, not in the least relieved by the shrewder, less pleasant look of calculation. Miss Elphinstone bent down to whisper, 'That's his sister, Mrs Leigh.'

'Who?' Annabella replied.

'The lady, I mean; the lady dancing with Lord Byron.'

So, there he was; she had seen him at last.

There was something about the hour (eleven o'clock) and the spring sunshine (cold and colourless) and the rectangles of dust, which had gathered under several tables and lay geometrically revealed when those articles of furniture were pushed against the French windows, that suggested nothing so much as a school hall and a morning's lecture. The music began in earnest. In the spirit of education, Annabella felt that she could do wholehearted justice to the dance. She didn't dare approach Lord Byron herself. Her best hope of an introduction, she believed, was to attract his attention by taking on a kind of public role in the party. Not that she was, in a general way, very forward. Annabella suffered, as her mother once put it, from a diffidence both chronic and mild. It might be easily overcome but never shaken off. And there was nothing like a 'task at hand' to rouse her pride to the suppression of those softer instincts that generally enfeebled her efforts at flirtation. The man in the gold waistcoat was, it turned out, the dancing-master: the source of 'professional instruction' promised in the invitation. A small but authentic German named Wohlkrank, he had been 'imported' by Lady Caroline 'for the season'. Herr Wohlkrank spotted in Annabella 'an ally'—a preference she found very flattering at the time. It struck her only later, in the aftermath of spent happiness, as a proof of something improper or unsuitable about her manners or figure. She couldn't quite keep out of her mind the form his flattery took. 'Such ankles, my dear,' he cried, clapping, 'and such knees!'

Yet what changes a year in London had rung in her! A year of proposals and rejections, in perfectly equal measure (not to mention of balls, of operas, and at-homes) had taught, as she once put it to herself, a quiet country lamb occasionally to interrupt her silences and 'baah with the rest of society'. Well, she was baahing now. In a rush of blood, she publicly and repeatedly confessed that though she had no ear for music she had 'feet for numbers'. The waltz had undone the spirits of many bolder girls than she, not so much for the intricacy of its steps as for the enforced pressure of the gentlemen against their breasts—a species of contact which, however desirable it might appear under the influence of punch and the heat of evening lamps, seemed more difficult to stomach before tea. It was gratifying to see how many graceful ladies appealed to Annabella for assistance, preferring her lead to that of the men who stood and stared along the circumference of the ballroom, drying their sweaty hands inside their pockets.

Mrs Leigh was not one of these. She seemed sufficiently occupied by her brother's attentions. 'Will you pinch me, my dear,'
Annabella heard her whisper, 'if I step on your foot?' 'You can be
sure I won't *kick*,' Lord Byron said. Part of the charm of the pair of
them lay in their subtly varied reflections of each other. Her face,
rounder and softer than his, placed the same emphasis on the ver-
tical line of nose and chin. They shared, too, those little apostro-
phes at the centre of their lips, which suggested either habitual
scorn or a sharp intake of breath. There was, in his case, an inclination to the former; and though *her* countenance tended towards
the more amiable alternative, its expression was compounded by
something shy or silly about the jointure of the nose and forehead,
a stupid flatness: as if the palm of her maker's hand had rested
carelessly against her face as she lay cooling.

Her figure, however, was very good and might, Annabella privately conceded, have roused the envy of an envious mind. Mrs
Leigh possessed that combination of stillness and grace which the
poets had begun to term 'ethereal'. Annabella had a passion for
the modern school, but she was by no means a slave to its jargon.
She guessed how much in the expression of a figure, or even of a
pose, lay outside the scope of intention. Most likely the poor
woman—a mother already of three or four—was simply too anxious to eat; and though Annabella could claim her own share of
nerves, she was far too sensible to let them rob her of an appetite.
Lord Byron referred to his sister as 'Gus' or, sometimes, 'Goose'.
She was unspeakably shy; there was no question of that. The
blood filling her face had given her skin the trembling surface perfection of a liquid brimming in its cup. The proper object of
Annabella's envy was the fact that Mrs Leigh's very shyness
seemed to centre upon herself the attention of the men surrounding her. Annabella had, with a stiffness of will, overcome her own
reserve only to find herself allied to the dancing-master and

instructing, often by hand and foot, the other girls: a proximity that offered her, if nothing else, too vivid a sense of what the feminine body in touch and smell suggested to a man.

No doubt Lord Byron played his part in attracting to Mrs Leigh the eyes of that assembly. Annabella could not keep her own off the pair of them. As Miss Elphinstone swung in her arms, she just glanced across her shoulder to see if either the poet or that helplessly beautiful woman were following her lead. Annabella lacked both sister and brother, and there was something in their easy, though not ungallant, intimacy that made her ache to feel its absence in her own life. She never forgot this first sight of him, in spite of the heap of other less happy visions that overlaid it: the famous, lame-footed poet attempting to lead his sister through the steps of the latest dance, while the music beat out of time to their affectionate and staggering embrace. Afterwards she reflected, with just enough good humour to sweeten her embarrassment, that the first words she had spoken in his hearing were 'one two three, one two three, one two three'—an association with the mathematical she later found it hard to shake off.

Chapter Two

—

SHE MET HIM AGAIN a week later at a lecture given by Mr Campbell at the Royal Institute; by this time, she had read his book. She sat in the row behind him—close enough, had she wished it, to trace the line of his neck with her finger. But her hands were cold with nerves in any case; and even the thought of touching his fair skin produced in him, it almost seemed to her, a chilly shudder. She imagined saying to him, 'I have read your book', a phrase whose insistent repetition in her consciousness precluded much attention to Mr Campbell. Instead, she argued at silent length her conception of the merits and demerits of *Childe Harold*. And whenever there was a pause in her thoughts or a hush in the hall, she had to restrain herself from leaning forwards and whispering in his ear, 'I have read your book. Would you like to hear what I think of it?'

She went home afterwards almost feverish with unspoken feeling. Her silence had produced in her something like a fit of temper; at least, she wished to be left alone with her thoughts—she wanted, quietly, to count them up. Home, of course, was the house of Lord and Lady Gosford, the friends of her parents, who had lately arrived. It surprised her, how little she had trusted her own show of gratitude at the family reunion. Her sleeping quarters, for one thing, had been shifted to the top floor; and as she turned on the landing, her mother called to her from her former bedroom and asked her to come in.

'Did you enjoy the lecture?' Lady Milbanke asked. She sat at her dressing table. Judy (her mother's family nickname) was never an idle woman: a worthy heap of correspondence lay turned over at her right hand.

'I did,' was her daughter's answer.

'And what did you learn?'

It was rare in Annabella not to volunteer for the general improvement her own units of edification. 'I learned,' she nearly answered, 'the shape of Lord Byron's head.' Instead she replied, 'Mr Campbell described, in the most personal terms, the Sinking Fund of the Imagination on which a poet could rely as he grew older.'

'Did you like his text? Did you agree with it?'

Theirs was a family in which such quizzing was treated as the proper commerce of affection and curiosity, but Annabella met it with an answer perhaps a little deficient in both. 'No, I did not. In that light, making verses scarcely strikes me as a nobler activity than making mayonnaise; it is only a question of the quantity that can be got out of the smallest expenditure of eggs.'

Judy, who was more efficient than unkind, turned to look closely at her daughter. Her eyes, Annabella couldn't help remarking, were narrowly set and gave to her forehead the appearance of a squint; her mother had not aged kindly. Her hair, cut short behind as a girl's, only emphasized something practical and unadorned about her station in life. Beauty in her presence seemed an excess rather than a quality. She was a keen horsewoman, and her complexion had suffered from exposure to the wind—one of Judy's characteristic oddities was that she insisted on Annabella's retaining the babyish milk-white perfection of her own countenance. 'I suppose, when called upon, you will learn a greater appreciation for the virtue of drawing out,' she now said, 'otherwise known as making do.' Annabella bowed her head, not for the first time conscious of being carefully and slowly brought along. There was a lesson appropriate to every stage. If she tolerated the management it was only because its first principle seemed to be a complete conviction in her own extraordinary possibilities. Judy was inclined to give her daughter's reticence the kindest interpretation (and the one most flattering to herself). She inquired if her daughter was suffering from a headache? and when Annabella meekly nodded, she was dismissed.

She had for some years failed to enjoy that perfect sympathy of spirits with her mother which her more idealistic notions of home life seemed to require of her. This proved an irritating imperfection. She could relieve it only like an ordinary itch, by scratching at it. Annabella, in the sanctum of her thoughts, sometimes indulged ungenerous feelings towards her mother—she was a sexless, overbearing, etc.—which soon shamed her into love again.

Retiring to her room, she found in it little enough to occupy her. Solitude always seemed to place before her, with the distinctness almost of a mirrored reflection, an image of herself to stare at; and she turned for a kind of relief to the other image that had begun to absorb her thoughts. She decided to spend the time before dinner writing up her impressions of Lord Byron in her diary, but she found herself hesitating to fix these in ink—not so much out of fear at having them read over, by her mother, for example, as at the prospect of having to admit them to herself.

After the lecture, she had become entangled in the stream of people pushing past. She only just escaped at the door to the hall, where she stopped a minute, hoping to let Lord Byron overtake her. But he had been caught up in what she could only presume was a group of his friends, who were lobbying him to make some kind of speech or recitation on the stage where Mr Campbell had been speaking. She heard him say, 'I believe you mock me.' He was smiling broadly, but his face was pink. Mr Campbell himself, however, clearly flattered by the poet's attendance, offered him a copy of his celebrated book, which he had been reading; and a handful of people waited at the door in case the famous young man could be persuaded into a performance. He bowed at last and without lifting his voice, in perfectly clear tones, declared his intention of playing what he called the part of Childe Harold in the manner of one Gentleman Jackson, whom he had overheard himself that morning, before a lesson, rehearsing certain scenes from the poem. He proceeded to recite his own verses in a broad angry accent that contorted the beautiful symmetry of his features. His friends drowned him out in applause, and his face broke into lines of laughter which so little suited Annabella's tender reading of the character, either of hero or poet, that she fled the pocket of onlookers into the cold spring day. She had not supposed him happy or light-hearted—qualities that threatened to nip her growing sympathies in the bud.

It was the image of their first meeting, then, at Melbourne House, that rose before her inward eye, and the thought of that dancing pair soon banished all temporary annoyance. There was something in their sibling familiarity, which seemed so natural and attentive, that led her to imagine that she possessed in the quiet of intimacy just those qualities which they took pleasure in 'drawing out' from each other. (That phrase of Judy's had come to mind. It often astonished Annabella how difficult she found it to escape the pattern of her mother's thoughts.) Augusta, or 'Gus' or 'Goose' (though she didn't yet dare to assert the privilege of a nickname) seemed a woman particularly susceptible to the comfort that Annabella trusted herself to be capable of giving. Her shyness, partly overcome, could help her to relieve another's; and it was characteristic, Annabella thought, of her better nature that her own black moods inspired in her mainly the desire to console others.

Of course, she was conscious, no one more so, of the little delusions excited by celebrity of any kind: of reciprocal interest or knowledge. And certainly Lord Byron had suffered his share of admirers. It might be kinder (or shrewder) to direct one's sympathies at *her* who was herself the object of Lord Byron's care. Annabella was enough of a gossip to be in perfect possession of the family history. Their father had remarried after the death of Augusta's mother. A second child, a son, was eventually born, but by this stage the first had been committed to the care of relations from whom her father had become effectually estranged. His children, inevitably, shared in that estrangement, for a period that Lord Byron had expressed himself determined to make up for. Not the least proof of his honourable nature was the extent to which, as Annabella herself had observed, he had lived up to his word.

She dipped her pen and wrote, 'My dearest Augusta,' and stopped short. Her diary, half against her will, had begun to shape itself into a letter. She need hardly stay shy, after all, of his sister, and the phrase itself seemed to entitle her to intimacies; it loosened her tongue. What she wished to make clear was 'that *she too* had known what it meant to suffer from the absence of a beloved sibling. She too understood the peculiarly affecting claims of a *partial relation*—those curious admixtures of likeness and dissimilarity, which in the happiest instances offered such a perfect medium between the pleasures of friendship and of family.' Annabella's mother had a sister who died young, and that sister had had a child, who was brought up as one of her own by Judy. And how welcome, at the time, seemed that increase to the family sum. 'Their cousinship quickly took on the deep sisterly feeling inspired by the remoteness of their situation: a charming house in

Seaham, a quiet charming village on the Yorkshire coast, where the only society for miles around depended on their obligations to the tenantry and the pleasure they took in their own.'

A loving house, undeniably, of which she herself was the 'cherished pet'; and if (her confession was growing in scope) Annabella 'occasionally quarrelled with her mother, as she had begun to do, it was only the result of that daunting example Judy had set of what a woman with all the privileges of rank and talent was capable of achieving. Her energy, her charity, her curiosity were famous in the parish; and few of her fellow parishioners had the heart to mock or resent that completeness of moral persuasion from which they themselves had so frequently benefited.' Annabella, as she refreshed her pen, refrained from adding (and only just whispered to herself) that her mother's fondness for a drink had recently taken on a more secret character; and there were, she now recalled, the remains of a bottle of sherry standing uncorked beside the papers on Lady Milbanke's table. Its medicinal scent had only just penetrated Annabella's picture of her mother's dressing room—adding its influence, strangely, to a sense of Judy's inviolable privacy.

'I shall never forget,' she wrote now, 'the morning my cousin left us to be married. I had prayed for that event,' she added, when it struck her as odd to be rehearsing such scenes for a stranger's benefit from the quiet of her room in Gosford House. Her childhood, however, had been so poor in incidents that she stored them up as a kind of precious coin—to be spent, from time to time, on intimacies. 'It was, I thought, to ensure her happiness,' she continued, and the simple truth of her confession began to impress itself upon her. 'But when after a long engagement the wedding finally arrived, when I passed her apartment in all the sudden disrepair of evacuation, the misery of my loss became insupportable to me. I remember feeling for the first time as if the actual scene was visionary. I made one attempt to confide my despair to her who was its object. I had been weeping and kissing Sophy's neck. My wet lips tasted the heat that they themselves had pressed upon her skin; there was nothing of her own. She was cool as ice. "What shall I do without you?" I asked. "What shall I do with *them?*" "Marry," was her answer, with a shrill laugh. It struck me, at twelve years old, as a contemptuous sort of reproof, and I shrank into an existence of solitary reverie that remained largely unbroken until my coming out. It being understood, of course, that my family relations, warm and enveloping as they were, seemed less and less to involve any kind of excursion from the kingdom of my solitude.'

'What are you writing?'

There had been no knock at her door, only a fat hand gripping the edge of it and the hesitant step of a large foot. It warmed her, unreservedly, that her father still trusted sufficiently to their relationship to admit himself unannounced into her bedroom. She looked up at Sir Ralph. His face, amiable as an egg, was turned on her; and she recognized in his loose cheeks and doubled chin the foolish excess to which her own appetites would incline her, unchecked. His eyes, wide rather than large, had a gentleness that owed a great deal to what Annabella thought of as their slowness of expression. He had a habit of repeating himself and did so now—'What are you writing?'—as he peered over her shoulder against the glow of her lamp.

'My diary,' she said, feeling not so much guilty over her slight evasion as forced unpleasantly into a consciousness of it. She smoothed her hand over the paper. What she wanted above all— and it had struck her more and more, lately, the pressing need of it—was a language in which she could reconcile the duty of honesty to her growing appetite for secrecy. There must or should be terms of confession in which neither truth nor privacy was sacrificed to the other.

'Mother thought you was looking hipped,' he said, 'and I wondered if you wanted a game of chess before supper. I know how it cheers you to beat me.'

'Yes, that is just what I *should* like.'

The drawing room was empty when they descended to it. A table had been permanently arranged against the tall corner window; it overlooked a chestnut tree, spreading its shade on the street. The chair creaked as Sir Ralph rested his weight on it; he always, as he remarked, over-indulged himself in London. There was something about the city in season that dispirited him: such energy and youthful gaiety. He had never himself in his own youth participated in the pleasures of it, much. That is, before he had set his sights upon her mother; and *then* he had condescended to 'enjoy himself,' as he put it, 'only as much as was required to gain his prize, and no more.' They began to play; Annabella as usual deferred to her father the opening sally. It was among the carefully nurtured family illusions that Sir Ralph was shy and slow in conversation. In fact, he had a tremendous patience for repetition and those layered confessions it was capable of easing away. The difference that age had wrought in him, he continued, was, that while he had always detested the buzz of social life, he had lately begun to be ashamed of his comfortable, solitary inclinations. And he drank too much and ate too much to occupy those appetites that flourished in him by way of compensation. Judy and he intended shortly to return to Seaham, once they had seen Annabella happily established. 'It did his heart good,' he added, and his daughter guessed at once that this was the conclusion towards which he had with some difficulty been working himself up, 'to see how . . . graciously Annabella had taken to *the scene*.'

His real intention, his daughter suspected, was only clothed in praise. He wanted to find out (perhaps her mother had sent him) just what it was that had put Annabella in a pet. It could only be, they reasonably supposed, a question of love. He may have hoped by admitting his own penchant for withdrawal to set the stage for her more romantic confession. And among the calculations that occupied Annabella, as her bishop began to take control of the board, was whether she was confident enough in her feelings to submit them to the test of her father's curiosity. Was there any-thing—and her attraction as yet could hardly be defined by its object, so slight had their acquaintance been—about her attitude towards that family which could lead to a more general exposure? She said, as she exchanged, with a knock of pieces, her castle for his knight, 'I have been reading, in the company of half of London, the adventures of *Childe Harold*; in fact, just this afternoon I fin-ished. Have you seen it? If not, I shall lend you my copy. I should like to hear what you think.'

He had not; it would give him the greatest pleasure, etc.

'In general, as you know,' she continued, 'I disdain to follow fashions; but there are occasions when they reach such a fever as to require of the spectator, at the very least, his opinion of the fashion itself. It was in this spirit that I began to read, but I soon found that there was more to sustain my interest than a mere social curiosity. It contains many stanzas'—Annabella's philo-sophical vein had always been indulged with scarcely discernible irony, and Sir Ralph listened patiently now—'in the best style of poetry; if anything, he is too much of a mannerist. That is, he wants variety in the turns of his expression. He excels most in the delineation of deep feeling, in reflections relative to human nature. I thought of him just now, Papa, because his case makes an interesting contrast to your own: he despairs of an excess of that capacity for whose deficiency in yourself you have expressed such regret. I mean, the capacity for taking pleasure. That despair frames the moral of his *Pilgrimage*—one which, I think, no one need shame himself for admiring. It has given me at least one sleepless night; and, as you have seen, a sleepy head-achy sort of a day.'

'There is, of course,' Ralph was quick to agree, 'nothing shameful in that.'

Annabella had grown accustomed to beating her father, regularly and with something like carelessness, at chess. She had his king now in a terrible thicket of pawns, and he was silent a minute as he considered his situation. 'No, there is no help,' he concluded. His face grew very red in thoughtfulness. The blonde grey hairs of his brows stood out palely and his eyes took on a blinking dimness: he seemed old, at odds and ends. Annabella was but thirteen when she first defeated her father at chess. Victory had surprised and delighted her; it had set up their relation to each other for years to come. She had just begun to bristle at her mother's constant example and used to greet Sir Ralph's returns from parliament with something like a lover's restless welcome. 'Shall we have a game, father, before dinner? Shall we just sit down—you see, I have laid out the table . . .' But she had lately had to suppress a strange sort of disinclination to watching him lose. Partly, to be sure, out of pity; but her sense of triumph did not lack the faint frictive energy of impatience, which she had recently learned to recognize in her mother's own treatment of Sir Ralph. He was no fool; his temper was good; his taste in matters of wit and poetry was both joyously inclined and well considered; but there was something about his good nature that inspired, even in the kindest and best-disposed of his acquaintance, the desire to abuse it. And Annabella could not help resenting in him a weakness that, she suspected, such resentment would help her to expunge from her own disposition.

In a guilty burst of more filial spirit, she said, 'I saw him, Lord Byron, that is, today for the second time. We danced together, I mean, we danced separately, at a waltzing party given by Lady

Caroline last week. He waltzed with his sister, a very pretty woman though shy as a wren. And then I read his poem and then I met him again at Mr Campbell's lecture. It was particularly gratifying for me, so soon after finishing, to test my sensibilities, my reading of his verse, against what I saw of his actual character, revealed in person.'

'And what,' Ralph asked, 'of his actual character, did you see revealed?'

After a hesitation: 'Mostly the back of his head.'

It was one of those little triumphs of her good humour that were only ever brought out by Sir Ralph. Even so, she suspected, in that half-second of consideration, an inclination to deceive. She wanted to keep from her father any sense of the seriousness of her . . . preoccupation—an intention that constituted nothing less than the first acknowledgement of it to herself.

At dinner, *Childe Harold* came up again in conversation—specifically, the moral character of its author. Lady Gosford had not read the poem, a fact which she happily admitted and which in no way restricted her interest in or contribution to the discussion. She was a round comfortable woman, in whom the pleasures of the table had preserved, by the outward pressure on her fattening face, something youthful and good-natured in her countenance. Lady Milbanke was, by force of opposition if nothing else, her great and particular friend. And though their relations, especially in the course of the Milbankes' extended stays in London, were not without their little frictions, the two old companions were on the whole each grateful for the correcting influence of the other. Their friendship took shape from their competing philosophies; and where Judy was, at least in principle, strict, abstemious and actively charitable, Lady Gosford indulged her own and others' appetites with equal complacence.

She now took the side of Lord Byron's admirers. 'No harm could come,' she insisted, 'of a miserable libertine, whose various immoralities serve only the cause of his unhappiness. Besides,' she added, 'my own experience suggests to me that his sins are more talked about than read.' She drained her claret and gestured for more. As the butler made his rounds, Judy (Annabella was pleased to note) placed her hand above the glass. An act of abstinence that her daughter delighted in, not so much as an example of her pretensions or as a step towards her reform, but out of admiration for Judy's self-control: no private weakness could corrupt Lady Milbanke's public sense of her position. 'You take him altogether too willingly at his own estimation,' she countered. 'I have glanced over the volume. That famous misery is only the fancy dress of his desires. He pinches himself into it as some women powder their faces, to look interesting. It is really the worst of his bad example that he has made a fashion of unhappiness. I should almost prefer it that the young surrendered to the greatest of vices; instead, they take on the aspect of them and study to appear melancholy. No, the real wickedness of *Childe Harold* is a peculiar form of hypocrisy in which everybody strives to seem much worse than they really are.'

'Do you not think him sincere?' Sir Ralph inquired of his wife. 'I do not.'

'But surely that is a question that cannot be answered merely from a perusal of the text. It requires a most particular knowledge,' Lord Gosford, who had kept silent, now intruded, 'of correspondence between word and deed.' A thin, straight-backed man, he presented to the company's view rather the surface shine of spectacles than his colourless eyes. Sir Ralph was somewhat in awe of him. Ralph was a conscientious but quiet parliamentarian; and though Lord Gosford spoke little enough in the House, that little was seen as being very much to the point. His influence was of the kind that consisted as much in the rumour of it as in its original force. His opinions were more sought after than known. In the friendship of their marriages, Ralph had made an amiable alliance with Lady Gosford—to be comfortable together; but their relations, they both suspected, lacked the electric charge of Judy and Lord Gosford's quarrelling.

'I believe,' Sir Ralph said, 'that we have to hand a source of that particular knowledge.' Annabella had already begun to blush, as her father proudly turned towards her. 'Did you not dance with him, my dear?'

'I did not,' she said. 'He danced exclusively with his sister.'

'But you have met him, have you not?'

'I have not had the honour of an introduction.'

'Come, come,' Lord Gosford interrupted. 'You have seen him; you have formed an opinion.'

Annabella bowed her head. Lady Milbanke looked at her, raising her thin lips into a smile. She enjoyed with a not unloving detachment any occasion for putting her daughter to the test. 'And will you favour us with that opinion, my dear?' Nor was Annabella, for all her shyness, reluctant to claim her share of the conversation. She had been the almost unhoped-for consolation of her parents' later days. After fifteen years of marriage, they had as good as resigned themselves to childlessness. And the sense of blessing, which her birth had bestowed upon the Milbankes, had only increased as Annabella grew to womanhood. Each stage of her youth had brought home to her parents a consciousness of that variety of life with which her late arrival had favoured them, and nothing had engaged their curiosity more than her coming out. Annabella, as she began to speak, felt the warmth not of nerves but of their combined looks; and she was sufficiently the daughter of her parents' love that she believed their admiration to be no more than her natural due.

'I have seen him now,' she said, addressing her eyes to Lord Gosford, 'twice. Once, at a waltzing-party got up by Lady Caroline, and today at a lecture. He appears to be a very independent observer of mankind—his views of life participate that bitterness of temper which, I believe, is partly constitutional and the cause of much of his wretchedness. His mouth continually betrays the acrimony of his spirit. I should add that I have seen him humorous, I have seen him playing the fool; but to my taste, unhappiness suits him better than its inverse. It certainly comes more naturally. His eye is restlessly thoughtful. He talks much and I have heard some of his conversation, which sounds like the true sentiments of the speaker. I should judge him sincere; at least, as far as he can be in society ... He often hides his mouth with his hand when speaking, a diffidence as pleasing as it is surprising in one little noted for the delicacy of his views.'

There was a silence in which Annabella ventured to add, with a degree of mischievous intent she could scarcely measure herself, 'He argued, as I hear, with all his family; this was the cause of his foreign travels. My great friend Mary Montgomery, you know, is acquainted with him and was very much shocked at hearing him say, "Thank heaven! I have quarrelled with my mother for ever."'

'There,' cried Lady Gosford, 'surely there can be no greater proof of his sincerity!'

Lady Milbanke bowed and smiled at her old friend, to acknowledge the joke at her expense. Motherhood was the subject of many of their disagreements; Lady Gosford was childless and occasionally bridled at Judy's maternal certitudes. She was glad of any chance to score a point off them. 'I suspect from what I've seen of her that Mary was rather amused than shocked,' Judy answered. 'My daughter seems happy to take Lord Byron at his word. I'm sure he could not have painted a better picture of one of his heroes.

Perhaps he even trusts the likeness himself—I should not venture to say.'

'In that case,' Lord Gosford declared, with the briskness of a final judgement, 'we may take it that you have every faith in his sincerity, if nothing else; which was as far as our question went.'

'That depends,' Judy replied, 'on whether sincerity is to be considered a talent or a virtue. If a virtue, by all means, credit him with as much sincerity as you like; I am sure his intentions are honest. But if we mean by sincerity a talent for examining our own feelings, for judging them in the full justice of indifference, and for expressing them as clearly, as precisely, as it lies within our power to do—then no, the question is only just begun.'

'Surely,' Lady Gosford said, 'no one can doubt Lord Byron's eloquence. Of that, the booksellers themselves have the happy proof.'

'No, in his eloquence I have every faith and have seen by my daughter's account some evidence of his power to persuade. But we are, I believe, generally accustomed in talking of persuasion to distinguish between the truth of its object and the facility with which it is gained.'

'And yet,' Annabella interjected, 'and I have felt the force of it myself, there is a kind of eloquence that can properly be said to *create truth*, even where there was none before. Perhaps that is what I meant to convey in my picture of his character and conversation. It is certainly the impression he makes upon everyone around him.'

'Well,' Lady Gosford announced with some satisfaction, 'there is only one thing to be done: we must make a trial of him ourselves.' It was suggested that Sir Ralph might provide the best means of introduction, seeing that his sister, Lady Melbourne, was well known to be Lord Byron's favourite adviser—by necessity almost, as her daughter-in-law, Lady Caroline, had begun to 'express such unguarded preference' for the poet. But Sir Ralph, though he was fond of his sister Elizabeth, said he disliked exposing any of his family to her taste for gossiping and begged very humbly to be excused from playing a part in their scheme. Annabella could not be sure whether a feeling of gratitude towards her father or impatience with him predominated in her at hearing this timid speech. At that point, Lady Gosford offered to 'speak to my dear friend Lady Cowper, who is on the best of terms with Lady Kinnaird—owing perversely, it is said, to her having formerly refused *Lord* Kinnaird, none other than the poet's banker. I trust, Lord Gosford, you have no objection to a supper party?'

He had none, and so the matter was decided upon—to everyone's satisfaction perhaps but Annabella's own. She had taken comfort from the thought of keeping to herself something for her mother to disapprove of.

Before retiring, Annabella stopped in again to bid her mother goodnight. Her rebellious impulses were always followed first by remorse and then by a childish wish for conciliation. She feared, as she declared to Lady Milbanke's back or rather to the reflection of her face in the dressing-mirror, that her reference to Byron's family quarrels might have struck her mother as improper; she had not wished to offend. Judy was gratified to feel the pull in her reins take effect. She still had the power of bringing her daughter in, but it was best exercised with kindness. She turned now towards Annabella. 'There can be nothing improper,' she said, 'in telling the truth.' Lady Milbanke looked always handsomest in her nightdress. There was something very dignified in her weathered countenance and long upright mottled neck: they exposed an indifference to self that was really the best pride.

Annabella lingered in the doorway, conscious of her face and hands, the softness of her youth. She asked, in a different voice, as her mother resumed her evening toilette, 'How much of life, mama, do you think may be understood from books?'

Without turning, Judy answered, 'That depends—upon the taste and discernment of the reader.'

'A reader with the best taste and the sharpest discernment may understand a great deal of the world, even without the benefit of experience?'

'She may. Although taste and discernment are often acquired only with reference to experience—without which, even the best minds may be easily misled.'

'An attentive observer, however, may learn a great deal from a very little life?'

Judy, smiling, stood up and took her daughter's hands. 'It is only a question of eggs,' she mocked. And then, 'Have you had enough of life already, my dear?' And Annabella, answering her mother's smile, replied, 'Sometimes I almost believe I have,' and kissed her goodnight.

Chapter Three

—

IN THE EVENT, Lady Cowper deemed it best to hold the party at her own house; and the Milbankes themselves had returned to Seaham before Annabella had a chance of renewing her acquaintance with Lord Byron.

Mary Montgomery called on Annabella at Gosford House; they were to make their way together to the party. Mary was a pale, invalidish, good-natured and sharp-tongued girl. She flattered Annabella's sense of kindliness twice over: by seeming to require her friend's devoted attendance and by indulging an appetite for gossip which was crueller and more honest than Annabella dared to trust her conscience with. This gave her several happy occasions for reproof. The great joke between them, to which Annabella contributed only her silent enjoyment, had to do with Annabella's suitors: their number, their qualities, their ardours, and their inevitable disappointments. Mary was something of a favourite at Cumberland Place, owing to the lighter spirits into which she coaxed her friend; and she amused the Gosfords on their short carriage-ride by counting over the ranks of Annabella's 'unhopefuls', many of whom they could expect to meet at Lady Cowper's. There were George Eden, Augustus Foster, William Bankes . . .

'You seem quite the fashion, my dear,' Lady Gosford said. 'Mankind bow before you.'

'At least they did last year,' Mary replied for her friend. 'But she has left so many famous wrecks behind her that no one now dares approach. I have high hopes of salvaging someone among them for my own uses. I dare say, nobody would want me else.' There was, in the gentle rebuke to which Annabella subjected her friend, not quite the sharpness of disagreement.

Lady Cowper had decreed that the young should justify their appetites before receiving any supper; and as the Gosfords and their two protégées mounted the wide steps rising from Hanover Square, they heard the bright beat of a dance in progress. They were shown inside; Mary rested her weight on Annabella's arm. Amidst the confusion of the scene, the girls soon lost sight of their chaperons, and then Mary herself disappeared into the mix. Annabella began to look for her. She was often surprised into sudden depressions by the ease with which even her sickly friend could enter into any kind of public amusement. The happiness of others tended to rouse her bitterest self-reflections, but these, at least, relieved a little her anxiety at the prospect of seeing Lord Byron again. She had spent the day carefully rehearsing a pretext for addressing him and had just returned to the question when she almost stumbled over his leg. He caught her gently by the hand and guided her to a seat beside him. After a minute's silence, which both of them occupied by staring at the commencement of a waltz, Lord Byron bent towards her and whispered, 'Do you think there is one person here who dares to look into himself?'

It was her own thought exactly, and she was startled to hear it given a public voice. His remark betrayed the kind of scorn that was her secret comfort. She relied perhaps too much on the drug of misanthropy to soothe her, whenever she felt that nobody would speak to her, that she had nothing to say. But she was doubly grateful for it now that somebody had spoken, in that misanthropy itself supplied the course of the conversation. 'You are too kind,' she answered, 'in restricting your contempt merely to the masculine pronoun.'

He bowed.

'I have not had the honour of an introduction,' she continued after a silence, which he did nothing to correct. She was amazed at her self-possession; yet she was conscious of a kind of giddiness, too, that was distinguished rather for the stillness and clarity of her thoughts than any confusion.

'I believe I have the advantage of you,' he said. 'There is no one among Lady Caroline's acquaintance whom she admires more warmly than yourself; and her praises have been so explicit that I flattered myself, my dear Miss Milbanke, we were already old friends.'

'Well, then, to return the compliment: shall I say that I knew you, if not by reputation alone, then by your poem, whose name is on everyone's lips?'

He hid a rueful smile with the flat of his thumb. 'You mock me, I believe; so I won't take offence, if only because you intend to give it.'

'My lord, not at all. There is only too much good in your Harold—so much, that he is ashamed to reveal it.'

'Then I won't spare your blushes. Your goodness is so generally believed in that the particulars of it often go unnoticed.' There was a pause in which he gathered his thoughts; they watched the dancing couples bow and part. In a more serious vein he continued, 'I heard of your kindness to Joseph Blacket with as much shame as admiration. Once, for the sake of a rhyme, I did him some injury, which as a poor fellow-poet, poor in the bitterest sense of that abused word, he had done nothing to deserve.'

Blacket was a cobbler from Seaham; he had dreamed of becoming an author and had studied hard to improve himself. Not only had the Milbankes taken on the expense of printing an edition of his verse, Annabella herself had copied and corrected the proofs. But his constitution being weak, he had not lived to publish a second—which might have built on the triumphs of the first and omitted those faults that Lord Byron had formerly seen fit to satirize for their pretension. 'The errors of our youth,' replied the nineteen-year-old girl, 'have this virtue: that they teach us to correct them. And if the lesson once learned is never forgot, we may at last deserve to regard them with complacence.'

There was no topic Lord Byron might have hit on that could have pleased Annabella better; the humanity of his feelings on the subject touched her to the quick. And yet there was something so perfect about the quality of attention he bestowed on her that she could not suppress a suspicion that in some large sense she was being teased. His conversation certainly had its ironies, but their real object, she consoled herself, might be nothing other than his own capacity for sympathy—which seemed quick and strong, but also selfish. The great danger, she knew, to a sensitive conscience was that it tended to suffer more for its own sake than for others'. *Poor Blacket.* He had never in life amounted to anything so valuable: he had become a token of Lord Byron's repentance. Annabella found, at least, that she was willing to accept it.

The next dance was beginning. Lord Byron had not stirred; he surveyed the scene with a detachment to which he soon gave a voice. 'The great object of life is sensation,' he said to Annabella, without turning towards her. 'Is it not? To feel that we exist, even though in pain . . . It is this craving void which drives us into society and out of it again. The principal attraction, I believe, of any pursuit—whether waltzing, gaming, husband-hunting, or war—is the agitation inseparable from its accomplishment.'

At that moment, George Eden (one of her young 'unhopefuls', as Mary called them) claimed Annabella for the dance, and she was drawn away—from the periphery of the scene into its centre. Mr Eden was a good-natured gentleman, if a little conceited. It was just like him, Annabella thought, to 'rescue' her from the attentions of the fashionable poet; he trusted to their shared opinion of his corrupted and corrupting nature. As she turned to look over her shoulder, she saw Lord Byron cross his legs and smile: an unhappy smile, which affected her painfully, as it seemed to imply a fresh disappointment. It was as if she had added her own piece of evidence to the proof of his loneliness. In his eyes, they were no better than the rest of the busy dancers, whose happiness depended on their motion, whose life was a continuing escape from that observant stillness with which Lord Byron regarded them.

Mr Eden, Annabella was forced to admit, danced beautifully. His conversation, however, was more declarative than interrogatory. 'In two weeks,' he said, as they circled each other, 'he was set to take orders, but he could assure Miss Milbanke that his ambitions were by no means limited to a quiet country parsonage. His modesty was only the plain language of his wants; he had trimmed his expectations in order to realize them in their essentials.'

Annabella was aware of his preference; he was the kind to flatter by confession. Nor could she deny that he was a 'very respectable match', as Lady Milbanke herself had once remarked. Mr Eden had sensible tastes and two thousand pounds a year to satisfy them. He was not unhandsome either, she considered, as they stepped to the top of the line and faced each other again. His broad, rough countenance conveyed solid virtues: a strong nose, with healthy, articulated nostrils; a large, expansive eye. Only his thin, fluent lips suggested a more delicate gauge. And yet, as Annabella perceived it, there was a want of something spiritual in his character. He knew his own mind and presumed to know hers with so firm a grasp as to exclude her own uncertainties: she had rather be doubted more. As she complained afterwards to Mary Montgomery, 'Perhaps if he were more unhopeful I should like him better; the fact is, he presumes to know.' Their characters were very much alike, he continued, as she felt her hand grow warm against his: 'sensible, clever, good'. And when she only smiled at him, he replied, after the music had stopped, 'That the best modesty included an honest sense of one's merits, as well as their limits.'

Later, over supper, she fell into conversation with Lady Caroline, in whom the charge of mixed company had produced an almost uncontrollable current. She had been over-exerting herself. Her features were small and finely expressive—the least and pettiest of her changing feelings declared itself in her face. Activity had given her a hectic glaze; she looked hot to the touch. She said to Annabella, 'How well I remember your waltzing. There never was a prettier instructress; I should love to learn at your hands.' Annabella, who was puzzled for a reply, was soon spared the need of one. 'And what do you think of Lord B? I saw you engrossed together. Was there ever a more miserable charmer? Or a more charming misery?' She linked her arm in Annabella's and together they surveyed the scene. 'He is somewhat in awe of you,' Lady Caroline continued in a whisper. Annabella, who distrusted her friend, was still aware of the concentration of looks they attracted together: the very good and the very bad girl in confederation.

'For that, I believe, I have you to thank. He praised your account of my virtues till I grew quite uncomfortable with so much imputed goodness.'

'Well, and was it less than the truth?' Annabella could not read

Lady Caroline's mind: C was one of those jealous women who prided herself on strong sisterly feelings. Her jealousies played strangely off her passion for female friendship. It seemed to Annabella that Lady Caroline wished to set her up as a rival for the purpose of beating her to Lord Byron's heart. It was a game Annabella disliked: she could not help but lose at it. 'You have had a most remarkable coming out,' Caroline continued. 'There has never been another like it. To the charms of youth and beauty, you have added those of an unimpeachable goodness; and it has acted upon the gentlemen as riches used to. There was never a more sought-after hand than your own, my dear.'

'I have never understood what is meant by my goodness. It seems rather an imaginary quality: my real state of grace, only God, and perhaps my mother, can claim to know. As for the rest— I suppose it is a question of manners more than anything else. Men blame me for it to soften the force of my indifference to them; and women praise me for it, so that the men no longer attempt to approach me.'

'Perhaps you will not be offended,' Lady Caroline replied, smiling, 'when I say that you reason like a man, since you know how often I have been charged with acting like a boy.'

Annabella still felt the pressure of Lady Caroline's arm in her own. There was something improper in her friend from which she would have preferred to detach herself, not least because her standing there implied a tacit consent, to Lord Byron if nobody else, of those behaviours which had begun to get the pair of them talked about. She remembered with an inward blush her reluctance to attend the waltzing party. It is not a ball, she had reasoned; her aunt was presiding . . . Considerations that, she fully admitted, could play no part in excusing her present visit: how easily she had been seduced into a second meeting! The first step is always hardest.

But her sense of virtue quickly rallied to a justification. She disliked the idea of Lady Caroline's friendship with the poet. His character, it seemed to her, was such that he was often tempted into sin by his finer feelings; and it would take a nice management indeed to prevent the one without suppressing the other. Annabella's interest in Lord Byron was still at that stage where she could persuade herself that all she sought from him was his own moral advantage. She excused herself. 'My great friend Mary Montgomery,' she said, 'possesses both high spirits and a weak constitution. I consider it my duty to rescue her from the combination of them. I see her across the room, irritably rubbing the backs of her hands, which is always a sign with her of great fatigue.' Lady Caroline released her on the condition that Annabella would call on her soon. They were practically sisters, and she was anxious to hear her thoughts on Lord Byron, about whom she delighted to speak, especially in a more comfortable seclusion. She was glad that their introduction had now been effected. Lord Byron had long desired it, and it afforded Caroline, at last, the pleasure of testing her opinion of the poet against Annabella's greater penetration.

It seemed to Annabella, as she bade her goodnight, that Lady Caroline was trying to throw her in Lord Byron's way. And she wondered how far she would be justified in accepting the connection, if only in the hope of offering his lordship a model of female conduct that Lady Caroline was particularly unsuited to providing. As she crossed the room, she for the first time noted that Augusta had joined the party; Lord Byron was talking in her ear. She smiled to think of the brother and sister, each as shy as the other, made all the more so by the mutual solace of their company. Augusta looked very beautiful in a dark blue dress patterned with spangles, in whose glimmer her eyes showed especially black. She was encouraging her brother to join the gentlemen; she did not wish to keep him from his friends. Annabella thought she could just make out Lord Byron answering, 'I have not a friend in the world', and was pierced by the persuasion that he was speaking the simple truth. But Augusta laughed at him and said, 'You only think yourself friendless, because no one else loves you so well as I.' In Annabella, a wave of jealousy followed swiftly on the back of her compassion.

Mary, on their journey home, quizzed her friend about Lord Byron. 'I saw him talking to you in his very best low tone,' she said, 'and wondered what he was being quietly significant about.'

'You are teasing me; everybody teases me,' Annabella replied.

'I thought you were held in such universal admiration that it was my privilege alone to mock you.'

'Well, Lady Caroline has now taken her turn. She loves him so much she would have me love him, too.'

'Is she not supposed to be of a jealous disposition?'

'She was very puzzling; I could not make her out.'

'And did she succeed, in making you love him?'

Annabella recognized in this a more promising inquiry. She prided herself on her truthfulness, especially when she believed it might cost her pains. In fact, she was glad to give her impression of the poet; she wanted to talk of him and analyse her feelings out of their confusion. 'He is certainly very agreeable in conversation and very handsome, etc. His manners prove him to be one of nature's gentlemen. I confess that I felt he was the most attractive person in that company.' Their coachman shouted at some disturbance in the street, and as she collected her thoughts Annabella congratulated herself on being confident enough in her affections to criticize them openly. 'I was not bound to him by any strong sympathy,' she continued, 'until he said, not to me but in my hearing, I have not a friend in the world! There is an instinct in the human heart that attaches us to the friendless. I consider it to be an act of humanity and a Christian duty not to deny him any temporary satisfaction he can derive from my acquaintance—though I shall not seek to increase it.' And then, when Mary only smiled at her, she insisted in a warmer tone, 'He is not a dangerous person to me.'

'I respect you so greatly,' Mary countered, 'that I wonder if the same could be said about him, in regard to you.'

As usual, Annabella felt, her friend had wilfully misunderstood her finer motives. But the carriage had arrived at Mary's home in Wilmot Street, where it deposited her amidst mutual good wishes before carrying Annabella on to Gosford House and a sleepless bed.

Chapter Four

—

THEIR ACQUAINTANCE, THUS BEGUN, had the full summer in which to ripen, but Annabella was becoming disappointed by its progress. She despaired of doing him any good by her example. His affair with Lady Caroline reached a pitch of excess that promoted it from the hushed gossip of the privileged few to the talk of the newspapers. Worse still, they both looked unhappy on it. Lady Caroline, whose charms were more animating than comfortable, had discovered to her cost the effects of repetition on even the warmest declarations of love. Her feelings had not altered, yet she could not disguise from herself the fact that the tone of their relations unquestionably *had*. The consciousness made her desperate. Lord Byron, who for his part hated a scene, found himself unwillingly placed in the midst of several. He was soft-hearted enough in the presence of affection to suffer anything for its sake, but absence quickly hardened him to sterner measures. And Annabella's aunt, Lady Melbourne, seemed to grow tired of plotting the cuckoldom of her son: she began to entertain other plans for the young poet.

Meanwhile, Sir Ralph and Judy had entrusted their daughter to the care of Lady Gosford. Annabella had written to her mother a full account of the evening at Lady Cowper's. 'What will you think,' she began, 'when I tell you that Lord Byron himself sought me out, in the gentlest manner, to sing my praises?' In spite of her differences with Lady Milbanke, there was no one Annabella preferred for confession. Her mother, it should be said, had the strongest appetite for hearing her daughter admired; and Annabella had long since ceased to feel any shame in appealing to it. 'I have met with much evidence of his goodness,' she continued. 'He sincerely repented his treatment of poor Blacket. You know how easily the noblest heart may be perverted by unkindness—perhaps the most easily a noble heart, because it is the more susceptible to ungenerous indignities. I believe that the criticisms he suffered from every quarter for his own first poetical effusions taught him only to visit similar judgements upon a young pretender. He freely confessed that he should have learnt forbearance instead. But while there are many virtues that depend on high feelings if they are to be acted upon, there are others, and forbearance among them, that proceed only from quiet spirits, which he has never known himself two days in succession. I have begged him to study tranquillity. There is nothing his noble intellect might not master if he applied himself to it, but he lacks direction. Alas, that none of his acquaintance seems inclined to give it! His conversation is very pleasing, but he wants that calm benevolence which could only touch my heart.' And then she repeated her assurance to Mary Montgomery: 'He is not a dangerous person to me.'

The passing of the summer tended to justify this conviction. She met him again and again, at suppers and dances, but he was too much the object of a general attention for one who prided herself on an indifference to fashions to make much way with him. And he seemed to continue shy of her. Once, at a dinner given by Samuel Rogers, the conversation turned again to a question of poetical sincerity. Their host, himself a poet, who was rather admired than read, gave his opinion that there could be no good poetry without true feeling; Annabella was greatly surprised to find Lord Byron take up the argument against him. He invited any of his readers to determine from any particular passage what his real feelings on the subject were; often, he had no notion himself of what he believed or did not believe when the *estro* took him. Besides, he could never answer for his own feelings for more than one hour together.

Dinner was finished, and the gentlemen had rejoined the ladies in the drawing room. There was something in the bleak elegance of Rogers's apartments to encourage 'philosophy', as Sir Walter Scott pleasantly declared. Annabella had read his novels, and Scott's open, manly countenance greatly impressed her. It was hard to imagine him lost in the business of fancy. He looked like a family lawyer, and his manners had the excellence of that profession: he was particularly kind to young ladies. He nodded at Annabella as he said the word. Her reputation as a blooming intellectual was sufficiently established to provoke the gentlemen into little tributes to it. She had found, however, that her opinions were more frequently honoured than asked for. And she began to summon within herself the courage to do justice to them.

Their host himself, a small, narrow, sour-faced man, who looked as if he suffered equally from hunger and indigestion, was perpetually engaged in straightening a picture, or resettling a cushion, or aligning a gem on the mantelpiece. It was quite a game with Lord Byron to shift one of these little ornaments in his progress through the room: to observe Rogers, like a restless ant, busily re-establishing order. The lamplight tended to exaggerate his shadowy fretfulness against the wall. Byron teased Rogers for being 'the ghost of small adjustments'—a quip that, not unkindly meant, served only to irritate the feeling it was intended to relieve. The older poet, Annabella guessed, resented the fact that

Byron continued to hold the floor over a question of inspiration. But nothing could divert the flow of inquiry.

It was suggested to his lordship that what mattered was his sincerity at the time of composition. Something of the force of his true sentiments, however changeable, could not be kept from the language. These would declare themselves in the gross power of the eloquence, if nowhere else. There could be no poetry without passion; and passion, whatever its moral tone, was little susceptible of being doubted if felt. Lord Byron smiled at this ruefully and said, 'I hold my tongue, I hold my tongue, I should not like the ladies present to suspect how much the gentlemen *put up* for show.' Annabella did not understand the tittering that greeted this remark and responded, lifting her voice to drown her nerves, that 'perhaps it was the business of a discerning reader to decide for himself the truth or otherwise of poetical sentiments. I mean to say, that there is something in the act of publication which may be said to reveal an author to himself more clearly than any examination of his own conscience, unaided by such reflection, in its literal sense, could ever hope to do.'

Lord Byron bowed at her gravely and said 'that he could never wish for a fairer discernment than Miss Milbanke's; that he feared she placed but too much faith in the power of an author's understanding to live up to her own; that her generous mind interpreted virtues where none were present, but that he himself would study to deserve them.'

A ripple of applause greeted this gracious speech, and Annabella blushed, not entirely for pleasure. He had touched on, however inadvertently, what Annabella conceived to be the great obstacle to their deepening acquaintance, as she later explained it to Miss Montgomery: 'He puts so much faith in my goodness, such as it is, that he has correspondingly little in his right to attract me.' George Eden had been among the party. The look he directed at her, after Lord

Byron's pretty compliment, was less one of reproof than calculation. Annabella bridled at any suspicion that she had fallen under
the poet's spell and gave him but a cold farewell when Mr Eden
excused himself early—hoping to anticipate, he said, by only a day,
the forbearance which is always extended to the clergy for appearing unsociable. He was travelling to Oxford in the morning for the
purpose of his ordination.

But she was caught out both ways that night. Later, she overheard Lord Byron attempting to appease their host at the expense
of his departed guest. 'Now there is a good man, a handsome man,
an honourable man, a most inoffensive man, a well-informed
man, and a dull man, and this last epithet undoes all the rest. It is
lucky for him that God loves him, as nothing human will.' Rogers,
who for all his severity of manner relished gossip, only simpered at
him; and it was left to Annabella, by a pointed turn of her shoulder, to communicate an appropriate disgust at such sentiments.
She had heard of this side of his lordship's wit but had never
before seen the evidence of it herself; and the worst of it was, that
he had hit upon her own awful suspicions of Mr Eden. She was
forced to count among the objects of her disapproval her own
hypocrisy. Afterwards, he apologized to Miss Milbanke for attack-
ing a reputation he could never aspire to himself, when he knew it
to be dear to her—and which he envied on that account. 'You are
too good for a fallen creature to know,' he added.

In the morning, she called upon Miss Montgomery—hoping,
by a limited confession, to relieve her mind of its most painful
uncertainties. Mary lived in a comfortable house on Wilmot
Street. As an only child, she was the spoilt darling of her parents,
although more conscious of the luxury entailed by that condition
than Annabella, in her own case, was willing to confess to. It was
feared she would not live long. Her constitution was very weak
and often laid her up a month at a time in the front parlour with

nothing but a constant fire and supply of books and gossip to sustain her. Her invalidity had at least one benefit, which she sometimes admitted, that it spared her the pressures which usually attend the coming out of a girl with expectations. She had no real expectations, it was not presumed that she would live to see her wedding day. She only joked of being slighted in Annabella's favour by every suitor to tease her friend; really, she had little desire to surrender her mental independence to any man, however much her material liberty lay at the mercy of her flickering vitality and the vagaries of the weather.

She liked to keep the front room of the house on the first floor for her own use. It was smaller but overlooked the street, whose traffic she took a steady pleasure in remarking upon. (She sometimes said that the only joy to be gotten out of *observation* was that it supplied her with *conversation*; she preferred talking to looking and indulged in the latter only as it served the former.) Miss Milbanke was offered, upon entering, either the seat by the fire or by the window. Only Mary's position combined the two comforts, and as it was a bright April morning, Annabella chose to join her friend at the view. 'Now, shall we occupy ourselves with something ladylike and improving? Have you brought your embroidery, or will you borrow mine? I believe not: you may claim the privilege of an invalid and do nothing but gossip.' She rang the bell, and when the servant came, called for coffee, which was eventually set down on the card-table between them.

'I don't understand,' Mary said, after hearing Miss Milbanke's story, which was something between a confession and a complaint, 'what the matter is. Is it that Lord Byron daren't approach you, because he fears you are too good for him; or is it the trouble that you are in fact too good for him?' It was just like Mary, Annabella thought, to insist on what she had been trying to evade.

'I could not say,' she replied at last. 'I flatter myself, perhaps, of being some use to him. And yet if he shuns me on that very account . . . There is also, I believe, some injury to my modesty in his opinion: I am hardly as perfect as he pretends me to be. It does me no good, I know, and can do our relations no good, for him to think me an angel; he plays up to the worst of my vanities and suggests, by that manoeuvre, that he knows me either much too little or much too well for my comfort.'

Mary smiled in admiration at her friend's subtlety. 'Does it matter, *which*?' she asked.

After a moment's thought, Annabella said, 'I believe it may.'

'And which of those alternatives should you prefer, after all?'

Finally, from Annabella, an answering smile, 'I can't say.'

It was one of those fine April mornings that gives way easily to a sudden shower. A tide of low grey cloud, still instinct with sunshine, had rolled in over the rooftops, and from it a flurry of drops fell to rattle the panes. A shift in the quality of light brought out a new cast of features in the two friends. Mary's face emerged, as vivid in darkness as it had been in brightness, but more intimate, more gravely ill; and Annabella herself appeared to Mary somewhat tired, not so much the pretty incarnation of her own complacence.

'I'm glad of that,' Mary said, holding her cup in both hands, 'now I shall have you all morning to myself. You won't venture out in this.' They watched the water soften the stones of the street and begin to gather into channels. 'And what of Mr Eden?' Mary continued. 'Shall I entertain any hopes for him? He seems so assured of everything in life that I feel a curious interest in *not* seeing him disappointed in the one thing most essential to his happiness. It's quite perverse of me, I know. We generally delight in finding the expectations of our friends frustrated, if only for their sake, that they may learn patience; but I often prefer to see their desires gratified. There is something very instructive in the spectacle of someone attempting to enjoy his perfect bliss.'

'And what of me?' Annabella responded. 'Would you sacrifice my own happiness to see to the end your little experiment upon his?'

'I don't suppose Mr George Eden would make you unhappy—you, who want for nothing, and consequently have no desires of your own to act upon.'

'That is unfair, Mary, but I know you are only teasing me into a reaction. Mr Eden is a fine, upright man and shall make no doubt an excellent preacher and a very comfortable husband.' She remembered Lord Byron's account of him—'now there is a good man, a handsome man, an honourable man . . . and a dull man'—and desired very much to repeat it now for her friend's amusement. Yet she feared an appearance of impropriety and so bit her tongue and continued, 'But I wonder if his understanding is not too confined to what is reasonable and proper. There are corners of my conscience I should not like him to stumble upon. I doubt very much if he would recognize what he found, and I fear he might blame me for his own incomprehension.'

Mary set down her cup to press her hands together and raise them to her lips. 'My dear sweet Bella,' she began—when her friend interrupted her, crossly, to say, 'Now you have got what you want and shall mock me for it.'

'Not for the world; only, I cannot make you out. A very good man and a notorious libertine have fallen in love with you. Both honour you for your perfections, so much so, that the one only just dares to approach you, while the other scarcely understands you. If you are a very good girl, you must marry Mr Eden; but if you are a bad one, Lord Byron may sympathize but won't love you for it. I think on the whole you had better be a very good girl.'

'I said you would mock me, and what if I am something between the two?'

'Heaven help you, my dear, if you prove human. But forgive

me: I should like, more than anything, to see you trust in your desires as much as you have been used to trusting in your virtue. I only wonder whether your sins stretch quite as far as you fear, whether loving-kindness and patience and charity are not predominant in you. Perhaps Mr Eden understands you well enough. I do believe you wish to be a little less perfect than you are.'

'This is the strangest flattery,' Annabella said, quietly giving way to tears. 'It feels very much like being cut.'

'My poor sweet girl,' Mary answered, in a different tone. She had a blanket laid across her knees; from among its recesses she discovered a handkerchief, which she offered with an outstretched hand. 'I had not supposed you were so unhappy on it.'

Annabella dried her eyes. 'I hardly know myself.' And then, when she deemed herself presentable again: 'Do you really think he is in love with me?'

Chapter Five

—

AFTER HIS RETURN FROM OXFORD, Mr Eden began to press forward in his attentions. There was something about the tone of their discourse that made it impossible for Annabella to put him off. They professed to share a sense of how little the pleasures of society in general were worth, and it was their agreement on the matter that seemed to secure for him perpetual recourse to the pleasure of hers in particular whenever he liked. He claimed her at the beginning and end of every dance; cornered her in conversation; and attended to her at dinner, on departure, in a manner that declared, with every word or gesture, that he knew his own mind and could answer for Annabella's. He was acutely aware, as he repeatedly professed, of being about to take his place in the world; the prospect had not so much shaken as confirmed his faith in his judgement. He had pared his wants to their essential and was gratified to discover the scope of enjoyment that promised from the remainder. Indeed, what surprised Annabella, as a fresh response in her, was not so much that she wished from obstinate perversity to dispute his confidence in her, but that her self-possession allowed her to transform that perversity into something useful and more deeply flattering to her vanity. She observed, with a jealous eye, every jealous glance Lord Byron cast their way.

Once, after a banquet at Lady Melbourne's, Annabella found herself 'short of air', as she said, and turned for relief to the narrow balcony onto which the French windows of the drawing room opened. Mr Eden had only just retired. He was conscious, he had told her, of possessing personal charms that rarely survived the conclusion of a meal. His conversation, he trusted, might benefit the digestion and enliven the supper-table but could not serve the higher spirits that prevailed afterwards. She had not answered, except to smile, and he took her silence as his cue to depart without her. The little blush of sadness that she felt at his disappointment surprised Annabella, and she sought the balcony to reflect on it alone. Her first response at finding Lord Byron already installed, contemplating the expanse of the gardens below him, all noiseless in the summer heat, was mortification at the thought that he would suppose her guilty of an approach. She begged his pardon and prepared to turn inside.

'Stay,' he said, quickly touching her shoulder with his hand. 'What I wished to escape, inside, has not followed me out.' For a moment, she thought he must mean Mr Eden, but before she could defend him, Lord Byron continued. His voice was beautifully modulated to the evening, low and musical. 'I have been imagining for the past half hour what the effects would be of my keeping an unbroken silence—if anybody would take note and join me in it. I had a most delightful vision of the entire company standing and staring at each other, as quiet as sparrows. But there, I am as guilty as the rest of them—you have come out for a minute's peace, and I have spoilt it, have I not?'

'My best answer, I believe,' Annabella said, finding her wits, 'should be to ignore the question.'

He bowed his head, and they stood side by side, breathing the still air. She exulted in the confidence that her power of silence would outlast his own. He had set them a little game to play, and she was determined to beat him at it: she could act the misanthrope as well as he. A minute passed, and then another. She heard the low waves of conversation from the drawing room behind her. Someone had sat down to the piano. There is nothing sweeter, she thought, than the sound of music *within*. She was thoroughly stirred up by the secret of their presence on the balcony. Mounting silence was like a spring of joy within her, bubbling up. She could barely suppress her pleasure in it any longer—until he broke it, in a casual tone that suggested no sympathy with the contest in her at all. Perhaps she was going mad.

'When we first met,' he began, 'I believe I asked you a question. Do you remember what it was?'

She nodded and summoned her voice. 'You said: Is there any-one here who dares look into himself?'

'And have you discovered, in the course of these months, a happier answer to make to it?'

Annabella reflected; the tone of her answer was everything. 'I met with one or two who, like myself, did not appear absorbed in the present scene—and who interested me in a degree. I had a wish to find amongst men the character I had often imagined, but I found only parts of it. One gave proofs of worth but had no sympathy for high aspirations. Another seemed full of affection towards his family, and yet he valued the world.'

'You might just as well have said,' he replied, smiling, 'I found an Augustus Foster, a William Bankes. I know them and pity them the more for being found out as well as turned away. But was there no one who answered your complete idea?'

She blushed and looked down.

'I believe I understand you,' he said. For an instant, she thought he had, but then he continued, 'And wish you every happiness in your garden of—'

The door behind them opened, and Lady Caroline put her head out. 'There you are, Annabella. The gentlemen have been complaining of a want of pretty ladies for waltzing with. No one is excused; we must all do our part . . .' Then, 'Even you, Lord Byron.'

Mr Eden's proposal arrived with the inevitability of summer, or its end. He applied first to Lady Gosford, as Miss Milbanke's chaperon in the city; and she warned Annabella to expect a caller in the morning, who had a question to ask of her. 'I suppose you know his business as well as your own,' Lady Gosford said. 'My only piece of advice, and I don't flatter myself that it will be taken, is this: do not answer hastily. I believe that a good night's sleep has never stood in the way of a decision.'

Annabella received him in the drawing room. She had put on for the occasion her simplest muslin. Her hair was tied up in cream ribbons. She wished to convey the impression, for Mr Eden's benefit, of a creature whose indifference was only the flowering of her innocence; she wished to suggest that the only answer she could ever give a man was, no. She had made up her mind to respond in the negative but, even so, was conscious of being supported by his attachment in that vanity which gave her the courage to refuse him.

Mr Eden, arriving somewhat late, had already put Annabella out of spirits. She had risen from her chair, on which she believed the light to fall most flatteringly, half a dozen times and sat down again on every seat in the room, to make a trial of it, before returning to her position by the window. He was shown in, not in the least sweaty with hurry and larger indeed than she had remembered him: a solid, proper man, quite unlike the creature of her imaginations. She rose stiffly to greet him and held out her hand. He kissed it with warm, dry lips and, as they sat down together, offered his explanation.

'He little presumed that his arrival attracted such a weight of anticipation that any delay would be felt as a burden, yet he wished to apologize for his lateness—if only because he had so often professed to Miss Milbanke the value he placed in satisfying the letter as well as the spirit of one's obligations that a departure from his usual rule would strike her as the worst hypocrisy. Word had only just reached him regarding an incumbency, the gift of which he had sufficiently despaired of receiving before the end of the summer, that he had only yesterday decided to anticipate it by the question he intended to pose her. Its arriving just in time that morning was the cause of his being late in setting out, but he was confident that Miss Milbanke would forgive a delay that allowed him to frame his proposal to her in a manner more becoming to her deserts. He had been offered and intended to accept, subsequent to their conversation, a vicarage in Sutton, outside Newmarket. The rectory, which he had visited himself on a number of occasions when poor Mr Torking presided there, God rest his soul, was a comfortable, dry and gentlemanly place, with a large orchard attached to it; and the income from the living would fully justify him, given his private resources, to keep an establishment in town. He mentioned these claims though perfectly conscious that Miss Milbanke would consent to marry only on the grounds of affection and that the charm of a fortune could never persuade her where the charms of the person had failed to; but he was sensible of the fact that a level of material comfort was, not only her proper due, but the best security for the increase of those sentiments a young couple could command on setting out in life.'

He paused at last. Annabella was almost overwhelmed into silence by the duration of this little speech. Lord Byron's humorous description of Mr Eden recurred to her for a second time, and it was with some difficulty that she held back the smile that might have rewarded his wit. But she was angry, too. She reflected that, in her relations with Mr Eden, her own opinions were rather praised than solicited. It was entirely like the man to ask for her hand in the midst of an earnest and rambling account of his own advancement. Still, she hardly knew what to say and decided that her best response would be an attempt at clarification. 'Was she to understand that Mr Eden proposed to marry her?'

His large, sensible face had contracted around the eyes. 'Forgive me,' he said, 'I am a little overwrought and have been all morning. I could scarcely swallow any breakfast.'

Annabella moved to ring the bell. 'If Mr Eden was hungry, he had only to say the word. It was quite shocking of her to have forgotten her manners; she begged his pardon. Of course, they must have some tea.' The archness of her tone brought home to her, as nothing else could have, how poorly the innocence she pretended to would serve her in this interview.

'No, no,' he said, touching her hand, which held the bell, to silence. 'He could not eat, or think, or breathe, until he knew his fate. He was conscious, no one more so, that his manner suggested a confidence which he was far from possessing. And he had expressed himself very badly, he knew.'

Annabella sat with the bell in one hand on her lap, while her other hand played with its cold tongue. She felt a rush of pity for both of them: for Mr Eden, for proposing; and for herself, for refusing him. 'The shortness of my answer, I fear, will do little justice to the weight and scope of the question, but I must say, no— and no amount of stretching the syllable out can make it any pleasanter to either of us.'

Mr Eden put his fingers to his mouth, as if to hold in place an intake of breath. 'May I ask your reasons?' he said, exhaling.

'I wish I knew them,' she answered in a livelier tone—a rare outbreak in her of simplicity. He was, unquestionably, a suitable match; her mother had said as much. And in the weeks to follow, she pondered deeply not over her decision but over the ease with which she had come to it. It occurred to her now to say that she loved another, but she knew quite well whose countenance the phrase would conjure up, in her own as well as Mr Eden's thoughts. Besides, she couldn't even then have answered for the truth of this evasion. She had been proposed to (she silently counted them up) on five occasions, and though the recollection of their professions of love had often flattered her into a better humour on a gloomy day, she remembered only now the real emotion they had provoked her into at the time: blind fear. What a terrible thing it seemed, to surrender your life to a man! How pleasantly she had always got on in the safety of her parents' love and free from the confinement of a husband's.

Mr Eden had to some extent recomposed himself. 'Might I hazard to describe them?' he said. His manner was much more like his accustomed manner, more concisely reasonable, and only then did Annabella guess the state of his nerves on his first proposal. His pupils had retracted considerably; they looked very small and calculating in his large eyes. 'I believe you suppose me generally in want of a wife.' She made a gesture of dissent, which he ignored. 'You suspect me of lighting upon you as the most suitable to hand; you fancy another will do just as well. I can assure you the reverse is true. I have too great a conviction in my own merit to risk my life with anyone else. You are unquestionably my superior, in beauty, in virtue, in sense, and if I venture to deserve you, it is only because I believe no one else so capable of doing justice to your deserts. If you refuse me, I may with confidence assert: I shall never marry.' As he stood up to take his leave, he added: 'I ask you to think on this, as much for your own sake, as mine.'

It was a speech she was never given the occasion to forget, but at the time it only made her task easier. She had bristled at his assurance, and as he took her hand, she said, practising her dignity, 'I respect you too much to compound the injury of my refusal by drawing it out.' She let go of him. 'I blame myself already for having, however innocently, led you to form expectations which I have always known I could not satisfy; my only excuse can be that I did not guess your feelings in time. You know me well enough to believe that I should not have spoken if I were at all uncertain of my own.'

He bowed and in a softer tone declared, 'When there is no more to be said, even I know enough to keep silent.' After he had gone, she moved to the window to see him striding into the road; there was, in his step, the little skip of a purposeful haste. She almost smiled—enjoying as always, after the initial scene, the exercise of her power of refusal. It bucked her spirits up, like a warm ride in cold weather. But in the morning she woke so low, so out of sorts, her first thought was that somebody dear to her had died; her second, that she had dreamed it in the night. And it required the better part of the day for her to compose her thoughts to a suitable order: it was only the uncertainty of his attraction to her, which had amused her and sustained their companionship; it was only that which she now regretted, in its passing . . .

Chapter Six

—

IT WAS SOMETHING OF A RELIEF when, a few weeks later, a note from her aunt arrived. London had gone quiet, and Annabella had grown first listless, then dull, then bored altogether, and subsequently irritable—after which it needed only a run of wet days to induce in her a steady depression of spirits. Lady Melbourne, from private motives she promised later to reveal, wished for Miss Milbanke to call on her. She had a little test to set her niece, which, she suspected, might prove as amusing as it promised to be instructive.

Annabella arrived at Melbourne House on a cold morning whose dryness suggested the real beginnings of autumn. The smoke of hearth-fires sharpened the air. She had not felt so light-hearted in weeks. She had walked all the way, as she confessed at once to Jennings when he showed her inside. He complimented her on her fresh colour, and she glanced at her reflection in the hall mirror, to test his praise. Her own eyes stared back at her, bright with exercise. As she looked, she felt the startle of an actual recognition, blinking back at her, and quickly turned to follow Jennings into the library.

Lady Melbourne rose to greet her. There was in her aunt's weak-chinned, amiable face something so expressive of her father that Annabella was obliged, as usual, to repress an instinctual confidence. 'My dear Annabella,' Lady Melbourne said, holding out her hand, which was still babyish and pale, in spite of age, 'how well you look; how delighted I am to get you to myself for a morning.' The family features, Annabella was forced to concede, not without a nod towards her own vanity, appeared to greater advantage in their feminine incarnation. Lady Melbourne wore her hair piled high on her head and wound round with pearls; she had, by the restless touch of her hand, to keep a loose strand tucked behind her ears. 'We have heard such tales of you!' she said, delightfully, as she guided her niece into a chair.

'Nothing, I hope, to my discredit.'

Her aunt only smiled at her, without opening her mouth; then she rang for coffee to be served. 'Ralph asked me to speak with you. He wrote to say, they feel themselves cut off in Seaham from London life; had no sense of what was proper to a girl.' What followed, evidently, took some formulation, for Lady Melbourne paused to make it. 'He complained of his own innocence,' Lady Melbourne began again. 'He once attempted, he said, a fatherly inquiry into the state of your feelings, but you put him off in terms that suggested the hopelessness of a second experiment. What your prospects were, what intentions you cherished, were his only concern.'

Annabella felt herself blushing.

'Come, come, my dear,' Lady Melbourne continued, as if to cut short her embarrassment. 'I can imagine what a sad fist he made of it. Ralph, bless him, for all his good nature, is not the confessor a girl would choose for herself.'

Nor was she, thought Annabella, bristling slightly, the kind of woman a brother would lightly confide in. Ralph, she suspected, would apply to his sister, whom he hardly pretended to trust, only under the influence of a grave and particular anxiety. 'He knows me

well enough, I believe,' Annabella said, 'to rely on his own understanding of my state of mind.'

'A faith in your father that does more credit to your sense of
duty than to his penetration.' Coffee came. Annabella sipped her
cup, considering her aunt through the heat of it in her face. Then,
to soften the briskness of her last remark, Lady Melbourne added,
'No, I think it's high time we took you in hand. You have been
coldly breaking hearts long enough . . .'

Perhaps George Eden has talked, was Annabella's first thought,
though it seemed unlike him. He had the kind of pride that would
rather conceal than advertise the wounds it received. Of course,
she could not keep from herself the flutter of a hope that Lord
Byron had been intended by her aunt's remark. Lady Melbourne
was well known to be his confidante, and she was perfectly capable of intriguing on his behalf—even at the expense, events had
proved, of her own son, whom Caroline had made to look very
foolish. How little the discomfort of a brother would count for in
her calculations—a reflection that led Annabella to guess the real
source of Ralph's anxiety. Her father wanted to know the state of
her relations with Lord Byron. Annabella experienced the new
and not unpleasant sensation of being the object (in prospect at
least) of disapproval. It seemed to her delightful, from the security
of her virtue, to know that someone suspected her of being, if
nothing else, a prey to temptations.

'Her coldness,' she said, intending to catch something of her
aunt's tone, 'was so generally believed in that any man who put
it to the test had only himself to blame for finding the rumour
justified.'

Lady Melbourne's reply suggested to Annabella for the first
time how little she had the measure of her aunt. Miss Milbanke
felt in it the not unpleasant force of correction: a very hot dry
wind against which she partly closed her eyes. 'It isn't only a ques-

tion,' Lady Melbourne began sensibly enough, 'of what you might be blamed for. You have made a very good beginning. Anyone with your interests at heart will be concerned to see how you follow it up. Naturally, what we all desire for you now is a brilliant match. Naturally, what we ask ourselves is the manner of man who could, shall we say, justify your interest in him. I am trying to discover from you what the nature of that interest is? What the scope and depth of your ambitions are? Think for a minute, Annabella; I have no use for a half-cocked reply.'

Annabella thought. As she thought, she looked round her, and the prospect from the window had the advantage of suggesting what the fruits of an ambitious match could be. A flagstoned promenade at the foot of the garden was bisected by an avenue of birch trees. These marched away towards the shimmering quiescence of a fountain—at such an angle that Annabella, from her vantage, fancied she could almost hear the military beat of guards parading up and down. Yes, there was an unmistakable air of protection, in no way diminished by the fact that wealth, that luxury, that beauty itself formed the shield to be reckoned with. The library in which they sat exceeded the comprehension of her view. There were corners and alleys in it, still to be discovered. She imagined the pleasure to be got from the possession of them; there was a scale of riches that could make, even of solitude, a continuing exploration.

Lady Melbourne, then, served both as a model and a warning of what a womanly ambition could effect for itself. Annabella believed herself, not unhappily, to be made up of the same materials as her aunt. They were both strong-willed, subtle, vain; yes, she was willing to admit that much. And if Annabella had been used to regarding the differences between them with some complacence, she now began to revise, not her opinion perhaps, but the certainty with which it was held. Lady Melbourne, unquestionably, had had a brilliant career. She had managed to attach, with a degree of immorality that her niece hoped at some point to calculate, the greatest figures of her day—with the result that the best of society, its soldiers, its statesmen, its artists, now revolved around her sun. Lord Byron was only the latest, and not perhaps the brightest, of her planets; and the prospect of shifting the centre of his orbit to herself was not without its attractions to Annabella.

There could be no doubt, of course, that the niece regulated her feelings with a greater propriety than her aunt had ever been disposed to attempt. But whether the difference between them should be attributed to an excess or an absence of certain qualities was becoming for Annabella a very decided point. Was there a talent for sin? Could virtue be considered a deficiency of it? Annabella, in the course of that summer, had begun to learn something about the force and variety of desire. It was only a question, perhaps, of how successfully she could translate her virtue into a style with which to engage the society around her—if she wished, that is, to make an equal name for herself in time.

Their coffee had grown cold. As Annabella sipped it, a man came into her view, dragging his rake across the gravel of the avenue; he appeared and disappeared between the trees. It was out of her silence that Lady Melbourne's suggestion seemed to grow. 'Would Annabella care—it should only take a minute or two—to make a list of whatever qualities in a husband she felt were necessary to attach her?' After all, it was a library, there must be paper and ink in it; Lady Melbourne promised to leave her to collect her thoughts.

Annabella might have resented such interference more if it did not involve just the kind of game that she delighted in. It seemed to promise her a sort of *playing at* life. Still, a touch of that resentment coloured the way she acted it out. 'Indeed, that's just what I would like,' she said and began, gently, to tease her aunt's expectations. 'It hits off my idea of what they call a literary marriage, exactly: between a woman, that is, and a list of qualities. I feel I have the character of the perfect husband so clearly in mind that sketching it would be a positive pleasure.' A literary marriage, in flesh and blood, was naturally what both of them had at the back of their thoughts: Lord Byron's name figured all the more prominently between them for being unmentioned. If only Annabella could persuade him to show his hand, without being compelled to give away her own! She believed that nothing could make *her* feelings clearer than the confession of *his*. She wished, above all, to determine the state of her affections. That was the prize, for which a certain amount of sincerity might be sacrificed. The worst she would be guilty of was ambiguity; her real fear was failing to stick to it under pressure of her aunt's conversation.

That she was, in the most important sense, at odds with Lady Melbourne, she had no doubt—in spite of the fact that one of the feelings her aunt inspired in her was a desire to confide. Annabella's confessional instincts were always strong, and though she hoped, at least in part, to overcome them, her greatest stroke was to guess from the first that nothing could conceal how much she had at stake as well as honesty—in a careful measure, of course, and strictly hedged about. She wished to indicate to Lord Byron how acceptable his attentions would be, without appearing to play for them. The fact that she still thought of the experiment as a kind of game suggested that she hadn't yet taken on the full weight of her aunt's advice. In any case, Annabella intended to win it. The idea of scoring off Lady Melbourne was just what a daughter of Sir Ralph was practically bound, by filial duty, to delight in.

In the event, it took her considerably longer than a minute or two. Lady Melbourne appeared, at shortening intervals, to inquire how her niece got on. Annabella waved her away, with a practised blush and a shake of the head. The fact was, as she 'confessed' to her aunt afterwards, that she had enjoyed the task of composing her lover from scratch. She doubted, she said, whether any man would ever exert himself as much in living up to her idea of a husband as she had in framing it. Lady Melbourne, smiling, sat down and picked up the paper to read. Miss Milbanke asked her to excuse the several blottings; she could not refrain from indulging her powers of correction. Flesh-and-blood gentlemen, she found, rarely suffered being improved upon so patiently. Her aunt said nothing; and so Annabella, after a minute, gave way to silence herself, surprised by the flutter of vanity she felt: that of an artist seeing her work examined.

Years later she remembered the scene and was constantly struck, not so much by the subtlety of her intent or its naivety, as by what the combination of the two had produced: a kind of prescience. Yes, she was young. She had had little sense of the force that her ideas would achieve in their reality, and her tone suggested most clearly the imaginative luxury to which a spoilt daughter had become accustomed. But the contradictions in her description had been only too faithfully played out in the conflicts of fact; and though the free expression of them had not, at first, been without its ironies, it was a mistake to dismiss out of hand the sharpness of her vision. She had seen clearly what lay ahead, and her best consolation lay in the fact that she had, she believed, lived up to her sense of desert.

Her aunt read out, selectively, her sketch of a husband. The paper lay in the flat of Lady Melbourne's palm. She lifted a lorgnette to her eyes to scan the page and began to declaim it in the off-hand fluent rhythms that carried her own conversation along. Her voice had a kind of smile in it; it was, almost perfectly, an expression capable of being put on and kept up. '*That her husband* was to maintain consistent principles of duty,' she read; 'that he must be pos-sessed of strong and generous feelings . . . And pray,' she interrupted her-self suddenly, glancing up at her niece, 'how was he to reconcile them, when these opposed each other?'

Annabella repressed a smile: she had reckoned on a little quizzing of this sort. One could scarcely suspect Lord Byron of 'consistent principles of duty'. She had hoped, by this opening sally, to put her aunt off the scent of what she was hunting for. But it mattered just as much to throw Lord Byron a little in her way— to hint that she might be willing to come round. No one, of course, could claim a more generous share of strong feelings than the poet himself. Paradox, then, was the note to be struck; and Annabella was conscious of the almost physical pull involved in taking with one hand what she refused with another. She hoped to require from her husband '*an equal tenor of affection*', but she ven-tured to assert that '*any attachment, which has not been violently fixed, can-not steadily endure*'. Lord Byron's capacity for, as Annabella put it, 'violently fixing' an attachment, the mother-in-law of Lady Caro-line, and his great confidante in their affair, had little reason to suspect, but she could not answer for his 'endurance' and was puz-zled by the freedom with which her chaste niece seemed to play on such themes.

'*I do not regard beauty*,' Lady Melbourne continued her recitation, '*but am influenced by the manners of a gentleman*.' Lord Byron unquestion-ably had both; and to confuse the matter further, Annabella had written, and now heard her aunt read back to her, that '*she was always, by nature, suspicious of any too perfect agreement between them. That is, she preferred good manners that seemed not merely the most flattering ornament to good looks*.' If Lady Melbourne was aware of having been matched for subtlety, she could console herself with the reflection that her niece had become lost in it. '*Genius is not in my opinion necessary*,'—she had at least come to the end of the page—'*and, I suspect, difficult to unite with the qualities I have mentioned. Yet I am afraid that some genius is requisite to understand a fellow-creature, and a good heart is not the best proof of penetration. A good heart, however, is what I absolutely require in the character of a husband, which leaves me, I suppose, much as you found me: unwed.*'

Lady Melbourne, in whose voice the smile might be said to have hardened with the strain of preserving it, now ventured to suggest 'that anyone who could make up the sum of these contradictions must be either a madman or an angel.' It amazed Annabella afterwards that she forbore, simply, to grin, as she directed her aunt's attention to the reverse of the page, on which a single condition had been written. This, Lady Melbourne, flustered at last, now read aloud: '*I would not enter into a family where there was a strong tendency to insanity.*' Annabella had feared, in the final minute, that in spite of everything she had tipped her cap too plainly at Lord Byron. She had hoped by this late addition to upset anything like certainty in her aunt's views. Lord Byron's descendence from Admiral Byron, or 'Mad Jack', was so well known that Lady Melbourne could not doubt the object of Annabella's reference, which had the additional effect of seeming to acknowledge the character against which each of them, privately, had been testing Miss Milbanke's description. 'Well,' Lady Melbourne said, asserting her dignity by rising first, 'I believe we must find you an angel after all, if you're not to become incorrigibly spinsterish, like your dear friend Miss Montgomery.' Annabella was sensible of the threat in these words; it was, perhaps, the clearest note of her little triumph.

It seemed wonderful to Annabella to have put her famous aunt into a temper, especially as she had in no respect compromised the innocence of her role. Sir Ralph might be the victim of other people's bullying self-assurance, but his daughter saw no reason to give way with him. Lady Melbourne left Jennings to see her out. Annabella watched her recede into a private room, with a delicacy of womanly grace that had just begun to stiffen into brittleness.

Jennings, as it happens, had a message for Annabella, which, he advised her, was to have an immediate reply. It came from Lady Caroline—the Lambs occupied the apartments on the second floor of Melbourne House. Lady Caroline had seen Miss Milbanke come in and had guessed with whom she was closeted; now, in turn, she begged for a minute of her time. Jennings showed himself in the confidence of his mistress's daughter-in-law by guiding Annabella up the broad stairs. She was conscious of a slight pressure on her vanity induced by the attention she was receiving, at one of London's great houses, from its most glittering figures. She felt the need to spill off, a little, some of the flow of her spirits; and so she remarked, as Jennings allowed her to pass on the steps, 'that it seemed quite a morning for little chats. She was unused to being the object of so much curiosity.'

Afterwards, she had occasion to remember his response. 'Miss Milbanke will no doubt grow accustomed to it—as much as one may, that is.' This was, as she later reflected, the first chord sounded of what became the deafening symphony of her life. The curiosity of strangers struck her more and more as a noise in which all other sounds, including the intimations of lovers, of friends, of her own conscience, were lost. At the time, she felt only the flutter of tickled vanity at what was expected of her, at the prospects to which she must learn to inure herself.

There was no one to direct or receive her when she reached the top of the stairs, but the door was open, and she pushed against it. She found herself standing at the fringe of a long Persian carpet, unrolled down the length of a hallway. It was adorned on either side by a succession of busts, the heads, as she noted in passing, of their famous contemporaries: Canning, De Witt, Fox, Sheridan, etc. Lady Caroline's husband, as Annabella knew, harboured ministerial ambitions, but the bust that presented itself most forcefully to her inner eye was that of Lord Byron. It would, she imagined, beautifully ornament any hallway, including her own; and she considered for a minute in that light the possession of him, as one might consider the purchase of a work of art. Yes, she decided, he would do very well as a husband in marble. A series of doors stood between the heads, and she walked the length of the hall—her sense of invasion becoming acute—to determine if any of them hinted at their mistress's presence. The thought struck her that Lord Byron himself must have come this way, many times; the apartments seemed designed to keep a visitor secret. She tried at random a succession of handles. One of them turned, and the door gave way, yielding at first a view of the gravelled walk behind the house, and then the closer comforts of a study: a thick rug, the remains of a fire, a deep chair, and a table, covered with papers, pushed under the window. A door to the side opened inwards. Annabella had just stepped forwards to glance at the contents of the desk. She had little time to register the shock of surprise at finding her name at the top of one of the papers, and her writing below it, when a voice from the inner chamber called clearly, 'You have found me out.'

Lady Caroline emerged now, barefooted, wearing nothing but a loose gown. She looked thin and pale. Only her lips made a plea for colour, being almost obscenely red. They suggested the slickness of fruit freshly eaten. Annabella was conscious of the way they centred one's gaze and deliberately withdrew hers—to meet the large eyes, startled and startling, of her hostess. 'You have found me out,' she repeated and, after the usual kisses and courtesies, added, to make her meaning plain, and by way of apology, 'Lady Melbourne presumed to show me these samples of your poetry, which I believe are delightful. I have just had them back from Lord Byron himself, who perfectly agrees. We have all been utterly charmed. What an extraordinary girl you are, he said. Who would imagine so much strength and variety of thought under your placid countenance?'

There was in her sisterly attention something to be fought off; it made claims, it called for and overcame resistance. Annabella, against her will, began to redden. She had been caught off guard. Lady Caroline offered her guest the chair and threw herself upon the low couch that ran along the wall opposite the window. Annabella's defences, already fatigued from her earlier interview, had been breached; what finally flooded in, gathering and rising in her breast, was a swell of high feeling. 'Everyone calls me placid and thinks me cold. I presumed Lord Byron to possess greater discernment.' Caroline, sweetly smiling, offered to correct his impression. At which, after a moment's silent rehearsal, Annabella more softly remarked, 'It is only that I may be said to suffer from vanities as other women suffer from nerves. It does me no good to have them played up to; it is like telling ghost tales to children. I feel too often, inwardly rising, a shriek.' And then, with her eyes all but closed and speaking by rote, 'I have felt the madness of pride to such a degree that I have struck my head against my bed-room wall till I staggered back.' She yielded to this Carolinish outburst more or less wilfully. That it was true, she could not deny to herself; but she volunteered it less in confidence than rivalry. Perhaps, she later reflected, it was the air of rivalry itself that gave her away. Caroline now clapped her hands together and gave her a look above the tips. 'My poor girl,' she said—and Annabella could not measure the extent of her irony—'what a little volcano you are, to be sure, under all that beautiful snow.'

Annabella was conscious, from this opening exchange, of hav-ing lost ground. The fact made itself felt. It seemed to alter the angle of her view and brought into sharper comparison how level had been the gaze she had directed at Lady Melbourne. Now, towards Caroline, she was distinctly looking up—a tendency to which, strangely, Caroline's air of apology only contributed. 'I wanted to see you,' Caroline offered at last, 'because'—her hesitation was only a calculation of her effect—'because I have a confession to make.' Annabella could not disguise from herself the quick fear brought on by this amiable introduction. It proved to her how much she felt she had to suffer at Caroline's hands, of exposure, if nothing worse; and exposure had often seemed to her the worst fate of all. 'I have told Lord Byron,' Lady Caroline continued, 'when he applied to me, that you were engaged to George Eden. I believed it to be true at the time; I have heard nothing to contradict it. But I cannot deny, as a second motive, a desire to spare you attentions that I supposed you to consider displeasing. It has lately occurred to me that perhaps I have been hasty—on both counts. I wished to do you justice and discover, from your own lips, the state of your attachments.'

Caroline's air, as she spoke these words, was all solicitude and contrition, but Annabella suspected that, in the largest sense, she was being practised upon. Indeed, she seemed to feel the closing of a door; she was being forced to choose, as it were, inside or out. Lady Caroline was attempting to push Annabella into one of two unpleasantnesses: into either a contradiction or a confession. If Lord Byron's attentions were, in fact, displeasing, then Annabella could hardly regret the mistake into which he had been led. But if she acknowledged the truth, that Mr Eden had been rejected, she invited Lady Caroline to entertain the crudest conjectures as to the other question. Annabella recognized that an outright lie, especially one so easily contradicted, was beyond her. The simple truth was, perhaps, best blindly adhered to; and blindness of a sort is just what she felt as she confessed 'that Mr Eden and herself had formed no understanding. They were under no obligations to each other, but she considered it, in all fairness to him, a question of honour to leave the matter there.' At which, she allowed a brief shining fullness to rise to her eyes, hoping that a little cloud of tender feeling might, for a minute at least, obscure a clear view of herself.

Afterwards, on her way home—Annabella's recovery had been quick; a softening of temper seemed the only enduring effect of her show of tears—she began to puzzle over her latest encounter. How little, it seemed, Lord Byron's mistress had to gain from the confession that one of her rivals was free to accept him. She felt for the first time the hand of true fear resting on her. It occurred to her that Caroline's cozy intervention had not been outside the scope of Lady Melbourne's design, that the pair had approached her in concert. And she began to detect, even in her own impulses, the pattern of a larger orchestration. The game they intended to play was still beyond her, but as a proof of its progress she had only to consult her own conscious feeling of exercised tact. She was living to win, and a manner both joyous and indifferent had crept into her conduct of relationships formerly sacred: with her mother, her friend, her suitor. This was new to her, and either the first mark of incipient adulthood, or something more troubling still. Though whether, in the event, it would matter so much if she *did* win, Annabella was not yet in a position to say. What victory itself would look like was perhaps the first of the questions demanding her answer.

Chapter Seven

—

AN ANSWER, THEN, WAS JUST what Annabella was soon required to make. Within two weeks she had received a letter from Lady Melbourne. She took it after breakfast into the garden to read. The weather was the very best of October. The light, in yellows and reds, played across the fall of plane-tree leaves on the Gosfords' square of lawn, and a pleasant friction between the two colours produced, it seemed, a glow of heat at the edges. The stone bench placed at the bottom of the garden was perfectly dry, and she had only to brush a handful of fat leaves from the surface of it to secure for herself a seat that she could adopt, and keep to, for as long as her purpose lasted, without fear of damp. She broke the seal of the envelope and emptied its contents on her lap. What seemed to be two distinct notes lay before her, composed on different paper and in different hands. She recognized in the first her aunt's writing, and though her breath quickened at the sight of the second (Annabella always enjoyed the constraint and deferral of pleasures), she decided to begin with the former.

Lady Melbourne (in what Sir Ralph called his sister's best 'harum-scarum' style) entered at once upon an explanation of their 'recent conference'. She had had at the time already in her possession the note which she now saw fit to dispatch to her niece, after a deal of soul-searching in which she had attempted to weigh and rank, if not to reconcile, the distinct duties of which she was severally possessed: to her brother, to her own son, to Lord Byron, and 'of course, to yourself, my dear Annabella'. She had hoped 'by a closer inquisition' into her niece's feelings to spare herself the need for 'playing any further part in the affair'. Had she been perfectly persuaded that Annabella could never, on any account, reciprocate the sentiments of which Lord Byron had entrusted to herself the communication, she would gladly 'have given the matter up, and let it rest, at once'. But she found she could not so persuade herself. Annabella's responses had been sufficiently obscure and uncertain as to admit the possibility that she might, given time and a better acquaintance with her own feelings and their object, learn to resolve the paradox of her desires in such a fashion as to allow to one, who consistently satisfied at least half of her contradictory demands, the favour of her choice. The proper period of that acquaintance she had at length decided to anticipate 'in consideration towards *him*, whose anxiety to know his fate seemed to preclude the patience which might be necessary to attain it.'

And so, such as it was, she laid the question in her niece's hands and trusted to her own judgement the resolution of her own doubts. She begged for his sake, however, that Annabella would consider well the extent to which she might feel free 'to canvas a general opinion' to help her to a decision. Lady Melbourne believed it to be her duty to remark that she had not, as far as that went, mentioned the matter to Sir Ralph. She hesitated— this was added in a postscript, which seemed to indicate a second sitting and a development of mood and tone—to presume to direct her niece's deliberations, but she felt it might not be improper to advise that Annabella had better 'take off the stilts on which she had been mounted' in their previous interview before she came to a decision. She knew from her own experience that such questions might easily be said to possess 'an imaginary quality' which obtruded on their proper consideration; it was best to address them with one's feet on firm ground. One wasn't, after all, playing games.

A game, however, was just what Annabella, briefly, felt the elation of having won. She could even, fondly, condescend to smile at her aunt's little gibe about stilts. Annabella's feet had never before felt so lightly the pull of 'firm ground'. Every circumstance, large and small, seemed to contribute to her happiness. The unusual, almost personable, warmth of autumnal air, the light mixing on her lap, and the expectation of what awaited her indoors (that little flurry of self-interested activity; what a blessing it was, being already engaged to Mary Montgomery for tea!) combined with her sense of holding in her own hands, not only her own fate, but that of the most celebrated poet of the age. She was young; the world was expanding around her, but she seemed to remain, however it grew, at its centre. Her faith in her own deserving had at last been met, and beautifully, grandly, at that. She was on the verge of a choice, but it was lightened by just enough uncertainty to spare her the burden of the full, particular weight of a *yes* or a *no*. Even so, she could not delay for ever, in the sunshine, her reading of the second note. She must, in the end, turn to it; and as she did, her heart began to race with no simple consciousness of joy.

My dear Lady M.—or, dare I write it?—Aunt,

I have always openly professed my admiration of your niece and have ever been anxious to cultivate her acquaintance, but C told me she was engaged to E. So did several others, all being generally convinced that E would make the best husband in the world. Under these circumstances I withdrew and wished not to hazard my heart with a woman I was so extremely inclined to love but at the same time sure could be nothing to me. The case is now different—as your daughter-in-law herself has tenderly 'put it' to me. I have trusted you to my secret and am entirely in your power. I do not care about her fortune and should be happy if the floating capital of which I am now master could by some arrangements turn out to be advantageous to both. Does Miss M. waltz?—it is an odd question—but a very essential point with me. I wish I had any hopes that it should be possible for me to make myself agreeable to her, but my fears predominate, and will I am sure give me a very awkward appearance. I wish you would undertake to say a few words for me. Could you not say that I wish to propose, but I have great doubts of her, etc.

Excuse my asking this favour, but you have always been so kind to me in every crise de Coeur that I trust to your being my friend in this case. Everything rests with A.M. herself, for my earnest wish is to devote my whole life to her.

Yours ever,

B

There was, no doubt, a great deal in this to please a young lady, but enough to trouble her, too. That presumptive 'aunt' suggested how snugly Lord Byron supposed himself to be 'in' with one branch, at least, of the family to which he aspired to attach his name. It spoke, if nothing else, of his confidence in her answer, but the reference also revived in Annabella her suspicions of acting, as she had put it to herself, in a larger concert—which isn't to say that she had ever paid heed to the rumours occasionally floated about the poet and her aunt. Lady Melbourne was, after all, nearly four decades his senior, and her charms, such as they may have been, had certainly aged into the wintry end of autumnal. Annabella herself, milkily complected, could hardly repress on occasion a tender abhorrence from kissing her aunt's papery cheek. The lengths to which a lover's attraction might reasonably be expected to go produced in her a shiver of disgust. But the breath of that disgust was drawn in fear, and her own distaste struck her—as she entered, almost unwillingly, this avenue of her curiosity—as perhaps the clearest proof of her naivety in these matters. She did not trust herself to guess the enticements a young man counted on in such relations. She was far from confident of possessing them in any useful measure. Lord Byron's appetites, it was generally understood, were well seasoned; and Annabella was perfectly aware that she could not, in the event of her accepting him, presume to satisfy only his sense of her virtue. There were other senses that demanded their due, and she was conscious, in her own life, of having starved them.

Her eye tended to stop, too, as she reread the letter, on that pretty piece of vagueness which Lord Byron himself had casually accented. Her aunt's daughter-in-law was, of course, Lady Caroline, but just what was meant by the way in which she had 'tenderly put' the 'case of Miss M.' to the poet was a subject that began to occupy Annabella's jealousies. The rumour of their affair was well established; its truth could be little doubted. What her interest might be in proving Miss Milbanke free to bestow her hand, Annabella had already questioned—bafflement had been her only answer. She had supposed herself too innocent to enter into any sympathy with the motives or appetites of that spoilt creature. But Annabella's curiosity, now excited, knew neither bounds nor bars and ventured forth in every direction. The worst imaginings began to appal her thoughts, in a manner that first and foremost convinced her of the depths of her own corrupting fancy. She was not, she discovered, above being involved herself in the scenes that her darkest fears luridly conjured up.

But there were other, simpler, reflections to upset her, which she turned to almost for the relief of her deeper anxieties. That business about the waltz: she would have liked to believe him capable of merely teasing her, quietly, through the medium of her aunt. Surely a man who had pledged to devote his life to her happiness could not so quickly have forgotten the circumstances of their first meeting? True, they had not spoken, but Annabella had played so prominent a part in directing the steps of the ladies that only a gentleman blind to their charms or madly in love with one of them could have failed to perceive her. Unless, indeed—and this was a more comfortable line of thought—he had been so occupied by his sister that he had no attention to spare for flirtations. A fact, if true, which spoke well not only of Lord Byron's sense of brotherly *tendresse* but of his general indifference to the world of beauty where there was one particular relation at hand to claim his solicitude. And, if he was teasing her, Annabella was too well aware of her tendency 'to mount herself on stilts', in her aunt's phrase, to resent for long the gallantry of a gentleman who discreetly tapped against them, by way of reminder. Finally, there was that off-hand business of the 'etc.', which she read over and over again, till she could make nothing of it but her instinctive dislike of abbreviation.

Chapter Eight

—

MISS MONTGOMERY, UNEXPECTEDLY, had been inspired by the fine weather to propose their venturing out in it, and Annabella was glad of the chance to relieve her considerable indecision by the exercise of her two legs. She had decided to put a term to her hesitation. Her sense of what was due Lord Byron precluded a lengthy period of reflection, and this limitation, practically a decision in itself, had given her an almost vertiginous dose of high spirits. Besides, she always felt vigorous, innocent and free in the company of her ailing friend. Her mood seemed to her, as they strolled through the fall of leaves into Regent Street, a hint of internal decisions struck, which would soon bubble up. That sense of rising uncertainty was among the effects she decided to ascribe to 'being in love': it suggested to her the first blustery onset of the positive. She was conscious, indeed, of the need for a sober corrective, which no one was better placed to administer than Mary Montgomery. But this fact could not entirely subdue in Annabella a childish impatience, which the stronger always feel towards the weaker. She supposed herself on the verge of a prominence that might for ever change their relation to each other; and it seemed to her somewhat hard, in the act of attaining it, to have to abide in their discussion of the question to the old proportions.

What she learned, however, from her conversation with Miss Montgomery struck her as a kind of reminder: this is the force of which a friend is capable. Mary, with one of her grateful ironies, had claimed the due of Annabella's arm; and as they passed briefly into Regent Street together, Miss Milbanke, guiltlessly enough, acknowledged to herself the pleasure she took in the contrast they afforded the passers-by. Her friend, with her clever and humorous features squeezed into the corners of her face: stooped, pale, dependent. Herself, blooming in the hothouse heat produced in her pretty round head by the necessity of a decision: free-striding, supportive, erect. Mary liked Regent Street only from the security of one of its coffee houses, where she could enjoy the view of every Tom and Jerry in their tour of the shops with, as she said, 'a little elbow-room to mock them in'. She was, in her reputation as an invalid, sufficiently the 'real article' that the press of people against her occasioned sensible distress. Regent Street, in particular, was very much the parade of the men. The ordinary rules of gallantry seemed not to apply. Even Annabella, protected as she already perceived herself to be by a subtle shield of self-importance—held up, as it were, by her idea of Lord Byron himself, and forged from the interest he took in her—was glad, at last, when the traffic deposited the pair of them upon the banks of St James's Park and allowed them the freedom of quiet.

Annabella, as they took their seat upon one of the benches that lined the water, remarked on the felicity of the weather. It was positively golden. The autumn had reached just that stage of the gilding when things begin to go brittle and break off. Pools of leaves at their feet equalled, beautifully, the sparseness of the trees. The ducks, too, seemed a pleasant proof of nature's gift for the *buffo*, the humorous touch. It was strange, Annabella remarked, that garrulous people never so prettily adorned a scene. Mary, for once, refused to 'make conversation'; and as Annabella continued to let the flow of her spirits spill out in 'small talk', she felt herself, unfairly, being cast in the role of the duck.

'I have heard,' Mary finally, and by a change of key, broke in, 'that Mr Eden has taken up the incumbency near Bury St Edmunds; that he has quit London.'

Annabella confessed to having seen him go. 'He had been,' she kindly added, 'delighted by the situation. It was almost all he could have wished for.' A recognition, on Annabella's part, of what lay hidden in that 'almost' affected her, it seemed, with something of her friend's mood for they lapsed again into silence. Mary, happily, let them. She had the air of someone waiting out the trivial, as if she trusted in what might be called her magnetizing force to draw the real metal to herself—the dross, for once, held no attraction for her. 'I have some news,' Annabella offered at last. 'I want your advice.' But humourlessness was just what she had not counted for, and she found her recitation of Lord Byron's 'approach' oddly interrupted by it. She had been expecting, at the very least, to quicken curiosity, which would have given air to the fuel of her confession. What met her, instead, was the silence of concern; she heard, echoed back at her, only the noise she was making. She almost gasped at the clatter, which seemed, indeed, to give her intentions away, as much to herself as to her friend: she planned to accept him.

When she was finished, the first thing Mary decided to question was whether his 'approach', since this was the word they were giving it, had not been suspiciously quick. Annabella had scarce seen him a dozen times and had conversed with him, it might be, on fewer than half of those occasions. Her fortune was, thank God, well known to be entangled enough that one could not imagine Lord Byron to be hunting after it; but (and Mary attempted to smile her insult into pleasantry) one presumed that Lord Byron had sufficiently 'the pick' of beauty that Annabella's claims to it, great as they were, could hardly be said to have decided him. Annabella began to redden. She considered for a moment a dignified return to silence. But she feared, with a burst of self-analysis, that her dignity could not outface her friend's, so she decided to make a point of her advantages—of her intimacy with the poet. 'He is inclined,' she said, with a confidential air, 'to open his heart unreservedly to those whom he believes good, even without the preparation of much acquaintance. He is extremely humble towards persons whose character he respects, and to them he has been known to confess his errors—and his love—with almost precipitate haste.'

This seemed all very well, as far as it went, but Mary would not admit that it went very far. His own precipitation could scarcely claim, as the price paid for it, a similar rush of imprudence from Annabella. Surely it was the part of the wiser head to defer any engagement until a deeper and more durable basis for it had been established. It seemed to Mary, distinctly, to be 'plucking at chances' to accept him now; it was unlike Annabella to seize at such things. By 'things', Annabella quickly took up, Mary surely did not merely mean 'good fortune'. Annabella should hate to find that she had acquired the reputation, among her dearest friends, of someone who refused whatever came her way from a sense of honour that was really only a mask for indecision and timidity. That word conjured an image of her father; and taking strength from real feeling, she saw her way to addressing an aspect of the question much nearer her heart. Conscious of emerging at last onto the higher ground, however exposed, Annabella added, that she had seen in these past weeks prospects opened before her—of love and beauty, enhanced by all that wealth, fame, and genius could accomplish—which she had hardly dreamed of. It seemed to her that the best she could hope for was to deserve them; she might for ever regret the failure to attempt it.

'My dear Bell,' Mary quickly and with greater warmth rejoined, 'you do me no credit to suggest that I have any fear for your deserts. You deserve worlds; it is rather that I suspect Lord Byron himself incapable of living up to you than the reverse.'

'But you must see, much as you love me,' Annabella now softly replied, 'that any association with a man of Lord Byron's prominence, whatever you may think of his prudence, offers possibilities —if nothing else, then, of seeing my own merits acknowledged— which I could never aspire to, without it.'

'I should have thought that the warm and particular regard of your dearest friends would have sufficed you.'

'You mistake me, kindly, lovingly, but almost wilfully, my dear Mary. I mean by possibilities the full extent of the moral education that any contact with a nature as expansive, as noble, as ambitious, as Lord Byron's must entail.'

Mary echoed the word, as if by a change in tone to give it its real meaning. 'Ambitious.'

And Annabella, fully conscious of her friend's understanding, and rising to it, repeated, 'Yes, ambitious. I confess it, Mary: I am ambitious.' And then, as if by a distant shot having narrowed the gap between them, until their ships lay enmeshed in each other, she began to board and address the argument, hand-to-hand. 'I admit to possessing a greater portion of ambition than you do, with this exception: that I should have thought you no less ambitious *for* me.'

'Did Mr Eden, then,' Mary answered her, descending to tactics herself, 'never declare his feelings to you?'

Annabella, frankly, stopped short at this. 'He did.'

'And you declined him?'

'I did.'

Mary, quietly, took this in and then, after a moment, said, 'I confess to having thought him a proper, loving, honourable, amiable man. I am sorry for him. I am sorry for both of you.'

Annabella perceived in this last general expression of pity a wrong note. It shifted at once, like all wrong notes, her attention from the music. It recalled to her the nature of the performer: a lively, clever, affectionate girl, who deserved the largest acknowledgement in return but was confined by illness to a dependence on her female friends. Annabella saw now in Mary's pity the hand of envy; and having found it out, she refused to believe that envy had not had its hand in the whole song. It was only a question of whether the fact could be gracefully acknowledged by some subtle distinction in her reply.

She was prevented at first from attempting it by the recognition, amidst the general foot-traffic, of Lord and Lady Gosford, approaching from the side of Piccadilly in their barouche. 'How delightful it was, the way the weather brought about these coincidences! It really was so fine,' Lady Gosford declared, as soon as her foot touched the ground, 'that she didn't know whether she mightn't after all attempt a walk. Nothing should give her greater pleasure than the young ladies' joining her.' She added, for the benefit of Miss Montgomery, that a little perambulation was supposed to do one a great deal of good: *a good walk* was the only medicine her doctor could not excessively prescribe. Annabella, seeing her chance for just the necessary 'distinction', pointedly took up the offer, as if their confidences had reached a natural term; there was nothing left to be said. The four of them set off together, with Mary taking the arm of Lord Gosford.

As they crossed the little bridge, he inquired of Miss Montgomery what the pair of them had been so busily gossiping over. Mary, archly, confessed a horror of gossip; they had, she said, been discussing poetry. The question had come up, of whether Lord

Byron's present popularity had not had a pernicious effect on his readers. It was Mary's belief that he had excited an appetite for sensations which had begun to vitiate the pleasure one had been accustomed to taking in the modest, the sensible, the durable, and the good. Annabella, lagging on Lady Gosford's arm, now looked over her shoulder for a chance to intrude. In a high, sweet voice (that tasted in her own mouth like apple-cider going hard), she remarked that 'among the strangest of what you call the effects of Lord Byron's company, upon myself, is that he tends to make me exceedingly pious. I am never more jealous of my own propriety, of my modesty, sense, and goodness, as you put it, than in the company of that reputed libertine. His manners are so perfectly those of a gentleman that one feels, in oneself, any deviation from that standard to the most painful degree.'

'It was not the effect of his company,' Mary replied, with the air of one insisting on her own game by continuing to play it, 'that formed the object of my remarks; rather, the influence of his poetry itself.'

Annabella had by this time drawn her hostess into the foot-path beside her friend. A little shifting all round became necessary, to steer Lady Gosford out of the bank of leaves at the edges. 'As for that,' Annabella resumed the discussion, when this was accomplished, 'I believe myself to be so tainted with the *blue* that I may as well aspire to some of the privileges of that tribe. It is our vanity, which we are best humoured in, to trust in our literary convictions as the honest may be supposed to trust in their consciences. I admit that the moral and immoral are dangerously mixed in Lord Byron's verses, although in a manner which, I think, we may call "true to the life". Vice is never indulged in but as a lesson to the virtuous. His heroes, at least, always suffer for their sins.'

'I believe his heroines suffer even more.' It was wonderful to

Annabella how coolly her friend had kept up the tone, though what followed had the air of a stronger sincerity. 'For myself, I confess,' Mary said, 'to having seen much in his writing that I should not dare to claim the comprehension of. Not all of us possess so fine a critical understanding as Miss Milbanke's, and there may be some who delight in his depiction of vice merely for vice's sake.'

They had by this point returned to their original station, by the bench overlooking the water; the coachman awaited them. Lady Gosford, who was shrewd enough to suspect in their discussion the heat of a deeper opposition, interrupted it to offer the use of her barouche as a conveyance home. They should be a little uncomfortable and close, but it hardly mattered on a journey so short. Lord Gosford, having business in town, declared his intention of walking, upon which Mary gratefully accepted his wife's invitation.

Annabella reluctantly followed her friend into the barouche. She had hoped to continue their discussion alone: if only, as she put it to herself, to pick the burrs off one's stockings after their pleasant walk. Mary's disagreeable reservations had a way of clinging, and Annabella could not rest until she had removed them, one by one. She was fatigued, she had sat down again, but there remained a little to do. 'It is better, surely, even for them,' she ventured to say, after an interval in which, one might have supposed, the conversation had been dropped, 'that Lord Byron's readers satisfy their tastes in fancy rather than fact.' At which Mary took it up again and, smiling sweetly, made an end of it. 'On that point, we may safely agree.'

They continued their short journey in silence. Mary, indeed, a little pale with exercise; her narrow face had contracted still more around the mouth and eyes. But for all her invalidish airs, she gave off, with her crossed arms, a sense of containment, of careful husbandry: she knew perfectly well her own store of fuel and quietly measured out for herself just what was necessary. You are intolerably self-sufficient, Annabella sourly thought—a phrase that suggested perhaps too vividly the prospect of her own dependence. Well, she had no ambition to live as her friend lived; she was confident, in this respect, of desiring better. Still, as she kissed Mary outside the door at Wilmot Street, it was all she could do not to hiss it. *You are intolerably self-sufficient.* But even the checked violence of that intention stunned her a little, as violence always does. She was glad in the end to have said nothing sharp. It would only have given her another cause for regret. It would only have forced the private acknowledgement of something she still hoped, even privately, to put off.

Chapter Nine

—

BUT SHE COULD NOT PUT IT OFF FOR EVER. The weight of indecision, secretly supported, had almost exhausted her by the time she retired to bed. She had never felt heavier in her life, but it was the worst of her weariness that rest itself could play no part in relieving it. She rose after a sleepless hour and struck a light, which she hardly blinked against. It occurred to her that she might, following her aunt's example, attempt to sketch the character of her proposed husband—if for no other reason than to occupy the dead hours of the night. Pressing her hands to her eyes, she breathed deeply and sat down to write at the dressing table. The freedom, of choice, of thought, that she felt, there at the bright centre of her darkened room, struck her even then as extraordinary: she might, after all, do anything with her life; she might, after all, take any place in the world.

'There is a chivalrous generosity,' she wrote, with an inward nod at Mary, 'in his ideas of love and friendship, and selfishness is totally absent from his character. In secret he is the zealous friend of all the human feelings; but from the strangest perversion that pride ever created, he endeavours to disguise the best points of his character, with such lamentable success, that these are generally misunderstood. Inevitably, he feels himself wronged, but he scorns to show regard to illiberality of opinion by condescending to a justification.' *Condescending to a justification*, as Annabella felt borne upon her, was just what she had set out to do; but the flow of her remarks loosened more honest reflections, and she continued. 'When indignation takes possession of his mind, and it is easily excited, his disposition becomes malevolent. He hates with the bitterest contempt. But as soon as he has indulged those feelings, he regains the humanity that he had lost (from the immediate impulse of provocation) and repents deeply. So that his mind is continually making the most sudden transitions—from good to evil—from evil to good. It would require in his wife a disposition both mild and forceful to correct such tendencies. The contradiction in these virtues suggests only too well the difficulty one must encounter in uniting them. My own disposition is, in this respect, the mirror of Lord Byron's, but that I should endeavour to improve it depends not one jot on my acceptance or rejection of his suit.'

This brought the question somewhat close to home, and she sat for a minute considering herself coldly, in the same light she had cast upon Lord Byron. Coldness, in fact, was both the quality and the source of her best nature: she could get by, at a pinch, on very little warmth indeed, and she continued to examine herself with scarcely a shiver. 'It shall be the duty of my lifetime to mend a temper whose chief defect is its vanity, a sin to which I ascribe my changeable humours and sensitivity to slights. I must also, I believe, attribute to it my reputation for generosity, for innocence, for good sense; but whether my vanity is the *cause* or the *effect* of these virtues has become for me of late a painful and uncertain question.' (Yes, she was equal to that: it was the doubt under her feet; it was the air she was falling through.) 'One of the benefits to be expected from any prolonged intercourse with Lord Byron is that he might, as they say, knock the wind out of me; I should be forced to draw new breath. I should be forced to draw new breath,' she repeated, as the bees of sleep began to buzz around her. But she shook her head against them and continued. 'Sensations, indeed, the striving after them, have been his guide from childhood and have exercised a tyrannical power over his very superior intellect. It is this craving void which drives him to gaming and love, to travel and to strongly felt pursuits of every kind. Yet amongst them are many which deserve to be associated with Christian principles. His love of goodness in its chastest form and his abhorrence of all that degrades human nature prove the uncorrupted purity of his moral sense.'

Yet even as she wrote these words, she heard the little interior vibration of an echo. Her sense of solitude—which, at the best of times, and despite her being an only and cherished daughter, had never been complete—had begun to seem hopelessly porous. What was always leaking in, from this side or that, were the feelings of other people. What flooded in now, almost overwhelmingly, were the feelings of Lord Byron himself. He was watching her; and she, demurely, had begun to adapt her step. She recalled now, at their first meeting, standing out a dance with him. 'Sensation,' he had told her, 'was his great object in life. To feel that we exist, even though in pain.' Yes, she had borrowed for her character of the poet his own confession. She had seen him only as he had chosen to see himself—or chosen, rather, to present himself to her. The stranger's hand, which she had felt from time to time resting on her shoulder, now revealed itself: it belonged to Lord Byron. He might, with his wide powers of persuasion, have orchestrated everything from the first—a sum in which she included her own small offering of love.

She was ashamed, almost, of being too innocent to guess a motive for it. That Lady Caroline's importunities had grown increasingly scandalous, scandal itself had made plain. That Annabella's spotless reputation might, for the contrast, serve to redeem his own, had already occurred to her; but only, she had presumed, at the expense of his continued relations with Lady Caroline herself. And yet—what was it Mary had said? That there was a something in the poet which she would not care to claim the comprehension of. Lord Byron could with his rough conscience handle a number of truths the mere glimpse of which would defeat Annabella's curiosity. And one of the lessons she inwardly noted was the need for more courage: for more courage and more curiosity. The scope of the game in which she imagined herself to be an innocent player almost took her breath away—the fact that Lady Melbourne might have been enlisted on his behalf; the fact that Lady Caroline herself might have seen, from her own vantage, the benefit of *joining in*. It was as if, by a strange alignment of the planets, a single blackness had appeared in the sky. The great variety of what she had failed to understand could be encompassed by its shape. The shape, whose absence clearly defined itself for her, was Lord Byron's. *He* had been keeping the light away. *His* was the darkness more palpably present when she blew her own lamp out; it was the darkness in which she fell asleep.

In the morning, however, the simpler glow of the sun prompted certain revaluations. It fell on her lap around the edges of a cloud. There was black at the edges and a soft chill within; but in the full surrounding light, pale and level with the approach of winter, she felt the kindness of warmth. How hungry she was. Worked up with nerves, she had hardly, the day before, touched her food. Hunger at least suggested her nerves were quiet. The work, her decision, had been done. Nothing was left but for her to admit to it—to bring it up. She blushed to herself at the recollection of what in the small hours had seemed to her clear-headed and now struck her as the madness of dreams. Still, the effect of it lingered, as dreams do. It was as if the violence she had checked against Mary had in the night released itself, had turned into fact. It demanded, as fact, its due, and she gave it. The private acknowledgement had been made. Lord Byron had proved himself greater than the scope of her choosing: she hadn't the measure of him. That was the fear which in the end decided her. There were other fears, greater and lesser, but none so decisive. She couldn't *see* him, that was the horror, and this blindness had infected her with the sense of being watched. The question remaining was whether what had prevailed in her belonged, most properly, to common sense or cowardice; they were pushing the same way. It was almost impossible to disentangle them.

'I endeavour not to yield to any decided preference till my judgement has been strengthened by longer observation, but I will not assign this as my only motive for declining.' This, after a good breakfast, is what she wrote to Lady Melbourne. She had returned—her composure just managed an inward smile—to the desk in her bedroom. The sheet of paper on which her night-thoughts had been scribbled lay in the basket beside it, crumpled to a ball. 'Were there no other objection, his theoretical idea of my perfection, which could not be fulfilled by the trial, would suffice to make me decline a connection that must end in his disappointment.' Was it true, or true enough, to satisfy her conscience, which was stricter, perhaps, with the letter of truth than its spirit? She supposed it was in the nature of great decisions that they bulked even larger than motives. One approached them, as it were, craning one's neck—to see around their corners for a glimpse of the motives behind them. These appeared, if at all, only after the decision was struck. 'I should be totally unworthy of Lord Byron's esteem if I were not to speak the truth without equivocation. Believing that he never will be the object of that strong affection which would make me happy in domestic life . . .' Quietly, kindly, in long unpunctuated phrases, she gave him away. Her first trial was past; it seemed to her at that moment the only one that would ever signify.

For a few days afterwards, the force of her decision sustained her. The only thing to vex her was Mary's obvious relief. Mary alone knew the secret of Lord Byron's proposal, and Annabella could scarcely turn elsewhere now to confess her reply. Still, it was very trying, she privately acknowledged, to be obliged to endure (complicitly, as it were) such a return to her friend's good opinion. The irritation of it, at least, busied her thoughts at a time when they might easily have turned inward with more painful heat; and it was a relief, perhaps, to keep up the argument in the quiet of her head not with *him* but with *her*. Had she done right? was a question that quickly presented itself, whenever other occupation failed her. In the first aftermath of her decision, it was a great comfort to her vanity to pity Lord Byron himself for the part she had played in injuring his. She read over, again and again, her favourite passages in *Childe Harold* and flattered herself that the plaintive, conscience-stricken effusions of his muse had been inspired by her. Well, they would be. It was satisfying, she sometimes admitted to Mary, to think of all the immortal poems he could write just because she had decided to break his heart.

Even so, she was conscious in the weeks to come of a loss of balance. It was as if a weight she had been pressing against had been abruptly withdrawn, and though she had caught herself, just in time, the absence continued to be felt: she was leaning, as it were, without the support of opposition. A push here or there would have knocked her down. Careful of that possibility, she decided to return to Seaham for the winter. London had 'ceased to amuse her'. This was her great protestation; she made it whenever she could. She meant by it, of course, to suggest worlds of private *ennui*, but her suggestions were rarely taken up. It was only, one supposed, the boredom a girl always feels when the balls of summer are over and the men have retired to the country to shoot. Well, perhaps it was, she once admitted, no more than that really. And yet, there were suppers still and the theatre; there were 'breakfast parties' and 'musical interludes' and tables of whist of an evening to be made up. But these gave her no pleasure now beyond the bright little cards of their invitations; she rarely attended them. She had never before considered herself to be one of those women 'in the hunt for a husband', and yet now that she had shied away at the last from catching hers, she discovered, almost to her relief, that the rest of the exercise was not worth the discomfort. She went home.

Home, then, promised a great deal: her familiar room; its quiet view of a loud sea; and the general shelter of living within her mother's arrangements. What she made of it would depend on that little distinction between common sense and cowardice—on the distinction, as she put it to herself, between a return and a retreat. It demanded, she was well aware, a very nice subtlety indeed to make out the difference. But she was a subtle girl; she never despaired of living up to nice distinctions. She hoped to return, then, with a more conscious conviction to what she had been: a country girl, unused to society, content with her own. She hoped to continue on the old lines—to make of London a mere interruption. *Unused to*, perhaps, was the only phrase on which time might be said to have wrought its effects. Another to meet her case could be supplied. Inured to? Untouched by? And yet there were moments—as the coach changed horses at Durham, two hours short of her destination; and she watched them being harnessed, through the fireside window, with the sudden happiness of impatience—in which she took comfort from the very idea of giving in to the weakest of her inclinations, when to be her *father's daughter* again seemed the only relation she could ever desire.

She soon realized, in a few days, no more, how little these distinctions counted for in the event. After the first happy rush of arrival, it grew clear that she could neither return nor retreat. All that was over. What was over, indeed, was just her capacity for taking comfort. It seemed almost as if her mother, her father, the rocks along the shore, the sea itself, had lost a quality. They had been stripped a little barer, by a kind of winter; and she couldn't but suspect her own heart of being the low sun of that season. In the long journey north, she had played out secretly the various stages of her confession. It was all a question of starting a scene. She had but to get herself remarked upon, for looking pale or thin, for failing in her usual lively spirits. Her father could easily be tempted into sympathies—her mother, into corrections. 'You've changed, my dear,' Judy might begin. Annabella had only to deny it, with a heat that would forge in the necessary reconciliation its own excuse for intimacy. The length she would go in confession was all that concerned her. She inwardly vowed—one of those promises she supposed at the time of being made for the breaking—just to stop short of his name. That was the limit she set herself. That was the size of the box in which she would treasure her secret. That was the size of the secret: his name.

And yet, to her childish surprise, they rather left her alone than otherwise. Annabella's quiet insistent inward flow of thought ran only into deeper silences. A succession of heavy gales had struck the local fisheries very hard. There had been several shipwrecks, with all their attendant widowings and orphanings. Annabella, for the first week, heard talk of little else. She was persuaded to survey the freshest scene. Under a stark white cloud a grey sea laboured. Upon the rocks, remnants of the fishing smack could still be seen, straining against the ebb to reach shore. The sand was littered with nets and spars and sails; and boots and pea-coats and hats. Annabella remained perfectly unmoved by the sight of them; they might have been left over from a play. Lady Milbanke saw it as her duty to take up a 'collection' (she was always collecting, Ralph complained) and to see that everyone was 'satisfied with their burials': the wives happily mourning, the children returning to school. Ralph himself was occupied by a tax-meeting at Durham. He was to give a speech at it, if only he knew which side of the question to support. He asked Annabella's advice. He wished to put the case before her. Her mother had long ceased to take any interest in the business—a remark at which, he was surprised to find, his daughter burst into tears.

'My dear Bell,' he said, 'oh my child.' He was conscious suddenly of his preoccupation, and ashamed. The shame got in the way of his reassurance. He put his hand to his mouth and looked at the poor girl: her round red face was too large, it seemed to him, for a child's grief. But he rose to his sense of it at last and joined her—he had been standing—on the sofa and took her head in his soft long-fingered hands. 'You have been here a week, and no one has said to you as much as a *how do ye?* You find your parents, no doubt, become very old and dull; and the worst of it is, very busy in themselves with being old and dull. My dear child, what is it?'

Annabella had always thought her father the most amiable of men. But no one, perhaps, got the virtue of it more than himself. He was complacent. He indulged his own weaknesses even more than he tended to indulge his daughter's. She had always supposed herself, if put to the test, incapable of holding anything back from him. Well, this was the test. And she found to her surprise that her struggle was all the other way. Something childish in her balked stupidly at confession, and the woman in her hardly had the words to insist on it. 'Please, carry on,' she began, nobly, perversely, 'I was really attending; I should like to hear you out. To the end.' But when he, sensibly, answered her only with silence, and her tears had dried up, she condescended to explain—with just that little excess of eloquence which always came out in her under the pressure she felt to suffer the least common griefs. 'It's my own fault: I expected too much.' She was, by this point, perfectly composed; weeping had cleared her head. 'I was conscious, you see, of having changed. What I wanted to make certain of was just by how little, the measure of which seemed to lie in the ease of my homecoming. Ease, of course, is a thing impossible to strive for. Perhaps I was guilty of striving. Something, you know, had passed in London that might be seen to have given, to any return, the shame of retreat. I was determined, by force of happiness if nothing else, to put off the shame of it. But the force itself, as one might suppose, struck me as proof of the worst. Under that sense of it, just now, you saw me give way.'

Sir Ralph only stared at his daughter. 'I don't think I understand you.' And then, finding his feet a little: 'What passed in London?'

'I had in London'—it was wonderful really, how lightly it all came out!—'a prospect opened before me, a very fine view. Or what might have been, on a clear day; though one can't expect, as Mary would put it, mountains without clouds. The mountain, one may say,' she had found a smile, 'was the picture of sublimity, but I mistrusted the path that ran up it. You have always, I know, presumed me worthy of the largest acknowledgement. It was offered, and I refused it, less from a sense of falling short—of deserving it, that is—than from the faith that real value would show itself indifferent even to the justice that can be done it. Well, I had that faith, but events have proved me very far from indifferent. And the worst of all my regrets has been, as I say, the shame that goes with them. At the time, I felt the largest grandeur of refusal, but it turns out to have aged rather worse than acceptance might have.'

'I can't make you out,' her father said, becoming impatient. 'Am I to understand that you turned down an offer of marriage?'

This was the point she had come to, but Annabella, as soon as she met it, guessed her own reserves. She could let it press harder still before giving in. A sign, perhaps the first, of her renewal: the strength to put him off. She was equal, for once, even to the necessary lie. 'No,' she said, 'it isn't that at all.' Her little secret began to grow from that moment, compacting from the privacy in which she stored it into an awkward irritable lump of obscurity. Her family felt only the discomfort it kept up within her. It made for just what couldn't be smoothed away—her obstinacy, to which they attributed the two long years of unhappiness that followed. They didn't see it for what it was, the deep digging in of independence. Lord Byron's name had the power, for Annabella, of all stolen treasure: it bought freedom with guilt.

And then, more bitterly, and with what almost passed in her for candour, she added, 'It isn't always and only a question of men. What was offered was much larger than marriage—call it fame if you like. And I didn't suppose I should miss it, but I do.'

'Well, then,' he repeated, 'I can't make you out. You're too subtle for me, my dear. You always were.' And then, happily, he hit on an evasion. 'Shall I fetch your mother?'

This brought on, in his daughter, a return of the childish. 'Please,' she said, 'don't!'

BOOK TWO

—

Marriage

Chapter One

—

IT WAS LORD BYRON'S PARTICULAR WISH, expressed in the confidence of Annabella's perfect agreement, that they be married quietly at Seaham. Cushions were all they required, for kneeling on; he was sure Lady Milbanke would be kind enough to provide them. There were to be no invitations. He had only to arrange a few of his affairs in London 'for their mutual comfort' before he could come north—just stopping at Newmarket on the way to take 'a bachelor's leave' of his sister, before he embarked on that remarkable journey 'from one into two'.

Annabella could hardly bear the weight of her own impatience. Two years had passed since she first refused his offer of marriage. After a period of silence, during which, as Lord Byron said, 'he was mourning his suit', a sort of understanding had sprung up between them. The unhappiness each had caused the other, by that offer and by that refusal, still bound them; and they looked to each other, inevitably, for certain sympathies. In time they became, as he eventually put it, 'epistolary lovers'. It had been one of the sorest trials of her subtlety to suggest to Lord Byron in the course of a long correspondence, without exposing herself to a charge of inconsistency, that the No with which she had met his first proposal might, under the pressure of a second, split like the shell of a truth to reveal the little nut of a *yes* within. But her subtlety had triumphed in the end; his proposal came early in the fall of 1814, and Lord Byron himself followed it shortly after to Seaham. Annabella had been sitting in her own room, reading, when she heard his carriage in the drive. Quietly, she put out the candles in her room before descending. She found him in the drawing room, standing by the side of the chimney-piece. He did not move forwards as she approached him but took up her extended hand and kissed it. A silence followed which she could not for the life of her break. That *he* did was the first thing she had to be grateful for. 'It is a long time since we met,' he said. 'For that, I believe,' she answered, commanding herself, 'I have only myself to blame.' To escape for a moment the strain of his company, she added, 'Let me call my parents. They are quite on fire to meet you. It is only that they don't dare to.'

'I am not such a gorgon as all that.' And then, finding a way to good humour, 'though frightful enough, I'm sure, in the relation of son. My own mother never liked to admit it.' This brought out a smile in her. Until he continued, 'But she's dead, God bless her— I know I shan't.' It was the first note struck of a tendency she began to fear in him: to break against harmony simply for the sake of it.

Within a week she had sent him away again to attend to his affairs in London, preparatory to their marriage. As soon as his carriage disappeared between the lines of the elms, she regretted her impatience to see him go—since it was only replaced by another, to see him come back. There was a great deal in her conduct as a lover that she could not think on without blushing, and in Lord Byron's absence she had nothing to do but think. She had been so silent with him, a silence that perplexed them both extremely, for neither knew how to break it. Her parents, of course, were charmed—he had set out to charm them. Byron talked of Kean and politics with Sir Ralph and village life with Judy, who, to be fair, had managed for the space of his visit to remain plausibly sober. It could not last, and Annabella's fear of a lapse, as she secretly expressed it to herself, seemed to her at the time reason enough for cutting his visit short.

Besides, he had seemed to her so strange, moody and unaccountable that they rarely had a minute's peace together. Peace, perhaps, was not the quality lacking—they had been only too quiet. In the summers when she was a girl, Sir Ralph used to take her sailing out in Seaham harbour with her cousin Sophy. Running south along the shore, they could just make out the humped shapes of the collieries through gaps in the trees on the coastline. Sophy, as the older child, more often than not handled the tiller; but when the winds were low, Sir Ralph put the sheet in Annabella's clenched fist and told her to pull till the sail flattened. What she remembered most vividly was the awkwardness of a perfect calm: every shift required a startled readjustment. Only when the wind filled again could they relax against its steady pressure. The sense she had in Lord Byron's company was of perfect calm. Each word or touch produced a light imbalance, and it required the lightest of words, of touches, to restore their tempers.

The analogy produced in her another fear. What was lacking was love, that was the wind that failed them. Without it, they could only keep their course by little adjustments. That she herself loved, the unhappiness of the past two years had given her ample proof. The failure was his, though when she offered (honourably, as she believed) to break off their engagement, the violence of his response shocked her into a deeper faith. He turned pale and fell into a seat; called for salts, brandy; said to her at last that there was no cruelty like virtue. He spoke unguardedly, in a tone that was new to her. Not even Lady Caroline, fiend that she was, would tease him into a proposal after two years only to spurn him again. He had staked everything; his life depended on her. Annabella, from a deep conviction of her own goodness, was colder than any coquette . . . Her tears finally calmed him. 'It was only,' she said, 'that she thought he did not love her.'

It was not a reproach. She had not intended a reproach, but he took it as such and gave one bitterly back: that she stared at him so silently. He could hardly make love to a statue.

She stared at him now, but at least she managed to interrupt her silence. 'She wished only to please him; she could not find the words. Consequently, she said nothing at all. And he was so peculiar with her.'

The word restored his humour—how often, in their relations, the temper of it depended on such a piece of luck, either good or bad. 'He should like to be a great deal more peculiar,' he said. She had been standing over him, and he now took her into his lap, which she submitted to, while he began to kiss her neck and cheek and temple. 'Sweet little round face,' he said, 'my little apple.' Annabella, quite ashamed of herself, silently endured these attentions, until he began to kiss her mouth—they had never kissed— which startled her into an equal greed that had left them both quite breathless by the time a foot on the stairs recalled them to their sense of place.

For the rest of that long week, whenever their tempers seemed misaligned, Lord Byron attempted a similar 'process of adjustment'. 'You are quite caressable into a good humour,' he said to her once. 'I think we shall get along very well.' She had taken him on her favourite walk over the cliffs. A late October sun had a low scurfy bank of cloud to keep the heat in. Their faces were bothered by flies, as he with difficulty clambered over the rocks, taking her hand from time to time or resting on her shoulder. The breeze on top of the cliffs was fitful, but the long sweep of the waves, flatly repeated, tirelessly arriving, suggested out to sea a steadier blow; and they had the sense of catching at the fragments, gratefully enough in that autumnal haze, of a much larger force. She had brought with her an apple and a purse of cashews, and they stopped once to sit with their backs against a rock and eat them. After a while, the extent of what she was capable of desiring began to frighten her. She made them go home again, each in a surly and childish mood, which was not unloving: they were turned, as it were, towards each other in sullen frustration. The waves and the shore. That evening she asked him to leave. The sooner they were married the better; she could not trust herself. He should 'arrange his affairs' in London as quickly as possible, and then come back to her when these were settled for what they both desired, a quiet wedding.

As the year 1814 drew to a close, she passed her twenty-first Christmas stuck at home, the precocious daughter of her parents' affections. These had begun to chafe; it was time she grew up. Lord Byron complained bitterly of the 'law's delay' (*Hamlet*, indeed, was the text on which they both drew for material), but nothing, save her most particular command, could persuade him to marry without having settled his debts. Newstead Abbey, his ancestral home, much as it pained him, must be sold, but the buyer was proving as indecisive as, by force of that indecision, Lord Byron himself must appear to her. Sir Ralph could not help remarking that in spite of Lord Byron's injunction to invite no one, they had better, after all, invite the groom himself; it would be a sad sort of wedding without one. Annabella, at last, commanded.

Lord Byron appeared, unannounced, in the afternoon of New Year's Eve. He had a friend with him, a young man, whose large straight nose cast a shadow over his chin. Annabella heard their carriage running over the gravel of the drive and watched them from her bedroom window. Still, she did not come down. She had a sense of his arrival that the mere physical fact of it couldn't live up to. Two months had passed since she had seen him, and she had spent the time attempting to discover what the awkwardness in her manner was that had produced its echo in him. She wanted to prepare herself—she wanted, internally, to meet him, her idea of him. Or rather, she needed a moment to enter into what she conceived to be his idea of *her*. She was conscious, of course, of the play between these two ideas, and of the fact that Lord Byron himself was quite likely to 'break up the game'. This was, as she put it to herself, just what she needed *him* for, the man himself: to break up the game. Still, she waited and listened to Dawlish, the butler, showing them to their rooms at the back of the house. It pained her that neither Sir Ralph nor Judy had moved to greet them—out of pique, no doubt, at his endless delays. She must learn to disregard their pleasure, to attend to his.

After a few minutes (she had not moved from the window), she heard the carefulness of his step, descending. One two, one two, on every stair. No other sounds; his friend must have stayed behind to change. If she hurried now, she might just catch Lord Byron alone. A glance in her bedroom mirror gave back to her an image of outward calm: she seemed fairly smothered up, from top to toe, or rather, from neck to ankle, in a long dress of green muslin that brought out the pink in her round cheeks. You strange quiet girl, she thought, is there nothing inside you? She counted to herself—one two, one two—sighed deeply and emerged into the corridor. It was only when she reached the bottom, from being out of breath, that she guessed she had been running—down the stairs helter-skelter to the library door. But she could not wait any more. She could not wait and pushed in. Lord Byron stood by the fire with his back to her. He was fatter than she remembered him, a fact just brought out by the pinch of his black waistcoat against his hips. Perhaps he had been unhappy, this struck her at once—and then: that he was still unhappy. She had seen him only two months before, but he changed shape lightly. It was a kind of nimbleness in him, the way he fattened, and peculiarly expressive in the largest sense of mood, of temper. With one foot over the other, he stooped to the heat. He turned to see who it was—saw it was she—stretched out his hand to her. For a second she hesitated, then ran across the room and flung herself sobbing into his arms. 'My lord, my lord.'

He gently disengaged himself from her embrace, but keeping her hand in his, he kissed it, cold-lipped. She was conscious of the fluster in her hurry, the smudge of tears around her eyes, and pressed her fists to them. 'I told myself that you would come today, that you must come. I knew that you would, you see, and yet, when you did, it was no less a shock.' She was expressing herself very badly, she knew, and thought of poor Mr Eden.

'I did not mean to upset you,' he said.

'No, that's not it at all. Only this time, you see, I know what to expect. More than before. I know *you*—' And then, breaking off, she smiled, too hopefully perhaps, 'I'm afraid I can't make myself clear.' But there was no answering smile; and she began to suspect that something had happened since she had seen him last. He had not in the least, as she put it to herself, attempted to enter into her idea of him—that was the fact that struck her. The fault, no doubt, lay in her own idea. She wondered if, for her part, she had failed *his*.

'Forgive me,' he said. 'I've had a dull Christmas at my sister's. Her husband, a very pretty piece of foolishness, was at home, and the children screamed at him, and the dogs barked at the children, and the servants beat the dogs. I have,' he added, 'a particular horror of children.'

For the first time, she looked at him with something like

detachment. (It relieved Annabella, after the foolish rush of her greeting, that she could return to it.) His hair was curlier than she had remembered it, his aspect altogether more boyish. Plumpness had rounded his cheeks and thickened his neck. His shirt was open, with a cravat tucked into it; his chest, broad and firm (she had felt her head against it), suggested a simplicity of character, of honesty, she knew him to be far from possessing. His face was a little pale, except here or there where the heat from the fire had reddened it. There was something in his attentions, as she remembered them, so feminine, which had been still more fully developed in the spirit of his letters, that the plain masculine effect of his presence came as a shock. It was not what she had counted on. The fear of giving her life to a man—to this man—renewed itself in her. She was conscious of desiring allies. Her parents had again proved tardy in their welcome, and she was turning to the door to say, 'I will just call out to my parents', when the door opened and the unfamiliar young gentleman with the strong-shadowed nose came in. The hair around his ears was shiny and wet from a hasty wash. This was one of the recollections that stayed with her.

The scene in general left its deep print on her mind: the restlessness of the fire in its grate; the sunshine of a muffled winter's day, the colour of bone-china, lying in pieces on the Persian rug at their feet; the intricate leathery gloom of stacked books. The library wasn't a room of which she was used to having the run. A bust of Thomas Gray stood on its pedestal by the door. He was a favourite of Sir Ralph's and had always impressed upon her a sense of adult ponderousness. She was frightened, as a child, of knocking him over, of being crushed. Perhaps that old fear contributed to a new one. For an instant, the sensation of being trapped between these two strangers in her home almost overwhelmed her. She stood on the rug between them: one by the fire, the other by the door. There seemed no escape, but she had collected herself by the time introductions were made. John Hobhouse was his name, a college friend of Lord B's, and a former travelling companion. Reaching out a hand, she welcomed him to Seaham Hall.

Her parents came down at last to dinner. Sir Ralph, himself by now embarrassed at their delay, did his awkward best to charm—it was the awkwardness itself that had its effect. The dining room was perhaps the worst room in the house; he apologized for it. One sat miserably close to the fire—one was, oneself, quite cooked. He had nothing much to praise his own cook for, but he would say this, he would just say this, she knew what to do with a fish. He had a particular horror of seeing a good fish spoiled, and the best, perhaps, he could say of Mrs Tewkesbury, is that she did not spoil it. 'She let the fish alone, thank God, she did not worry it with too much sauce.' He could never stomach too much sauce; and then, as if the idea had put him in mind of it, he confessed that he had not read *Childe Harold*. At this Annabella began to blush. His tastes were old-fashioned—but he had promised to do so, if Annabella promised to explain it to him. An attempt had been made. They had been so long waiting for Lord Byron to appear that Sir Ralph had decided at last to dip into his book. Only he could not agree to Annabella's explanations. It was quite hopeless. He had his own opinions, he could not help it, and began to insist on them. The experiment was broken off.

'It is a father's right,' Lord Byron intervened, 'to disagree with his daughter. I should not, for myself, presume to attempt it.'

'Yes, well.' The interruption had broken his flow, but, catching at a chance of wit, he said, 'And yet, and yet, you would not take No for an answer.'

'Father!' Annabella cried, but Lord Byron spoke over her, 'It was only a disagreement over the irregular verb *to love*, but Miss

Milbanke has finally taught me the proper conjugation: I did not, I do not, I will. I should rather, I confess, have stopped short at *I do* two years ago but have resigned myself to the charms of the *future perfect.*'

Annabella could not decide whether the sting in his wit was intended, but she was too good a grammarian to pass up this chance at correction; and then surprised herself by the confession it teased her into. 'I hope you do not mean to say that you *will have* loved me. It would break my heart. I mean for myself always to love you.'

He bowed at her. 'We shall attempt our own construction, to be called the *perfect eternal.* And shall love each other all our lives, I'm sure, as much as if we had never been married at all.' Lady Milbanke, at last, rewarded him with a little smile, just flattening her cheeks to raise the edges of her lips; and Sir Ralph himself gave out a snort. But Annabella could not read him. He frightened her into a wakening sense of the force of other people. Yet it was just this awakening, she bravely told herself, that had persuaded her in the end to accept him. She meant for the first time in her life to be taken along—as it were, by hand. In any case, she could not have stopped at home another year without going mad. There were so many days to be filled, and she had lately begun to entertain the notion that she could fill no more, not with books or music or mathematics. She might just stick inside one, a Tuesday afternoon perhaps, without the means inside her to reach to Wednesday. And yet the years had slipped by quickly enough. 'I am so glad you have come,' she said suddenly to Lord Byron. 'Each day I waited for you, thinking, I could not wait another day. It seemed impossible; and yet, just as impossible to me, that you should ever arrive and sit here, to be looked at or talked to.'

Lord Byron turned on her his large grey eyes, with love or pity in them, but said nothing.

Hobhouse she greatly took to. He had, after an initial shyness, much of the talking to himself. His father was a Whig MP, and John was in the first bloom of his own parliamentary ambitions. He had come from London full of stories of the House. Sir Ralph, in the middle of dinner, broke into one of these with, 'Tell me your name again, sir? I am sure I have heard it before. Would you spell it out?' It so happened he knew Hobhouse's father well. They had opposed each other on several questions with a very good grace. He thought it always a sign of character when a man could 'disagree agreeably', and they often sought each other out, after a fractious vote, and ate a good dinner and never said a word about it. Yes, a perfect gentleman; it was a pleasure to meet his son. The final test of a man's character was, of course, the character of his son. Sir Ralph was glad to see it 'lived up to'.

The fish was followed by minced pies, left over from Christmas, indifferent Stilton, and very good port. Lord Byron inquired after Lady Milbanke's health. He had heard she was ill; he hoped she was better. Annabella froze. Judy's fondness for a drink had in the past two years taken on a more public quality, or rather, her mother's privacy was no longer large enough to contain the whole of her appetite. The effect on her character had been a gradual diminishment of force; and though Annabella at first rejoiced shamefully in her own comparative powers, she had lately, as her wedding approached, begun to mourn the loss of an example. One had the sense, observing Lady Milbanke, of a tremendous underwater struggle, in which all her old strength was being brought violently to bear—though one received now only the muffled report of it, a few small waves, rather than, as before, its full immediate weight. She had sat very still through dinner, hardly trusting herself to say a word, and drinking steadily. She was very well, she thanked Lord Byron, only it had been a cold winter. Her circulation was not what it should be; one had only to look at her face to see how she suffered for it. It was a terribly draughty house. She had not felt warm, properly warm, since September. Her hands and feet seemed not to belong to her, she'd grown so clumsy with them. Her only recourse—but here Sir Ralph interrupted her to say that he had heard 'something odd that day from Dawlish, who had heard it from the cook, when she sent for the fish. An Irishman has been inquiring in the village for Seaham Hall; he claims to be Lord Byron, on his way to be married to the daughter of the house. Mrs Tewkesbury, who saw him herself wandering around the harbour and talking to the fishermen, said he couldn't have been any younger than fifty; he wore a long thin grey beard and a dirty grey coat. Even so, Dawlish has been cleaning my fowlers all afternoon. One can't tell, he says, what an impostor will stop short at.'

'It's a form of madness,' Lord Byron said, 'I am only too well acquainted with.' Annabella, whenever he spoke, attended him so closely that she could scarcely make out the words. There was a public character to his charm she could read very little into. He seemed to be playing a part—himself. The intention itself made up a kind of mask, which hid him none the less for being framed to suit his face. Occasionally, in a moment's shyness, in his stutter, she believed to catch a glimpse of the push involved—she sensed a boyish reluctance in him to perform a duty. The scale of the task staggered her conceptions: what concentration it must require to hit always upon one's characteristic response! His moment of hesitation, his stutter, was where she hoped to prise open a space for herself, for her companionship. 'My misanthropy, which is more poetical than personal,' he continued, 'is so generally believed in that the most wretched men attach themselves to it, as beggars sometimes dress themselves in cast-off clothes, to look like gentlemen. I'm afraid the borrowing does no honour to either of us. Should you like to make sure of me, however,' he added, smiling, 'you are welcome to inspect my foot. It is the too hasty signature of my Maker and serves me as a proof of authenticity.'

After dinner, they staged a mock-marriage in the drawing room. Hobhouse was given away as the bride. Sir Ralph was in fine spirits and acted the part of reverend. Dawlish was the father, and Lady Milbanke played a limping Lord Byron—a joke at which Annabella noticed the poet wince. The lovers themselves sat side by side on the music bench and watched. Dawlish decided to look for the epithalamium, which his master had spent the several months' delay in carefully rewriting. It was discovered eventually on the music stand of the harpsichord and read out to a very mixed reception. Lord Byron managed to revenge his humour upon it. Sir Ralph blushed. Hobhouse was more judicial. Only Annabella kept quiet—she could think of nothing to say. It struck her as almost blasphemous, the mockery that was made of the ceremony on which she had pinned her hopes of a new life. But her begrudging reticence shamed her just as much, and she turned at last to face the harpsichord and play a wedding march as her own tongue-tied contribution to the entertainment. The music somehow sobered them all to silence. The tune was wrong, too mournful and grand, and they sat and dutifully attended to her. It was all she could do to keep on playing without breaking into tears. In the smattering of applause that followed, she managed to rub away the softness in her eyes with the flat of her palms. At eleven o'clock, Dawlish brought in a bowl of champagne-punch, which kept them lively till midnight, when they shook hands together and listened to the bells of St Mary's ringing in the New Year. Judy, red-faced, had fallen asleep in her chair.

It snowed through the night. Lord Byron had asked her, before going to bed, when she liked to appear in the morning. Ten o'clock, Annabella had said; she was very fond of a walk at breakfast. If he liked to join her, she would be glad of his company. And in spite of their late night she came down at ten, if only to live up to her word. If only to get him for an hour to herself, for she felt they had come to an understanding—the first of their intended marriage. She waited for him in the drawing room; it was the morning of New Year's Day. She had a secretive nature and decided to class it among the thrills of love that it expanded the scope of privacy: from 'one', as Lord Byron had put it, into 'two'.

One felt all through the house the effect of the snow. It threw ghosts of itself against the walls, against the rugs on the floor. It reminded Annabella of a high repeated note on the harpsichord. There was a kind of sweet insistence in it from which one eventually began to wish to avert one's sense. And yet there was, in spite of the chill of the house, a new softness in the air that seemed a little like warmth. The fires had only just been laid and burned more brightly than hotly; Annabella, as the morning grew older, watched them settle in the grate. Her mother had for several months been accustomed to taking her breakfast in bed. Sir Ralph slept poorly, especially after a night of drinking, and tended to rise early and work in the library and sleep there. Annabella believed she had heard him, shifting his easy chair to be nearer the fire. She waited for Lord Byron to come down till the clock struck eleven, then she put on her boots and went out into the world on her own.

A low snowy sky hung over the elms of the drive. But the air was grey and spotless; the falling had stopped. A layer of white brought out the irregularities in the ground, in the gravel and grass—a thin crust like toast, she thought to herself absurdly, as she stepped upon it. She took a quiet satisfaction from making her mark on the road. After the gate, which she opened herself, was a small hut, intended once for a gatekeeper. Sophy and she used to hide in it as children and spy on the carriages, which in Sir Ralph's electioneering days often thronged the drive. Now it stored mostly a collection of sticks, boots, shawls. One was always forgetting things; one hated going back to the house. A small round window by the door let a little light in. There was still the bench inside that the children had brought there to stand on: they could not see out of it otherwise. Annabella, feeling the air on her neck, decided to wrap herself in another shawl. The smell of the hut, of mud and leather mixed, of enduring cold, brought on—she was very sensitive to recollections—a flood of sentiment. She had hidden there to watch Sophy drive out to be married; Annabella had refused to come in her carriage. 'What shall I do without you?' she remembered saying to her cousin. 'What shall I do with *them*?'

'Marry,' Sophy had said, laughing.

Marry, she repeated now to herself. Yes, it was time.

The snow had thickened even over the beach, except where the waves had washed it away, leaving a rim of ice. There was little wind. The rollers seemed, more out of duty than desire, to repeat their advances on the shore. In the low-hung cloud, the horizon looked very near, almost palpable—looming and vague at once. Annabella imagined how quickly the land behind her would disappear from view if she sailed out to it: a prospect which, she supposed, would awake in Lord Byron the simplest of yearnings. She herself had never left England before. Well, she must learn to reconcile him to quietness. That, she suspected, would prove the task of her marriage. She walked down the middle of the sand, to keep clear of the waves, and began, as she used to, composing verses in her thoughts. As much as anything else, it was a test of her memory. 'Let my affection' was the phrase she had been mulling over. The last word suddenly acquired a crispness, a clarity, brought out by the sound of dry snow compacting under her steps. 'Let my affection be the . . . the bond of peace . . .' And then, as they sometimes did, the lines came almost unbidden, which seemed to her at the time the best evidence of their beauty, of her sincerity.

Let my affection be the bond of peace
Which bids thy warfare with remembrance cease.
Blest solely in the blessings I impart,
I only ask to heal thy wounded heart.
On the wild thorn that spreads dark horror, there
To graft the olive branch and see it bear . . .

She turned back only when her feet grew cold. The thought of whom she was about to marry struck her afresh. She was in a position to give the first poet of the age her little tribute to their love. The fact obscurely supported her in the silent continuing argument she kept up with Mary Montgomery; and she walked home again in better spirits, feeling she had scored a point.

At the gate, she stopped to return her shawl (which was, after all, too dirty for house-use) to the hut. Just as she opened the door, she caught a glimpse of two young men at the end of the drive, setting off. One of them moved a little more slowly, resting his weight, it seemed, on his hand in the air: the stick was too thin to be seen. Without thinking, she slipped inside and waited for them. She felt her heart in her throat, beating quick. It was only, she supposed, the childish desire to surprise which rendered her childish again; that and memories of Sophy. She sat down on the bench, rather demurely—it was too low for a full-grown woman. There was no other sound but the pulsing in her neck. She touched her thumb against it, to feel its vivid agitation. The delay grew almost unbearable. She began to count the seconds: it could hardly take them more than a minute to reach the gate, but she had told a hundred before she heard their boots in the snow.

'Can you guess which way she has gone?' It was Hobhouse speaking; his words carried very clearly in the cold air. Annabella, then, almost called out to them. She had half prepared the smile with which she would open the door but needed a moment to find her breath again. She mustn't sound flustered; it was only a game she had played. Often she noted in herself a slight hesitation to enter *his* company again: it was like dipping a foot in cold water. One needed to accustom oneself. That she was shy of him still, she considered a proof of her love.

'It doesn't matter to me if we run into her. I suspect we shall see enough of each other in time.' This made her stop short. She bit her tongue and resolved to hear them out. The strain of keeping quiet turned her shyness into something else, into guilt, into outrage. She was not accustomed to eavesdropping, and she feared the lesson to be learned from it. Other people were always more indifferent to one than one imagined them to be: she sensed for the first time, beneath her, a cushion being removed. Lord Byron sounded brisker, less musical than usual—as if the voice he addressed to her was an instrument played, which away from her ear he handled more carelessly.

'I suppose you must marry,' Hobhouse said.

'I spent last summer at Hastings, with Hodgson, bathing and advocating to me, often at the same time. He calls it the most ambrosial state.'

'Marriage, you mean—not bathing? Well, Hodgson.' And then, 'If you must, you might as well marry *her*.'

The opening and closing of the gate provided a pause, which, in the thick of their conversation, they made use of, stopping to have the question out. Annabella, sitting with her hands between her knees to keep them warm, had lowered her head and closed her eyes to listen. She heard the foot of the gate scraping over the snow. And then, with something like the sweetness in his manner she was accustomed to hearing, Lord Byron said, 'What do you think of her, Hobby? You needn't spare me. I know you too well to trust your opinion.'

'I'm not such a fool.' There was a silence in which Annabella could almost feel, between the two young men, the comfort of their friendship swelling. Hobhouse was the first to break it—not with an answer, but a question of his own. 'What should one look for in a wife, I wonder?'

'Gentleness, I suppose.' She could hear Byron shift on his feet, thinking, rutting his stick through the snow. 'Liveliness. *Cleanliness.*' Hobhouse laughed. After a pause: 'A little comeliness.'

This seemed to make Hobhouse's way easier, for he ventured his opinion at last. 'I think you've done well.' Byron must have looked up, to prompt elaboration, for after a moment Hobhouse hesitantly gave it. 'Her feet and ankles are excellent. The upper part of her face is very good—expressive, if not exactly handsome. She seems very . . . *clean.*' He was ashamed, perhaps, of descending to mockery, for he continued more earnestly, 'She gains by inspection.' And then, with greater assurance: 'I believe she dotes on you.' There was a clear small clang as the gate shut, but Annabella thought she could just make out Lord Byron's answer. 'A little silently, for my taste.' As their voices began to retreat again, he added, 'I like them to talk, because then they think less.' Annabella, as quietly as she could, stood up on the bench and pressed her nose against the window. She might have been ten years old; it might have been only a game. Lord Byron was an inch or two taller than his friend. They walked arm in arm and seemed in no hurry at all. She felt a needle of envy working in her heart, at the ease of male companionship. They descended between the trees, and just as their heads dropped below the line of the snow, Annabella heard herself: gaping for air, sucking and shaking, dry-eyed. She had in the end to close her hands over her mouth, as if in prayer, to soften her sobbing—at the thought of what she had put herself at the mercy of.

The coldness of a loveless eye: she had never seen herself

through one before. She followed their footsteps back into the house, an exercise which, at least, restored to her the face of calm. Sir Ralph met her in the hall. Lord Byron had just gone out; he had hoped to find her. No matter, she said, she must have just passed them in the woods. And then: 'I suspect we shall see enough of each other in time.' Her coolness puzzled him somewhat, which she knew—a fact that helped to relieve the worst of her feelings. Her father, however, had begun already to resign the rights of his paternal curiosity. He was not the kind of man to pull at the tender root of a secret. For that, she relied on Judy—or used to rely. Annabella's most pressing, most selfish concern, was that her mother had lost the strength to check her. She might have been inclined to put a stop to the business in hand; Judy had once had that power.

Annabella retired to her room. At her dressing table, in front of the mirror, she stared into her own eyes, unblinking. It was Hobhouse's words, at first, that ran through her thoughts: 'the upper part of her face', etc. The force of the specific seemed very painful to her. It reduced one to scale, and a sense of scale is just what, as she put it to herself, the soul can bear very little of. But then, her humour reviving somewhat, she considered her feet and ankles, 'excellent' both. And there was consolation to be had, on several fronts, from Lord Byron's character of a wife, which suggested only too shameful a contrast with her own paradoxical account of a husband to Lady Melbourne. Gentleness, liveliness, cleanliness, a little comeliness. Surely, her modesty could demand no more of his good opinion. And it was, she decided, among the benefits to be expected from her marriage that she could rely on her husband for such grace and sense. Simplicity, indeed, was just the margin she looked for, and if the confinement of marriage could teach it to her, she need not resent her cage. If only, as Lord

Byron said, she could unlearn a little of her silence—and she came down to lunch with her equanimity somewhat restored and a resolution to cling to.

They were married the next day, in the drawing room. Lord Byron, as the hour approached, was summoned and found at last in the garden; his wedding-shoes, as he came in, still dripping from the snow. It was a game they had been playing together, perhaps the most intimate of the day: to append the word to anything. The wedding breakfast; a wedding sneeze. The wedding snow. He complained, in a voice a little shaking with humour, of having caught in the outside air a 'wedding chill'. The vicar of Seaham was the son of old family friends—a surprisingly young man with fat ruddy silken cheeks and a cheerful stammer. 'He was only very cold-tongued,' he said at the beginning. 'He needed a minute, a minute, a minute, before the fire, to warm up.' A Mr Wallace. Hobhouse looked very upright and splendid in full dress and white gloves. Annabella, feeling strangely composed, found time to make a compliment on his appearance, which he gallantly returned. Simplicity, she said, considering herself in the mirror above the fire, had been the effect she aimed at. She wore a muslin gown trimmed with lace at the bottom and a white muslin curricle jacket and nothing on her head.

There was only one little unpleasantness. As the room was being arranged, Sir Ralph—to keep, as he said, the conversation afloat—mentioned something Dawlish had told him that morning on coming back from the village. The conclusion to his story about that Irish impostor. No one could discover his real name, which had become a material concern, since he was found last night in the straggle of bushes outside the gate to the harbour, quite dead. There wasn't a sign of violence upon his person, though he stank of laudanum. A copy of *The Bride of Abydos*, signed, it seemed, in Lord Byron's own hand, lay inside his jacket-pocket. Lord Byron was observed to turn very pale at this. He had inherited, he said, from his Scottish side, a foolish streak of superstition. He was persuaded to sit down; brandy was brought. (Annabella, almost glad of the chance to exhibit her tenderest concerns, thought she heard him muttering something to Hobhouse, who answered with a shame-faced smile.) But the real awkwardness was to come. Lady Judy, who had been keeping carefully quiet, turned on Sir Ralph. It was just like him, she said, to be spreading such distasteful gossip on his daughter's wedding day. He lacked all decorum and would sacrifice every fine-feeling for the sake of one of his 'stories'. Sir Ralph looked duly chastened; the egg of his head seemed to tremble. He had lately begun to express his uncertainties, his hesitations, physically; one almost felt the *vibrato* in him and took from it a kind of musical effect. 'My dear man,' he kept repeating, 'I never dreamed it would upset you. It was only some wretched mick.' Though even this incident had its consoling force: Annabella was glad to see her mother insisting on the old relations. Judy looked pale that morning, almost drained of blood, but steadier than she had in months. Perfectly composed, only a little stiff, which suited the occasion.

The rest of the ceremony passed off well enough. Brandy brought a touch of colour to Lord Byron's cheeks. He praised Lady Milbanke for the wedding-cushions, or rather, the two small squares of woven matt that she had provided for them to kneel on. 'One shouldn't,' he said, 'expect too many comforts in setting forth on such a journey.' Annabella couldn't quite make out the object of his irony, but Judy offered him a little smile. Mr Wallace had a rough amiable manner and an air of inconsequence, which greatly lightened the formality of the wedding-service. Annabella spoke her part distinctly well. She had been accustomed, ever since childhood, to acting out small scenes in the drawing room for the benefit of her parents and their friends. Lord Byron seemed more affected, although when he came to the line 'with all my worldly goods I thee endow', he cast a wry look at Hobhouse. By eleven o'clock, they were married; the bells of St Mary's rang an extra peal for them, and they kissed and shook hands all round.

Annabella retired shortly after to change. She could see from her bedroom window the carriage waiting for them below; Dawlish was loading their cases in it. Her uncle Lord Wentworth had lent them Halnaby Hall for the honeymoon. It was forty miles away on winter roads. The phrase of the previous morning recurred to her, that she had scored a point, only 'this time,' she supposed, summoning an image of her friend Mary, 'it was the match-winner.' There was almost a kind of anger in her throat as she thought of the words, a kind of ache. She returned in a few minutes, dressed for travelling in a dove-coloured pelisse. 'I believe it did vastly well,' Lord Byron said quietly to her, leaving his hand for a moment against her side. A taste, she imagined, of the contact that awaited her.

Dawlish opened the front door for them, at which Hobhouse appeared to present her with a copy of Lord Byron's poems, bound in yellow morocco. 'A wedding gift.' And then, to lighten the mood, he added, 'I believe you have lately acquired the original.' She nodded but in a sudden agitation could not think what to do with it, or how to thank him. She held it for a moment thickly clasped across her waist, until the young man took pity on her and relieved her of the book, to deposit it himself in the rear of the carriage. Her mother seized her now by the arm; she seemed on the verge of tears herself. 'Did I not behave well?' Judy kept repeating. 'Did I not behave well?' Annabella kissed her passionately; she was conscious of tearing herself away. It seemed as if someone was pulling her from behind. Sir Ralph kept shy of her. He had a word with the coachman instead. 'Keep off the Durham road,' she heard him saying. 'It's very bad in the snow.' As they took their seats, Hobhouse reappeared in the window; he was holding Lord Byron's hand. 'I wish you every happiness,' he said, turning to Annabella.

'If I am not happy, it will be my own fault.'

He only let go when the carriage moved away.

Chapter Two

—

THEY WERE ALONE TOGETHER, almost for the first time, but until they passed the gates Lord Byron continued, from a sense perhaps of being still in eye-shot, to stare straight ahead of him at the underside of the carriage roof. The line of his profile was vividly distinct against the white background. How well I know it, she reflected lovingly, then remembered having seen it, for years, on his frontispiece. The thought struck her: I have married a famous man. As they were turning into the road, a violent crack of sound erupted behind them. It startled Annabella into breathing; she had half been holding her breath and now leaned her head out the window to look back. The servants, in a ragged line at the front of the house, stood darkly, holding muskets to their shoulders. They had just fired off a volley. Annabella, in a surge of high spirits, laughed, at the—she could hardly have put it into words herself. At the *show* of it, for such a quiet virtuous studious country girl. Lord Byron, determining to break their silence, found only something to recite. 'Such a sight as this,' he said, 'becomes the field, but here shows much amiss.'

'I'm sure my father,' she began to say—very eager, if nothing else, to placate him, until she noticed he was smiling, faintly. She smiled more broadly at him, indifferent for once to the fact that smiles only made her round face rounder. Then he took her hands in his. 'You should have married me two years ago,' he said. For a moment she thought he meant only a kind of whimsy, a regret that the happiness they now shared had been put off, needlessly, for so long. And she wanted an endearment to respond in kind.

'What shall I call you, sir?' she said. 'I can scarcely call you, however much I might think of you as, *my lord.*'

'I suppose we'll find names for each other in time.'

Again, his manner puzzled her, but she took his remark as a corrective, the first of their marriage, from his larger store of experience *in such matters.* ('My love', 'my sweet', she had wanted to say.) And Annabella found that she was willing, to an extent that surprised her, to be guided by him. She felt herself pushing a little, impatiently, at Lord Byron, a fact gently brought home to her by a certain pressure on her own affections. It could only be caused, however innocently, by his rebuff. They had time, he seemed to be saying, as much as they could want. She was hurrying him. The coachman, she noted in passing, had ignored her father's advice and taken the road to Durham after all—a disobedience which, in its way, duly comforted her. She was travelling outside a sphere of influence that she had been accustomed to thinking of as *the world itself.* To escape it had been, in many ways, the object of her marriage. She had escaped.

The snow, which had held off in the morning, now began, lightly as spiders, to descend. On landing, the new flakes, many-footed, stood resting on the old. The road was still passable, though they encountered little traffic in the course of the day. Everyone, it seemed, had decided to stop at home, and this only contributed to Annabella's sense of venturing forth, of embarking. Trees to either side of them broke darkly against the muffled sunshine, which was of that charged oppressive whiteness that suggests the imminence of a thunderclap. It seemed to Annabella not the least of her anxieties, drawn out over the length of that endless journey, that no thunder came—that the heavens continued to thicken silently, while the snow softened underfoot. That cushioning, above and below, rendered their voices (on those rare occasions when they spoke) and the knock of the horses' hooves and the cries of their driver both quiet and curiously distinct. Only the light changed, as the day wore on and the pallor of the horizon took on a deepening yellow stain.

At Durham, as they trotted through it, the bells rang out. Lord Byron at last broke his silence. 'Ringing for our happiness, I presume?' She could not read his tone. Was he asking for corroboration? Of what? The fact of the intention, to honour their wedding day—or the fact of their happiness? She decided to understand him simply. 'I expect we have been looked-out for.'

He smiled at that. 'I expect we have.'

She was beginning to tire from the strain of his presence. There was a moment, as the shuttered shops sped by, when she thought of stopping the carriage and getting out. They were running along the High Street and passed the millinery store, above whose bright-red shop-front Mrs Clermont lived. She was an old friend of the Milbankes and had been Annabella's governess for many years. Annabella considered it a kindness to visit; she sometimes journeyed to Durham only to take her a cake and a bag of tea and sit for an hour with her. It seemed to her the most natural thing in the world to knock against the roof of the coach and descend, leaving Lord Byron to proceed to Halnaby alone. To talk with Mrs Clermont in her little room overlooking the street. Annabella had, after all, a great deal to gossip about. The most natural thing—not nearly so strange as the other. But she did not knock, and the carriage continued regardless, and the houses of Durham grew scarcer on either side of the road, then disappeared altogether on the ascent towards Crook. They drove for a space along the river. It somewhat consoled her to see its current flowing thickly the other way, back to Seaham and the sea.

Once, to relieve the silence perhaps, Lord Byron broke into a kind of song. Annabella could not make out the words. It had an Eastern ring and reminded her of just those poems through which she had first come to know him. 'Will you teach it me?' she interrupted at last. He started, as if he had forgotten her, and said roughly, 'You wouldn't much like to know what you were singing.' She bowed her head at this, humbly and hurt, and he, seeming to repent, took her hand in his and kissed it. He left his lips on her skin, looking up at her, and then, with growing fervour, began to kiss her palm, dropping it as suddenly again. 'You might have saved me once,' he said. 'Now it is too late. I fear very much you will find out you have married a devil.' Annabella endured all this silently, but no explanation followed, and she hadn't the heart to require one. She had the sense of waiting him out.

What she was waiting for, not just in name but in shape and force, oppressed her thoughts. His too, perhaps; and she hopefully supposed it the source of the awkwardness between them, just as it might prove the solution to it. Her first tastes of passion, such as they were, had surprised an appetite she little suspected herself of possessing. She had proved, as Lord Byron said to her, 'quite caressable into good humour'. Just what else she might be caressable into began to occupy her more and more as they left Durham behind. There was nothing he couldn't do to her; there was nothing, she guessed, she would not let him do. She was conscious, even then, of reserving for herself a passive part. The burden of anticipation, the task of supporting it, seemed to her active enough.

There were in the course of a long journey several mute exchanges that seemed, as Annabella put it to herself, to 'bear upon the question'. Lord Byron had kissed her hand; she had observed him, feeling heat rise to her face. Once, the coachman taking too quickly a bend in the road, she had found herself resting her head against him while he kept quiet and still. In the act of righting herself, Annabella put her hand against his thigh. As she gathered her weight, the carriage lurched again. Lord Byron, curiously inert, supported her shoulder and head upon his breast; and closing her eyes, she for a moment remained recumbent upon him by a forced inaction. The seconds passed. Neither stirred, until the carriage, turning the opposite way, by its own speed released her from his involuntary embrace. Nothing was said, but the silence itself persuaded her that whatever she felt, of uneasiness, of attraction, was shared by him.

At the inn in Rushyford, they changed horses. Stepping out briefly into the snowy air, she observed him wince. 'I hate the cold,' he said. And she, rising at once to meet him in sympathy, replied, 'It must be very painful for your . . .' until he stared her out of the end of her sentence. She didn't yet dare. They spent a few minutes inside, warming their hands together at the fire with their backs to the room. She wanted at least to make a show of conversation; it was their wedding day, after all. There were people about. 'How much longer to Halnaby is it, do you suppose?' To which he repeated, 'You should have married me when I first proposed.'

She, at a push, found something to smile at this time. 'I think you mean that it can't be as long as two years.' And then, when he did not look up, she added, 'Surely *now* there's no need to regret the past. We have time enough.' But the coachman then returning, Lord Byron was spared an answer and preceded his bride briskly into the carriage.

The sun set before them in a muffle of cloud, though for a bright half hour they squinted against the pervading whiteness. It was an eight-hour journey to Halnaby from Seaham, but through the long day she looked at him perhaps a dozen times: he so insistently stared in front. Annabella had not known what to expect of their enforced solitude. It had not been this—this electric silence. She had supposed herself rather in danger of too readily complying to his greed for her (that was her phrase for it) and had wasted her anxieties in composing, ahead of time, a number of subjects on which they might calmly discourse. None of them now, as she counted them over in her head, seemed appropriate. She could almost smile, with the wisdom of a wife, at the girl she had been. Of course, Lord Byron was right. Such silence was just what would suit them. It had the tendency, in her at least, to arouse her own greed for him, though as the dark set around them, that greed appeared to her in its plainest form: she was terribly lonely and cold. She wanted, more than anything, a word of comfort from him, a little warmth.

Nightfall, it seemed, had its own effect upon him. In the darkness she ventured to examine her husband more closely. Curly hair partly obscured his high forehead and the peculiar fineness of his ears, which were harp-like, distinctly shaped. His blunt, masculine nose and square cleft chin suggested the soldier or the statesman more than the poet. But his lips and large eyes were almost indecently soft and boyish, eloquent of vanities and sympathies and enthusiasms—to say nothing of a painful susceptibility to his own changing temper. There was bitterness, too, written in the lines between his brows and around his mouth. Feeling her gaze upon him, he burst out, 'This is intolerable!' And when she shrank, at the edge of tears, into her corner of the carriage, he turned towards her for the first time in an hour with an urgency of manner that was not ungentle: 'I wonder how much longer I shall be able to keep up the part I have been playing.'

It was all she could do to summon a little voice. 'Have you been playing a part, my lord? I wish you would not. I should not have thought we needed parts to play.'

'Come now,' he said, 'you have only been pretending to love me. You cannot love me as I am.'

And then, in her highest tone (which she for the first time suspected of priggishness), Annabella replied, 'That is what I have vowed to do.'

'Brave girl!'

His face in deep shadow was almost unreadable—was he mocking her? She finally took her courage in both hands. 'Have you been only pretending to love me?' Her voice, as she asked it, was perfectly steady and clear; there was not the tremor of an appeal. They had come to the point, but only then did Annabella guess how awkwardly she had felt it intruding, regardless of the way she wriggled—ever since his first proposal, throughout their protracted engagement and that long day's silent journey. Afterwards, she remembered the question and marvelled at how simply she had faced it.

'How can you ask me that?' he said, at his wits' end.

Her nerve failed her then; Annabella decided to take this as reassurance enough. There were tears on both sides, which he caressed them out of, kissing them off her chin, her cheeks, the line above her lip. She put her palms to his face and with her fingers rubbed the wet out of his eyes: she had never touched his face. His hand, with the force almost of anger, ran down her neck and the length of her spine. He began to grip her thigh from behind her, and she felt for the first time the indifference to everything else of the appetite he had awakened. There was nothing like sentiment in it, very little like love, and she waited with shut eyes to feel what else he might do to her, when the coach slowed to a halt and the coachman knocked his fist against the roof. Halnaby Hall had appeared, in its own light: eight splendid windows in two rows, casting a mullioned glitter. The servants (a half dozen of them) stood on the balcony above the drive to greet the happy couple.

Lord Byron barely gave them a glance as he hobbled inside. Annabella, still breathless, managed to compose herself before she stepped out into the snow. Wondering a little: what had she done to displease him? And she began to blame herself for putting on, at the coachman's knock, too quickly a public face. Perhaps she had even *looked* her relief. They had in their communications always been sensitive to slights and misunderstandings, and she was conscious of having entered an arena in which the least gesture was liable to misinterpretation, if only because her grasp of the language was still very weak. The butler, who had been hovering on the steps, now introduced himself—a Mr Payne, a large-headed, large-handed, slack-jawed, somewhat ageless young man, whose manner communicated cheerfulness and hesitation in equal measure. He took upon 'himself the duty of welcoming Lord and Lady—I mean, Lady Byron, to Halnaby Hall' and wished them a pleasant stay, which he would do everything in his power to ensure. He was perfectly at their disposal; they were to consider him 'quite their own'.

Leaving the servants to manage their boxes, Annabella followed Lord Byron inside. Lord Wentworth, her uncle, had been regarded in their family circle with as much awe as pride. He was Judy's brother and incalculably richer than Sir Ralph; Annabella, in fact, had only once in her childhood been to visit Halnaby Hall. This was in the first flush of favour that attended Sir Ralph's election to the House. The invitation itself, greatly cherished, had seemed to usher in a new stage in the Milbankes' fortunes: such was the hospitality it entitled them to. But as her father's amiable helplessness began to declare itself in the bumbling of his career, no second invitation came. Lord Wentworth contented himself with keeping up their relations at a respectable distance. It seemed to Annabella by no means unlikely that only her marriage to so great a figure as Lord Byron had persuaded her uncle to offer them the use of Halnaby for a honeymoon. She bore him little gratitude. Annabella, as a girl, had been amazed and strangely hurt by Judy's deference to the abrupt old man; it was very unlike her mother. Judy, however, had always regarded her brother as a model of virtue and rough gentlemanly common sense. It was by the contrast to him that Sir Ralph had occasionally suffered in their otherwise loving marriage.

Annabella had turned eight years old in the course of that stay and was given a very grand, very miserable birthday party to celebrate the fact. Lord Wentworth, who was childless, invited his county friends, and Judy insisted that Annabella thank him publicly for his kindness. At the end of her party, for which she had been too nervous to eat more than a piece of her birthday cake, Sir Ralph, painfully complicit, lifted Annabella underneath her arms and stood her on the piano stool to deliver her thanks—which she did, as Judy afterwards commended her, a little quietly but very prettily, to her mother's great satisfaction and pride. By supper-time, however, the small girl was running a fever, and Annabella spent much of the night being sick and the last two days of their visit in bed. Feeling again childish with the memory, Annabella thought of that cake, which was made of almond paste and decorated with currants, as she began to explore the house in search of her husband.

Lord Wentworth had classical tastes and an appetite for grandeur. The stairs in the hall were overlooked by a high-hung portrait of Sir Thomas More, in rich and gloomy reds, by van Dreisdale; there was a bust of Aristedes on the landing. It was a puzzle indeed, a lesson in the effects of time, for Annabella to consider them again from her larger view. There was something too insistent in the appointments. More modesty would have conveyed a more satisfied ambition. Her family, on every side— she had only begun to suspect it, after her contact with Lord Byron and the circles in which he moved—was guilty of puffing itself up. She knew now, or could guess, what real fame, what real influence, looked like. Only a wide view by Canaletto of the Grand Canal in Venice offered her any pleasure: it showed a fine cold day in early spring or late autumn (there were no trees to judge by). A gust of sea-wind had sketched a little uncertainty, a little urgency, into the man-made channels. One could feel a heavily bearded, bow-legged gondolier just allowing himself to sway with it, keeping his feet by giving way. It hung over the door-way to the drawing room, in which she found Lord Byron, resting his foot on one of the sofa-cushions. He rose this time quickly to greet her and shut the door behind her, and all her old childish-ness, the sense of it, returned.

After he was through with her, she sat for a minute recompos-ing herself on the sofa. He had gone upstairs to change. Little had been said between them: she took this as an indication of prefer-ence and was very quick, in these matters, to guess at his tastes. The greed in his face (that was the word she had decided to keep to) left her no room for doubting his—sincerity; and in fact, a dim sense of her own expressions, of pleasure and pain, suggested at least that sincerity of a kind had not been lacking in her. Some-thing had been done away with, a veil had been torn aside, of fine-feeling or hypocrisy, she could not yet be sure; and for a moment, as she sat there shivering, not quite giving way to sobs, if only because of the close heat of the well-laid fire, she was conscious of being for the first time (and she could put it no clearer than this) unadorned. Her sense of it proved how 'dressed up' she was accus-tomed to being—discomfort, not painless, remained from her undressing. She hugged her corseted stomach with crossed arms.

'Have you been only pretending to love me?' she remembered asking her husband. There was, if nowhere else, in Lord Byron's clear appetite something for her to be sure of; and from a depth of loneliness of which she had never supposed herself capable, *that* at least struck her as something to cling to.

Chapter Three

—

FOR THE REST OF HER LIFE, whenever it snowed, Annabella thought of Halnaby, of her honeymoon there. It snowed every day. The effect was relentless, a steady covering-up. They could hear it against the windowpanes in gusts of wind, as if it were trying to get in: a soft scratch like a dog's paw on the glass. She imagined, each morning, taking pity on it, letting it in—and saw herself sleepily disappearing, only the shape of her features remaining, marbled by snow. Sometimes, after lunch, she used to step outside just to feel it against her face, that quiet release in the air. The whiteness of Lord Wentworth's grounds expressed in the simplest way the unmaking of her world. The trees and the roads and the grass were gone. What was left was only a very large house, a few servants, and the two of them.

At dinner on their first night, Lord Byron finished the bottle of wine set between them and called for another, which Payne brought. Byron glanced at it and said, 'I think we can do better,' and persuaded Payne to lead him into the wine-cellars. He had a way with servants when it suited him; and when it didn't, they quickly learned to forgive his ill-temper. It was one of the first things Annabella knew to be grateful for. With all her best politeness, she was conscious of the little resentments her manner aroused. Her husband seemed to charm by giving open offence. Payne and Lord Byron were gone for some time. Annabella, alone again, quietly ate—a dish of salted pork and mashed turnip. She heard them laughing together as they came up the stairs and felt, briefly, a pinch of envy. They emerged both with a bottle in each hand. Annabella, with an anxious tender voice, wondered aloud whether her uncle had intended to give them the run of his cellar? She could not help herself and disliked her own manner. Anxiety gave her tone the edge of correction. Byron, with a free, easy air of injury, presumed they had something to celebrate: Lord Wentworth, he said, appealing to Payne, would not stint them. Besides, he had no intention of spending the honeymoon *dry*. By the time he began to consider his bed, he had drunk two of the bottles and opened the third. Annabella, meanwhile, contented herself with a glassful. She anticipated, in a confusion of fear and longing, a repetition of their performance on the drawing-room sofa.

In the end, on rising, Lord Byron asked her, 'Do you mean to sleep in the same bed with me? I hate sleeping with any woman— but you may do as you please.' The remark, no doubt, was intended to achieve a distance. It had, he could see, its effect: Annabella felt in herself the stiff little stalk of her dignity quivering upright. 'Shall we say then,' she answered, 'that I'm at your disposal?' At which, by that perversion of pride and sympathies which marked his character, he attempted to make up some of the ground. He hardly imagined her, he said, accustomed to sharing a bed with a man. 'Perhaps she had had enough surprises.' Their journey had been fatiguing, and Annabella had seen, he supposed, as much of him as she cared to.

Annabella was shocked to find how quickly her dignity drooped; it needed only a touch of gentleness. In a childish voice, she said that she would not like to spend the night alone. The house frightened her; she felt very far from home. It was a long time since she had stayed at Halnaby. She had been very small before, and unhappy. And—she would not know what to *think* to herself, alone.

He looked at her and then at the bottles on the table. 'Well, I am not quite yet savagely drunk,' he said. 'As you wish.'

They undressed separately and retired at last in the light of the heaped-up fire; it cast a red glow through the curtains of their bed. 'I suppose we are not in hell?' he said to her, as they lay side by side. 'Not in hell,' she repeated, and then more firmly, 'I have never known such happiness.' It was an assertion, not of fact, but intention. She was conscious, already, of wanting his grace, his power of charming a sentiment into truth, but she wished to make clear to him what it was she offered: the strength of purpose, of application, of consistency that he lacked. Love itself, she seemed to be saying, lay within the scope of her will. A monument of love—that was what she had determined to build out of their marriage.

She awoke at false dawn to find him sitting up in bed, the moonlight brightly reflecting in the snow and falling redoubled into the room. They had forgotten in their embarrassment of the night before to draw the window-curtains. For a moment, she imagined her father had come to sit with her, in her fever; had fallen asleep beside her, and woken up. Then—'My love, my love,' she said, reaching out to touch his back. He turned to look at her, staring, it seemed, without recognition. She scratched at his nightshirt, as he pushed aside the draperies and stepped out of bed. Annabella was too sleepy to follow, but for the next hour, drifting in and out of dreams, she heard him: pacing the halls, coming sometimes nearer, and receding again. A watchful, warning presence. And then, turning over in her sleep, she knocked against him and allowed her arm to fall across his face. He didn't wake, but at least he had come back. Later, she found him lying in the crook of her arm; the skin of her neck was wet, from his mouth or his tears. She guessed, for the first time, that he was unhappy and muttered every kind of endearment, stroking the hair out of his eyes and tucking it behind his ears. Grateful, at least, for the power of comforting that comforts the consoler. In the end, though, he couldn't be woken, and she rose up without him and went down to breakfast alone.

Afterwards, she could scarcely recall how they passed their days. There was of course, as her husband put it, *that there sort of thing*. The language she had despaired of knowing grew of its own into a system of phrases and looks that veiled, in flimsiest decency, what they otherwise might have been too embarrassed to admit to. Greed was her private word for it, but it became, between them, a kind of public face to their desires. 'Are you greedy?' he might say to her. And she: 'I am a fat greedy child.' His confidence that they would find names for each other in time was justified by the event. Pip he began to call her, for her pippin-apple face, her bright round cheeks. An endearment, once offered, which she clung to; it stuck from her own insistence. 'Should you like Pip to read to you? Shall Pip sit on your lap?' And sometimes: 'Pip is happy, her husband pleases Pip.' Was there nothing, Pip wondered, she could call *him*? Goose, he remarked, with one of his characteristic airs, between tenderness and irony, was the name he reserved for his sister. 'Well, then,' she said, not to be outdone, 'I shall call you Duck.' Once, when he had tired of her, he said, 'Pip mustn't be greedy.' And the shame she felt in asking, after all, only to please him made her burn and retreat, until he coaxed her into something like loving-kindness again. Though it wasn't, quite, only to please him, she must acknowledge to herself. Her appetites were not unsensual, and she discovered to her great surprise that her own strict regulation of character had masked a nature only too willing to indulge itself. At the very least, she grew dependent on her right to give him pleasure. Between coaxing and retreating, on both sides, they pushed the hours along.

Her image of her husband was rather sketched than painted in full, the outline on a frontispiece; and she considered it, among other things, the task of her honeymoon to fill in and complete the picture. That Lord Byron was not in the steadiest of spirits she could not hide from herself. Her own changeable temper, she must own, was only the reflection of his; she was the sea that imaged forth his clouds and might have been serenely happy had he been clear and calm. 'And yet, perhaps,' she philosophized, 'she had been guilty, in her old life, of too much consistency. She should not complain then that her struggle to overcome it involved her in contradictions.' Contradiction, clearly, is what she *was* involved in. Her husband's manners, when he wished them to be, were so easy that one imagined an easy man. She found to her cost that he was not. Annabella saw that he was unhappy and guessed that it had nothing to do with her. She was generous enough not to mind that—at least, to tell herself she did not mind it yet. The duty of her marriage, in this light, was simple: to make of his state of mind her own affair.

Once, at breakfast, he received a letter that put him very much out of humour. She asked him: 'Who it came from and what it said? She was his wife: their troubles were shared.' And he began to recite, in a bored hurry, the particulars of his, he begged her pardon, their various debts, which amounted to nothing short of thirty thousand pounds. Six thousand charged on his home at Newstead to a Mr Sawbridge. Another thousand in his mother's name—a Jew debt, by the bye, of which the interest must be greater than the principle. Then another Jew debt, six hundred in principal, and no interest (as he had kept that down) to a man in New Street. He had forgotten his name, but it should be known to him on half year's day. There were others, too many to count over, which he had collected (this was his word for it) before his majority. They had been negotiated by his landlady at the time, a Mrs Massingberd, whose daughter he had once paid off with somewhat less expense. Various debts to tradesmen of various descriptions, some of them transcendently usurious. Meanwhile, against these, he had collected his own share of the *uncollectable*. There was Hodgson, a clergyman, who owed him sixteen hundred pounds, and his friend Webster, to whom he had lent a thousand. Nearly three thousand to his sister Goose, from whom he had the letter in hand, which stated what he had already supposed: that her husband was in no position to honour it, having gambled recklessly at Newmarket. In any case, he never wished to see that sum again, but there were others he shouldn't mind having repaid. Webster's bond was worth a damn or two, though he never wanted, nor asked, any security of Hodgson. Although, as for that, he had lent him an additional two hundred at Hastings last summer, which Hodgson had promised to repay punctually in six weeks, and which he had repaid with the usual punctuality, that is, not at all. Lord Byron was generally supposed rich. It always amazed him. His money was eaten away by interest, and the rest had been swallowed up by duns, necessities, luxuries, fooleries, jewelleries, whores and fiddlers. His marriage settlement, or rather, he begged her pardon again, theirs, was totally inadequate to meeting these expenses, and as for what is politely called expectations, Sir Ralph and Lord Wentworth seemed to grow healthier every day, and he verily believed they were at this moment cutting a fresh set of teeth.

At this point he ran out of breath. Annabella had only been staring at him, growing closer to tears, until Lord Byron abruptly excused himself and left the table. For a minute she gazed at his empty chair, before she noticed the letter still lying on his plate amidst half-eaten fruits and the rind of a cheese—he had forgotten to take it up. She watched it for a minute, as if to see what it might permit. How quickly, she was honest enough to concede, the threat of tears vanished without the pressure of his presence! Her honesty, she found, had been set a more difficult test: the duties of a wife might be variously construed. Perhaps, after all, he had intended for her to read the letter; and to stand on a dignity that he did not believe she possessed would not allow her to fulfil, in the largest sense, her obligations. This supposition supported her, for a time, which was just long enough to enable Annabella to rise and walk to his seat.

The letter was indeed from Augusta and addressed *Dearest and gentlest and best of human beings*, a line whose insistent rhythm reminded Annabella of the morning-waltz at Melbourne House almost three years before. She had seen *her* then, her husband's sister, standing in her husband's arms. One had the sense, looking on them, of a kind of feeding; one felt the flow of nourishment between them, and one's own exclusion from it. Of course, they had been dancing together: naturally, they appeared a little entangled. Still, there was something for her to strive towards in that image of their affections . . .

Meanwhile, she had begun to read, and her train of thought was interrupted by the attention increasingly claimed by the ramblings of the letter to hand. Augusta, as it happens, had little to say on the score of her husband's debts:

> Of course you did quite right to go about everything quietly, and John has sent me a very loving picture of what you looked like, and what everybody looked like. Miss Milbanke (whom I long to call sister) was said to be very prettily and properly got up in muslin, with a simple *&* curricle jacket—you see, I have quite insisted on hearing everything, and John complains of all the niceties I

required of him, which made him feel like a Mrs.
somebody in a play, I can't remember which: you know,
a terrible gossip. Mrs. Milbanke, he says (do you call her
mother?), was drunk throughout: can it be true? I have
heard she is such a formidable respectable lady. He
thinks and I agree with him that you have done very well
with Miss Milbanke, though it's a great pity that Miss
Elphinstone took fright, whom I very much hoped would
suit you, because I know her and love her better. You
aren't so very frightful, I told her myself, and perfectly
manageable to anyone who wishes to attempt it. The least
kindness will govern you, or so I have always found, and
you have never had the heart to contradict me! But you
did very right, I was saying, to proceed so quietly, and
I was only sorry George was here when you stayed at
Christmas. The worst of his debts to you is that they
confined him to home. You should have liked a sisterly
farewell, which he made quite impossible.

But can it be true? Are you married at last? I hardly
credit it. I awoke that morning in a very low spirit,
without remembering the occasion for it. It was very cold,
you remember, and here at least snowing a little forlornly,
which I know you hate—and then I did remember, in a
rush, and must sit down again to clear my head. He is to
be married today, I declared to no one. I made a miserable
breakfast, sitting in George's seat so I could look at the
clock. And I remember saying to him, George will tell
you, how I said to him, at ten o'clock, it is just gone ten
o'clock, he will be dressing now; and at half past ten, I
said, how shameful for it to be so cold, for I am sure he
would like a turn in the garden, alone, above all things;
and at eleven o'clock, they will be calling him down, I

wonder if she is dressed already? Then the children imposed and made a mess of something, I hardly remember what, till it was suddenly a quarter to twelve, and I said, I suppose they are all assembled. What a dreadful word that is: assembled. You may imagine my feelings when the bells at noon rang, which I knew to be your wedding hour. I turned quite pale I am told, George particularly remarked it. All was agitation within me, as the sea trembles when the earth quakes, though I managed to keep down the worst appearance of it . . .

Annabella was dimly conscious, as she lowered her hand to the table, that Lord Byron had entered and was observing her. She sat with her back to him, had heard his step; but her husband had done nothing yet to declare his presence, and so they could continue, if they liked, in silence—he standing, she sitting—without any appearance of rudeness. There was nothing, she consoled herself, very horrible or improper in the letter, barring that shameful aside about her mother—all the more shameful because it wasn't quite true. She had the sense, however, that any correction would only involve her more deeply in explanations. These were, above all, what she wanted to avoid. Augusta's 'agitations', her quakes and waves, were easily accounted for by a reference to Annabella's own feelings at the marriage of her cousin Sophy; and it seemed the most natural thing in the world for 'Goose' to prefer in a sister-in-law an old friend to a stranger. As for Miss Elphinstone, Annabella could hardly resent a woman for having failed to become her husband's wife.

And yet the effect of the letter, the shadow and chill it cast, was quite as strong as a real shadow and a real chill. It reminded her of the conversation she had overheard between Hobhouse and her husband outside the gates at Seaham House. What was shocking was really just the fact of the conversation itself. The way they had carried on without her—that she lived in their thoughts without any rights of contradiction. She saw herself, for the first time, through their eyes: a good quiet kind of a girl, an acceptable match. Her own self-opinion, perhaps, was what lacked proportion. And yet she was mindful, in spite of that little evasion (of dropping her hand to the table), that the letter contained something she could challenge him with if Lord Byron complained of her snooping. She didn't suppose he would dare to—afterwards noting, how quickly she had reconciled herself to the role of spy. In fact what he said, when he broke their silence at last, surprised her in another way. It was not quite an apology or an accusation. 'I was a villain to marry you, I could convince you of it in three words.' And then, when she failed to look round: 'Anyway, it is too late now. And I hate scenes.'

She did not say, what is too late? And she made no scene. She had the virtue of forbearance, when it suited her, and was conscious of waiting him out. It seemed to her the clearest intimation of success, that in a contest of patience, at least, he was sure to lose.

Chapter Four

—

THAT THERE WAS SOMETHING weighing on his heart, she did not doubt; though whether indeed what seemed to him so terrible was a large secret or a small one, Annabella could not be sure. She feared the small secrets more. The other, his works had beautifully acquainted her with: the burden placed on a noble nature by the recollection of an ill-spent youth. She considered it among the purposes of her marriage to train him into a more reasonable view of his own bad character—she suspected him of delighting a little in his reputation for sinfulness. He certainly, in the first weeks of their honeymoon, played up to it. But his nature was really too generous and fine to sustain the part for long without internal violence. Annabella hoped to teach him that a greater regulation of his own temper, though it might involve a sacrifice of high spirits, would preserve him in the end from his worst demons.

She had begun to concern herself over his drinking, although her least remonstrance threatened to call forth, in his justifications, the example of her mother—she could only reprove the one behaviour by acknowledging the evil of the other. On the whole she kept quiet; at least, she said less than she might have, than she wished to. He had discovered in the cellars a cache of Tokay vintnered in the year of his birth, and vowed to get through it by the end of their stay. He drank heavily at lunch, afterwards retiring to the library 'to work' with a flask of 'right sherries', as he called it, in hand. By suppertime, he was rarely steady, and having ordered Payne to open several bottles of burgundy and let them breathe, he 'hated to see them go off' and finished, sometimes, even the remnants of Annabella's glass. She found herself against her will attempting to keep pace, if only for the sake of his sobriety; and though he was rarely, as he put it, 'savagely drunk' by bedtime, they indulged what they called their 'greed' for each other in a manner that suggested rather the anger than the kindness of love. What surprised Annabella was how quickly she had come to feel dependent even on those rough tokens of his affection.

Their isolation was great; they saw no company, and the house was too large to be thoroughly kept warm. The hallways, lofty and overlooked by high windows, were particularly bitter, and Annabella used to run from the fire in her bedroom to the fire in the sitting room without drawing breath. They relied on each other for heat if nothing else; and Annabella was almost grateful to the cold, in that it prompted Lord Byron sometimes to huddle beside her on a chair or rug and permit his wife to fold her arms about him. These were her happiest interludes. They might lie for as much as an hour together, wordlessly—she, waiting for him to speak, for fear of breaking the spell that held them. She was always, Annabella had learned, saying the wrong thing and began to practise her silences. These, she discovered, could also offend. 'I only want a woman to laugh,' he once said to her, as they were thus entwined, 'and don't care what she is besides. I can make Augusta laugh at anything.'

What she wanted was to be, as she put it to herself, 'more nat-ural', but it wasn't a thing one could act, and she was conscious in the weeks to come of using too much muscle. The fact, palpably, made itself felt. She was constantly tired. And occasionally tiresome: she sensed it herself, by the tension kept up within her of a leash in the hand. She was pulling at him, and it struck her eventually that the fault of that contest lay only partly in the creature harnessed. At least, sometimes, he managed to pull her *along*. She had never before considered herself a burden, and the real lesson it taught her, in feeling him shoulder his share, was how great was the weight she used to carry on her own.

In the afternoons, he was engaged in working up a number of songs on biblical themes for a set of tunes composed by one of his friends. He sat in the library in his overcoat, drinking and writing. At first, she used to join him there, reading, or standing at the fire with her back to it, so that she could look over his shoulder at the half-finished verses. 'I don't want you,' he finally said to her. 'I hope we are not always to be together—that won't do for me, I assure you.'

Later, he relented (it amazed her sometimes, his indulgence) and allowed her to transcribe his pointed scrawl in her fairer hand. They spent long, almost happy afternoons together, in perfect silence, both writing. He insisted that she keep her distance and pushed one of the tables under a window for her to serve as a desk. It overlooked a slope of lawn running down to a brown sketch of elms, which bordered a frozen stream. She watched the short days set behind the trees, a dirty light that spread its stain up the snowy hillside to the shrubs in the beds below her sill. Then it climbed up the wall. When it reached her, she stopped—till the sun set, she could see nothing more than the ache of yellow in her eyes. Her knuckles grew stiff with cold, and she began to drink hot grog after lunch to keep fingers and heart warm. Contented enough to sit near him, and sometimes quite blissful, when the beauty of his verses flowed on to her page as if they had but freshly occurred to him. She felt, almost, the force of them in her own hand, as if she held it against a fall of water.

They spent several afternoons in this companionable silence, which Annabella liked all the better for the steady view it gave her of Lord Byron's best, most patient and considered self. She supposed herself to be, in copying his hasty script, a conduit to another age. There was something indeed in the mere act of *writing out fair* that suggested the role she was playing, careful, loving, neat, in preserving his name. Hers was, she could almost imagine, the fist of posterity. And yet at other times she felt only too vividly the personal element; these songs became, she grew convinced, Lord Byron's private language of love and apology to her. He could express himself in them with a free-hearted clarity that the pressure of her affections otherwise forbade, and she occasionally suffered from the curious feeling, as she picked out a line of his text, of being complicit in his own opinion of her—of playing, as it were, both sides of the marriage question, husband and wife, and admiring from this detachment equally the suffering of the victim and the eloquence of her abuser.

It was their custom, after breakfast, to remove to the sitting room and read. Sometimes Lord Byron, from a general restlessness or a more particular sore head, asked his wife to read aloud to him, while he sat in the easy chair, pushed up to the fire, and closed his eyes. His manner at these times was wonderfully indifferent and relaxed, and Annabella could not help, occasionally, attempting to provoke him to a response. He crossed his legs at the ankles with his feet against the fender; he rested his clasped hands on his stomach and pointed his chin in the air. It was the heat he basked in, but his wife, she thought, might be forgiven for thinking that in the general sum of warmth her own poor contribution of love was just another quantity. One morning, after a

sleepless unhappy night, Annabella chose an album of their letters, which she had put together in the long delay preceding his
arrival in Seaham. She even dressed up for the occasion, in jewels
and ribboned braids: she was determined to begin an assault upon
what she considered the constant quiet level of unhappiness in
their relations. What she wanted him to feel was just how large a
quantity her love made up. The scale of it was something which, in
her way, she might admit to being proud of, and perhaps a note of
that pride made itself felt in her voice.

'I wish for you, want you, Byron mine, more every hour,' she
read out, very prettily, in clear carrying accents. 'All my confidence
has returned—never to sink again, I believe. A confidence in the
power of my affection to make *me* anything, *everything* that you and
I wish.' He did not stir; he might have been asleep. 'Do I understand you? you asked. Surely I do, for without understanding of
the completest kind, I should fear to love you less, if you proved
any different from that which has made me love you.' It was a
queer sort of recital. Annabella felt the queerness of it, and that
within her praise was a sting of reproach; but there was also, she
hoped, the balm to soothe it with. 'I have no such fears.' She
repeated: 'I have no fears.' And then, continuing, 'I have always
insisted (you may guess how often I am quizzed about your character) that you are the most lovable of men,' whereat Lord Byron
interrupted,

'Then if I were unfaithful, you should not resent it?'

His eyes were still closed. She did not at first answer, until he,
sitting up and looking her in the face, insisted. 'I ask only for
information.'

She still considered her reply. At length, carefully, slowly,
Annabella offered: 'I have been taught to believe that a wife had
better not notice deviations which are more likely to be repented
of if her own conduct continues kind and constant.'

'Then you would *let* me be unfaithful?'

'No—that is a different thing.' She was perfectly equal, Annabella discovered, to meeting his stare. 'Even as your friend I should love you too well to let you do what would injure yourself.'

He smiled at that and repeated, 'Oh, as my friend . . . You have a very pleasant notion of injury. It might surprise you to hear that Augusta has no such scruples.'

She had nothing to say to this.

'Does it surprise you?'

'I cannot answer for her conduct.'

'Be careful,' he said, with imperfect consequence, 'before you attack my sister. I think you will find that it does not help your case. She is the only woman who has ever loved me—*as I am*. A love of the completest kind, as you put it, must include an understanding of one's little sins, to call them no worse. No other love is worthy of the name.' And then, very coolly, 'I thought you would be more malleable.'

It was that word, she later reflected, which set her off: malleable, to a point, is what she had intended to be. Hadn't she taken pains that very morning to dress the part of loving wife, just as a woman might, to her advantage, appear in it? The failure of her little experiment upon their happiness, as she framed it to herself, was perfectly evident. And the consciousness of wasted energies, as much as anything else, induced in her a quiet show of tears, to accommodate which she hardly needed to increase her breathing. The effort to support her role (kind, just, loving, temperate) was sometimes too great for her. But her misery seemed to irritate him further. 'This is intolerable,' he said. 'I will not be *tear*-beaten into marriage.' And then, from a greater depth of unhappiness: 'You provoke me, you know you do, by your damned tolerant virtuous tireless suffering. It is too much; I will not stand it. I cannot stand it.'

'You forget,' she said, with a hint of anger, 'that we *are* married.'

'For the moment. I will live with you, if I can, until I have got an heir—until I have got an heir. And then—and then—we shall see.'

At lunch, they never mentioned the scene, and after lunch something happened to lighten their mood. Lord Byron had discovered a billiard room at the back of the house overlooking the terrace; in it were stowed dirty boots and overcoats, some of them piled across the table itself. His lordship had asked Payne to see that it was cleared up. After his meal, he decided he wanted a walk, if only for air. He was sick of the close heat of fires, which had not, he said, 'the fragrance of a honeymoon but the settled smell of marriage'. He wouldn't dream of troubling his wife, he was only going 'to stomp once around' and come back in. Annabella watched him go; she was too unhappy to move. In a minute he returned and taking her hand led her back along the corridor very quietly. There were sounds coming from the billiard room, but he drew her outside, into the cold, and then along the balcony to a window. He signalled for her to look in. She was shivering already, in her muslin gown, from the chill, and it may have been the shivering that induced her to giggle. The window gave on to the billiard room. The table had been cleared, and Payne was playing a game in the company of Miss Minns, who had been assigned to Annabella as a lady's maid, although she was a stout beet-faced woman of forty-five. They were clearly in high spirits. There were boots and coats everywhere on the floor, and instead of using sticks, they played with their hands, rolling two balls rapidly against each other from opposite ends of the table. Occasionally, a loud crack announced a successful hit. Annabella could hear the concussion through the windowpanes, although their laughter, which attended these collisions, could only be seen and not heard. Lord Byron leaned over her and whispered, 'I suppose, Pip, they are very much in love?' which only made Annabella giggle more. Payne, for all anyone knew, might have been a respectable grand-father, but he looked no more than twenty-five years old. The contrast between his threadbare youthfulness and Miss Minns's solidly maternal charms seemed irresistible to Annabella—although the longer they stood watching, and the colder she became, the contrast that struck her most was rather between the couple outside and the couple within. Lord Byron seemed to feel it at the same moment.

In the afternoon, her husband as usual retired to work, and Annabella joined him in the library. The light crept up the hill. As she sat by her window, looking out, he came over to her chair and laid a set of verses on the table, which she with the promptness and indifference of a scribe began to copy onto a fresh sheet. It was only as she reached the second stanza, with the sunset work-ing against her sight, that the meaning of the lines began to make itself felt.

> I saw thee weep—the big bright tear
>   Came o'er that eye of blue,
> And then methought it did appear
>   A violet dropping dew.
> I saw thee smile—the sapphire's blaze
>   Beside thee ceased to shine.
> It could not match the living rays
>   That filled that glance of thine.
>
> As clouds from yonder sun receive
>   A deep and yellow dye,
> Which scarce the shade of coming eve
>   Can banish from the sky,

Those smiles unto the moodiest mind
  Their own pure joy impart.
Their sunshine leaves a glow behind
  That lightens o'er the heart.

It was an apology, perhaps, as much as a token of love. What was it he had said of Augusta, that he only wanted a woman he could make laugh? Well, Annabella had laughed, and the lines were very pretty, and for a day at least she could believe them to be true.

Chapter Five

—

MOST NIGHTS LORD BYRON WAS too drunk to sleep well. He woke before dawn and, too restless to recompose himself, would crawl out of bed and begin, as she once put it to him in the morning, 'to haunt the corridors'. He complained of noises in the night. It was a big empty house; he feared intrusions. The only sounds Annabella heard were the creak of his steps in the halls as he paced up and down them—sometimes, as she learned, when he retired again to bed, by the gleam of it, with a dagger in his hand. The hint of excess in his unhappiness she was not too in love with her husband to overlook. He dressed himself in it as one might in rich clothes, and she saw it as her duty to teach him a simpler habit. That she was in love with Lord Byron her own urgent desire to console him made perfectly plain. One night as he returned to her, worn out from his vigil, she moved to lay her head against his breast. She wanted him to feel her warmth, but he only said, more gently than he was used to, 'You should have a softer pillow than my heart.'

He talked a great deal of his sister and once, in a happier mood, compared Annabella to her: they had the same round face and shy, perplexing manners, though he had 'unpuzzled Augusta' and hoped to do the same for his wife in time. Of course, they had their differences, too, he said, and added, looking at her teasingly, that his sister, for example, always wore drawers. She blushed and in her confusion suggested that they invite her to Halnaby for the last week of their stay. It might be a relief to them to have a little company, and she was fully determined to claim Augusta as a sister. Lord Byron at first demurred, in some alarm. He warned that a visit from Gus would not contribute to their 'hymeneal harmony'; that Augusta made claims upon him, as her brother, which he could not resist; and that Pip might find her Duck a bird of altered feather in his sister's company. In short, Annabella did not know what she was about. But Annabella was determined. She had no such wifely jealousies as Lord Byron imputed to her, and she would be glad herself, it might surprise him to know, to have about them in the large cold house what he once described to her as the 'softening presence' of another woman. Miss Minns's manners, she feared (venturing boldly into a little joke), were not quite so comforting or comfortable. She wrote to Augusta that evening, and for a day or two, in fact, her husband seemed to her in better spirits: Lord Byron drank less and slept more and spoke of what they might do when his sister came.

They even spent an afternoon at the billiard table, though Annabella insisted on learning to play in the orthodox fashion. Lord Byron obliged by standing over her and guiding the cue in her hand—in its own way, she supposed, striking through the ball, a scene just as affecting as the one they had witnessed together. Duck, however, despaired of instructing his wife. Pip played too rigidly, by calculation, as it were, and had not the easy manner to bring a shot off happily. Besides, she proceeded too slowly, she spoiled the sport of it. Annabella herself felt that she was 'getting in her own way'. Her corset, for one thing, struck her as awkwardly constricting. She guessed that her own patience, for improving, was quickly beginning to tire her husband's, for teaching her. And he began to play more seriously, commanding the table for great stretches, and beating her steadily. It was a question of grace, he said—that is, one must give to a skill the appearance of luck. Angelo, his fencing-master, who despised the brute bulk of the boxer, had a phrase for it, applied to swordplay. He called it 'muscling', his English was very rough, but it perfectly suited the action, and Annabella might be said to be 'muscling the shot'. Her husband's lecture only determined her to beat him more, though that determination seemed to have the very effect he was describing. He found her anger charming, which provoked her exceedingly, until he placated her in the usual way. Later, she overheard him instructing Payne to clean off the baize. He had had his wife on the billiard table, he said, and there had been a little 'untidiness'.

The next day a letter from Gus arrived. Her husband was stuck at home and would not spare her; there were also the children to be considered, a constraint with which Annabella, she had no doubt, would shortly sympathize. No, it would not do, much as she longed to, she could not get away. Although, perhaps, on their return to London, her brother might be persuaded to stop for an extended visit? If only, as Augusta charmingly put it, for the purpose of 'introducing a sister to her'. That was the hope she would cherish in the meantime; Annabella must know how attached she was to 'dearest B'. Gus then struck the note of confession—in part, no doubt, Annabella ungraciously reflected, for the purpose of disarming. She had been almost overcome by emotion on their wedding day. Augusta made no apologies for the fact. Only, raised as she had been by the generosity of strangers, it had made an epoch in her life when she learned of a nearer relation: a younger brother (or a half-brother, at least), living all the time within a day's journey, and entering just those interesting stages of life which women were barred from enjoying themselves. His school, his university, his travels—Annabella could imagine how much Gus delighted in his letters. They came to depend on each other alone for the comforts of family, and the thought of losing Byron to a stranger had made her go dark, for a minute, as the bells rang out the hour of their wedding. She had sat down with her children in a heap upon her lap and she could not hear or feel them; they tugged at her hair, they pulled at her face, she clung to them so hard. Her only consolation, which she promised herself afterwards, was the right to claim Annabella 'for her own'. She planned to insist on it . . .

Well, Annabella had been disarmed, and it struck her eventually (when she had time and occasion to regret her defencelessness) as a proof of how lonely she'd been, that she felt so intimately the force of Augusta's appeal. The comfort of women: she had been starved of it, for these, the hardest weeks of her life, and she sat down instantly to answer Augusta's letter. The marriage of her cousin Sophy when Annabella was twelve, her childish unreasonable insistent sense of abandonment, gave her a 'text'; and she rejoiced in her own 'confession' in that it allowed her to show how little she minded Augusta's. From that moment they fell into the habit of writing to each other every day. At breakfast, letters from Suffolk began to appear, addressed to Lady B. Annabella would read from them to her husband as they ate—selecting whatever, she said (conscious of scoring a point), she felt might amuse him. Afterwards Annabella retired to her dressing room to answer the latest. Not the least of her pleasures in the correspondence lay in the fact that she saw how deeply her husband resented it.

But she had other motives besides, nobler and gentler both, and altogether more desperate. Her husband was unhappy. His misery was infectious: she had caught it herself. Gus in her first letter had mentioned how easily he might be managed, and

Annabella had undoubtedly sunk to the point that she was willing to take advice. In the album of love letters, which she had made up for Lord Byron, she came across the character she had once sketched of him, before her first refusal. It was crumpled, of course (she had rescued it from the bin), and her acquaintance at the time had certainly been slight enough, but she could almost smile now at the thought of how much she had seen:

> When indignation takes possession of his mind, and it is
> easily excited, his disposition becomes malevolent. He
> hates with the bitterest contempt. But as soon as he has
> indulged those feelings, he regains the humanity that he
> had lost (from the immediate impulse of provocation)
> and repents deeply. So that his mind is continually making
> the most sudden transitions—from good to evil—from
> evil to good. It would require in his wife a disposition
> both mild and forceful to correct such tendencies. The
> contradiction in these virtues suggests only too well the
> difficulty one must encounter in uniting them.

Of course, she had not guessed at the time the particular form his sudden transitions would take: from the acting out of his sensual nature to the revulsions he suffered from *post coitum*. Nor, indeed, that she would come to consider the first in the light of a good and the aftermath as its consequent evil. It seemed a measure of her unhappiness that she often looked forward to the violence of his desires as a respite from the indifference of his larger neglect. That her own disposition, mild and forceful as she strove to make it, only added to his irritation, she was perfectly aware; but she had not the trick of making him laugh as Augusta could. And it struck her as something to be grateful for, that in the three years since she had written her character of Lord Byron, she had learned, at least, to rate the virtue of a sense of humour.

If only she could make him laugh! Was it, she wanted Augusta to tell her, a trick that could be taught? She had taken a position (this is what she tried to explain to her 'sister'), she wasn't quite sure where, only it was in his way, and for whatever reason, she wasn't budging. Not that she didn't try to, only somehow she couldn't help it—she was stuck where she was. Augusta had responded that it wasn't only a question of making him laugh; it was also a question, of course, of laughing oneself. Annabella could not help but acknowledge the good sense of this remark, and yet, in spite of her best intentions, there were times in which she couldn't see her way to doing justice to the humour of her situation. For example, and she decided on balance not to publish this episode to her sister, one night, after his sleepless rambles, Lord Byron had returned to their bed. She had felt his absence, as she often felt it, and had been lying awake. But with her eyes shut and her breathing regular, he had reasonably presumed her asleep, so that when she reached out to touch his face, she felt him shrink from her in disgust, and she opened her eyes to the look of horror in his own. She had had, she could now admit it, a moment of weakness then, for she allowed herself to ask what she should not have asked: 'Why do you hate me?' To which he replied almost tenderly, 'I do not hate you, Pip. Only, I do not love you either, which may be worse.' Her lesson, at least, had been learnt—never to ask him anything she did not care to hear the answer to—but she wanted to inquire of Augusta, nevertheless, whether she should have found the heart to laugh at him then?

That his unhappiness had not everything to do with her, she could with some complacency reflect on. He had always been unhappy; she had the poems to prove it. There were times, however, when this seemed scant consolation. Once, towards the end of their stay at Halnaby, she came back from a lonely tramp over the fields—Lord Byron rarely ventured outdoors in those three weeks because of the snow—to find the library and the sitting room empty. It was a large quiet house, and yet the quiet seemed to have taken on a different character. She began to be frightened for him and feared that he might have attempted to do himself some harm. She went upstairs. He was not in their bedroom or any of the bedrooms (there were a great many), and the silence around her, she noticed, had almost silenced herself: she was hardly breathing. In her dressing room, where she went to rouse herself with a dose of salts, she found him at last, sitting on the day-bed with a gun in his hand and Augusta's letters scattered across his lap. 'You will not like it if we visit her, I promise,' he told her, calmly enough. 'Remember later that I warned you.' But her silence—she did not know what to answer—suddenly provoked him. 'Was ever anyone so tormented? It isn't human; it can't be borne,' he cried out. 'I forbid you to write to her. I forbid you to see her.' She remained in the doorway, unmoving—shaping, she hoped, a look of compassion on her face. 'Have you nothing to say? You know I can't stand your patient preening airs.'

'What would you like me to say?' she was in the midst of asking, when the gun went off in the direction of her dressing table. The mirror cracked. Something else had smashed and Annabella was just looking to see *what*—a soda-bottle, they afterwards discovered, broken at the neck—when she noticed that a piece of glass had caught her in the hand. She pressed it at once against her side, where it bled brightly onto the dress. There were footsteps at once. Miss Minns came running, red-faced, so that the hairs around her lips stood out darkly, and pushed into the room. Annabella, feeling faint, had collapsed into the chair at her dressing table; her image was variously reflected in the broken mirror.

Lord Byron sat behind her with his head in his hands. The gun, an old boot pistol with a plain wooden handle, lay at his feet. Miss Minns saw the bloodstain spreading along her mistress's waist and screamed. Lord Byron (Annabella could see him in the glass) looked pale as a milk-bottle; he did not stir. Then the real commotion began, which Annabella only dimly perceived. Her head seemed wrapped in cotton, not ungently. In fact, she had the strangest sense of some merciful intervention, which prevented the full force of events from reaching her; she remembered being conscious of a kind of mercy, of having been spared. 'You must leave this house at once,' Miss Minns began to hector, 'this day, this minute. I will not stand aside and watch him murder you.' And then, with a certain reasonableness, which Lord Byron in a calmer moment could not help but admit to and admire, Miss Minns continued: 'I should not be able to look your mother in the eye if you was murdered. I waited on her when she was a bride, and I'll wait on you. But your father was a respectable husbandly man, and this man is a monster. A monster.'

In the end, only Payne could remove her, by absolute force, lifting her with both his arms around her generous waist; they heard her shouting as she was carried downstairs. 'I will not stand aside. I will not stand aside.' A minute or two passed in relative peace before either Lord Byron or Annabella acknowledged the other. It was she, however, who rose first: her husband, she saw, was shivering with tears. She sat beside him and laid her arms around his neck and her cheek against his ear. He was deadly cold to the touch. Lord Byron turned and covered her face in kisses; she had to close her eyes against them, the wet from his own was stinging her into little blindnesses. Even Miss Minns was quieted at last. Only three days of their honeymoon remained, after all, and they did not leave, and the days passed.

There was, indeed, even in his misery a certain thrill—in his capacity for feeling it and giving shape to it. Such things she wrote in his name! And among the consolations of her marriage was the fact that her husband could hit so brilliantly the heart of their despair. Just to feel what he felt seemed enough to her, just to borrow his grace of feeling. Towards the end of their stay in Halnaby, she copied out a poem for him, which he had titled simply 'Stanzas for Music'. It began: 'There's not a joy the world can give like that it takes away.' She sat at her library-window and wrote it out in a mist of sentiment, almost happy, with the white of the snow in her eyes. But it was the last verse that stuck in her thoughts and came to stand, for the rest of her life, as an image of Halnaby, of the heartbreak she had suffered there and would never suffer from again.

> Oh could I feel as I have felt or be what I have been,
> Or weep as I could once have wept o'er
>   many a vanished scene—
> As springs in deserts found seem sweet,
>   all brackish though they be,
> So, midst the withered waste of life, those tears
>   would flow to me.

Her honeymoon, she always remembered, had been bitterly unhappy; and though she never forgot the fact, as the years passed she began more and more to miss, not perhaps the misery of those weeks, but the freshness of feeling that had permitted her the sharpest sensation of it. The life that followed grew unquestionably drier with age. 'Springs in deserts found seem sweet,' her husband had written. And yes, there were those, too, which they had occasionally, almost against their worst intentions, stumbled upon and taken nourishment from.

Annabella had determined to beat her husband at a game of

billiards. She had often, while he was scribbling, retired to the billiard room to practise. And in spite of her habit of 'muscling the shot', as he put it, she had managed to improve. She was very sensitive to her own capacity for error, and by dint of great concentration of mind and slow particular attention to the dispositions of her body, she had acquired an action of cueing that was more steady than graceful. On the eve of their departure, after he had drunk a considerable quantity of what he called his 'birthday Tokay', she invited him into the billiard room to observe, as she said, her technique—and was gratified to find that her nerve did not fail her under the pressure of his gaze. Annabella's improvement was unquestionable. Her husband applauded her for it. He drank a toast to it.

She offered to play him. He refused, preferring to watch. She committed a number of shots and repeated her offer. He continued to refuse. She said she would beat him, that she had been practising steadily and was sure to beat him; she wanted to beat him. And it was, strangely, her insistence on that word that for the first time brought home to her how much she had suffered at his hands—for his lovelessness, as much as anything else. There was, almost, a relief in the repetition. She was joining in the fight and felt again that fine upright stalk of dignity quivering within her. He, however, coolly put her off with praise, until she became incensed and tried to provoke him in turn. 'It was ungentlemanly to refuse; really, he had the manners of a sailor. Hobhouse would never dream of refusing.' He sat at his ease with crossed legs, laughing, and admitted that he was only somewhat afraid of her. 'You are terribly . . . provoking,' she said, stamping her foot. 'I will not be put off, I will *not*'—although in the end, she was. She could not help herself, she began laughing, too. Not quite, as it happens, at her husband's high humour, but rather at her own absurd angry helpless attempts to make him love her, to argue him into love, by beating him at billiards. He might have guessed as much, for the consolation he offered in the end seemed out of proportion to the injury inflicted. 'You married me to make me happy, did not you?' he said at last, when he had kissed and caressed her into a more sombre pliable temper. She nodded and he continued: 'Well, then, you do make me happy.' And the recollection of that moment, as the coach bore them away from Halnaby, through acres of fields in snow, and woods hidden under it, and roads covered in it, was almost enough to make her smile.

Chapter Six

—

THEY HAD BEEN STOPPING AT SEAHAM until a house in London could be fitted up for them. Lord Byron had been for several weeks on his best public behaviour in front of Annabella's parents—with one notable exception, which was just strange enough to be passed off as a joke and which, consequently, had hardly upset the genial illusion of their domestic harmony. (He had lifted, in the midst of a drunken parlour game, the wig from Lady Milbanke's hair.) The cost, however, of this show of gentlemanliness had been, from the wife's point of view, that he presented to her in private an utterly blank face—the reverse of the card, as it were. And she was honest enough to admit to herself a preference for this state of affairs, except on those evenings when, with scarcely a word spoken and a countenance of stone, he insisted on taking up, as he called it in the morning, his 'conjugal subscription'.

At last, through Lady Melbourne's intervention, a house was arranged: a little large, perhaps, for the needs of their establishment, but pleasantly situated and with a view of Green Park. Lord Byron anxiously anticipated their return to London. His financial affairs remained considerably unsettled, and his business agent, Mr Hansen, was more inclined to consider his duty than to act upon it—he was not a man to be left to his own initiative. Besides, spring in London was not a season to be thoughtlessly missed. 'Only think, Annabella: a London spring.' The theatres like rivers were swelling; the fashions were blooming. Tom Moore and Hobhouse and Dougie Kinnaird were shooting 'new leaves'. The tone he took persuading her to return, its hackneyed enthusiasm, reminded her with a sudden vividness of the airs he used to adopt in their courting days, when he played the gentleman for her. She marvelled now, with a kind of *nostalgie*, that she had ever mistaken the role for the man. And then he surprised her again by stepping out of it. He freely confessed that he had been at times an awkward sort of brute. The fact was, which he admitted in the teeth of his poetical proclamations, that he could never for very long endure the confinement of women. He preferred women in the company of men: they set them off to such advantage. Annabella, by this stage, was sufficiently patient or inured to abuse to draw a little consolation from the prospect of his reform—even if it came at the cost of being lumped together, in her husband's view, with the generality of her sex.

The only question remaining was whether, on their way to London, they should stop at his sister's house at Six Mile Bottom for a week or two. She was determined to make Augusta's acquaintance, or rather, to seal in common intercourse the friendship they had already pledged each other in correspondence. Lord Byron had deeply opposed the plan, and it struck Annabella as the first sign of her successful influence that she managed to override his opposition. Indeed, Augusta herself, as the prospect of their visit approached, appeared suddenly reluctant. Her husband had decided at the last minute to put off a shooting-party with some friends in Northumberland. He had just bought a horse from a stabler in Newmarket. It wanted breaking, and he didn't trust anyone but himself to do it properly. Added to which, her aunt, Miss

Sophia Byron, had proposed a visit, which had been promised for several months, and which she could not hospitably defer. In short, much as she regretted the fact, if Lord and Lady Byron chose to descend upon her now, Augusta would not 'have a hole to put them in'.

It struck Annabella as curious, the disinclination with which brother and sister (who, after all, made such a show of their affections for each other) treated the possibility of a reunion. She wrote to Augusta directly, accepting of course though not without a taint of suspicion 'her sister's word for the necessity of a postponement. Yet she bitterly regretted any delay that would prevent her from claiming, in person, a relation she had decided to cherish above all others—with the exception, of course, of the marriage-bond itself.' This marked, in its way, her first hesitant insistence on her rights as Lord Byron's wife, and she was puzzled, afterwards, by the taste of irony these modest phrases left on her tongue. Her own sincerity was never among the things she had been taught to question. What surprised her, really, was only the pleasure she managed to take from having, as it were, acquired another lens through which to regard herself.

She was rewarded at last with the news that Augusta's husband, Colonel Leigh, had decided, in view of her aunt's visit, to accept his invitation to the shooting-party after all; and that Miss Sophia herself had been frightened off coming by the very bad beginning of spring and the state of the roads. If Annabella felt equal to them, she was welcome to pay them a visit, though the house, as Lord B would tell her, was too large to be kept warm and too much the product of ill-thought-out renovations and additions to be made as comfortable 'for a young bride as she could wish.' In short, 'the coast was clear,' Augusta wrote, with a strangely resigned air, 'and they might as well come now as later.'

Lord Byron consented to Augusta's offer of hospitality, such as it was, with an ill grace, and as they set off in the carriage for their four-day journey, he permitted himself a great display of unwillingness. The weather had turned, but only the skies had the beauty of it, sharp and cloudless and blue. The roads and the woods surrounding them had begun the painful transformations of a thaw. A few shoots and shrubs nosed brownly out of the slops and muds; even the tough young buds of the trees had the appearance rather of a cancer or a general deformation than of the natural and vigorous onset of the spring. 'Take care of Annabella,' Lady Milbanke had called after them, as the carriage descended the drive.

Byron frowned, with the quickness of someone looking for an irritant, and muttered, 'Whatever does she mean by that?' Annabella, with an effort of will, bit her lip. She had turned, in any case, and stretched to look out the window. Her father and mother stood against the steps of the house with their arms at their sides. Sir Ralph stooped a little at the neck: his pale long face vividly suggested dolour. Judy was motionless, compact with disapproval. Annabella hoped they might wave or rest on each other affectionately, and she watched them, for a minute, until they disappeared behind the columns of the gate.

It struck her that the face she had been presenting to her parents' gaze had been as blank, even in their private interviews, as a strict regard for filial decorum could make it—if only to keep from them a sense of how unhappy she was. It was as blank as the face Lord Byron presented to her. These reflections dovetailed into a single fantasy, which she elaborated during the long silence of the road into a vision almost as definite as a comic print: mother and father, husband and wife, seated around a table and playing a hand of whist with faceless cards. It was the wilful perversity of their good manners, as much as anything else, that amused her. This, as she now considered it, was the first gift she had given her husband:

to conceal from her parents how unhappy they were. For proof of success, she needed to look no further than her mother's parting words. Judy had addressed herself to Lord Byron, as if any approach to her own daughter must, from this point forward, be made through her daughter's husband. Nor had they waved farewell. Her last cool sight of home might have given her little sympathy for a man on the road to visit his sister; but she had steeled herself by now to the prospect of facing alone the task of supporting, as pleasantly as she could, their intimate relations. 'Come now,' Annabella chided him, hoping to mother him out of his mood, 'why do you look so gloomy?'

'I feel as if I was going to be married,' he said.

It was a sign, perhaps, of how far she had come that she managed to laugh at that, and the laughter effected what nothing else could have—'to make him,' as Augusta had once advised her in a letter, 'a little less disagreeable.' Even so, as the days passed in the tedium of confinement, in a steady repetition of bad meals and dirty beds, amid the fitfulness of continuous sleep, his reluctance to arrive began to express itself in a more painful and less conscious gloom. He was as restless as a cat before a storm and stretched himself anxiously, as often as not, in the direction of his wife's comfort for a little caressing. She had never known him so sweetly dependent and felt again a validation of the firm line she had decided to take: restricting him, among other things, to three bottles of wine for each day's journey, a total that included anything he hoped to drink at luncheon or supper.

They stopped for the night at Sutton on the eve of their arrival—a very pretty respectable prosperous sort of a town, with a Norman church at one end of the high street and a graveyard at its feet that seemed, as B remarked, 'no bigger than a picnic cloth'. Annabella remembered that Sutton was where Mr Eden had taken up the promise of an incumbency; and she coyly remarked to her husband that evening as they dressed for bed her curiosity to attend a service in the morning, which was a Sunday. 'She believed she knew the vicar, a Mr Eden, who was said to be a decent and gentlemanly person. His sermons, at least, were rumoured to be very enlightening.' The confusion over Mr Eden's proposal and the obligations it was supposed to have put her under were over two years old, and Annabella had counted, or so she told herself, on being able to mention his name, innocently enough, without awakening any ridiculous suspicions. Lord Byron only grunted a response. Later, though, as they lay in bed on Sunday morning, he grew 'greedy' for just such attentions as might have been calculated to put off a young bride from appearing too hastily dressed at church. He asked afterwards (it was his first allusion to the subject), 'if she had had occasions to regret the patience with which they had waited and teased from each other their confessions of interest and love?' He lay at that moment with his head against the angle of her neck; her hand rested on his brow. She answered, with a directness that surprised and exhilarated her, that she had a far greater fund of patience still remaining, that she intended to continue waiting, that she would even, if his reluctance demanded it, continue to tease him, until she was perfectly satisfied with his protestations of love. 'I believe you will, too, Pip,' he said. And then, turning over to look at her, he said, 'Well then, I think I *am* in love with you. Are you satisfied now?' he added, as an afterthought.

'Not yet, not yet,' she answered, smiling through tears.

They reached Six Mile Bottom in the afternoon of an uncomfortable, chilly, humid and windy day. The house, Annabella saw as they approached it, was indeed rather large than distinguished—it looked like a farmhouse that had grown on to a barn. The yard, in which their carriage drew up, was dirty and wet. A three-legged dog undipped his head from the horses' trough and stared at them, before bending to drink again. Smoke from the chimneys settled around them; Annabella, nervously, coughed. Byron said to her, 'I will go in and prepare Gus,' and limped out, leaving her sitting there.

She had felt his unease for the past hour. He had been pretending to sleep, and she had watched him closely to see how long he was willing to keep up the pretence. At last she had said, in a perfectly clear and ordinary voice, 'I believe I saw your sister once at one of those morning waltzes Lady Caroline delighted in bullying us into. In the drawing room of Melbourne House. We were not introduced. I was very young, and you were dancing with her, exclusively, and had attracted a considerable share of the general interest. I believe I was shy—that is, I considered it beneath my dignity to play up to the fashion for you. I had a deal of dignity then; at least, I discovered there to be a great many things that were beneath it.'

She had added, when Lord Byron continued silent, 'I recall she was very pretty,' at which he opened his eyes.

'She looks like her brother.'

Byron himself now broke her train of thought, emerging from the house alone. He needed, perhaps, half a minute to cross the yard; she watched him coldly. 'She was not downstairs,' he said, approaching, and gave her his hand. She stepped down. Together they walked back the way he had come—Annabella checked her eager stride to keep pace beside him.

In the hall, which was dark and awkwardly proportioned, being wide rather than square, Byron began to look through the post, collected on a table beside the stairs. Annabella noticed Mrs Leigh at the top of them; she had rested a moment against the balustrade and now descended. Her features were soft and regular, her neck was good, and her figure, though not tall, was elegant. She wore a muslin dress, simply embroidered, which fell around her ankles—the only element in her appearance that suggested the effects of age and motherhood. (Annabella remembered Hobhouse's praise of her own, conscious of playing the miser, of counting over the pounds and pence of pride.) A pale-blue headdress brought out, with modest assurance, the colour in her face: she had the Byrons' complexion, a bright pallor with a high finish and touched with pink. Annabella, unsure of herself and whether to go to her sister, waited at the foot of the stairs, where Mrs Leigh met her, reaching out a hand. She did not stoop to offer Annabella a kiss, and Annabella could hardly rise to insist on one.

Lord Byron meanwhile had opened a letter and begun to read from it, without looking up. Nor did Augusta glance at her brother. She said, instead, how happy she was to meet 'her new sister'. Her voice, like Byron's, was low and musical, an effect brought out in part by nerves, which gave to its tone a deepening uncertainty. What surprised Annabella, whose faith in Augusta's good intentions was by no means complete, was the rush of real sisterly feeling the introduction inspired. Gus offered to lead Annabella to her rooms; she was sure the journey must have fatigued her. Her brother, she knew, being an inveterate traveller, had only the dimmest sense of what a woman suffered in the squalor of a public house. Byron at this looked up from the letter he was reading. 'Nonsense, Gussie,' he said, 'you'll soon find that Lady Byron is perfectly indestructible. I have put her to every test.'

Annabella followed her hostess to the top of the stairs and along a dark corridor to the door at the end of it. Her room, at least, was clean and bright, though it overlooked the stables. Against the odour of which and the restless noise, Augusta now shut the window—an act of modest kindness that drew from her sister-in-law a sudden kiss. 'It was the kiss,' Annabella said, not without a touch of reproach, 'she had meant to bestow upon her new sister on sight.' She had guessed at possibilities: that Mrs Leigh might offer her an outlet for those feelings her brother so irregularly reciprocated. A sister, in fact, from her earliest childhood, had been the highest dream of escape from that solitude which Annabella had practically come to believe was her natural state. And what pleased her especially was that she felt already, rising in her, the confidence to assume in their relations the part of the elder and wiser. This, in truth, is what her insistence on kissing Augusta was supposed to seal. Gus only said, 'I should see to my brother now,' and added, by way of apology, 'he can be very awkward in company, especially with his sister! and dislikes particularly greetings and farewells. He becomes very abrupt and seems rude without the least intention of it, only we have been so used, you know, to being on our own.'

Having washed and dressed, Annabella descended to the drawing room. There was silence within. She listened at the door for a moment before entering, to find her husband inside, limping along in pain behind the sofa, back and forth, while Augusta sat with her back to him and her head bowed. He tended to suffer afterwards for the forced repose of a long coach-journey. The sun had set and the curtains were drawn against the night; a fire burned damply in the fireplace. The house was neither cold nor warm but a something in between—one was just as likely to sweat as shiver.

Annabella felt the general oppression of accumulated life. Paintings and prints, mostly of horses or hunting scenes, had been added haphazardly to the walls. There was, in that preference for subject, a general neglect of the subtler art of arrangement. Annabella discovered, in the course of her stay, a Romney hidden away in a corner of the chimney-breast, while a large sketched print

of a mutton-legged English setter was given conspicuous prominence. One sensed in these appointments the insistence of
Colonel Leigh; nevertheless, Augusta inhabited the house with so
comfortable an indifference that Annabella could not help but
admire her for it. She had yet to make herself at home in her husband's tastes. Occasionally, perhaps, the equine passion was taken a
little far: a child's rocking horse, draped with a lady's shawl, stood in
place of a stool at the pianoforte. One had the sense of arriving at
any empty seat just in time. Annabella sat down on a low-backed
chair covered in green baize, having removed from the cushion an
unfinished piece of embroidery and set it on a card-table nearby.

A decanter of spirits was open on the tantalus. Lord Byron disengaged the spring and poured himself a glass. When he saw his
wife, he stopped, with pointed attention, and offered her the
drink. On her refusal, he drank it down and continued his parade.
Augusta began with an apology. 'My dear sister, you'll find us very
dull here, I'm afraid.'

'Gus and I are used to amusing ourselves,' Byron added.

'What he means is only that the children adore him. He plays
the part, very happily, of uncle and slips quite noiselessly into family life. We haven't, I fear, the advantages of a town. Our days are
mostly taken up with a great deal of bustle in a very narrow round.
I confess I have got used, simply, to chasing after the children, and
B is often good enough to join me in that thankless task.' She
laughed. Annabella was surprised to see her sister-in-law capable
of so much manner—she had the first real inkling, not of fear
exactly, but of that responding pride which measures itself against
the confidence of others. Augusta seemed hardly so shy as she at
first appeared.

'I should like very much to see the children,' Annabella sweetly
replied. 'My husband and I have been constrained, since our marriage, to make do with each other. It is something of a relief to be

forced to make do with other people.' And Annabella herself was equal to a laugh.

'You forget, my dear, the entertainment we enjoyed at Seaham at your parents' house. Your father, in particular, diverted us with variations on a speech he had given at Durham the fortnight preceding, concerning certain enclosures and the provisions necessary to implement them. Such games we had, too; it was quite like Christmas.'

The irony in his tone created a silence, which Augusta at last ventured to break. 'I have never laughed so much as I did on hearing how my little brother plucked the wig from Lady Milbanke's head. You kept yourselves very well amused, I believe. I was quite astonished to discover how many occupations he had acquired: walking, dining, playing draughts with your mamma. Though I am vain enough to think he did not entirely forget his Gus.'

'He was a perfect little child,' Annabella replied, not to be outdone. 'He has a child's gift, too, which never fails to charm, of declaring his wants in such a way that it is quite a pleasure to satisfy them. Poor little B, he grew in the habit of saying—wants this, wants that. We all doted on him.'

'I am so glad. You have hit on, at once, just the way to manage him. Never mind what he says and see that he eats enough. He has a terrible passion for starving himself, which must be resisted. One suffers much more oneself for his hungry humours.'

Byron, meanwhile, who hated ordinarily to be caught out on his feet, continued to pace behind the sofa. Annabella heard the rustle of the curtain against his leg as he brushed it aside, again and again. 'Shall we call the children in?' he said at last. 'There is one among them, Pip, I should particularly like you to meet; she is a great favourite with me. It is said, though I am no judge, that she takes after her uncle. I believe that any imputed resemblance is more flattering than plausible. Medora is reckoned very beautiful.'

'They have just been got to sleep,' Augusta said, 'and I should like first to have a quiet minute with my sister—'

'You have nothing to say to each other,' Byron interrupted her, raising his voice; he rested his hands on the sofa behind her neck. 'This is intolerable. To be smothered like this in female kindnesses. I will not be managed!'

Augusta flinched, with a stiffness that suggested how rigidly she had been holding herself—she closed her eyes as if the blow had been real. His sister's excess of manner had been, Annabella supposed, only the careful containment of a woman on the verge of tears. His wife, she reflected, not without pride, was more accustomed to such outbursts. She picked up the piece of embroidery and held it against the light, to see how much remained. Grateful, for once, to be allowed to disregard his anger. 'You may do as you like, my dear.' It was left to Augusta to answer him. 'You always do.'

Chapter Seven

—

AT SUPPER HE BEGAN TO DRINK IN EARNEST. Annabella found, as
she attempted to tighten them, that he had quite slipped his reins.
His sister also learned that the hand with which she was used to
comforting him had lost the power of direction. A painful meal: of
roast chicken, slightly burnt, and underboiled potatoes. There was
something, indeed, in the quality of cooking that expressed the general mood of helpless unhappiness. It was as if—and Annabella
afterwards, on one of their quiet walks, ventured to make the
reflection to Augusta, she was sufficiently pleased with it—a large
wild bird had flown into the room and, unable to escape, had begun
to beat them with its wings. The effect of which, understandably
enough, was to draw the new sisters more closely together. They
exchanged in the course of the meal a series of underlooks, in which
a genuine and shared fearfulness was mixed with the real pleasure
of conspiracy. Lord Byron, who never drank himself to insensibil-
ity, could not help remarking on these glances and feeling
(Annabella almost pitied him for it) the extent of his masculine
exclusion.

In the evening, they sat in the drawing room and watched him
drink. Augusta had claimed to fear that the three of them might

find it very dull together. At least they did not find it dull. Annabella was angry enough to be grateful for that fact; she was almost light-hearted with anger. And there was consolation to be had from seeing her private suffering made public. He insisted, once again, on waking the children. He particularly wished to introduce Medora, his daughter, his goddaughter, to her new aunt. He had been in a fever to see her all day; she had been the real object of their journey. There would be time in the morning, Annabella said. They had, after all, at their disposal a comfortable fortnight. It was unnatural, he maintained, to keep Medora from him and would do the child no good. He dimly remembered, he could not have been more than one or two, being woken, after one of his revels, during one of his reappearances, by his own father—'who was no doubt as drunk as I am now'—and roused out of bed, to be held and cried over. How old was Medora now? he asked. 'Not yet one,' Augusta quietly answered. 'She was born last April?' he asked; his sister nodded. 'Aye,' he added, turning towards the door, 'and got, I remember, in that summer of revelry, 1813.'

Augusta, deferent to his wife's claims, sat very quietly where she was. It was left to Annabella to attempt a restraint. She seized him by the hand, entreating. It was only a question of waiting till morning; surely, he could wait as long as that. Mrs Leigh would hardly thank him for putting her to the trouble of getting the child to sleep again. 'As for that, as for that,' he repeated, inconsequently, 'he had had enough, for one night, of the kindness of women. It was the worst thing imaginable for a child to be left in female company. God knows, he had suffered for it himself.' In shaking her off, with the violence of impatience, he caught her a blow with the back of his hand. She fell into a chair, and he took the occasion to escape. For a minute the women sat in silence, listening. Annabella never forgot how quietly Augusta had endured this outbreak of her brother's temper. Mrs Leigh breathed audibly

through her clasped palms, less in horror, however, than calculation: she was following from the noises overhead Byron's progress
through the house, through her children's rooms. There was a
general disturbance. He did not know the bed he sought for, and
then, a minute later, as he made his way downstairs, one sharp
particular cry grew clearer and louder.

He was weeping himself with the weeping child in his arms
when he pushed through the open door. 'Is it Medora?' he said to
his sister. 'I could not be sure; I believe it is.' The child was hysterical. The blood in her face gave to her cheeks a purple translu-
cence; the noise her lungs poured forth was enormous. Annabella
felt, at any cost, the desire to silence it. She imagined closing her
hand over its mouth and winced a little as, in her fancy, the child
bit into it. Byron, helplessly, kissed the girl's eyes, which were as
blue as his own; their tears ran together. Augusta said only, 'Yes,
you have found Medora.' She remained on the sofa. It surprised
Annabella that she played in the scene so passive a role. For her
part, she had never seen Byron so tenderly repentant. She was
almost grateful for the exhibition in that it offered such a vivid
reminder of her husband's capacity for sincere remorse. At last,
from a consciousness of futility, he resigned the child to its
mother's care (it had grown almost too breathless to shout).
'Console it, console it, console it,' he repeated and sat down himself beside her, just as Augusta was rising to return the baby to its
bed. 'I suppose you despise me?' Lord Byron said to his wife, when
they were alone together.

'Not at all,' Annabella said, careful as always against the noise
of his violent feelings to express herself with something like exactness. 'I pity your sufferings and pray for their relief. There is so
much original goodness in your composition that your indul-
gences afflict no one so painfully as yourself. Only, you lack the
power of regulation, which would concede to the better part of

your nature the control of the worse. The violence of the contest between them is, I believe, the chief cause of your distress.'

Augusta, after an interval of ten minutes, returned to a room in which the expression of feeling had considerably dried up. No direct mention was made of the interlude preceding. Byron rose to offer them all a drink. They demurred, and he poured a glass of brandy for himself. 'Have you ever, Gussie,' he said, holding his wife by the cheek, 'seen such an angel's face? Not the prettiest angel, certainly, but without doubt the best. I have never known anyone so good; she is quite implacable with goodness. She watches her own heart as jealously as a miser his millions and counts over, from time to time, her good intentions.' Annabella cast on her sister-in-law a glance that conveyed with unmistakable pride how much she endured. 'There is nothing she will not forgive me,' he continued. 'Not even you, Gussie, could forgive so much, although you have never had the occasion. Except, perhaps, for a single particular offence, sometimes repeated, in which your part, I believe, was not entirely guiltless—even if I have suffered more for it in the end. Do you know, Gus, that on our honeymoon I practically shot at her? I was terribly provoked, though, by those letters you wrote her, with scarcely so much as a note to poor old B. Now that was not right, that was not fair, was it, my dear?'

One of the effects, Annabella found, of the siblings' company was subtly to hush her; they had, after all, a deeper habit of conversation. In the course of his ramblings, however, Augusta endeavoured to keep up a quiet sort of under-conversation with her brother's wife. 'Do not imagine,' she turned and said to her at one point, 'that I have forgotten our first meeting. It was at a waltzing-party in Melbourne House, just at the beginning of that rage. We were all hopelessly behind-hand; I dared not dance with anyone but my brother. How the ladies admired you! You seemed to pick up the trick of it at once and put the rest of us to shame.

There was a little German man, our instructor, who singled you out for praise; I blushed with envy. The Byrons, you know, are terribly shy. We cannot bear a general attention, but we long for it and fear it in equal measure. You will forgive me, my dear sister, if I hated you a little for dancing so well?'

Annabella blushed in turn, acknowledging both the compliment and the ambivalence, she believed, it had just failed to conceal. Despite their sisterly protestations, she sensed in Augusta a jealous reserve. Gus held, as it were, a hand out to each of them, to husband and wife, in order to comfort them and to keep them apart.

'It was one of my particular conditions,' Byron broke in, 'that my wife should waltz. I expressed myself exactly on that point and directed Lady Melbourne to make inquiries. The answer came back, and I have since found the truth of it justified. Pip dances beautifully, as you say—quite like an elephant, by crushing.'

'I don't know what you mean by that, I'm sure,' his sister replied.

'You will learn.'

At ten, a clock rang out behind her. Annabella later remembered the awkwardness of their conversation by the fact of the silence that allowed her to count the chimes. Lord Byron, in whom drunkenness produced a sort of cruel watchfulness and strong ironic sympathies, began to give a voice to the whisper in her lips. 'Seven eight nine ten,' he said, and then: 'you needn't stay up on our account.'

He was sitting by Augusta on the sofa; his hand rested on his sister's, which lay on the cushion between them. Annabella had not supposed herself capable of fresh suffering, but the thought of being sent away from them afflicted her with the most childish anxieties. 'I am not in the least fatigued,' she insisted, blinking back tears.

'You have had a long journey,' he said, 'particularly for one in your condition.' Augusta looked up sharply, and he continued: 'She is too innocent to guess the cause of it, but there have been certain restrictions in our personal intercourse. A kind of resistance or awkwardness in that respect, as you and I know, my dear, often prefigures the grosser show. You can see for yourself, Gussie, how changeable her temper is, and the least kindness or cruelty sets her off.' It was all Annabella, who hadn't the least notion of being *enceinte*, could do to keep back her tears and turn on the pair of them a smiling, shining face. 'Not at all, not at all. If I have fallen quiet, it is only out of admiration. I suffered, you know, very much in my childhood for want of a sister. It is a relation that has always had a peculiar fascination for me, and to see each of you so happy in the other's affection does my heart good. I am guilty, I know, of slipping at times too easily into the role of observer; but I am perfectly cheerful in it, though it makes me a dull silent staring sort of companion.'

'You say that always,' Byron broke in, 'with a great air of confession, as if you had not said it an hundred times before. I can never imagine anyone wanting a sister quite so much as you pretend to do. We choose not to believe you.'

'Perhaps,' Augusta said, with an air of true kindness, 'you had really better retire. Your journey has been long and the best sleep is always the sleep of arrival. We have, as you say, a comfortable fortnight in which to deepen our acquaintance. I'm sure, in the course of it, you will observe more than you wish to of the little humours of a brother and sister. I'll see that your husband follows shortly after.'

Byron, however, took this as just the proof of alliance he was seeking. His drunkenness had climbed over the sullen foothills into a kind of windy elation, which was no less savage. 'Come, come, we don't want you, my charmer. Now that I've got Augusta, you'll find I can do without you in all ways.'

She must in the end give in. Annabella hardly trusted herself to utter another word. Augusta, all gentleness, lit a candle for her and promised, in the open doorway, to soften Byron into something like sobriety before she sent him to bed. As she made her way up the shadowy unfamiliar stairs, Annabella resented, as much as anything else, her own childish weakness. She had meekly obeyed those from whom she sought comfort, in spite of the fact that what she submitted to was nothing more than their desire to be free of her. In the tally she began that moment to keep, she conceded to her new sister the opening point. As she undressed, however, in the cold strange room, the misery she felt seemed both simpler and harder to measure. The bed was lumpy and smelt of children, of their peculiar sweetness gone rather pleasantly stale. She found a stray brown curl against one of her pillows and rubbed it off between her palms. What if Byron was right? Sitting at the edge of the bed with her feet hanging free, she crossed her arms and held them against her middle. It seemed a lonely sort of burden to be growing within her.

Only by lying on her back could she settle the mattress into any sort of quiet, and quiet is what she wanted. She was listening with the full still fierceness of her considerable attention to the restless silence of a large country house—from which at last emerged a low inarticulate current of conversation. They were talking together, but their voices, by the time they reached her ears, had been thickened by the floorboards between them into hums and ahs. What she heard was a language reduced to its simplest sound and repeated; what it conveyed, eloquently, was only the fact of comfort, of intimacy. He had rested his hand against the back of hers on the cushion between them. Her face was the mirror of his, only softened, it seemed, by a dullness (almost silvery) in the reflection. From time to time a burst of laughter startled in Annabella the sense of lying awake. It sounded all the sweeter for the muffling of distance. 'I only want a woman to laugh,' Byron had said to her. 'I can make Augusta laugh at anything.' Laughter, she reflected, is just what one cannot, with the best will in the world, put on. A great shame: she trusted in nothing so much as her strength of will. But the laughter dried up, and she struggled in the darkness to keep track of the time that had passed—could it have been as long as an hour? had she fallen asleep?—before she heard her husband's uncertain footstep on the stairs.

Chapter Eight

—

IN THEIR COURTSHIP—and Annabella could consider the facts of
it whenever she liked, consisting as it did mainly in an exchange of
letters, which she carried with her in a large blue calf-skin album—
Lord Byron had presented himself to her as a man bearing the burden of a terrible secret. It had been at the time a positive pleasure
for her, one of those rare occasions in the correspondence when
she felt sure of the ground beneath her feet, to offer to relieve him
of that burden as best she might. Her conscience was pure and light;
she had plenty of strength left to support a few more sins. Now, in
the face of his variable and violent moods, she saw it as her duty to
honour that promise—if only for the sake of their common peace.
The fact was (and she could acknowledge this truth almost with
an inward smile) that he *did* behave towards her like a man with a
burden to bear. He played, in other words, his part; and she felt
now keenly the obligation to live up to hers.

In the mornings, Byron slept late, and Augusta and she had the
freedom of his absence in which to establish their friendship. The
children, at last, were properly introduced to their new aunt.
Georgiana was the oldest, at six years, and conscious of that honour, the best behaved, though dirty. She was proud of her reading,

and Annabella encouraged her in it, believing her to possess a character that might, with a little regulation, shape itself into propriety. Augusta Charlotte resembled her mother most, with sharp blue eyes and a face that had already begun to suffer the lengthening and rounding that would soften it into a perfect oval. She was pretty and silent and perfectly indifferent to instruction, which she endured and then ignored. George was the only boy, and Gus's great favourite: he was just beginning to speak, and his mother adopted with him such childish barbarisms that Annabella could not quite restrain a show of disapproval. Augusta took so happily to the cooing of children that she seemed to prefer it to ordinary speech, and what appalled Annabella was the air Mrs Leigh had afterwards, when reverting to conversation, of adjusting, however fluently, to a foreign tongue. Her most natural expression seemed to be the comforting, meaningless sighs of motherhood. Annabella, with some jealousy, suspected Lord Byron himself of reposing in their relations on his sister's simplest sympathies.

Byron was also jealous of the children, of the attention they demanded from Augusta, and his wife discovered that any interest she showed in them served to reinforce his sense of exclusion. It was a relief, indeed, to find him jealous of Georgiana, for sitting on her aunt's lap and reading to her. His appetite for affection was so great that he could mind any loss of it, and Annabella consoled herself, in playing up to it, with the reflection that there could be nothing sinful in teasing kindness from him. He had little real interest in his nephews and nieces, however, with the exception of Medora; and he grew tired, even, of his own jealousy. Spaces opened up around the babies for Augusta and Annabella to get along in. When he was drunk, they learned to be grateful to the children for inspiring in their uncle the gentleness of indifference. Despairing, he retired to the library—they heard him sometimes reading aloud to himself to attract their notice. Medora alone awoke in him his talent for attachment. 'I should like,' Annabella said to Gus, 'to have him painted when he is looking at Medora. The tenderness of his expression is remarkable.' Byron overheard her. 'You did not suppose, on the strength of our marriage, that I was incapable of love?'

The sisters, increasingly, took comfort in each other. The grounds at Six Mile Bottom had been carelessly maintained, but there was one dry path running through it, past a grove of fir trees, which obscured from the house a view of the farms behind. Whenever the weather was fine, the pair of them, arm in arm, seized the chance of escaping the glooms of the drawing room. Nature would, regardless of man's neglect, refresh and beautify itself, and the first primroses as the fortnight wore on began to appear. The thick of their leaves flushed darkly in the gusts of spring. They were both, in spite of their new-found relation to each other, grateful enough for female company that they managed to keep up, on the surface of their intercourse, an easy intimacy; and it amazed Annabella how often it allowed them, almost painlessly, to touch on the deeper questions that afflicted them.

Augusta puzzled her more the better she knew her. The jealousy or ambivalence, to which she had at first attributed her sister-in-law's reserve, struck her perhaps as merely the effect of shyness. There was in her manner an artlessness which Annabella seized on, from the beginning, as the means of that ascendancy she hoped to establish over her. Annabella herself, whatever her other virtues, could never aspire to artlessness. She had observed since childhood with great curiosity the growing divide between her real thoughts and their expression. The measure of her virtue, of the strict accounts she kept, was only the care with which she attempted to adapt one to the other. Yet she could find in her sister no sign of that care, no sign of such a divide. Augusta seemed unashamedly devoted to Annabella. The strangest effect of that devotion, and the really charming naivety with which she gave it a voice, was to silence for a time in Annabella just those reservations on which her sense of superiority usually relied.

'I think I never saw or heard or read of a more perfect being in mortal mould,' Augusta confessed on one of these walks, 'than you appear to be.' Even in that 'appear', Annabella, flattered in spite of herself, observed the ingenuousness of her good intentions. 'I have been raised, you know, in London as the indulged dependant of very grand relations. For all their kindnesses, I was never presented with a model of true female conduct and was forced to rely as best I could on my own nature, such as it is. What I wanted, in short,' she added, 'was a guide, a philosopher, and a friend; and I'm afraid my brother, loving as he is, was never suited to the role. I am delighted to call you sister, but what I long to call you, above everything else, is friend.' Then, in a lower voice, she continued: 'You know how much my brother and I are attached to each other, and I had feared that, by his marriage, I should be asked to give up a precious share of that attachment. And yet even in the friendship of a brother and a sister certain affections might be said to run their course, and I have found, in fact, by your addition, that my sisterly feelings have been renewed and strengthened, and diverted more properly to their object. To you, my dear.'

Annabella was almost disarmed. She had believed to trace in her new sister the conscious airs of a rival. Perhaps, it occurred to her at last, the air she moved in was really her own. She had, in truth, no one else to blame for finding the proofs of rivalry so generally prevalent in her acquaintance. The 'play of manner', which Annabella had imputed to Augusta on their first encounter, she now assigned a simpler source: the efficient grace of perfect innocence. But then, the idea of 'innocence' hardly did justice to the particular quality of Byron's sister. Augusta seemed to possess, truly, helplessly, the virtues of gentleness, of sympathy, of honesty.

One found in her so little the effects of regulation only because the materials of which she was composed so little required it. And yet there was in her unwitting goodness a real indifference to her own virtues, which might just as easily, Annabella presumed, allow to the darkest and most sinful desires their free expression.

Each night the pattern of their arrival was repeated. After supper, her husband sent Annabella up to bed, where she lay listening, as best she could, and drifting in and out of sleep. Their laughter, she was relieved to hear, broke out as the week wore on more rarely than at first; and Byron, when he came up at last, seemed anything but happy. He took up less and less (it was a phrase she echoed back at him) his conjugal subscription—a fact that Annabella could attribute, if she liked, to that awkwardness or restriction which he had complained of in their personal intercourse. Still, she offered to do what she could to please him. She placed herself entirely in his hands, on the one condition, that he trusted himself freely to hers. There was nothing, she bravely gave him to understand, they need stop short at, and among the duties she promised willingly to perform was the part of his confessor. It had occurred to her, as if for the first time, that Lord Byron was suffering not in show only but from the real burden of a secret sin; that the pressure she applied against him to trust in her might finally persuade him to confide it; and that she might not much like the truth of his confession. She had been proceeding in marriage with the air of a swimmer who closes her eyes against the torrent, to stave off the more painful blindness that would afflict her if she opened them too soon. But she must open her eyes at last, and the courage to see, to feel, to understand, was just what she had always counted on to make up for the absence in her character of gentler and more feminine virtues. Really, she could almost laugh: Lord Byron could not have chosen for himself a wife more different from his sister.

Even so, the full extent of what his confession might stretch to nearly took her breath away. A few mornings after their arrival, Augusta received a parcel in the post; Lord Byron was particularly anxious to watch her open it. It seemed to put him in the best, most mischievous of spirits. He had reached the stage in which Annabella was grateful even to those good humours that exercised themselves at her expense. Augusta, with the unforced excitement of a child, tore off the string and wrapping. There were two brooches inside, of simple gold and marked with little crosses. They each contained a strand of woven hair and differed from each other only in the letter inscribed upon them, an A and a B. 'Do they please you?' Lord Byron said to his sister, with real gentleness, and pinning to her breast the second of these. 'Are they pretty? The hair, of course, belongs to both of us, though I can't distinguish yours from mine. We are so much alike. Do you think Pip can guess what the crosses signify?' Augusta blushed at this, though Annabella could not be sure that it wasn't only from the pleasure of adjusting the brooch on her dress and observing the effect of it in the hall-mirror. Afterwards, Byron asked his sister to pin the other brooch, inscribed with her initial, against his coat-pocket. 'You remember,' he said, while she was fussing under his chin, 'of course, how we passed our time at Newstead?'

For the rest of the fortnight, Augusta never appeared without that mark of Byron's affection: the little gold pin etched with crosses and containing a braid of their hair. It began to haunt Annabella and suggested to her imagination the most horrible intimacies, of a type from which her own poor relation of wife could only exclude her. She watched for it with a jealous eye and walked distractedly down to breakfast every morning, lost in the most absurd speculations. Had Augusta forgotten, perhaps, to wear it? or to what piece of her dress had she chosen to attach it that day? Her obsession with that testament to her husband's brotherly feeling grew into a source of real shame. She supposed herself, at times, to be going mad, and she hardly dared to explore the scope of her suspicions for fear that the symbol she had fixed on, as the proof of them, would seem to a stranger's eye so slight and innocent. Only once, on one of their walks, was she emboldened to raise the subject with her sister, in the belief that Augusta herself had introduced it.

It was a bright morning after a wet night. The breeze, though cool, had the expansion, the lightness, of a warmer wind, and had tempted them into the open air from the fire of the drawing room— where they had been waiting, awkwardly enough, for Lord Byron to descend. 'I am sorry to say,' it was Augusta who broke the silence, once they were safely away from the house, 'that his nerves and spirits are very far from what we could wish them. One mustn't, of course, breathe a word of this to him on any account.' After a pause, she continued: 'He has every blessing this world can bestow. I have been, among all your other virtues, admiring your forbearance. You very judiciously abstain from—pressing him at the present moment. He would likely, if pushed, give away a great deal more than the truth.' Annabella was honest enough and vain enough to take pleasure from such praise, though she knew quite well that a little pressing, on various points, was just what she had decided to permit herself. It occurred to her, of course, that Augusta had only been dressing up a piece of advice as admiration. But she believed her sister-in-law to be one of those women who acted, as it were, from cause alone; Augusta seemed incapable of calculating, to such a degree, her effects.

They had been walking through the darkness of the grove of firs. A noisy gust scattered upon them a few drops of wet, and then they emerged, happily, into the wide green space of fields. Augusta had been relieved to find, she added, stopping and taking her sister's hands, that Annabella didn't mind too much his little insinuations. It was only his confessional instinct, which was very strong. He could never bear to keep a thought to himself and 'suggests all sorts of doleful things, which have no reality but in the fervency of his imagination.' Still, he could not help believing them to be (and Annabella never forgot this phrase) 'as bad as if they were true. One is only playing up to the worst of his famous melancholy by taking him at his word.' A little laughter, she had found (adapting her brother's meaning), could shake off a great deal of misery. He was only unhappy by conviction; luckily, his convictions were neither deep nor steady. 'It was perhaps the duty of his wife *not* to trust in him. He is easily managed, so long as one doesn't mind what he says.' Augusta had set between them the very question that had occupied Annabella—what, exactly, had Lord Byron been saying?—though whether it was with an air of putting the matter to rest or taking it up at last, Annabella could not determine. She was tempted, indeed, to take it up, but it seemed at the time too decided a step. Lying out, then, and unre-marked upon is where she left it.

Afterwards, she had occasion to reflect that her confidence of assuming in their relations the decisive role had suffered some-thing of a blow. Consolation lay, perhaps, in the fact of her youth: she was not yet twenty-three, and Augusta had, for all her naivety, the benefit of seven long years of motherhood behind her. There was also the simple fact of Annabella's loneliness. She had entered by marriage a family of strangers, and she could not condemn her-self too severely for deferring to their sense of her position. After a silence, which Augusta had allowed her to fill, Lady Byron only observed that 'it was a relief, after the wilful confusions of the pic-turesque, to stare out at the long level prospect of working land.' Gus, however, was not to be put off, and Annabella felt, by her insistence, duly chastened. 'The fact is,' she said, with one of her bursts into clarity and candour, 'he hopes by these games to set us against each other. I am quite determined not to be pushed. You mustn't be either, my dear.'

'You mean,' Annabella offered at last, 'by the brooches?'

But it was the wrong note. 'Oh, the brooches . . .' Augusta made a gesture with her hand. 'You've seen for yourself, I'm sure, how generous he is.'

The game of setting the sisters against each other began that night in earnest: Augusta's warning, it seemed, had ushered in the event. It was as if her brother had set out especially to make her meaning clear.

After supper at Six Mile Bottom, it was their habit to retire together to the drawing room, where Augusta would join them again after kissing her children goodnight. Lord Byron drank brandy and fell asleep over a book, and his young wife used to occupy herself more soberly at the desk in the third window, answering letters. She was a dutiful correspondent and marked the receipt and reciprocation of each letter in a diary she reserved for the purpose. She also recorded the subject of the exchange, along with any personal reflections it had inspired in her. Annabella had been used, in the course of their honeymoon, to read to her husband extracts from their protracted epistolary affair. She had hoped to remind him—trusting, with reasonable presumption, to the effect on the poet of something like literary proof—of his love for her. The diary allowed her, if she liked, quickly to find, amidst the mass of her correspondence, a certain line or sentiment. She had often referred to it before selecting a passage from their letters, whose tone and substance, she sup-posed, would be most soothing to his exacerbated feelings.

This diary was his abhorrence. He particularly resented the way she recorded in it and reflected upon those letters from his sister, which she had been receiving almost daily during their stay at Halnaby and afterwards at Seaham. Her remarks on Augusta's style and penmanship were not always flattering, especially at first. And as he had been observing, with a jealous eye, the increase of intimacy their relations had enjoyed from the habit of daily intercourse at Six Mile Bottom, it occurred to him to expose to his sister what he believed to be the real character of his wife's affections, by reading out to Augusta the quiet ironic commentary Annabella had made upon their correspondence. One evening, Augusta came down from the darkened quiet of her children's bedrooms to find Lord Byron, it seemed, being assaulted by his wife. He stood laughing in front of the fire with his arm raised above his head, while Annabella, at his back, clung to his shoulder and attempted to reach the book he was holding in his hand.

The sight of her sister-in-law persuaded Annabella to desist. She disliked, above all, any show of disharmony in their married life—or rather, any show of her own deeply felt resentment at his treatment. So long, she believed, as she could seem not to mind him, there might really appear to be nothing to mind. Byron, released, sat down in one of the easy chairs by the hearth and began to read quietly. Annabella, with a forced laugh, complained that her husband 'was being terribly provoking. She had never known what it was to have a brother, and now she was almost glad of the fact. They contributed very little to one's peace.' Augusta could only smile at that, with a grave little smile; she wanted to see what Byron was reading. After a minute, he gave them a specimen of it, in an off-hand manner that suggested he had just come across something amusing. 'Her penmanship is fluent rather than strict. It is the writing of a child too soon thrust into the duties of womanhood, with her character hardly yet fixed. One feels, almost plaintively, the appeal of her innocence. She is as supple as a child and wriggles from one feeling to the next without any concern for consistency, just as they suit her purpose. I should not exactly like to call it innocence myself—and yet I am almost grateful for it and feel, instinctively, the superior strength of regulation.

There is something, indeed, in the tone she takes in relation to her brother, an overripe sweetness, an air of too much certainty, that suggests our intercourse will take the form of a contest of loves . . .'

At this point, Annabella, who had not yet sat down, made a fierce little rush at him and, with a cry, rescued the diary from his hands. Augusta said nothing, and Lord Byron, who, after all, had offered scant resistance, seemed pleased enough with the progress of his experiment to permit its momentary interruption. In fact, he spent the rest of the evening in the best of spirits and kissed Annabella into something like quietude again, leaving her only to resent that her husband's good humour was instantly persuasive while, with the best intentions, her own high spirits struggled to awake in him any sympathetic response. Augusta and she never once referred to the matter. Their growing intimacy, in fact, was marked, like the leaf of a blighted tree, with little spots or blemishes of silence. These seemed to be everywhere multiplying, so that the sisters found, in spite of their increased familiarity, less and less to communicate to each other as the fortnight wore on— a consequence, no doubt, in keeping with Lord Byron's intention.

The evenings are what Annabella learned particularly to dread. Lord Byron, who rose late, spent the afternoons in a state of slothfulness more or less pleasant. The first effect of drink on him (and he drank steadily: a flask of brandy stood by his bed to relieve not only his bouts of insomnia but the shock of daybreak) was cheerful enough; only the nights brought out his savagery. After supper the next day, he took it into his head to amuse his wife and sister by reading to them extracts from his own correspondence with Augusta. Byron had discovered the box in which she kept their letters, somewhat jumbled together. He had spent a very pleasant afternoon, he said, reading them through, tidying them into sequence, and selecting, from the crowd of trivial affections, a few 'choice bits'. Annabella had given him the idea. He flattered himself, he added, that she would be interested to hear the details of a relationship that had been the refuge of his youth (confined, as he had been, to the company of an ill-bred, ugly, violently doting mother) and the consolation of his manhood, after the effects of sudden fame had thrust upon him, as it were, an uncomplimentary view of the decency and good sense of her sex. He wanted her to see, above all, what it was he had given up for her—that she was not the only one in their marriage who had relinquished for the sake of it what he called 'the comforts of home'.

It was Augusta's turn to be horrified. She came down after supper to discover Lord Byron in his easy chair, with the box on the floor supporting a glass of sherry, and a heap of letters on his lap. 'I am sure,' she said, wringing her hands together, 'there is nothing of interest in them to anyone but ourselves. I am such a bad hand; you always complain of it to me. You'll strain your eyes.'

'Nonsense, Gussie,' he said. But she would not sit down, and as he began to read, she stood by his shoulder with her back to the fire, looking unhappily on. The flatness in the jointure of her nose and forehead had a stubborn, childish persistence. If *this* was her protest, Annabella considered, she could be made to endure a great deal quietly. Lord Byron took no notice and managed to put into his voice something of his sister's most gossipy manner. 'I wonder, my dear, if you know Miss Elphinstone. She is reckoned very beautiful, though shy. At least, she hasn't any of those practised airs you often complain of in women. She eats with great appetite; she rides five times a week; and she scarcely puts seven words together from one afternoon to the next. She has become a great favourite of mine. When we walk out together in St James's, or go promenading through the park, all the men stare at her and listen to me; which, I believe, is much the best way round. Her father, they say, is rich as Croesus. I know for a fact that he buys a new horse once a month. In short, I recommend her to you in the character of wife, which article, I am told, you have been shopping for. You might be pushed to get more than one word out of her—though that, I believe, is as much as you need.'

'Come,' Augusta said quietly, 'put them away. For my sake, if not hers.'

Byron, ignoring her, picked up another letter. 'Well (he writes in reply), you have lined them up very prettily, only they won't stand still long enough for me to take a sight of them. As Krausnitz said, outside the walls of Vestograd, "I'm dammed if I'll shoot at them, when they won't keep their heads up." I wonder at your diligence, which makes me glad, I am sorry to say, of your own priceless piece of foolishness. Colonel Leigh has spared me, at least, the trouble of finding an imbecile for you. Much as I love you, I should not like to perform a similar service, my dear. But, as you say, I can "judge for myself" and a pretty piece of judgement it is. You shall hear. Last night at Earl Grey's, or rather this morning (about two by the account of the said Aurora), in one of the cooler rooms, sitting in the corner of a great chair, I observed Mr Rogers not far off colloquizing with your friend, Miss Elphinstone. What seized me I know not, but I desired him to introduce me, at which he expressed much good humour. To my astonishment, after a minute or so, up comes Rogers with your Miss E at the *pas de charge* of introduction. The bow was made, the curtsey returned, and so far "excellent well", all except the disappearance of the said Rogers, who immediately marched off, leaving us in the middle of a huge apartment with about twenty scattered pairs all employed in their own concerns. While I was thinking of *nothing* to say, the Lady began—"A friend of mine—a great friend of yours"—and stopped. I wondered, heavy-hearted, if she meant my Carolinian, for there was something in her tone that suggested an indiscretion, as if she were putting between us the name of a lover. But then I remembered your letter and ventured, "Perhaps you mean a relation." "Oh yes, a relation," she said and stopped again. Finding this would never do, and being myself beginning to break down into shyness, I uttered your respectable name and prattled I know not what syllables. We went on for about three minutes, until we parted in a cloud of courtesies, for never did two people seem to know less what they said or did. Afterwards, I was surprised to find a real melancholy descending, for though I never much liked talking nonsense, I wasn't used to feeling it so painfully. On reflection, the cause of it struck me as simple enough. What strange parts I play, my dear sister, to please you—or rather, to satisfy your respectable sense of what will do me good, though I have always much preferred your disrespectable senses . . .'

He stopped there and read silently for a minute. Augusta tried to take the letter from his hands. The petulance with which he resisted her proved, if nothing else, that his good humour had soured. Pushing her away, he upset the glass of sherry on the rug and threw it, empty, into the fire. The sound of its breaking startled Annabella, for the first time, from the stillness of horror. Augusta, with tears in her eyes, sat down with her back to her brother. He picked up another letter and began to read. 'My dear brother, I never supposed it possible, but I heard this morning that you are going to be married. A great *parti*, Hobhouse informed me (was it you who sent him?) with a gentleness which suggested that he guessed the probable effect of his news. Her uncle is said to be very rich. I am glad of it, for your sake—and for mine, too, and managed in the face of your friend's curiosity to appear happy, with such success that the appearance of it survived, by several hours, any necessity for keeping it up. Though when the mask slipped off at last, I seemed to have no face at all beneath it and was almost surprised, indeed, when little George and Augusta Charlotte, waking from their sleep, recognized their mother and ran into her lap.' Byron put down the letter and picked up another. 'Do you know,

Gus, I have some doubts whether this marriage will come off. The father's estates, it seems, have been dipped by electioneering. Part of the remainder is settled on Annabella, though whether that will be dowered now, I do not know. There is an uncle in the case, who is, happily, both rich and childless, and dotes on his niece; but his health is uncertain. He is a widower and may live to an hundred, and, in short, it isn't only a question of money. The bride, I believe, has her doubts (she is reckoned very virtuous and makes herself loving only by a great violence of will); and these may be played upon in such a way that the public burden of disappointment, such as it is, would fall to the groom. And—send me only a word, Gus. A word from you is all I need. Have you ever known such happiness as our quiet little escapes from other people? at Newstead? and Bennet Street, and once, on the road between Cambridge and Newmarket, on the floor of a post-chaise?'

Byron stopped and looked at his wife and, keeping his eyes upon her, said, 'Well, Gus, I am a reformed man, ain't I?'

Annabella never forgot the silence that followed. She felt herself to be suspended in it, and trusted to her natural diffidence or air of reserve only to discover that it had taken on a kind of public quality: to say nothing seemed really the most explicit language of acknowledgement. It was up to Augusta, in the end, to break the spell. 'I believe I have noticed some improvement,' she offered at last.

Worse was to come. (Later that night, for the first time, she began to set down for the benefit of lawyers her impression of Lord Byron's behaviour during their stay at Six Mile Bottom.) At ten o'clock, as was his wont, he ordered his wife to kiss him goodnight and retire; but the action (Annabella had learned dutifully to comply and was almost relieved, by this time, to make good her escape) put an idea into his head. Augusta was sitting beside him on the sofa, and he bade her kiss him, too, so that he could compare 'at first hand' the differ-ence in effect between a sister's and a wife's embrace. He seemed in dangerously high spirits, hot-tempered and strangely loving. He had worked himself to such a pitch of good humour that he would brook no resistance against the demands of his affection. On such nights, Annabella had learned to expect, whenever he came up to bed, the consolation of being asked, with that tender grace of which he was always capable, to live up to her uxorial duties.

There was something so impossibly brazen in his experiment that a kind of disbelief carried the sisters through it. Lord Byron had pulled Annabella against his lap, where she remained; and he took it in turns, kissing her, with an almost comic exaggeration of conjugal passion (to which she was far from indifferent), and his sister, who sat beside him. In fact, the weight of Annabella against his leg was involved in his every movement, and she could not pre-vent herself, as he addressed Augusta, from leaning awkwardly against her sister and becoming entangled. 'A kiss for you,' he repeated, 'and a kiss for you; a kiss for you, and a kiss for you,' in a babyish manner that reminded Annabella of nothing so much as the cooing clucking language with which Augusta comforted her children.

They could do nothing but comply, patiently, and endure, miser-ably—that was the part to which Annabella usually resigned herself. There seemed no clearer proof of her husband's unhappiness than the lengths to which he went to inflict it upon them. What surprised her, as she tasted in his kiss something of the warmth off Augusta's skin, was the infection of Lord Byron's high spirits. Someone began to giggle. She heard a tremor in her own voice and found herself, against her will, playing up to the role he had assigned her. Closing her eyes, she kissed him and waited and kissed him again. What she had shut them against was the eye of conscience: this, she imagined, is what it's like to go unobserved. For a minute, Annabella struggled to keep down, within her, a tide of feeling. Her feet, as it were, had slipped, but something had caught her up; she supposed it to be nothing less than a kind of communion. Loneliness, she had always believed, lay at the root of suffering. She was living, at least, in the heart of things now and could hardly complain of the fact that it involved her in certain complications. Hedged about with duties and virtues, as she generally was, she sensed the relief of rising clear of them. She felt his face against hers and took it in her hands and kissed it and let him go and waited again.

Then the minute passed, and a different sense of her situation began to overwhelm her. Augusta, she believed, had permitted herself in the context of the game the fullest expression of sisterly love, and the first chord struck of the dissonance in which the scene broke up was the note of rivalry aroused in her breast by the sound of her breathing. Her husband's state of excitement was undeniable. Annabella had slipped between his legs and was forced to stoop under his arms as he reached towards his sister. Their laughter had become hysterical; and Lord Byron, it seemed, satisfied with the results of his experiment, had been acting for some time on the preference it established. In any case, Annabella's patience for waiting her turn had come to an end.

She opened her eyes at last, but what she saw had little to do with what she had heard. 'Gussie' (Byron repeatedly invoked her pet name) was sobbing, and the deep breath of her passion was brought on only by tears. Her brother had been attempting to quiet her, and the real measure of Annabella's unhappy position was her exclusion not from the pleasures of a game but from its miseries: she had been kept out of their consolations. Annabella could not move until Byron let go of his sister, which he refused to do until Gussie had contained herself. So she was obliged to wait until her sister's sharper sense of the horror of their violation had subsided, characteristically, into a breathless little laugh. 'Oh my dears,' Augusta said, drying her eyes with her palms. 'I had not guessed how much I needed a good weep.' Then she added (it was impossible to say, how subtly or simply), 'I felt very strongly being absent at your wedding. Think of these only as wedding-tears.' Annabella, with great difficulty, managed to keep back her own as the blood rushed to her cheeks. (What kind of a fool do you think I am? she thought.) Rising, with the dignity of awkwardness, she bade the pair of them goodnight, as she had been ordered to do, and left them together on the sofa.

Later, in the mirror on her dressing table, Annabella stared for half a minute at the puffed red face staring back and refused to pity her: what she required now was the great impersonal clarity of justice. Then she took up her diary. For an hour she wrote down, as carefully as she could, an account of the evening's entertainment—from an 'impartial' view, in a manner she supposed appropriate to an affidavit. 'Confirmation forced on her by documents and testimony of her having been a dupe and a victim. A feeling on her part of immeasurable horror . . .' She described Lord Byron's behaviour, the state of mind and character it suggested, and what she had suffered at his hands. She touched also on Augusta's collusion and the suspicions aroused by it, snuffing her candle at last, with a flurry of anger, to act on a sudden determination. The murmurs of brother and sister in the drawing room below her had died out; the silence itself, as sharply as a bell, brought her attention to the fact. Inspired by the promise of the law, she rose from her chair and opened the door to her bedroom. Documents, testaments and feelings were all very fine, but nothing, it struck her, might serve her so well in the future as the proof of her eyes.

As she tiptoed downstairs, the quiet of the house seemed to cast, as brightly as any lamp, a large flickering shadow of sound at her every step. Something about the role she was playing coloured her sense of righteous injury—it began to look like fear; it began to look like guilt. Her courage, she was almost relieved to discover, was equal to both, to the fear and the guilt, as she crouched at the door of the drawing room and put her eye to the keyhole. She had not stopped to ask herself, amidst the thrills of her impromptu mission, what she was hoping to see. What she saw, however, touched in her a very different faculty than hope. Lord Byron, she could just make him out by the legs of the sofa, sat huddled on the floor with his head thrown back. He was weeping, quite noise- lessly, and what most appalled her were the childish little convul- sions of his frame: he seemed almost patiently inconsolable; he had a great deal of grief to get through. Augusta had his head in her lap, but all she could see of her sister were the hands in Lord Byron's hair. These, indeed, rested tenderly against him, though Annabella could not help but perceive, in their quiet and com- forting pressure, the force that had put him in his place. Annabella suffered most, to her great surprise, from the sense of her own intrusion—it made itself felt, if nowhere else, in the dis- comfort of her knees. She had witnessed, she had no doubt, a proof of *something*, but she was willing to admit, as she made her way chastened back up to bed, that whatever it was might not in the end help her case.

Chapter Nine

—

IN THE MORNING, OVER BREAKFAST, Annabella asked her sister for a favour. She had been wanting to go to church. She particularly wished to hear a certain clergyman who preached at Sutton, but the journey, of course, was too great for her to undertake it on foot, and she was perfectly aware that the Leighs had not at their disposal a gig or barouche for the convenience of a guest (Annabella laughed) who wished to go twenty miles out of her way to be a little nearer to God. Even so, she had a great desire to go to Sutton. It was a point on which she could give no explanation beyond a simple repetition of the fact. It *was* out of the way; she wished to go. And she wondered whether Augusta might not solicit from a kindly neighbour the use of a conveyance. She could only assure her sister that she would not request it without the strictest regard for necessity. It had become, for reasons Augusta could, perhaps, appreciate, essential for her to purge her mind of certain—doubts or suspicions; and she needed, she believed, the comfort of a familiar face to inspire in her the confidence to make the completest expiation. There (another laugh), she had, after all, explained herself! It remained for her only to add that she would be doubly grateful to Augusta if, when Lord Byron came down, she could inform him merely that his wife had gone to church and was expected to spend the day in prayer.

Augusta nodded, demurely. She perfectly understood. Within the hour, a stately high-backed barouche, fitted to a pair of geldings from the stables of their neighbours, the Bassets, was waiting outside their door. Annabella was to consider it perfectly at her disposal. Colonel Leigh had much obliged Mr Basset in the past by advising him on the purchase of horses; it seemed the least he (Mr Basset) could do was to offer them to Mrs Leigh's sister-in-law. Annabella, meanwhile, had dressed for church and wore a smart new tamboured dress and the curricle jacket she had been married in. She thanked Augusta and kissed her goodbye. Gus said, 'I thought you should be lonely here for familiar faces. I'm afraid my brother and I are wretched company. It is the worst of family relations that, for the sake of them, one never puts on the least effect of manner or charm. I am sure you must find us very dull. A drive will do you no end of good.'

Annabella called her answer from the window, with an air of sweetness: 'It will be a relief to you to spend a quiet civil day with your brother, as you have been used to doing. Goodbye.'

The barouche pulled out of the yard and entered swiftly the open country surrounding Six Mile Bottom. As the house disappeared behind a hedgerow, Annabella felt a great weight lifted and was somewhat astonished by what emerged beneath it. The perfect calm she had kept up all morning (without, it seemed to her, the least unnatural effort) dissolved at once, and she hugged herself and shook from side to side, grateful to the clatter of the horses for permitting her, as she afterwards put it to herself, a little clatter of her own. The motion of the gig, in time, absorbed the rhythm of her sobs; and she passed from one to the other with the gentleness of imperceptible degrees. A line came into her head (addressed to whom, she knew not) that might safely serve to describe her stay: 'What I suffered at Colonel Leigh's house was unimaginable.' There was solace in the thought of a future that would allow her to speak so clearly of such a present. The day was brisk, with sudden alternations. The large hand of the wind bent back, and released, the stalks of the trees edging the farmers' fields, and flattened, and uplifted, the meadows of grass between them. Rain fell amidst bursts of sunshine, and the clouds at times took on a luminous darkness. She stared out the window of the barouche while the hour sped by.

Out of these prospects emerged the sense that she would have to face up to things squarely—that she had not been facing up to them. She was not yet willing to convict her husband of a total failure of love, but the evidence of a partial failure was so plentiful that she hardly needed to go over the particulars. There were times when, it pained her to admit it, her presence occasioned in him the acutest distress. A corner in her character rubbed awkwardly against a corner in his. They were both a little raw with the rubbing, although Annabella was sufficiently in love to wish to remove from her nature anything that protruded uncomfortably into his own. That, at least, is what she told herself, though she recognized even then that the little brute fact of her incompatibility might not be extracted from her (the image of herself she had in mind, for this purpose, was of a plain, pleasant, weathered wall of brick) without a general tumbling down. What she would suffer in that tumbling down she dared not think. Her suffering, she supposed, had already been ample enough—enough for what, however, was just the question that she had, for the past few weeks, been putting off.

What puzzled her still was the extent of Augusta's complicity. Her kindness had been so constant and particular, it was difficult not to trace in it the effect of guilt. Annabella was mindful, however, of reading into her sister's behaviour only the motives in her own conscience that might produce such behaviour in herself. In fact, Gus's open show of misery at her brother's treatment appeared to be the most natural expression of a clear heart. By contrast, her own awkward attempt at dignity—the way she stood on it, as it were, and attempted to make off with it—seemed evidence of duplicity. Surely, if the worst were true, Gus would never have indulged her brother in such a kissing-contest. If the worst *continued* to be true. (Wasn't that, after all, the question that counted?) And what could be sweeter in a sister than her little confession of attachment? 'Think of these only as wedding-tears.' The phrase, unhappily, called to mind Lord Byron's own: his wedding shoes, the wedding breakfast, the wedding sneeze, his wedding chill. No, Augusta herself was not what worried her most. It was only what might be inferred from *her* behaviour, about her brother's, that mattered—a reflection that brought home to Annabella for the first time how much she was willing to accept. Her powers of forgiveness seemed to her extraordinary: there was nothing in their past she need stop short at. Nothing, not the darkest stain of sin, would appal her, so long as she could persuade herself of his determination to reform, which she depended on as a proof not so much of his compunction as of his love.

It occurred to her, with a burst of simplicity, that the question she must put to herself was only this: how little of *that* could she live on? She was reminded suddenly of the lecture at which, for the second time, she had diverted herself by staring at Lord Byron (or rather, at the back of his head). Mr Campbell had spoken of 'the Sinking Fund of the Imagination on which a poet could rely as he grew older', and she had afterwards complained to her mother that the noble art had been reduced to nothing more romantic than the task of making mayonnaise. 'It was only a question of the quantity that could be got out of the smallest expenditure of eggs.' Annabella had become used (she was relieved at being able to give the problem so comical an aspect) to getting by on very little indeed. She congratulated herself, without any false pride, on the fact that such economies depended on just those virtues which she had always striven to cultivate. She did need, however, a little love, after all. By the time she arrived at the church, she was even equal to a smile: she needed at least one egg.

The coachman left her at the broken steps of the cemetery; he promised to wait for her afterwards in the drive leading up to the poor-houses. Annabella, whose tranquillity was always improved by the necessity of keeping up a public face, thanked him and made her way on the dry gravelled path that ran between the gravestones. The air was cooler in the porch of the church, and she sat down for a minute on one of the stone benches that lined the walls. His voice emerged from the rumble of noises that escaped to her through the half-opened door. Mr Eden was preaching his sermon, and the sound of it awoke in her such a sense of familiarity that she smiled at the idea of having heard his sermons before. It struck her that she might really have been sitting within, on a quiet Sunday morning in Sutton, had she accepted his proposal; and she imagined, waiting for her, a Mrs George Eden, who would turn towards her with a composed, superior, unafflicted look and welcome her in. The thought fell across her like a shadow; she quickly rose and stepped inside.

The nave was narrow and high and drew the eye instantly upwards. The light of day, of cloudy brightness and cloudy darkness mixed, had been softened by the church windows into a fine-grained grey that seemed to filter like slow sand through the air. Everywhere an echo of his voice came back to her, so distinctly that she was almost surprised, looking down, to find how small a figure he cut at the foot of the pulpit. She could just make out at that distance the scope of his high forehead and the slight excess of flesh at the end of his strong, straight nose. She ducked into a seat and stared at the backs of his congregation, in whom she believed to trace, by the modesty of their attendance, a quiet respectable piety. Country-best was the manner of their attire; there couldn't have been more than two dozen congregants scattered irregularly among the lines of pews. She supposed them to make up just such a sum of reverence as Mr Eden, at least as he appeared in her memory of their brief acquaintance, decent, moderate, assured, would have comfortably counted on to honour his debt to God.

She had expected to feel, at once, a sense of relief at the prospect of confession, of condolence, he presented to her. In fact, she felt with the sharpness of a kind of homesickness the irritable mild impatience he had always inspired in her. His sermon, on Jacob's seven-year struggle for Rachel, when she attended to it, seemed sensible; only it was a little long. He had an air of hardly trusting himself to be understood without the nicest, most complete explanation, and she imagined, impiously, that Mr Eden would in the presence of his Maker insist on confessing his sins with a strict legal regard for exactitude. Her nostalgia lay in the contrast he made—that is, in the consciousness of it he awoke in her—with the man who was now her husband. 'Now there is a good man, a handsome man, an honourable man, a most inoffensive man, a well informed man, and a *dull* man . . .' Mr Eden reminded her of just those tendencies in herself she had hoped in her choice of husband to resist. For a minute, she considered slipping out of her seat again and into the open air, and bidding the coachman to return her, as quick as the horses would trot, to the marriage from whose unhappiness she had so desperately sought relief.

It was only then it occurred to her, with a blush of shame or pleasure, she could not be sure which, that Mr Eden had seen her; that he was watching her with his large clear eye; that he hoped to keep her there, in his presence, in his sight, for as long as he could; that his sermon was, in some measure, addressed to her and protracted for her sake. She felt herself beginning to tremble, she scarcely knew why, and bowed her head and listened to him (to his voice, to its patient, careful modulations, and not his words) with her eyes closed until by the sound of shuffling around her, of rising and gathering about, she guessed that communion was at hand. Rising herself, she waited demurely her turn. Approaching him and summoning courage, she looked him in the face. He looked in hers, but the duties of the benediction left him no room for a personal remark, and she tasted the wine and bread in subdued agitation, which made a difficulty of swallowing. Then she was ushered away again.

Afterwards, she kept her seat. As the congregation filed into the bright, uncertain light of an early spring Sunday (the opened door cast a long shadow, as it were, of sunshine down the aisle of the church), she waited for Mr Eden, who was caught up in conversation with his parishioners, to come back to her. She heard his step at last but did not turn around. 'Lady Byron,' he said, 'what a great pleasure it is, what an honour it is. You cannot imagine what a surprise it was, what a delightful surprise, when I saw you approach to take communion. I had heard indeed,' he was facing her now, 'I had heard that you and your husband were staying with his sister at Six Mile Bottom, but I did not dream . . .' There was in this, in the urgent jumble of his sentiments, if not in the sentiments themselves, just enough flutter to satisfy Annabella's vanity—at least, it seemed to her that the best way to begin was by appealing to his.

'You mean, I suppose, that I have come a long way to see you. Yes, it *was* you I came to see, and the journey was really longer than you imagine.' She rose and claimed the privilege of his arm. 'Is there somewhere we could quietly talk?'

His humour, for once, was equal to the suggestion. 'Do you mean the confessional?' He smiled, and she was touched by the large simple decency of the man. 'No: I think, between old friends such as ourselves, a little walk, perhaps, if it isn't wet, among the peaceful dead, is really the best inspiration.'

'Do you know, a confessional is almost what I had in mind.'

He stooped a little, emerging from the arch of the door into the open air. In the light of day, she could see more clearly what the effect of two years (not to mention the rigours of his vocation) had been upon her friend. His face had taken on a countrified complexion. The thin line of his mouth had settled into an expression of professional kindliness, both vague and durable. Looking down, she saw that his shoes were caked around the sole with mud; blades of grass had become entangled in the laces. She remembered the promise he had once made her, of an income sufficient to meet the expense of a residence in town, and presumed that the narrow round of his duties had kept him from seizing his opportunity. He would hardly dare to appear in the best society in such a condition. She smiled at the thought of calculating from the state of his shoes a larger picture of the manners with which he might present himself. He had an air, generally, of retraction: as if he had learned to survive on worse food and company, on poorer ambitions, and on fewer thoughts than he was wont to do.

The skies had cleared a little. A patch of blue had spread itself like a picnic cloth (she was perfectly aware, to whom she owed the fancy) over the trees of the cemetery; and the lanes between the graves were just dry enough, away from the long-haired grass that grew around the stones, to permit a lady to pass. 'I must congratulate you,' she had left it to him to begin, 'on your marriage to Lord Byron. I heard of it only recently, as a piece of those rumours that brought the news of your residence in Six Mile Bottom. I have become, I'm afraid, something of a gossip.' He looked at her and laughed. 'It is one of the sins of the church, though you would be flattered to know, I'm sure, the part you play in such tattle. Lady

Byron has attracted a great deal of interest and admiration. She is said to be very beautiful and clever. He is said to be very—well matched.'

'I imagine,' she had found, she believed, her opening, 'the rumours say more than that.'

The kindly look he gave her suggested his willingness on such subjects to keep quiet. Annabella was fair-minded enough to acknowledge that the impatience he aroused in her had less to do with his tact than with her own awkward urge 'to confess every-thing'—a total that might become clear to her for the first time as she attempted to 'add it up'. She was forced, in the silence that fol-lowed, to turn her questioning on him. He gathered his thoughts for a minute into something like succinctness: he was very happy, he said; he was very busy, and quiet, too. Perhaps he had—shrunk in scope, which was just as well, he believed, as he was perfectly aware of the tendency his profession had to stretch out, if nothing else, one's speeches. But—he smiled, suddenly, and broke off to say, that he should for once attend his own sermon and take his own advice to heart.

Annabella had guessed the nature of the speech he might have launched himself into, and she was starved enough for flattery to attempt to draw him out. She begged him to continue. She had acquired since he had seen her last a sharper appetite for good advice, if only because she believed herself to be so greatly in need of it. He answered her deprecation with another little smile, which proved to Annabella at once, in her anxious impatience, that he was still refusing to take her at her word. He said he had only stopped short for fear that the sentiment he wished to deliver himself of, though perfectly complimentary, required nev-ertheless a delicacy of expression which he no longer trusted him-self, with his country manners, to keep up. He wished to say only that he had, since . . . since he had seen her last, acquired a still greater admiration for Miss Milbanke's, he begged her pardon, for Lady Byron's good sense. He was not one of those men who, from a duty of modesty, rate themselves below their deserts; but he was willing to admit that her—and he hesitated, not over the word, but over the propriety of addressing her with it—that her genius would never have found a suitable expression in the life he had proposed she share with him. Though he had had at the time his reservations over Lord Byron's character, he had none whatsoever over . . . over Annabella's ability to deserve the scope of ambition she would enjoy as his wife. And the fact that she had chosen to accept him in marriage had proved to him that she was confident of being able to repair and to regulate a disposition which, apart from the defects of his youth, of his upbringing, of his too early taste of fame, had such a generous nobility to recommend it. In short—but here Annabella, with a sudden and desperate break in the tone of their discourse, interrupted him.

'I cannot repair him; I cannot regulate him. He is ungovernable. He is impossible.'

He stopped at last to stare at her. His face showed that he had taken in her appeal, and guiding her by the hand, he led her to a bench, which, situated in the shadow of the church's western wall, had escaped for the most part the brief showers of the day. They sat down. Mr Eden put his hands together and raised them to his lips. 'You must know that in my professional capacity I am often called upon to listen to confessions in which I have a personal stake. I admit, without pride, that there is in my temper a peculiar willingness to detach itself from such considerations. It is, perhaps, the virtue of the clergyman and the curse of the gentleman that I lack what is thought of as the common touch. I believe it is the effect only of the fact that my sympathies, which, I flatter myself, are reasonably developed, remain proof against their own self interest.'

There was in Mr Eden's manner something that reminded Annabella so vividly of her own, or rather, of her own old manner, that she considered for a moment how well they might have suited each other. Yet the impatience he continued to awake in her suggested how greatly she had stood in need of a corrective—a reflection that recalled her to a sense of her position. It was owing to the violence of that corrective that she now sought relief from Mr Eden. Still, it was with a little contrary effort of the will that she began her confession; and she retained to the end the right to stop short at the fullest disclosure, if only because she supposed that the horror it would inspire in him would be too much like the horror she would have felt before her marriage at the situation in which she found herself. What she would miss in him was the benefit of her own experience. She was not quite as innocent as she believed him still to be, and Annabella discovered to her surprise a kind of pride in her own fall that made her hesitate to implicate herself in the outrage with which he might respond to the facts of it. Yet wasn't it really for that—to arouse such outrage, to witness it, to judge its force and relevance—that she had come to him? In any case, by the time Annabella answered him, she had decently recomposed herself.

'The question I have been putting to myself,' this was how she began, 'is why, after all, did he marry me? I don't mean to say that there weren't in the beginning certain testaments of his affection. His temper is variable, and I learned, as his wife, to regard what mathematicians would call the *mean* and not the range of his dispositions. But he has of late—and I am perfectly aware of the tenure of our marriage, and the sorrow that might be suggested by the need I feel to distinguish between its beginning and its present course—so little favoured me with the extraordinary grace of his affections, that I have wondered whether some change in circumstance, some failure in my own—'

Here Mr Eden showed himself capable of the largest simplicity; perhaps he had learned a little more in his professional duties than she had given him credit for. 'Has he been violent?'

The sense of her suffering renewed itself in her. Annabella bowed her head; she felt the prick of tears. 'It isn't his violence that I fear. It is his—indifference.'

'How long, then, has he been—indifferent to you?'

'It isn't even his indifference. His sister, in whose house we are staying, makes great claims upon his affection. At least, I believe he *feels* them; she may, after all, be innocent. And—'

'Innocent of what?'

A pigeon in the church eaves cooed hollowly and then, with a flap, resettled on the grass beside their feet. Mr Eden, idly, lifted his foot, and it flew away. The word had been on the tip of her tongue; but the moment, the quiet necessary to a confession, was almost spoilt. She hadn't after all the strength to say it aloud, and she leaned towards him on the bench and whispered something in his ear. For a minute, he hardly shifted. She expected to feel the instancy of relief, but really what she felt was only the sudden fear, or rather, the hope, that what she had said had not put her beyond the possibility of a retreat. She hadn't guessed till then how much she relied upon the chance of that.

What he repeated, in the end, wasn't quite what she had whispered to him. He had come, perhaps, in his own fashion, a long way from the practical innocence with which he had once professed his love to her. 'You think there has been—something horrible between them?'

She nodded.

'And you think that—it has been continuing in your presence?'

Afterwards, on the journey home again, and in the years that followed, she remembered her answer to him. There was a great deal she might have still been spared, but she had seen in his eyes the chance of her evasion. Mr Eden, by asking the question for her, had acknowledged its significance. Between the worst that she knew and the worst that she could imagine, there was a great gulf fixed; and his strict sense of the difference left her a little room to live in hope. Hope, in fact, her half-lie made clear to her, was very much the element in which she moved. She wasn't yet willing to resign to Mr Eden, for all his decency and dignity, her claim to the less modest virtues of Lord Byron. She came home, in fact, with a clear sense of the contrast between the two men; and the occasional impatience she had felt with one of them explained to her in part the resentment she was capable of arousing in the other. She would never have believed it possible on setting forth, but she returned to her husband after her 'church-excursion', as he came to call it, supported by a stiff new resolution: to devote herself to married life with a freedom, as Mary Montgomery had put it to her, that gave to her desires the privilege she had once accorded her sense of virtue.

'No,' she had said to Mr Eden. 'Not in my presence; I am sure of it.'

That night she had her first chance to test her resolution. Her visit to Mr Eden (Annabella, after the fact, made no secret of the object of her 'church-excursion') had put Lord Byron in one of his most loving humours. It was his disposition, as she expressed it to herself, to deem that whatever he *had* was worthless. Only the threat of losing them brought home to him the value of his possessions — she was almost eager, by this stage, to lump herself among them. Indeed, she saw it as a measure of the difference between them that he answered such threats with what she had described to Mr Eden as the 'grace of his affections'. Jealousy, Annabella knew, inspired in herself really the worst of her vanities. After dinner, he asked her to play for them and instead of occupying himself with his sister on the settee, he stood over Annabella's shoulder and turned for her the pages of the songbook. 'Who could resist you, singing,' he said, when she, at last, complained of fatigue and faced him. He added, with that simple honesty which even the most watchful soul sometimes slips into: 'It is only the stiffness of one of your dignities that makes me bristle.'

'I had never supposed,' she began, 'that dignity was something to be objected to.'

But he had, for once, enough good humour to laugh her out of it. 'No, my dear, only you'll admit, it can be a little uncomfortable for us poor sinners'—she wondered, for a moment, whether this was a class that included his sister and felt a pang of envy at her exclusion from it, until he continued—'for us poor sinners, who dream of resting on you.'

She took his hands at this; she was almost in tears. 'Rest against me. There is nothing I should like better. You—you mustn't believe that my dignities are any more comfortable to me than to you.' They looked at each other, and to apologize for her show of feeling, she added, letting go of him and wiping her eyes: 'You see, I am sure, how easily *I* am managed. The least kindness unbends me.' She feared, as she said it, that a note of unintended reproach had crept into her voice, but he was equal to the justice of her correction. 'I can be kind or loving,' he said, 'only upon inspiration, which dries up. I am sorry for that.' He continued, with the patient curiosity of famous men, regarding their own characters, in which the interest, they confidently presume, is sufficiently general: 'My temper, luckily, is vicious on the same condition. I always dry up, Pip. You can count on that, at least.' It was a kind of apology, Annabella supposed—at least, it was the only one he made for what she had suffered at his sister's house. And it struck her, then, as a proof of how little she *did* count on, that she was willing to take comfort from it.

They were leaving for London in the morning, and that night, for the first time, Lord Byron came up with his wife to bed. It was a sign (she quietly exulted in it) of her triumph over Augusta: she would win in the end. *Hers* was really the permanent relation, the one he must live with. And the fact that he felt the force of that necessity was made plain by the new note he attempted to strike in their relations. He was trying to find a way to love her—that was the desperation by which she excused, in the first pain of the aftermath, the violence done her. She was dressing for bed with her back towards him. She could feel him watching her, for once; his voice seemed to grow out of that feeling.

He said that he had become accustomed, in his travels through the East, to some of the local customs or practices, which had the reputation among the English as the worst of those vices against which a foreigner must, as it were, shut his eyes, if he is to keep up with the natives the pretence of civility. Well, he laughed, he had not shut his eyes, and without, as it happens, the least sacrifice of civility. It was only the pretence of it that one relinquished. He remembered that his friend Hobhouse used to complain in Turkey that he had no notion of comfort because he could sleep where none but a brute could—and certainly where none but brutes did. Thus they lived, one day in the palace of the Pasha (who had taken a particular fancy to him) and the next in the most miserable hut of the mountains. The hospitality they received was consistent, at least, in this respect: that Hobhouse refused from certain scruples to enjoy the full extent of it, wherever they were. Well, he had had no scruples, and he frankly confessed that he *had* enjoyed himself.

There was something in his manner that suggested to Annabella a forced good humour. He was embarrassed, and she felt she could play her part no better than by putting him at his ease. She turned to face him, and he, more quietly, more sombrely, reminded her that she had offered to do what she could to please him; that she had placed herself entirely in his hands; that there was nothing they need stop short at. This was, as she saw it, the first test of her resolution to give herself to him in love. And she found the duty of answering her husband made easier by the fact that she perceived in him something of the same intent. Yes—it was her look that said it; yes.

They had no other need of explanation. Indeed, Byron's meaning was perfectly made plain by the act itself, and it occurred to her afterwards that there are things that can only be done *unsaid*. Her silence had the effect of veiling, even in her memories of that night, the extent to which she had been complicit. Annabella could not, of course, have agreed to what she could not imagine, but neither could she have refused the unimaginable. What that was struck her, when it became clear, as sufficiently unspeakable; and she could come no nearer to admitting to it, in her thoughts, than by supposing it to be the answer to a question she had just stopped short of asking Mr Eden. What, after all, she had wanted to say (she had got no further than imagining the laugh with which she might have said it), if the worst *were* true, could the effect of it be on herself, on the security of her own virtue? Surely *theirs* was not the kind of degradation one could oneself begin to suffer from. Well, as her husband slept beside her, resting on her as she had begged him to, Annabella had the leisure of sleepless-ness to reflect on how wrong she had been. Wasn't that, in its way, just what she had suffered from? Wasn't she now just as degraded as they?

In the morning, however, the first flush of pain had receded, and she could more calmly attempt an answer to these questions. If she would no longer pride herself on being better than her hus-band, at least she was no worse. An equality of sins, she reasoned, as well as virtues, is what the harmony of a marriage depended on.

There were freedoms to be got by stooping as well as rising, and wasn't the best she could hope for to learn to enjoy them? It is true, she was no longer confident of being able to present to her mother, for example, the strictest account. But the consequence was that she had already ceased to make it, in the constant unwritten confession that gave shape to her thoughts. Really, she was almost relieved, at what her husband had decided to call 'the last breakfast', by the new internal stillness. She had been dutiful, she had been loving, but she had also been counting over her wrongs; it was the noise of the tally, perhaps, that had most oppressed her. She vowed, henceforth, to keep quiet—it was almost thrilling, to taste on her lips the power of her own resolution.

Augusta had permitted the children to breakfast *en famille*. Byron, for once, had risen in time to join them. His reluctance to leave was palpable; it took, in fact, the form of Medora, whom he held on his lap and fed with a tenderness that Annabella publicly remarked on. 'Yes, he spoils them all,' Augusta said. 'It will do them good, I believe, to get used to their father again.'

'Oh, they are used enough,' Byron said. When Medora began to cry, Augusta attempted to remove her from him. There was an awkward gentle sort of tussle. Byron clung on, and Augusta, with the first real sign of impatience, gave way at last—she was ready for them to go. Byron held Medora's soft head in his hands and covered it in kisses; the girl continued to cry. Hers seemed the voice of a larger, more general unhappiness, and the women were both relieved when the coachman arrived to signal the readiness of the horses.

Augusta saw them into the yard. It was a fine bright cold spring day. The sun was almost pale enough to look at and cast a vivid colourless light that picked out the beams of the house and threw fierce little shadows. Annabella was surprised to feel, in their parting embrace, a surge of sisterly feeling. 'I wish you would not,' she said, smiling through tears, 'leave me alone with him.'

'If you should ever want me,' she said, 'you've only to send. I'll come at once.'

There was, however, something in Augusta's answer, an earnestness, that struck in Annabella's ear the wrong note. It made of her own sweet words too significant an appeal. It quite brought the surge of feeling low, and the best she could do, to give a point to her displeasure, was only to say, 'Oh, I'm sure you'll come more than that.'

She waited in the coach for Byron to take his leave. After a minute he entered, a little flushed, but calm enough. 'Well, Pip,' he said, 'what do you think of her?' She was spared, at least, the need of an answer. As the horses began to shoulder their burden, he leaned out the window and waved; she left to him the privilege of last looks. It occurred to her that if she had wanted a proof of his love, she need search no further than her own conscious feeling of complicity in the state of their several relations, in the sins of that house. They were involved, all three of them, in a struggle for something: was it absurd to imagine that something as Byron's love? She could almost, in the light of that thought, pity him—it wasn't a quantity, she supposed, one took pleasure in seeing divided and counted up. What a relief it was, after all, to get away from that place! She could only be sure they had passed out of sight when he turned back in.

BOOK THREE

—

Separation

Chapter One

—

THE CRYING OF THE GIRL was the voice of those December weeks—a noise of complaint Annabella found particularly tiresome, given how painfully she had learnt to keep her own voice down. Augusta Ada cried and ate and slept; her mother did little else, only more quietly. After New Year, which she celebrated on her own, with a cold supper and a half-glass of hock, her first since the child was born, three bailiffs installed themselves in the house. Mr Torchard, a narrow, stoop-shouldered man with a rolling belly, was the only one who spoke to her. They always took to themselves the most comfortable chair, but he stood up from time to time to let her nurse in it. He had a newborn himself; it was a terrible intricate business, giving suck. He put his finger in the girl's mouth and watched her pull at it. For a moment, Annabella wistfully imagined that the child was among the articles of which he had come to dispossess her. Ada, she supposed, would never love her: she was Byron's daughter.

January sunshine peered briefly each day into the drawing room, which was reserved for her. It bled everything of colour and suggested, more generally, the light in which she saw her life: very cold, very clear. She was conscious, of course, of the changes a season could bring; conscious, also, as she put it to herself, of the force of internal seasons; and though the days, each day, grew a little longer, it was the equivalent within her that failed to lengthen and brighten. She had the wit, nevertheless, in writing to her parents to dress up in something like gaiety the worst of her fears. 'Dear father!' she wrote, 'you will hardly recognize me, I think. You know the pains I was used to taking over my complexion. Now, without the least care, I find myself beautifully bleached. Dear me, how pretty I look in that glass! I had heard of a mother's vanity but supposed its sum, entirely, made up of the precious child. I have discovered (it is a kind of relief, after my confinement) a sufficiency left over for my own use. Believe me, I use it.'

They planned to visit her parents at Kirkby and 'parade the dauphine. B particularly wished, he said, to show it off to the "dear old man"—a phrase at which, my dear old man, I know you will be affronted.' She noticed only afterwards, as she read the letter over, that the girl had slipped neutered into her thoughts. *It*, she had written, and repeated the strange syllable under her breath, to drum it out of her: it it it. She remarked on it only as an error that required correction; in future, she would correct herself.

For some time, she had been communicating with her husband through notes, and it was through one of these that she learned his intentions had changed. The pressures of business must keep him in town. 'When you are disposed to leave London, it would be convenient that a day should be fixed: if possible, not a very remote one. This damned money-business! You know, better than anyone, how it oppresses me. I hate the thought of it, and it leaves me no other thoughts. As Lady Noel has asked you to Kirkby, there you can be for the present—unless you prefer Seaham. The sooner you can fix on the day the better. The child of course will accompany you.' Her room had a desk pushed under the window. It overlooked, across the busy breadth of Piccadilly, the quiet of the park—which was in that dark winter (she sometimes kept up a flow of talk, using 'the child' as an excuse) 'rather white than Green'. Ada lay in her matted basket on the desk, staring at the mild pervading colourless January light. Annabella answered Lord Byron's note with a single line: 'I shall obey your wishes and fix the earliest day that circumstances will admit for leaving London.'

In the absence of his affection, she depended utterly on Augusta's. Augusta had come to stay, both to ease the progress of her confinement and to distract Lord Byron during the necessary tedium of the lying-in. Her sister's presence had inspired in Annabella a feeling of helplessness which she gave way to almost consciously: conscious, that is, of conceding a point to her in the struggle for Byron's attention. But lovelessness had made her childish; childishness made her loving again. Goose was also her best source of news, of views into Byron's heart—to say nothing of the fact that Mrs Leigh had, many times over, suffered the pangs of motherhood and could relieve Annabella, from time to time, of the worst of them. Mr Torchard had sometimes the decency, amidst these ministrations, 'to leave the room to the ladies'; he followed on delicate legs his full-sailed belly out the door. His absences, brief and rare as they were, often produced in the patter of their intercourse a sort of intimate hush. It gave them an air of secrets and confessions.

'He has been violent; he has been cold,' Annabella said, indulging a little in the drama of her suffering, while Goose held Ada on her lap and squeezed the child's small feet and hands. 'But he has never before treated me with such sustained indifference. I should prefer it almost that he abused me worse than he does the bailiffs, but to be regarded by him as an equal nuisance is more than I can bear.'

Augusta did not answer; she had bent her face to the girl's and blew hot air against it. Annabella continued: 'He takes no more interest in the baby than he might in the bed she sleeps in, which is forfeit to creditors. There is nothing, one feels, the creditors might not claim. They have claimed this,' she touched her heart, 'they have claimed *him*. You know that during my lying-in he sent me a note to say that my mother had died. My first thought on the birth of that child was the misery of being motherless myself; nothing but lies, thank God. And then he comes up to behold our daughter and says, as casual as you please, sweeping the cold air into the room with him, "The child was born dead, wasn't it?" I am becoming shrill; God help me, he has made me shrill. I used to have a subtler art of complaining. And the worst of it is, I look on that girl and think: she will never love me; she is a Byron. I will beat on her heart all my life, and she will never love me.'

'I am a Byron,' Augusta said, giving way to tears herself, which she did very easily. 'I love you.' These protestations, which drew the weeping women, bent over the child, still more closely together, required nevertheless a certain strength and clarity of voice. Lord Byron had made a habit of relieving his anxiety by tossing soda-bottles against the ceiling, a pastime he tended to engage in whenever he sensed the two sisters conspiring and felt his exclusion. He sensed it now; they could hear the bottles breaking below them. The sound they made was like the footstep of a giant ghost pushing his way blindly through the room. He was present, invisibly, and clumsily violently helpless. Already that winter, he had run through several cases in this manner. Under the noise of it, Augusta whispered into Annabella's ear, by way of apology: 'You don't know what a fool I've been about him.' She drew her hair back from her forehead with both hands to look her unobstructed in the eye. It was the closest she came to confession, and there was, in the embattled intimacy of the two sisters, an ample sense of confederate thrill to have tempted her into it. But Annabella put her off by kissing her forehead and holding her hands over Augusta's ears—what she meant was, that *she* did not want to hear. She had never before felt so tender towards Augusta. The large swelling love of forgiveness rose within her. She had so much to forgive; it was a mode of feeling that always brought out in Annabella the proportionate heat of affection. She wanted to kiss her again—Gus looked sometimes very much like her brother. And then the child began to cry.

'I shouldn't worry.' It was Augusta herself who introduced the humbler note. She lifted Ada over her shoulder, stood up and began to move about, swaying the skirts of her dress from side to side—an ostentation that suddenly irritated Annabella. 'It often takes the father this way,' she continued. 'Colonel Leigh, I remember, was so drunk with our first that he put her to sleep in the piano-stool. I don't like to think how long she had been crying before I found her. He was all contrition; it was the noise he couldn't bear.'

'But you must have heard her at once.'

'No,' Augusta was beginning to laugh. 'He had been playing scales.' And then, more soberly: 'They learn to love them. The best you can do is take them away at once, until they seek them out themselves.'

'I fear myself. I fear that once I have removed with her to Kirkby, I shall lose the heart to return.' She added, in a lighter tone that struck both their ears as false, 'I don't suppose my mother would permit it.'

Augusta had stopped swaying, though the girl continued to scream. 'It is impossible to think,' she said, 'in all this noise,' but the noise continued, and for a minute the two women distractedly, thoughtlessly listened to it. The January light fell into the room as softly as dust; it seemed to gather, settling, upon them. How easy it seemed, just then, to imagine a long life, spent in similar duties and maintained at just that pitch of tolerated suffering.

'Would he follow me there?' Annabella said.

There was in the look she gave Augusta a kind of appeal; and she wondered, afterwards, whether this was precisely the corner into which Byron's sister had hoped from the first to push her. 'I asked him myself, this morning, whether he had any thought of going to Kirkby. He said, Not at all, if he could help it. And then he talked all sorts of strange things, fell on me as usual, abused the colonel and the children, which you have heard before. But he mentioned quite coolly his intention—of going into lodgings by himself.'

'I see your significant eye. I know perfectly well what you mean by it: that I should make good while I can my escape. Is that not it? That I should leave him to you?'

Augusta at this made no sort of innocent protest, but still drew up short of agreeing. 'I have never known him so black and gloomy.' She shifted the child from one shoulder to the other. There were times, and this was one of them, when Annabella could only wonder, for all Goose's softness and sweetness, at her simple good sense and general competence—at just those qualities, in fact, she was conscious of lacking herself. 'You mustn't suppose that I spare him,' Augusta continued. 'He has behaved very badly and cruelly but does not love himself the better for it. He is full of false love; it is a kind of indigestion with him. When he is very unhappy, he gives off tremendous boasts.' She laughed. 'I said to him, whatever you have suffered is nothing compared to what Lady Byron has suffered, and at your hands, too. But he's reached such a pitch of vanity that he can think only of himself. It seems to him intolerable to be living, as he is, as you are, together, in this house, among the bailiffs and the—he could never bear the crying of children. He is too soft-hearted for it. One of the things he said was that he considered himself "the greatest man existing". I tried to tease him into a more sensible humour; you know how quick I am to laugh him out of his horrors. "Excepting Bonaparte," I said. But he only answered, after a moment, "By God, I don't know that I do except even him." There was a wildness in his eye. He seemed capable of any violence against anything—' but at this Mr Torchard returned, bearing on an unsteady saucer a cup of tea. 'Ladies,' he said, sitting down; and Augusta was forced to whisper, 'I should not like to answer for him. Indeed, I could not . . .'

On the eve of her departure, he came down to bid her goodbye; he looked greatly altered. She had come to believe that his proud shy careless dishevelment was the product of strict regulation—of that 'art of the self' in which he was so conspicuous a master. But his margins, she felt, for once had been overstepped; he was a page scribbled over. His face had fattened. The whites of his eyes were red and suggested, by the fine web of veins running through them, a fracturing gaze. He limped into the room and stood in front of the fire with his back towards her. 'I believe we both feel the cold somewhat?' he said. Annabella, ever since her brusque reply, had been fretting over the note. She was sensitive to the fact that she always took her tone from him and had vowed, henceforth, to seek out her own natural voice—to be loving, that is, even when he was indifferent; or angry, when he was quiet; or contented, when he was miserable. But it was no longer clear to her what her natural voice might be, that is, what it might say. What she said was, 'Would you like for a minute to hold the child? I am tired of it.' And then: 'If nothing else, she will keep you warm.'

He turned and looked down at his daughter. Her little lips frowned under the weight of her cheeks. She was sleeping; her high pink square of forehead wrinkled in her sleep. 'I wonder where it was begotten,' he said. 'If it was at Newmarket, no wonder it should be like Augusta.' And then, after a pause, with a touch of that unfeigned curiosity regarding himself which distinguished his happier moments: 'Do you know, I have never held her in my arms?'

'Would you like to now?'

'No, no,' he said, 'I shouldn't dream of separating a mother from her daughter.'

Annabella had the sense, as he stood silently with his back to her in front of the fire, of a duty being fulfilled. It needed no imagination to guess at *whose* prompting. Perhaps he was counting the minutes; a Harrison clock, a wedding-gift from Lord Wentworth, stood squat on the mantelpiece. He seemed to be staring at it; and then, indeed, picking it up in two hands and turning around, he broke the silence to say, 'I wonder how much this might fetch at auction. It is ugly and square, and there is something peculiarly brutal in its regular loud ticking, but the world is peopled by strange tastes. Unless, that is, you should object? It came from your uncle?'

'It did.' And then, taking up her earlier vow, she said pointedly, 'I have no objections to anything any more.'

Lord Byron smiled at that, with something of his habitual condescension. 'I have been thinking, lately, that there never were before two such clever people who knew themselves so little.' He returned the clock to its shelf. 'I used to give you too much credit for self-penetration. Augusta takes a reasonable view of us both. I believe I am perhaps a little better than I pretend to be, which isn't saying a great deal. And you, my dear, may be a little worse. Now, don't take offence at that—I believe you have not—you are smiling.'

'Only, a dear friend of mine once said to me that I wished to be a little less perfect than I am. I was wondering what she might say to the fact that, in your estimation at least, I had got my wish.'

'Nobody, I believe, could accuse you of getting *that*.'

This, effectually, put an end to their conversation; but he lingered several minutes more, holding his coat-tails out with his back now turned to the fire, and gazing at his daughter on her lap. Annabella kept his silence. She was hoping that the object of his contemplation might inspire in him a word of tenderness for its mother. Her own voice and opinions, she was clever enough to realize, would only serve as a check to the freer expression of his more loving moods. She hardly dared to look up at him—she could not have kept from her glance an air of expectancy, which might annoy him. Nor did she like to keep her eyes bent on their daughter: she might be seen to presume too much upon a shared interest in the child. There was nothing left for her to stare at but the fire, so she stared at that, while the clock ticked and she waited for him to break the silence.

'When shall we three meet again?' he said at last, in the heavy mocking tones he reserved for his little habit of quotation. It occurred to her only after he had gone, that she had no answer to his question and that she had wasted the time she might have spent fixing in her memory a last personal look at his famous face.

She fell that night into a deep sleep and awoke in the morning exhausted. He had promised her that a carriage would be at her disposal to remove them to Kirkby. She saw it at breakfast, below her, in the street. It was raining. The driver sat under his hat, hunched over; the rain dripped off the brim of it onto his hands, which quietly held the reins. The snow in the park had the slickness of ice, and there were ugly scars in the surface of it, where the mud had leaked through. The day seemed colder for the wet, which had crept into the air of the house and got amongst one's clothes unpleasantly. Annabella had changed her dress three times before she believed herself to be warm enough to face the world. Mrs Clermont, a family friend, a spare fussy tall bent woman, had been sent to London to accompany her on the journey. She had seen to the girl. From her window, Annabella watched her carrying the child under an umbrella into the carriage; she imagined hearing faintly through the sound of the rain the voice of her daughter, complaining. It was time for her to go, but she stayed another minute, looking out blankly on the weather, before she went. On her way downstairs, she passed the door to Lord Byron's room. There was a large mat outside it on which his Newfoundland dog used to lie. For a moment she was tempted to throw herself on it and wait at all hazards, but it was only a moment, and she passed on.

Chapter Two

—

HER PARENTS HAD TAKEN a house at Kirkby Mallory, near Tees-dale, where their good friends the Gosfords spent the country sea-sons. It was a large plain-looking L-shaped hall with a clock tower and a new roof, which glinted in the carriage-lamp as Annabella's party turned at last into the yard. The rain in which they set forth had given way, in the course of their long journey, to clearer colder weather. The yard had not been swept, and the wheels, as they came to a stop, with the horses sweating and steaming, creaked in the snow. Ada had been asleep upon their arrival, and Annabella left her with Mrs Clermont as she made her way, darkly, into the kitchens. They had been taken to the back entrance, and this was the first sign—Annabella, in spite of her misery, was quick enough to note it—of disordered management and what it suggested about the state of her parents' affairs.

She was sitting in front of the fire in the parlour—no others had been lit, a girl said, 'everyone was living upstairs'—when her father came down at last to greet her. Sir Ralph had an air of affec-tionate embarrassment. His daughter knew him well enough to guess the cause of it. Her reception had fallen short of the expected warmth, although she admitted privately that nothing could have lived up to her sense of homecoming after so bitter a leave-taking. 'I'm sorry, my dear,' he said. 'Your mother particularly requested to be awoken when you came, but I have taken it upon myself, for once, to disobey her. She has not yet quite recovered from her—indisposition at Christmas.'

It was always a source of disagreement between them, how to refer to the malady from which her mother suffered. Annabella was inclined with the doctors to call it a nervous condition, but Sir Ralph, for his own reasons, tended to touch on it more lightly and treated her episodes as nothing more significant than a series of unlucky ailments. There was, in any case, no shortage for either of them of terms to shy from. Still, as he went on, she guessed that a change had been wrung in his own conception of the illness and perhaps in the illness itself.

'She had been sleeping very badly, but Dr Kendall is confident (thank God) that the crisis is passed. She wants rest—it may take some time—and I decided,' he attempted a smile, 'to defy her, come what may. We had tried her at first on a course of emetics, which had the consequence, certainly, of increasing her thirst for natural waters; but she felt the indignity of it, and slept so badly, and looked so wasted and thin that the doctor, who, to be fair, has shown a laudable willingness to experiment with new ideas, prescribed a simpler diet, at night, of laudanum. She sleeps, perhaps, no *better* than before but *longer*, undoubtedly, and has begun, as her dose has declined, to recover an appetite.' After a moment, he added: 'There was some fear at first of damage sustained to the . . . nervous system, but your mother has really been—progressing so well and so—bravely—that the doctor holds out hopes of a complete recovery.'

The effect on Annabella of this little speech was to quiet within her the story of her own affliction, which had been bubbling away to the rhythm of the four-in-hand for several hours: 'I am your daughter again; he has sent me away.' It was a lesson, and she was not too fatigued by her journey to make a note of it, that her suffering lay at the centre only of her own life. One could not expect the world to turn around it, and she vowed, inwardly, to preserve 'the secret' of her sorrow. Or rather, she resolved, at least, to demand from her mother a great deal of affectionate pressure before she could be persuaded to give in to it. 'My dear,' Sir Ralph said suddenly, 'let me kiss you; I have not so much as kissed you.' He bent his large foolish amiable head to her own. Her hand, as she responded, clutched the tuft of grey curls over his ear. She closed her eyes and felt on her face the scratch of his cheek; he had not shaved. It seemed to her then that she was home at last and safe. Tears sprang to her shut eyes, at the thought of what she had suffered, in relief at the prospect of suffering no more. Her father sensed the fierce little urgency with which she clutched at him. 'My poor girl,' he repeated, 'my poor girl; whatever's the matter?' in a tone she had learned to recognize, by its sweet helplessness, as the voice he adopted whenever he supposed some greater or more difficult competence might be required of him.

'Nothing,' she said, retreating again and finding in her sleeve a handkerchief. 'Only I am cold and tired and have eaten nothing since tea.' She made a face for him of sniffling unhappiness. She was playing the game they had always played together, father and daughter. Hers was the voice, as he used to call it, of 'the miserable good girl' who, he would add, 'always got what she wanted'. What she wanted, however, she realized now, was her mother; it was the voice she used to keep at bay his deeper curiosity, which he for the most part was perfectly willing to suspend. 'I shouldn't mind,' he said, 'a little something myself, if only to help me sleep.' He was older than she had remembered him. His complexion, which had always been made up of reds and whites in equal measure, had a dullness now that softened the contrast between them. He looked as if he had been caught out in the sun, a little dry. 'The fact is,' he added, and this confessional mode was new to him, too, 'I haven't been sleeping well lately. Your mother often—needs me in the night.'

It wasn't till lunch the next day that Judy arose to welcome her daughter home. Annabella had got up early and gone for a walk through the grounds. The heavens had that peculiar white cloudless pallor of a northern winter. Annabella, after her confinement, was just beginning to enjoy again, as she put it to Sir Ralph—when he had asked her, on such a raw day, 'to stop within; the snow will spoil your boots'—'the use of her legs'. Empty skies and cold exercise gave her the sense briefly of having 'cleared her head'. Lord Byron had been used to teasing her, whenever she reproached him for unkindness, that she was very welcome 'to run back to her mother like a spoilt little girl'. Well, she did him the justice of acknowledging now that she *had* run back. And if he had played his part in pushing her to it, she was willing to believe that he had only meant to put her 'to the test'—a test her love had failed. The fact was, her reception at Kirkby Mallory had failed to live up to the contrast she had imagined between her parents' and her husband's affection. She had awoken in the strange bedroom, with its view of the frozen woods, still lonelier than she had been at Piccadilly Terrace. Augusta was not there; Augusta alone had understood.

When she got back, she sat down at the card-table in the sitting room and wrote him a letter. She had been composing it quietly in her head, against the background of an attention always a little occupied by the task of finding dry snow to step in.

Dearest Duck,

We got here quite well last night and were ushered into the kitchen instead of the drawing room by a mistake that might have been agreeable enough to hungry people. The house, I believe, would just suit you; it is large enough for any number of mothers-in-law and babies! Such a W.C! and such a sitting room or sulking room all to yourself. I have managed to keep for my private use a whole morning, undisturbed, to write to you and to Gus. If I were not always looking about for B, I should be a great deal better already, a great deal steadier in temper and health, for country air. Miss finds her provisions increased and fattens thereon. It is a good thing she can't understand all the flattery bestowed upon her, the 'Little Angel'. Love to the good goose and everybody's love to you both from hence.

Ever thy most loving
Pippin . . . Pip—ip.

Lies, mostly; she had been welcomed, if anything, somewhat sparsely. And the attention of the house was so forcibly directed at the convalescence of its mistress that there was little warmth to spare for a poor small child. But it was in the note to Augusta, which she slipped inside it, that she allowed herself to communicate her true feelings. 'I have left a home behind me, in a very disordered and uncertain state, and have arrived at another home, in equal uncertainty and disorder—but its troubles are not my own, NOT my own. Consolation, dearest Augusta, lies chiefly in the fact of having resigned to you the task of looking after him. Never was there a creature who took such taking care of as my husband your brother—excepting perhaps *myself*, which is really the root of all our troubles, I believe, just as you have been, as far as you were able, the solution to them . . .' Writing these notes had on her the effect of a secret kept. She sealed them and resigned them to the butler to post; by the time Judy descended, to take a little something at lunch, Annabella felt sufficiently shielded by her own private troubles to face up to the contemplation of her mother's.

Her mother's appearance, however, was not quite what Annabella had been expecting. She moved, it is true, with a delicacy that bespoke her stretched, discriminating nerves and sat down to eat with both her hands on the table. Her red windblown face had grown paler and softer by enforced confinement. It had now the almost embarrassed and adipose complexion of something unused to exposure. Her short hair had lengthened, roughly. She had got fatter, too, but the fatness suggested a kind of health, the renewal in her of decent appetites. The butler, a surprisingly small man referred to as Mr Arthur—he had a reed-like upright posture and musical voice—spoke quietly to her but without gloves, as it were, without too gentle a deference. There was nothing of apology in her own manner. She ate well, too, with a steady patient hunger: a meal of hot broth, warm bread and cold chicken. She picked for some time over the remains, carefully cleaning her fingers, after each bone, in a bowl of water one of the maids brought out to her. She drank several cups of tea and had in general the air of a woman with time on her hands—she seemed pleasantly, expectantly uncertain of how to fill it. What astonished Annabella most, in her mother's mood, was its expansiveness; she had imagined a humbler retraction. Judy wanted to talk and was particularly pleased to see her daughter, she said, 'because Ralph was beginning to tire of me.'

'Nonsense, my dear,' he answered. His own appetite, in Judy's presence, seemed diminished; he had contented himself with dipping a little bread into his soup and leaving the crusts on his plate. Annabella counted them. It was unlike her father to be careful of his food. It suggested how much of his life, of his household dealings, had come under the scope of necessary calculations. He had accepted the role of preaching restraint to his wife and could hardly make an exception of his own example. One could not resist, after a while, giving in to a general habit of moderation. Judy's health had needed so strict a management that he had begun to manage himself and looked the poorer for it.

'Not at all,' Lady Milbanke replied. 'You hope to keep me quiet, not for my own sake, but yours. I believe I have *talked you out*. Besides, I have things to tell Annabella that I shouldn't like you to hear.'

'Naturally.' He blushed, then replied more sharply, 'I'm sure you have a great deal to complain of.' Annabella was unused to seeing, in the open oval of his face, the tightness of withheld reproach. She resolved not to blame him. Patience, she had learned first hand, like a cut flower, begins to lose colour in time.

'The secrets of wives,' Judy said, with a nod to Annabella, 'are not always and only complaints.' Then she added, with a deliberate humility, 'I have only become shy, lately, of depending too much on you.'

Her father, she noticed, had drunk nothing at lunch; the retraction was all his own. Afterwards, he confided to Annabella that her mother had one way of talking 'in the sunshine' and another 'in the moonlight'. For his part, he slept poorly and was often a dull dog in the day; at night he had his wits about him. 'But the nights,' he added, 'were growing shorter—she improves.'

Such confidences were the air she breathed in; she hadn't yet had the space to breathe *out*. Judy's secrets, as it happened, *were* mostly complaints. Annabella's private afflictions, in the week that followed, were buried under the weight of her mother's, which nevertheless touched curiously upon her own. Judy had presumed when she married her father that his modest assurance was nothing but a kind of ambition. He was very well connected. It seemed to her that, at a certain level of society, nothing but decency and common sense were required 'for getting on'. Ralph was decent and sensible; his reticence struck her as a kind of easiness or carelessness. It was only the poor, she argued by analogy, who counted their money; the rich could make a show of indifference. She had been very ambitious herself, that's what she wished to say, but was willing to take from him a lesson in the finer graces of it. Only, she had mistaken him from the beginning. His aspirations, such as they were, belonged to some private arena from which she felt increasingly her exclusion. Her notion of a life well lived did not tally with his, and she was made to appreciate the vulgarity of her conception. He settled into marriage, congratulating himself on a job well done—which seemed to her only an excuse for leaving all the other jobs to her.

This, with several digressions, was the story Annabella heard in the course of a housebound week. The London rain had followed them north, where it turned to snow. It fell in a clatter from the roof and piled up outside the sitting-room windows, which were fogged and wet to the touch, in drifts as high as the lintels. The room (she gave Sir Ralph her opinion) was simply too large for the fire to heat it—the truth of which was vividly illustrated one morning when the maid had to stand on a chair to sweep cobwebs from the ceiling with her broom. Judy had decided to take the house in hand again and presided, from the comfort of her convalescence, over a fever of activity, which drove her husband to the dusty quiet of his study. In fact, he was glad to be relieved, for once, of the duty of keeping Lady Milbanke cheerful, on which Doctor Kendall had particularly insisted. When Ada cried, Mrs Clermont brought her in to feed. (Her present trouble, Judy confided, began when she was encouraged to drink porter while nursing.) Otherwise, Annabella had her mother to herself. She pushed two armchairs to the foot of the hearth, and they baked and froze together, taking it in turns to warm each side. Annabella never once said to her, though the words were constantly on her lips: I have left my husband; he has sent me away.

Instead, she endured silently her mother's misplaced admiration. Lord Byron, Judy understood now, was an image of the kind of man one ought to marry if one hoped to cut a figure in the world. It was no use angling for decency or common sense; these qualities brought one at last to Seaham or Kirkby Mallory. She had done what she could in Seaham to shape a role for herself in the little society she found to hand. She liked to think that, until her troubles (that was her phrase for it), she had made a success of it—as great, at least, given the poverty of local resources, as the success *his* sister had had at Melbourne House. Sir Ralph couldn't abide Elizabeth, and Judy blamed the modesty of his political ambitions on the contrast he hoped to suggest between himself and Lady Melbourne. It had lately become a source of consolation to her mother that Annabella had decided to follow the example of her aunt's career. A woman could only get on in the world, she had learned, by playing a part *behind the scenes* of public life. But one needed something to work with—one needed a scene, or a stage. It was no use sitting at the heart of a web like Seaham. She had run, quite simply, out of things to do.

How grateful she was for once to have so much time on her hands. They could talk properly, as they used to when Annabella was a girl. Tea was served them and buttered cakes, set down on the table between them. As a girl, Judy continued, lifting a piece to her mouth, she had never been told that what one depended on a husband for, in the first place, was the scope he gave to one's talents. A woman, of course, has no other scope. She touched a napkin to her chin. *Scope*, if she might call it that plainly, rather than riches or love, was what one should marry for. Though the quality, as such, had this to be said against it: it was harder to measure than riches, harder even than love. A fool might offer scope; Lady Melbourne had married a fool. Sir Ralph, she granted, was none, and there had been a time, before the last election but one, when she supposed herself on the brink of his great career. She called for more hot water. They had almost beggared themselves to make a name for him, but Sir Ralph, it turned out, was just the kind of man that names don't stick to. He is the kind of man whom other men trust in his private rather than his public capacity—they will listen to his jokes and not to his advice. Hot water came; she filled the pot and waited, then poured herself a fresh cup. Annabella refused one. Not the least of her regrets over the whole affair was the fact that it left them, as far as Annabella's dowry was concerned, a little short of pocket. She only hoped that money matters had not cast their shadow over the first year of Annabella's marriage.

'No,' Annabella assured her, mindful of Dr Kendall's warning. 'Not much.'

Each day, after lunch, they returned to the same two chairs by the fire and the same themes. As the week wore on, Annabella, who said little by comparison to her mother, began to insist on keeping her daughter beside her. I have left my husband, she thought; he has sent me away—and the confession, unspoken, kept her from exchanging other more commonplace intimacies. She had nothing to say but that, and she did not say it. Her baby, however, its mere presence, and the habits Annabella exposed while nursing it, struck her as a kind of confession of her new life, of her new role; at least, it was the only one she made. Sometimes Ada slept between them on the floor to catch a little of the hearth's heat. When she cried, Judy took her on her lap and made faces. Annabella could never remember seeing her mother so unconscious of her dignity. Perhaps she was really improved. Although, of course, an indifference to her own dignity had been one of the signs, her father had said, of the last stages of that illness or nervous indisposition whose history she had, in her own way, been attempting to give.

Sometimes, indeed, the conversation brought Judy's confession to a sharper point. 'Your father's career,' she said (she had lost her shyness of repetition), 'has not been entirely what I could have wished it. For one thing, it has afforded less employment than a woman of my capacities requires to occupy them.' Then she went on, and Annabella pricked up her ears: 'I have gone to this honest extreme, of composing a trouble of my own making.' Her mother stared at the fire; she would not look at her daughter, and the heat of it had reddened entirely one side of her face. Annabella held her tongue and hardly breathed. She had hoped for some time to hear from her mother the clearest admission; it might bring relief. There were secrets, of course, that she kept herself, and she needn't look far to determine from whose lips she had learned the habit of concealment. 'Well,' Judy continued, with a laugh, 'it has kept me busy these last few years, which is something to be grateful for, particularly as you have, by degrees, begun to give me less trouble. I found it very painful to watch you *slip the reins* in search of a career that I myself had had the ambition, but not the luck, to pursue. You have made a name for yourself, at least. It will "ring through the ages"; Lord Byron will make sure of it. I don't like to think,' she turned to her daughter now and smiled, 'of the *names* he will give to me.' After another pause, she added, 'though I don't suppose I was ever as drunk as I pretended to be—I mean, at my worst.'

Annabella took up, from this strange bold speech, the quieter word. 'I don't pretend to understand you.'

'Oh,' her mother answered, 'you needn't fear for me now. At my best, I know perfectly well, I was bad enough.'

Her own confession, in the end, depended on a respite from her mother. Sir Ralph had intimated to a few of their friends that Lady Milbanke was well enough to receive familiar visitors. Company would do her good, he wrote. She was growing tired of Sir Ralph, and Annabella, perhaps, was growing tired of them both. On Sunday, after church, the Gosfords paid their respects and stayed to lunch. It was the first time Annabella had dined in the dining room, whose views, over the gardens behind, were a little spoilt by the hothouse adjoining it. It was a house, Judy was complaining as they sat down, in which every modern convenience had been awkwardly added on without the least consideration of taste. In fact, one found in its design only a show of convenience. The kitchens had been rebuilt too far from the dining room. French doors had been added where they were not wanted; consequently, the sitting room was as cold as the cellar. The grounds themselves, which had been arranged according to the most expensive fashions, were large and variable and as bleak as a mountainside. Eight months a year they were too muddy for any respectable woman to walk in—excepting perhaps the coldest depths of winter, when the paths froze over. Annabella had guessed, by the end of this discourse, the purpose with which her mother had embarked on it, and could not help but admire her: she had wanted to set her guests at ease, that she was her old unhappy critical self entirely and required no special kindness.

Lady Gosford had such natural tact that one never suspected her of using it, and she was perfectly willing to disagree with everything that Judy said. She much preferred a modern house and could scarcely recall how they ever got on without Kidderminster carpets and hob grates. Sir Ralph, meanwhile, attempted to interest Lord Gosford in parliamentary speculations. He was hopelessly behind-hand in such matters and was eager to hear etc.—a strain of talk that excluded Annabella, happily enough at first, until she began to feel in her continued quiet the rising absurd voice of neglected egoism. One might have supposed, she told herself, that a greater share of the conversation would have devolved to *her*: a reflection whose truth she had every reason to regret when it finally was. Lady Gosford sensed Annabella's exclusion. As a childless woman, she declared, pleasantly enough, that she had no right, and consequently no intention, of inquiring into what she called the commonplace particulars. Such as, how often the child fed, and other questions less fit for mixed company. Instead, she wished simply to know, did the girl look like her father? How well she remembered, it was but three years ago, at their house in Piccadilly, where Annabella had been staying, their . . . excitement at dinner over the fact that one of their party had made the poet's acquaintance. Speaking of whom, she had heard that day from the vicar's own lips the voice of a general anxiety: when might they expect such a famous addition to their humble society? Annabella, dry-throated, just managed a tearless reply: business would oblige him to remain in town indefinitely. She kept her eyes fixed firmly on Lady Gosford; her mother was looking at her.

Later, a due parade was made of Lord Byron's daughter. Ada, wrapped in a blue cloth that brought out the brightness in her eyes, was handed about in the sitting room. Mrs Clermont hung unquietly back, to relieve anyone of the burden should they tire of it, until Annabella sent her away again. She was happy for once to preside as Ada's mother. The child fell asleep in her arms, and her face, in sleep, contracted in such a way as to exaggerate her resemblance to Lord Byron: the faint scornful puckering of his lips, the stubbornness of his chin, his fresh colour. Judy, by now unaccustomed to company, was on fire with talk; at least, she was too restless to stare (as she said) at babies. She had resumed, if nothing else, the show of her old assurance and offered to lead Lord Gosford on a tour of the hothouse, the care of which had been her particular consolation in the months preceding. When Ada awoke, loudly, with her tongue in the O of her mouth searchingly stretched, Sir Ralph volunteered (quick as usual to recognize the duty of his absence) to leave Annabella to nurse the child in peace. 'He had always been very awkward,' he said with a laugh, 'about babies, when they cried. He *would* try to reason them into tranquillity, but they preferred milk to reason.' Lady Gosford offered to sit with her, and he helped her to push the two armchairs, which had been pulled out for company, back to the foot of the hearth.

When they were alone together, she confessed the great pleasure it gave her to see Annabella's mother restored. 'It was a terrible affliction. No name did it justice; there is something shameful in the names.' There was no shirking about Lady Gosford—that is, she wished intimately to convey that she saw no need for any shirking. Her plump shapely hands lay folded across her lap. She shifted her feet now and then to relieve her legs from the heat of the fire. Ada was nursing steadily, with that blind selfishness which always moved in Annabella the tenderest feeling of pity. What she thought was: 'You mustn't depend on me, little thing. You mustn't depend on me.' She hardly heard what Lady Gosford, who seemed determined to speak frankly on the subject, was saying—which was only that she had never admired Lady Milbanke more than she did now. 'It must be a great comfort to you, to be reminded of the strength of purpose of which your mother is capable. I am glad to see you taking after her. Your father is the most amiable gentleman of my acquaintance. His virtues are entirely, if I might put it this way, of the *winning* kind. There is a softness in his manner, a willingness to please, which is, I believe, generally considered the virtue of our sex. I regret to say, however, that we have need of sturdier qualities. It is only the gentlemen who have the luxury of gentleness. Women depend . . . but my dear, what's the matter?'

Annabella had begun, silently and without the least air of

hurry, to weep. She had never in all her life, she believed, been so talked at; and she was conscious, as she gave way to tears, of hiding behind them. Lady Gosford had retreated into the dimness that lay outside the small quiet light of her own misery. Even at the heart of it, though, Annabella knew quite well that she was raising, as brightly as she could, the flag of her surrender. They must all, she supposed now, come rushing to her; they might never let her alone. Ada continued to nurse and she continued to feed her: Annabella's supply of milk, of tears, seemed equally deep. Lady Gosford had risen, and she sensed her approaching now, awkwardly enough, to relieve her of the child—repeating helplessly, 'My dear, you must let me help. What's the matter?' It was a cruel, selfish comfort not to answer her. Annabella guessed that she might never again feel so simply, so sweetly her own affliction: she hoped by her silence to draw it out just a little longer. And Lady Gosford, at last, despaired of consoling Lady Byron herself and went out to find her mother.

Chapter Three

—

IF HER MOTHER HAD COMPLAINED previously of a 'want of occupation', Annabella was struck by how quickly Lady Milbanke recognized the rich seam of activity that her daughter had now opened up to her. First, the Gosfords were sent home under the cover of Lady Byron's exhaustion. She had only just arrived from London. She was tired, and there is a kind of fatigue that can, of itself, produce an appearance of misery. Judy turned frankly to Lord Gosford in the doorway: she had learned in the past few months that one may make a *habit* of tears. Annabella, who overheard her, was persuaded for the first time of her mother's complete recovery by the fact that she was willing, coldly, to make use of it as an example. Their delight, Lady Milbanke continued as she ushered them into the parlour, in Annabella's company had led them to overindulge in it. What she wanted was nothing more than quiet and rest . . . Although, once the Gosfords were gone, Lady Milbanke dispatched Sir Ralph to his study and refused to allow her daughter to retire until she had heard from her 'a full confession'. She had lately favoured her daughter with the most intimate confidences (there was a note in her voice both of reproach and self-reproach), and these perhaps had drowned out the gentler noises that Annabella had been trying to make. Had she been holding something back?

Just what a 'full confession' would require of her was the problem that Annabella, in the midst of her distress, was forced to confront; and she was still sufficiently the wife of Lord Byron and the sister of Augusta to keep from Judy the secret of her worst suspicions. To admit to these might, in any case, deny her the luxury of a reconsideration. Fortunately, Lord Byron's conduct had furnished her with enough material for a reasonable account of sincerest sorrow, and that is, to the best of her ability, the account she gave. Her husband had, from the beginning, freely expressed how little he was suited to the part his vows required of him, and his subsequent behaviour had only justified these professions. He had never actually beaten her. That is, he had never done so intentionally; but their great pecuniary embarrassments, and the strains on the marriage produced by her condition and, subsequently, by the birth of their child, had reduced him to a kind of madness in which the threat of violence against her was really the least of the fears she laboured under. They had practically ceased to hold any common intercourse with each other. They communicated chiefly by notes, but his state of mind was so disordered that it announced of itself, in the most explicit manner, the chaos of his unhappiness.

She did not wish to go deeply into particulars, but she was willing to cite, as an example, the fact that during her confinement he had relieved his anxiety by breaking soda-bottles against the ceiling of his room, which lay directly under her own. She had heard them crashing beneath her; she thought they were gunshots. Annabella did not mean to suggest that his intentions towards herself had ever been murderous. It struck her on the whole as more likely that he would injure himself. His sister's presence in their household had the effect of goading him into a kind of intimate and demonstrable confession of the viciousness of his character. *His* was the sort of conscience that reproached itself as deeply for what he had imagined doing as for what he had actually done. Although—to be fair to Augusta—her patience, her gentleness, her formidable common sense, more than made up for the . . . the pressure her company produced on their mutual relations. (It was throwing Augusta, just a little, in Lady Milbanke's way. In spite of her protestations of love, Annabella could not refrain from exposing her sister-in-law to the brunt of her mother's curiosity. She had lifted no more than the edge of that veil—who knew what would happen if the wind caught hold of it?) In the end, that pressure had grown intolerable. She could not with any certainty declare whether she had of her own free will escaped that unhappy home, or whether her husband had deliberately dismissed her from it. These were 'the gentler noises' which, she discovered, in spite of her reddened eyes and sore-tipped nose, it was something of a relief for her to make.

Supper brought the three of them together again. Sir Ralph was particularly subdued, and just shy enough of his wife's more intimate knowledge to resign to the women the tenor of their table talk. Annabella had left it to her mother to lay at his feet the list of Lord Byron's abuses—his menaces, furies, neglects and infidelities—and was surprised to find that nothing had yet been said. Only Judy showed much signs of an appetite, and Annabella retired, leaving her pudding untouched and pleading as excuse the fatigues, as she put it, of her 'sudden display'. She had dined, she said with a brave ironic smile, on tears; and Sir Ralph, who disliked such airs, gave her an impatient look, not unmixed by the pain of his exclusion. She supposed it might drive him at last to make inquiries of her mother, and was gratified to hear him, after the necessary interval, storming through the house to find her, where she had decided to wait for him, in the tidy back parlour by the fire. She listened with a little smile of indulged love. 'Bell,' he was calling, opening and closing doors, 'Bell, Bell, Bell,' until he found her, with his large kindly face so puffed up that the unshaved hairs of his cheek stood on end.

His indignation could be counted on to do justice to whatever his daughter had suffered, though Annabella presumed that he would, in his accustomed manner, make of an excess of feeling an excuse *not* to act. In fact, nothing could have been more explicit than the avowals he demanded of her, never to return to him, never to answer his letters, never to speak to him, if she didn't want either the blood of her father, or her husband, on her conscience. His fury brought home to her, as nothing else had, a sense of her helplessness. There was a kind of violence in the sheer fact of it. She could almost feel in the weight of each moment the irresistible gravity of events, pulling her forward; and she responded to her father's anger with an equal passion of supplication. 'He was mad, he was mad, he was only mad,' she repeated, clutching at his hands, while he, strangely, attempted to fend her off. 'He does not know himself.' She finally managed to extract from her father a promise: that if Lord Byron was deemed, by those medically competent to judge him, to be insane, she should be allowed, in the event of his recovery, to return to him. Otherwise—and this was, privately, the vivid little phrase she allowed herself—he was lost to her for ever.

Sir Ralph retired at once to compose a letter, in which he would begin to address the question of their separation. Annabella stayed up by the fire. Mrs Clermont had put Ada to bed, and for the first time since her outburst to Lady Gosford, Annabella had a minute or two to herself—she practically counted them up. Her quick burst of feeling had offered a little relief. On the whole she confessed herself satisfied by the turn of events. She had at least restored herself to the centre of their small world; and the sense of living at the beating heart of things brought home to her, as nothing yet had done, how long she had suffered on the peripheries of Lord Byron's stronger passions. Nothing she suffered or felt could stand up to the heat of his sufferings and feelings. She was conscious, however, as the thought crossed her mind, of having at last found an occasion that might bring out, in their brightest colours, her own quiet and enduring qualities. Then her father came in with a draft of his letter, which he read to her; and the simpler truth of what was happening to her entered and pressed, by another inch, deeper in:

> Circumstances have come to my knowledge which
> convince me that, with your opinions, it cannot tend
> to your happiness to continue to live with Lady Byron.
> I am yet more forcibly convinced that after her dismissal
> from your house, and the treatment she experienced
> whilst in it, those on whose protection she has the
> strongest natural claims could not feel themselves
> justified in permitting her return thither . . .

Her mother joined their little conference in her nightdress and took the letter from him. It should not be sent without due consultation. 'You mustn't in the meantime,' Judy added, 'write him so much as a line. You must leave all that to me.' She intended to make an early start on the road to London, where she would engage the services of a lawyer.

It amazed her (she told herself afterwards that she should not have been amazed) how quickly the legal element intruded upon the question. Indeed, the law had a sort of taste, of itself, which flavoured the subjects it treated, and she grew conscious, in the weeks to come, that the savour of her predicament had been almost imperceptibly altered. She was learning to count up her wrongs with a little dry irony. Annabella believed that she had a natural talent for the law. It soothed the worst of her exacerbated feelings to be able to exercise, besides the wounded faculty of her sentiment, something like her old subtlety upon the matters of her heart. She was acting, for the first time since her marriage, in confederation with her mother—who, to do her justice, had taken up the cause with all the energy stored up in her dormant years.

Judy reported almost daily from London, addressing herself to Sir Ralph; what Annabella heard was only the echo of these letters. Reverberations, she supposed, rang out both ways, and she caught, from a postscript that her father read out to her, the low sound of those reports which Ralph must have sent back to Judy, regarding herself. 'Let me entreat you to calm your mind. Don't look for imaginary bugbears, Annabella, when so many real ones exist.' Nor could her mother, in the headlong rush of her new-found purpose and under the guise of a kind of reassurance, resist the odd humble boast: 'I assure you I have never been saner. My brains are particularly clear.' Their letter to Lord Byron had been submitted for legal adjustment. Judy would return when she could with the corrected text, which Sir Ralph was to copy in his own hand and sign himself. Nothing—she presumed that her daughter might take some consolation from the delay—could be formally undertaken until she had rejoined them. In the meantime, however, she had consulted a number of doctors on the strength of the testimony of Mrs Leigh (who seemed to Lady Milbanke a shy foolish calculating bundle of pieties), regarding the state of Lord Byron's health. There seemed little hope that his treatment of Annabella could be the unhappy effect of a mental *malaise*. At least, if it were, the medical opinion, with one voice, despaired of finding a cure. She must proceed, then, as if all parties to the issue had proceeded, in their common affairs, in their proper minds and had acted on their soberest intentions. It would be wise, accordingly—and this was her mother's own strange phrase, which Sir Ralph duly repeated with the letter in hand—for Annabella, henceforth, to conduct herself 'in the best legal fashion'.

In practice this meant that she was once more forbidden from writing to her husband—an injunction that brought out in her the shameful confession of the intimate tender playful letter she had sent him upon her arrival at Kirkby Mallory. Had she a copy of it? She had, and was forced to stand idly by while her father read it, leaning lightly against the mantelpiece, warming his coat-tails in the fire. There was nothing in it, she supposed, for which a young wife need reproach herself, although she regretted now the dry little reference to 'mothers-in-law and babies'. But what embarrassed her most was just its tone, which seemed natural and affectionate. She winced particularly, as she imagined his progress through the lines, over that silly loving nonsense of her signature: Pippin . . . Pip-ip. When he was finished, he looked up at her; and she was duly alerted to the increase in her filial respect by the difficulty she inwardly admitted to in returning his stare. 'This does not read,' he began, kindly enough, 'like the letter of a woman . . .'

'No,' she interrupted him, blushing. 'Only, you must understand the fears we all had for his sanity—for our safety.'

'We?'

'I mean, Augusta and I. We had acquired a sort of habit of kindliness towards him, if only because we tended to suffer more when it was broken.' She was moved by her own account, which was, after all, nothing less than the truth. It seemed to her then that the fullest confession might really exonerate her, so she attempted to make it. 'You must understand the particular form his . . . malady takes. He rather swells with his own unhappiness and grows expansive on it, just where others (among them, I believe myself) are inclined to contract. Everything, you see, the least word said, touches him nearly. One learns to give him the largest berth and to approach him, if at all, only with the—gentlest hands. You see by my letter the . . . gentleness he has taught me, which I practised, it must be said, willingly enough, for my own sake as well as his.' She was equal, at that, to the largest admission—and, feeling it rising within her, she made it. 'You see, I love him, still. I have always loved him; I always *will* love him.'

'Oh, my dear,' he said, taking her cheek in his hand. (She had lifted her chin, bravely, to look up at him.) But he could not resist asking, as much from the simplest curiosity as from a father's desire to correct in his daughter her unhappy illusions: 'And did he ever love you?'

'If I leave him,' she promptly replied, 'perhaps we may find out.' He had never admired her more. Her curiosity, it seemed, was still greater than his, but before he could give a voice to his admiration, she had continued, in just the same sensible considering tone. 'Is it very bad? I mean, my letter. Does it—affect our case?'

'I'm afraid it may. Your mother has consulted Sir Samuel Romilly, a very eminent lawyer, who has proposed another, a civilian, by the name of Lushington. She has written to say that the least suggestion on your part of a willingness to make it up could be interpreted by the courts as grounds for refusing a separation. If it comes to the worst.'

'Oh, if it comes to the worst,' she felt for the first time a temptation to give up her secret to them and almost yielded to it, regarding her father with a significant eye, 'I believe we can meet him, squarely.'

Chapter Four

—

LADY MILBANKE WAS TO SPEND the week in town, to see to the legal side of their affairs, and Annabella, who had always enjoyed the mild weather of her father's moods, passed the days pleasantly in his company. Ada, in their relations, made a congenial third. Her grandfather grew more comfortable with the child as she fattened and learned to smile, and Annabella was supported in her affliction by the illusion of keeping up, with Sir Ralph, a sort of conjugal arrangement. It was broken only by the child herself, who introduced at times, with a sudden fierceness, the note of her own absent father.

Annabella had never till then given much attention to what might be called the little feathers of character her daughter had revealed. These were still hidden, as it were, under her wings; they would grow out eventually to the full bright plumage. But missing the girl's father, perversely, as Annabella had begun to do, even the quick living unhappiness he brought out in her (which had been succeeded, in her parents' house, by a pace of grief for the most part slower and duller), she learned to take a greater interest in his child. It was, after all, the only piece of Lord Byron that Augusta had no share in—she was almost willing to put it as plainly as this.

Ada slept and fed, and her bouts of more violent complaint were rare enough that one could almost suspect the poor girl of calculations, by which her supply of useful and choleric protest was husbanded and meted out. She was, in short, a very good quiet kind of a baby, if a little reserved, which was just what her mother had been, Sir Ralph remarked, at the child's age. He leapt, whenever they offered themselves, at comparisons—out of shyness, perhaps, unless they seemed to him merely a painless and natural occasion for pressing his case. How could she *not* be quiet, her mother did not say, when her father had been so loud. Ada's eyes had lately begun to meet and blackly answer a curious stare; and Lady Byron was grateful for the excuse it gave her to avert her own from Sir Ralph's more intimate glances. She could almost feel, from his gentle hand, the stones dropped within her. They were sounding her out, and she wondered, indeed, how many she was supposed to endure, painfully reverberating, before they might grow sick of hearing the reports.

The voice that was silent, of course, was Lord Byron's own, though she imagined her father had had the privilege of hearing his views. Her father, she knew perfectly well, was reading her letters, on no less eminent an authority than Sir Samuel Romilly's; but no one had yet extended the freedom to her of reading theirs. What she absolutely refused to do—it was the one thing on which 'she had put her foot down'—was to give up her communication with Augusta. It seemed, on the one hand, too generous a concession to leave the field, and she knew quite well whom she meant by that word, entirely to Gus. On the other, she could not quite resign herself, at a single stroke, to giving up both of the Byrons. One at a time was surely enough; and there was, in the secret she harboured deep within her, a power of hurting poor Gus that inspired in her already the anxious loving desire to be forgiven. 'I have wronged you,' she wrote, 'and you have never wronged me. It

makes me feel I have no claim to what you give.' Her wrongs thus
far had been slight enough, but she knew quite well her power of
adding to them. What she was testing, really, was whether or not
an admission, however vague, of the *worst* had prepared in her the
ground for attempting it. How much was her conscience strong
enough to bear? She was, if nothing else, giving it a steady exercise;
and the feeling, as she stretched it out tentatively in every direction, reminded her of nothing so much as the first few weeks of
her marriage. She had been forced on their honeymoon to admit,
at her husband's insistence, just what she was capable of. There
was little at the time she had stopped short at—a proof of her
character that gave her every reason to fear for Augusta now.

Even so, she knew herself well enough to recognize that when
she was threatened, she retreated into her conscience; and she was
just as willing to acknowledge where the gravest threat to her lay.
She was giving up love, for her parents' sake, as well as her own. By
clinging to Augusta she hoped to salvage, from the wreck of it, a
plank on which to float. Her temper was such, she had always congratulated herself, that she could make out of any trial the food of
health. Consequently, she was surprised to find herself, during a
long cold month at Kirkby Mallory, being starved of something.
And what she was starved of his sister might learn to supply.
Augusta, she supposed, if she did her duty, might be her little
reward—she was hoping to keep her, that is, as a sort of memento,
all to herself. She had something of her brother's look; she had
something of his manner and lightness of touch, and still more,
after all, of what was really his distinctive quality, a willingness to
be loved. But Augusta was useless to her while she lived with *him*—
a reflection that had everything to do with the fact (and this, as
the weeks passed, was the note that grew only louder and more
painfully insistent) that she was unspeakably jealous of both of
them for continuing to live with each other in Piccadilly, in what

was, after all, the house of her marriage. Jealousy was always the sin to which her virtuous nature was most likely to surrender. And there were times, at night, in the confinement of her room, when she clung to Ada so tightly, as the last living relic of those relations, that Mrs Clermont herself, at hearing the child's cries, was forced to intervene, to rescue the girl from the clutch of her mother's arms, and to leave the mother herself on the floor of her room, beating her fists against the back of her head.

It was these paroxysms (she could hardly, in a house as echoing as Kirkby Mallory, keep them quiet) that suggested to her parents, after her mother had returned from London, the possibility that Annabella was holding something back. She could see them, with every word she spoke, counting up her miseries; and they could not conceal from their daughter, miserable as she appeared, that they were coming up short. How quickly, how lightly, indeed, had Annabella accepted their intervention—their meddling, she might otherwise have called it. She had met them halfway, and that fact alone pointed to a fall more deep than any she had yet revealed to them. It wasn't so much that they doubted her. Only, they seemed to recognize, in the show of her continuing submission, a kind of excess. In spite of their gentleness, they had the air of people determined, in accounting for their involvement in Annabella's affairs, that everything should *add up*: even though that total, as they knew quite well, was composed of nothing less than the sum of their daughter's unhappiness.

She might have taken a greater offence at the tone of calculation, which her mother especially could not keep out of her sympathies, if Annabella hadn't so completely inherited the tone herself. She was also vividly conscious of withholding just such a secret of her husband's cruelty as might be expected to square even Lady Milbanke's most extravagant claims for her daughter's redress. For the moment, at least, she was confident of putting her off; and she rejoiced in the fact, as a testament to her powers of healing, that she could still indulge herself in the vanity of such a possession. It seemed to her sometimes that she had kept back, at a general feast, the last precious cake for herself; and she was waiting for everyone to grow hungry again, before she could, with the greatest credit to her generosity, begin to share it around. She knew, however—this was one of the thoughts she was wrestling with—that she might have kept her rich little secret too long, to take *only* credit for preserving it so well. Just what the fact might suggest about her own complicity in the passionate guilt of the Byrons, she couldn't yet judge herself coldly enough to admit to.

The law, at least, offered some consolation. It gave her, if nothing else, something to talk to her mother about. 'I would not but have seen Lushington for the world'—this was, in the end, the report that brought Lady Milbanke home again.

He seems the most gentlemanlike, clear-headed and clever man I ever met with, and agrees with all others that a proposal should be sent by your father for a quiet adjustment. But observe that he insists on Lord B not being allowed to remain an instant at Kirkby, should he go there, and he says you must not see him on any account— and that your father should remain in the room with you. If you see him voluntarily or if he is suffered to remain, you are wholly in his power, and he may apply to the Spiritual Court for a restoration of conjugal rights, as they term it, and oblige you to return. The law, I'm afraid, is against the wives. But a great deal, he says, may be done with a public man by the fear of exposure, which we need not, I presume, fear at all? He is confident, in your case, of coming to terms, though less so of saving your daughter. He insists, again, on what we have already told you—that

you must not answer his letters—and was surprised to
find that I had given this advice before I left Kirkby. He
said it was the best possible. He wants to meet you: there
are questions only he can ask. I am coming, my love; you
have only to wait for me.

Waiting, it's true, she almost smiled at her mother's percipi-
ence, was really all that she had. Well, she was good at waiting. Ada
slept in the lap of the chair beside her; her cheeks were besmirched
with pimples, which clustered around the depression of her nose,
beneath her eyes. Mrs Clermont, when she came in to relieve her,
could be trusted to wash the child's face. It was just after breakfast,
and a part of Annabella's thoughts were occupied by the apple-
dumplings that had been promised them for lunch that day. She
had never been so hungry in her life.

Still, there was a great deal in Lady Milbanke's account to
occupy a woman who had thus far consented to cut herself off
from the source of original news: her husband's letters. She had
to admit that the threat of losing her daughter struck her with a
less thrilling fear than the thought, thus delicately put by Dr
Lushington, that Lord Byron could insist on the restoration of
his conjugal rights. There had been nothing, certainly, in Augusta's
communications to suggest the least possibility that Lord Byron
might come to Kirkby; and she wondered whether he had been, to
her father, more eager to propose a conciliation. Lord Byron had
written at least three letters since Annabella's flight from Piccadilly. Sir Ralph had seized them all. They sat, under a stone on
which, in her childhood, his daughter had painted a red turtle, on
the desk in his study. Annabella could see them, whenever the
door was open, as she passed by it on the way to the warmer fire in
the back parlour. Certainly, if Augusta hoped to keep him to herself (and it would, Annabella reasonably enough supposed, in

spite of her jealousy, be the most natural thing in the world for a sister to attempt it), Gus could do no better than presenting him, as she had done, as the indifferent victim of his own wilfulness. 'I don't know whether,' she had written, 'I should say, he is miserable for you, or for himself, or whether he is miserable at all. I suspect, my dear sister, it might be best for your sake that he wasn't at all? He is, of course, a little, and might be more; only, he has resumed, out of what you will, the worst of his bachelor habits, and is nightly drunk with the very men a wife should keep him from.'

Annabella could not conceal from herself that she had, at this, the most important crisis of her life, willingly resigned to anyone who would accept it the burden of her decisions; and the fact was brought home to her when the woman who had taken on the greatest part of them returned from London. Lady Milbanke had never looked better. Her colour was entirely restored, and she moved, from the ledge of the coach to the house, with the fresh vigour of a woman who had lately been given the largest licence to make herself useful. Annabella, watching her from her bedroom window, confessed inwardly to a sinking heart at the thought of what she might be capable of conceding to Lady Milbanke's persuasion. The peace she had occasionally enjoyed in her mother's absence was only the calm of postponement. Her return, at least, signalled the beginning of the grand event. A 'quiet adjustment', indeed! Her mother had a talent for compressing, in the most innocent phrase, such violent quantities. If the contest for her future was to be played out between Mrs Leigh and Lady Milbanke, Annabella began to fear what the defeat, which she considered almost inevitable, of her sister's views might eventually bring down (it was sure to be a great heap) upon Augusta's own head.

It was almost by way of apology that Annabella, that night, recounted for her sister's sake the shock of her mother's arrival.

I almost fainted when she first came in, and looked paler than usual when I meant to look better. I don't know that my heart has done beating yet. I found her in the sitting room with a mouth full of buttered bread. She was terribly hungry after her journey, but the note of apology in her voice, for putting me off, was perfectly calculated, as you may guess, to make me anxious. I waited for her to finish, and she showed herself every bit willing to take her time. At last I could bear it no longer and said, 'Is there any news from London?' To which she replied, with every appearance of sympathy, 'I believe the news is all on your end. Have you made up your mind?' I scarcely dared answer, 'To what?' before she continued, 'To come to London. You must, by this stage, have received my last letter. Dr. Lushington wishes to meet with you. He is the most dry, consoling man; it is quite like putting your hand on a book. But he cannot act, he says, without the fullest information. Believe me, I tried to spare you and offered to supply it myself, but he, all gentleness, maintained that you alone were in a position to render a full account.' Well, my dear, you may guess how this made my heart jump and the blood rush. It was all I could do to nod away my blushes and say, 'I should not myself desire to lift a hand against him,' before giving in to tears. Which she, with a touch of impatience, thus met: 'Your character is like proof spirits—not fit for common use. I could almost wish the tone of it lowered nearer the level of us everyday people. I have not slept on a bed of roses through my life. I have had afflictions and serious ones, though none so severe as the present. But in my sixty-fifth year I have endeavoured to rally—and shall rally, if you do. There are

troubles that must be faced up to oneself. Now, my love,
here is a Sunday's sermon for you, and here it shall end;
for I am mucky with travel and in need of a bath.'

How quickly had Judy picked up her old motherly air of impatient and critical admiration. Annabella read over her letter and
wondered, with her pen in her hand, whether or not the strictest
conscience should have balked at recording her mother's compli-
ments. She had said, more or less, just that, and Annabella had
always taken comfort from the simplest prescriptions of truthfulness. 'Proof spirits', she supposed, as a term of flattery, also carried
with it a suitable threat: hers was not a character to be taken, as
Judy had said, in everyday doses. And then, for it seemed proper
as a means of persuasion to add this sly note of praise, Annabella
continued:

Your kindness must always mean more to me than that of
any other. Of myself, I can only say that I feel well enough
to go through my present duties, and that is all I wish. I
am content. There are subjects I am more inclined to
speak of than myself—but I have resolved not to do so
unnecessarily, and alas! I have nothing to suggest which
can alleviate their pressure on you, my dearest Augusta. I
am advised not to enclose the least word to him . . .

She saw much too sharply into her own motives to deny the warning such a letter might carry to Augusta. But it also contained, and
this struck her at the time as the real sweetness of the gesture, a
kind of betrayal of her mother, which she, for once, was happy to
make. By breakfast the next morning, Sir Ralph had copied out fair
their legal demand for a separation. Mrs Clermont, who was
becoming quite invaluable, carried it personally into town to post.

It was on the evening of that day, in the dead dark hours, that Annabella gave way for the first time to the full passion of her misery. She could be heard plainly throughout the house, until Mrs Clermont came in to silence and console her.

Augusta, for her part, showed herself capable of unsuspected persistence. Sir Ralph's letter to Lord Byron was duly returned—by Augusta. She had intercepted it and now pleaded passionately for more time: 'She feared terribly the effect it might have on her brother.' Annabella was ungenerous enough to reflect that she might mean nothing more by that phrase than the effect it would have on his sister. It seemed to her, as much as she loved the poor little Goose, that no one had more to suffer from the process of law than Augusta herself. Well, the poor little Goose, as it turned out, was not entirely helpless. More and more this seemed to Annabella a game of letters, and she was taking note, with increased attention, of the tricks to be played. Sir Ralph and Judy, considerably put out—and one of the odd effects of their irritation was that a portion of it should be directed, however irrationally, at Annabella herself—simply sent it back. This one hit home, the proof of which lay in the shortest of notes from Augusta: 'He demands to know if they have acted according to your wishes.' A line that allowed Annabella, when Sir Ralph showed it to her, the greatest indulgence in her own powers of brevity. 'They have,' was all her reply. Silence followed, for an awful week. She presumed that her father had confiscated, if her husband had made one (and that was, with her, really the question that counted), Lord Byron's more personal response. She wondered what he might say. She wondered if he might care. They had kept each other, after all, in the dark for so long.

Illumination, when it came, was prodigious; it almost brought her back. Mrs Clermont had gone to London to prepare the ground, as Lady Milbanke put it, for Annabella's visit: she had been sent to make arrangements with Dr Lushington. In her place, a girl from the village had been briefly employed to take care of the child, and it was she who brought to its mother, one dry snow-bright morning, the letter from Mrs Leigh. Her parents were closeted in Sir Ralph's study. She could see, through the opened door, her father seated in his easy chair; Lady Milbanke stood with her hands clasped behind her. The girl from the village (her name, Annabella had particularly inquired, was Clare; Lord Byron had such an easy rough intimate manner with servants, and she had struggled, in his absence, to reproduce it) presented the letter to her on a gilt tray. It had her name on it, in her sister's hand. Annabella had begun to say that . . . that it was the custom of the house to offer to Lady Milbanke the first gleanings of the post, but her embarrassment at such a poor explanation made her stop short. She could hear the voice of her mother (rich and full, as she always imagined it, of the blood in her throat), but not what she plentifully said; and the thought, suddenly, of a chance to be snatched at nearly robbed her of breath. 'Thank you, my dear,' was all she answered, nodding and taking the letter in hand. She was sitting in the front room, sidelong to one of the windows that overlooked the broad drive, which was patterned muddily by the curves of carriage-wheels. As if she needed only a little more light, she rose to one of the benches and sat, facing out, with her back to the open door of her father's study.

Augusta had managed to enclose a note from Lord Byron; this was, in the rushed consciousness of wrongdoing, what his wife turned to first.

All I can say seems useless, and all I could say might be no less unavailing, yet I still cling to the wreck of my hopes before they sink for ever. Were you then never happy with

me? Did you never at any time or times express yourself
so? Have no marks of affection, of the warmest and most
reciprocal attachment, passed between us? Or did in fact
scarcely a day go down without some such on one side and
generally on both?

Do not mistake me.

I have not denied my state of mind, but you know its
causes. Were these deviations from calmness never
followed by acknowledgement and repentance? Were not
your letters kind? Had I not admitted to you all my faults
and follies and assured you that some had not and would
not be repeated? I do not require these questions to be
answered to me, but to your own heart. The day before I
received your father's letter, bidding me for a separation,
I had fixed a day for rejoining you. Recollect, that all is at
stake—the present—the future and even the colouring of
the past. The whole of my errors, or what harsher name
you choose to give them, you know; but I loved you and
will not part from you without your own most express
and expressed refusal to return to or receive me. Only say
the word, that you are still mine at heart—and 'I will
buckler thee against a million.'

His hand, it was true, was ever careless; and in spite of the brightness of the morning, which glanced off the snow-bound yard and
onto the page, she sat and picked over, with an almost passionate
attention, each overwrought expression. There was guilt in the
pleasure, which gave it a childish urgency. She had him, Annabella
almost felt, to herself just once more, and the mere fact of the letter in her hand and the presence of her parents in the next room
involved her lucidly in the pick of loyalties. No one knew better, of
course, than the Byrons the little claims made by a secret kept; and

she felt, indeed, that while she held so tightly to *theirs*, she could not be said entirely to have given him up. That was the hope, that was the fear, that thrilled within her.

She had once remarked of him, and the visit of the Gosfords had brought back the memory, that his was an eloquence which might be said to 'create truth, even where none existed before'. And though there was little enough that she recognized in his portrait of their marriage, she could not help but admire and weep at the picture he tenderly held up, like a hand-mirror, for her closer inspection. Ah (this was the sigh that escaped her), so that was her face! There was nothing, she realized, that she could offer against it that would breathe with such rich life; she almost lost the will to argue the matter with him. If this was to be a contest of persuasion, she had been made forcibly to feel, there could be only one winner. Although, and this struck her too, she had never in her life had so clear a chance of standing up, as it were, for a different virtue: her own.

She sat on her bench, quietly counting over the wheel-ruts in the drive, for perhaps ten minutes. At the end of that time she rose—she was hardly aware of the moment of decision—and, bearing the letter openly in her hand, made her slow way to her father's study.

Chapter Five

—

WHEN SHE EMERGED AT LAST from the cold days that followed, the vital change had been made. Annabella just managed a joke about having lately acquired, in addition to hunger and thirst, a third appetite, for legal matters. One might have supposed, from the quantities consumed, that no human appetite could have been better satisfied than her hunger for the law; and yet, as week followed week, and her opportunities for gratifying it only multiplied, she began to suspect that just what would always elude her was satiety. She had the sense, as she had once expressed it to herself, of starving for something, and was equal to the acknowledgement, in the midst of what was really her mother's legal pursuit of the explicit, that that *something* was something else.

Dr Lushington, with his long, small-featured face and conspiratorial hands, had brought home to her, as nothing else might have, just how far she had already committed herself. It was, on his part, the final means of persuading her into a still greater commitment, which she duly made. The silence with which he took it in gave her the clearest vision of just how tremendous her own silence had been. What followed could only involve a kind of diminishment: her secret reverberated, after a fashion, into various noises. Her mother, predictably, began to rattle the loudest. Well, she had given it up, her last bit of cake, as she had once whimsically put it. She had made, and she felt this intensely at the time, the final break, but just what was broken in her, she discovered with a kind of relief, wasn't everything; she had feared that it might be. It was a great deal, of course, and she was almost gratified by the scope of it, which encompassed, among other things, her passion for legal subtleties. She was willing, happily, helplessly, to let them take their course; and she crawled, as it were, battered and drenched but still breathing, from the side of that stream.

She had been staying, for the sake of her visit to Dr Lushington, at Gosford House, and was resolved afterwards not to return to her mother. London, after the quiet of Kirkby Mallory, offered her certain consolations. If her intent was really to address herself to a new life—to treat, that is, the year of her marriage as no more than an interlude—she was determined not to shy from a city that might be supposed to hold for her such unhappy recollections. One of the first visits she paid, consequently, was to Lady Caroline; and she could almost smile, as she made her way on a bright uncertain April morning past the stalls of Piccadilly to the quiet cove of Melbourne House, at the memory of an earlier appointment. It was just three years since her awkward interview with Lady Melbourne on the subject of which qualities she believed herself to require in a husband. Her current preoccupation, of course, was rather different, but there was something in the passage, as she imagined it, from expectation to disappointment for which she was not ungrateful. She was a woman, as Lord Byron himself had made painfully clear to her, who depended upon and delighted in her own superiority, but she might be allowed a little credit for the fact that she was also willing to enjoy the contrast with a former and more innocent self.

It was another contrast, however, that morning, from which

she drew, as she hoped, the necessary lesson. Lady Caroline received her, as she had before, in the little study that overlooked behind her the gravelled walk. A fire burned in the grate, shading from yellow to grey in the squalls of light, of darkness, that blew in from the changeable cold sunshine. Her cousin wore, once more, as little as she decently might, and the frail pearl-coloured chiffon dress hung off her narrow shoulders in such a way that Annabella was almost tempted to try it on. Caroline herself, it whimsically struck her, was only the rack on which it hung. Her thinness now was nothing but the clearest manifestation of unhappiness. Like her bones, it showed through—which made Annabella grateful, as she thus humorously remarked on it, for the fat of concealment. She had never, at least, lost her appetite.

If she had come 'to see for herself', as she inwardly put it, what a life lived in the shade, in the aftermath, of Lord Byron's love might look like, Lady Caroline offered her a most beautiful picture. Her long face had stretched into a narrowness that allowed her, it seemed, but a single muscular expression; Annabella remembered how quick and various the play of her countenance had been. It was almost the task of her visit to read into that face its abiding message. The impression she quietly took in was of a frantic force rendered desperately still: a moth, huddling beneath its wings in the death of a flame. This was the image that struck her, and to which, in time, she had her own reason for recurring. Caroline, however, proved perfectly capable of the odd nervous flap—Annabella confessed herself occasionally startled by them.

'I should like to ask your advice,' Lady Caroline began, after initial pleasantries, with her knees drawn up to her chin and her chair drawn up, as far as it might go, to the foot of the fire. 'Your moral sense (you see, how freely I admit it) has always been sharper than mine—even, I believe, concerning events in which you have a personal stake. Lord Byron has confided in me *that* which if you merely menace him with the knowledge shall make him tremble. But I promised him solemnly, at the time, never to give him away; and I have been trying to calculate lately, in the light of your . . . situation, the force such a promise should continue to hold.'

Annabella restrained a smile. She might almost congratulate herself on how far she had come—the proof of which lay plainly in the fact that Lady Caroline presumed her still innocently ignorant of the depths to which her husband had committed himself with his sister. There was, perhaps, something unflattering in the thought that, by Caroline's estimate, a woman as virtuous as Annabella could never have guessed the truth and remained, for so long, a party to it. Lady Byron, at least, was still innocent enough to make a pretence of it, and push her cousin into naming the deed. 'You believe me, then,' she said, biding her time, 'to be in want of threats?'

'Affairs with Lord Byron,' Lady Caroline said, and Annabella felt, rising within her, the first little flare of contention at her choice of a word, 'end always with threats, on the one hand, and indifference, on the other. I never had the luxury, as a means of keeping up relations, of a child; and I supposed you, wrongly it may be, in want of security against the chance that he might claim her.'

Annabella was equal to the simplest confession. 'Dr Lushington has hopes, and these are the hopes I live in.'

They rarely looked at each other. Caroline, who apologized at one point for the chill in the room, fixed her eyes on the fire; and Annabella, who had perched at the end of the chaise longue, which offered likewise a view of the gravelled grounds, was moved to imitate her by a strange sort of sympathy. A quiet flame on a bright morning just suited something ghostly in her mood. She was conscious of being at the heart or centre, as it were, of a particular mode of feeling. They could almost pride themselves on being, as lovers of the famous poet, the best, most powerful illustrations of his work; and there was, in the knowledge, the intimate complicity of shared privilege.

'I would like to help you,' Lady Caroline offered, 'and I'm perfectly willing to admit that my intentions in the past have never been so pure.' Annabella sensed in this a helpless sort of boasting, regarding an earlier triumph; but she met it, humbly enough, with the private reflection that whatever Lady Caroline had to tell, she had more amply, more exquisitely, endured first-hand. Her silence was suitably expectant, and Caroline continued, 'I wondered if you could relieve me a little of the guilt—either of staying quiet, where a word might save you, or of breaking a promise I was solemnly bound to keep.'

Annabella flattered herself that this was the sort of question on which she could exercise her wit with the greatest distinction, and she answered it with the slightly awkward sensation of being indulged in her vanities. 'We are taught,' she said eventually, 'that virtue follows always a single path. Where it appears to split, we may be sure of being offered, among the alternatives, a turn for the worse. Truth has only one path, though it needs at times a sharp eye to distinguish it from the false. By making vows we bind ourselves to keep to a single road, many miles before we can guess the course it will take. Yet God allows us only, by his sanction, to commit ourselves to Truth, and where such a vow appears to prevent us from honouring that commitment, we are entitled to ask whether his sanction was ever given.' After a pause, she added: 'You may guess that these are questions which have occupied of late my sleepless hours, for the vows I took I called on my God to witness. But I take comfort from the thought, that He who sees everything sees just as clearly the darkness in which we look for His intentions.'

It was then Lady Caroline's turn to smile, and Annabella drew on all of her fine propriety not to mirror her in it. She felt almost, in their delicate courtesies, the pleasant formality of a dance, which reminded her of nothing so much as the fated waltz, which Caroline had put on and where she had first met her husband. If only, and this was the thought that threatened to break out in her face, Herr Wohlkrank himself were present to guide their steps! Their tone, she was perfectly willing to suppose, was dreadful enough. She felt, although a party to it, the tiniest trace of pity, like a thread on the lips, for Lord Byron himself. He had always complained, after all, of the scruples of women, from which he had suffered both ways—in what they refused him, and in what they obliged him to accept. Oh, Byron's women! and the sensation recurred within her of living, at a high pitch, in the very refinement of that mode of feeling which Lord Byron's eloquence had made so brilliantly public. It rose up in her like a bright little streak of effervescence in a glass of champagne. What was really delightful was the thought that Lady Caroline, in spite of her huddled-up air, must be feeling it, too, that they were feeling it together. Their sympathies, however, had been sharpened by nothing so much as the habit of rivalry; Annabella recognized the danger of being cut.

Caroline began to address herself to the fire in a low tone. From the time of Mrs Leigh's arrival in Bennet Street, in the year 1813, Lord Byron had given her various intimations of a criminal intercourse between them, from which he had, at several stages, attempted to desist. These intimations had broken at last into an open avowal, which he had offered Caroline in a hope not unkind of blasting at the root that affection for his person, which had swelled on occasion (and still continued to surge) into an ungovernable obsession, and from which they had both violently, separately, suffered. But the overwhelming force (and this was,

Annabella flattered herself, Lady Caroline's best attempt at a little thrust) of his brotherly affection prevented him from giving up the only relation in which he had found, with an equal ease, his passions sated and his heart consoled. There was a pause; and Annabella felt obliged, for the sake of her own pretended innocence, to fill it with a suitable measure of horror. Just what that measure should be, it struck her for the first time (with a shiver of the real thing), she was no longer, in fact, innocent enough to gauge; but she wished, in any case, to make a display of repugnance that would still give a point to what was really her larger experience of her husband's delinquencies.

'The truth of this (and the only hope of its suppression, if it is true, is that such depravity must be *faced* before it can be proved) would expose Lord Byron and, which is still more to be feared, Mrs Leigh, to a condemnation so severe that its taint might reach, I dread to think it, even to me. I fancy, my dear Caroline,' she had decided to admit to what she could not conceal, 'that you had counted on, perhaps, a less calculated aversion; but the fact is, my relations with Lord Byron have taught me, if nothing else, never to be shocked.'

Lady Caroline looked up at her guest. Annabella's last words might really have struck her as nothing more than a challenge to be met, for she continued: 'There were worse crimes. He confessed to me once, in that sickness of his own sins which always inspired in him a run of talk, that from his boyhood he had been in the practice of unnatural crime. The boy Rushton, by whom he had been attended as a page, was one of those whom he had corrupted—for the sake of an appetite which, as you have no doubt heard, I was guilty in my desperation of playing up to, in the mistaken belief that a more natural outlet for those passions might suspend in him the unnatural desire to satisfy them. I do not believe that he has committed this crime since returning to England, though he indulged in it unrestrictedly in Turkey. His own horror of the act still appeared to be so great that he several times turned quite faint and sick in alluding to the subject; and the worst to be feared, from an impersonal view of his separation, is that it might push him to return to those scenes in which he had so little proved himself capable of self-restraint.'

Annabella was almost gratified to find, in the course of this speech, her powers of disgust renewed. They were as fresh and strong as ever, although she was prevented from making a show of her feelings by a little twist of the knife, in whose use Lady Caroline remained so beautifully proficient. 'I confess,' Caroline continued, 'that I have always shrunk from the contemplation of an act which is not only repugnant in itself, but whose practice is sufficiently vague that one might be said to regard its specific details with a horror that approaches incomprehension.' This was, in the first faint glimmer of understanding, the reflection that brought a hot sudden blush to Annabella's cheeks. She had wondered once, after the shock of her suspicions of Augusta, just what, if the worst were true, the effect of it might be on her own steady virtue—in the falter of which (she hardly dared, even now, to give a name or a thought to what they had done together) she believed at the time to have found the sharpest answer. She had hoped, indeed, to keep *that* secret, if only by virtue of the fact that it was just so unspeakable. What struck her most forcefully in her cousin's last remark (it was about as cold and vivid as a bucket of water) was the sense that Caroline had managed, almost, to give it a voice. Annabella began to see, as if the low grey land were spreading around her, just how exposed in the general dawn of their separation her own private self might become.

There seemed to her afterwards no clearer measure of just how great, as she privately put it, her emergence had been than the fact that Caroline's words struck her so entirely as a challenge to be met. 'I see, my dear,' she managed to get out, when her hot little blush had grown cooler, 'just the necessity you felt of breaking your promise. It isn't, of course, for my sake that I thank you. The most hardened wretch would not have consigned my own poor girl to the education she would likely receive at the hands of her father. And neither of us, I believe,' she added, with what was really, in the circumstances, the sweetest of smiles, 'is a hardened wretch.'

That was the phrase on which their interview ended, though it hung in the air and seemed, as she rose to take her leave, rather to swell than recede. It gave them both a colour and, perversely, brightened them by the contrast it suggested: as a dark frame might bring to life a portrait of rosy cheeks. What things those two quiet and frail examples of the feminine had proved capable of considering, in the whitest light of their curiosity—considering, and enduring, and plotting to adapt to their own advantage. They were certainly hardened, and one of them, at least, was wretched enough. Caroline had remained, as Annabella turned in the door, huddled palely in the light of the fire, at which she continued to stare. Hers, it seemed, was the kind of loneliness that had begun to grow, at its edges, quietly permeable. It spilled out even in company; she returned to it almost before she had lifted her cheek to receive the quick kiss of farewell.

Annabella stopped then, for a moment, in the space her retraction offered, to consider her cousin. Here was a fine fractious restless powerful nature, and this is what had become of it. She had compressed herself, remarkably, to the expression of a single theme. One practically winced, taking her in, at the repetition of that high thin note: no child had ever amused itself at the piano with so stubborn a finger. Annabella was determined to give to the music of her own suffering a larger harmony; she was confident, at least, of drowning out every competing noise. The lesson, really, was that if a life could be spent in mourning what was lost, then the least that might make it acceptable was a kind of pre-eminence. She was living, once more, to win. This was the thought that offered, as soon as the door shut behind her, its own consolation. As she strode the length of the corridor, the sole soft quick living thing amid the procession of statues that lined its ochred walls, she indulged in the whimsy of one day taking her place among them. Lady Byron, at least, was a title that no one could take from her; it would look very fine on a bust.

At the bottom of the stairs, in the tiled, echoing hall of Melbourne House, Annabella was startled by the sudden entrance of her aunt. Lady Melbourne swayed against the frame of the door, which led to her own apartments. 'I hope you know what you are about,' she said. The pallor of her countenance was almost ghostly. It was like a vision of her father, long-faced, with the little thickening aged bruise of bone under her eyes, and the dishevelment of loose hair and too much powder. 'Lord Byron will never suffer for you as you suffer for him. Caroline can tell you, it's a thankless task.' And then, inconsequently: 'Remember, it's a very long life.' She had the staring interrupted air of instant waking; perhaps she had been listening out for Annabella's step. 'I hope you know exactly what you are about,' she repeated. Annabella was so surprised by her appearance, its urgent disordered sincerity, that she could only back away from her aunt, bowing and offering respects, as Jennings held for her, against the changeable spring winds, the opened door.

Chapter Six

—

WHAT SHE WAS ABOUT BECAME, in the next few weeks, mercifully clearer to Annabella. Lady Caroline's secret was safely confided to Dr Lushington, who promised to make the force of it felt by a canny suppression. He held out great hopes of what he called a 'complete satisfaction'. That, of course, was beyond his power to secure; but Lord Byron himself had given, within days, a generous off-hand assurance that he had no designs on the child. It was his intention to go abroad again, and the life he planned to pursue, though large in scope, was not sufficiently immense to include within it the encumbrance either of a wife or of a child. On April the 21st (the onset of spring, to Annabella, carried always a heavy burden of recollection; it suggested to her only the renewal of old griefs), he signed the separation papers, and within a few days he was gone. Dr Lushington, who had sent to Dover what he called a 'professional witness', wrote at last to Annabella these consoling words. 'Lord Byron, as promised, has departed these shores amidst a general hubbub made up of the curiosity to see him—which was so great at the inn where he had resided, that many ladies accoutred themselves as chambermaids for the purpose of obtaining, under that disguise, a nearer inspection of what they supposed might become, as one of them put it to the agent I had sent to make sure of him, a "famous farewell".'

Well, she had made her own farewell, some months before, and without the recourse to any disguise whatsoever. She must learn to accustom herself, henceforth, to the way women 'threw themselves' at the man who was still, as far as her title to him was concerned, her husband. Annabella was sufficiently acquainted with Lord Byron's habits and appetites to admit that the truth of 'his relations' was at least as rich and various as the rumours to which they gave rise. There was one rumour, however, in particular, that touched her much more closely. It was all she could do, in fact, not to squirm at the pressure, and the only relief she discovered was to make of her great discomfort a sharp occasion for acting. Lord Byron, it was said, intended, once he had established himself on the continent (at Geneva, in all probability: he was supposed to have taken a fancy to the prospect of boating, placidly enough, on an inland sea), to send for Augusta.

Lady Byron decided to call on her old friend Mary Montgomery. She had seen her, perhaps, once or twice since her marriage as they made the rounds of the London scene together, but the presence of her husband had seemed, in Mary's eyes, to make of her friend's perfection a significant difference. Annabella, who had always been pretty and clever and good, had become famous, too; and it was a part of Mary's modesty—though Annabella felt it at the time, painfully enough, as a kind of reproach—to hesitate to approach her in the dazzle of Lord Byron's reflected brilliance. Miss Montgomery, of course, had never married, and Annabella had been conscious of indulging, as a balm to her wounded feelings, a sweet tooth for pity at the prospects of her invalid friend. The recollection of this, in the aftermath of her separation, sufficiently shamed her—although she was honest enough to admit that where the sense of shame was so general, it was difficult to be particular about its cause—that she had failed since her return to London to pay a visit to the broad pleasant house on Wilmot Street.

Miss Montgomery had not changed: that was the truth the sight of her gave instantly back. Annabella was shown on her arrival into the little front room on the first floor, where Mary sat, with a chair for her feet, by the fire. It was a grey watery changeless sort of a day, rather dark than cold. Lady Byron, who had walked all the way from Cumberland Place, blushed in the close air of Mary's apartment, which smelt entirely, and sweetly, of her friend: of buttered cakes and books and the branches of fir she scattered from time to time across the fire, where they smoked and glinted. Mary shifted the rug from her knees and swung her feet to the floor and just rose up, not from her seat, but on tiptoes, to offer a hand to her friend. 'Sit here, my dear,' she said, pulling a fold of the rug from the empty chair with an intimate insistent manner that almost brought a tear to Annabella's eyes, at its easy resumption. 'I have been stretched out all morning till I am perfectly roasted. And I want you near to me today, very near.' It was her quiet little mention of 'today'—quite as if she had been coming every morning for weeks—that peculiarly touched Annabella. It suggested that even *in absentia* their friendship had grown and demanded the freshness of variety.

Mary herself, however, was just what she had been. It was almost as if, Annabella reflected, invalidism in her friend was nothing more than the language of constancy. She looked frail, pale, and cheerful in a deep-red dress with puffed sleeves that showed to delicate advantage her slender arms. She looked gently declining, though wasting away seemed to involve her only in the ease of a downward slope. She looked tidy and careful, well-layered in a cashmere shawl, and politely amused: she looked, in fact, utterly unchanged. Three years had passed since the pair of them had sat in that room comparing the virtues of Lord Byron and Mr Eden, and for the first time in months Annabella was grateful for what had been so eventful a passage. She could congratulate herself, at least, on having picked up along the way an accumulation—of what, she wouldn't have liked to say, except that she felt in the presence of her old friend by contrast a kind of addition. She was *not* what she had been, and the difference might also be counted as an increase in force. Mary, she remembered, had been used in their friendship to exercise the superior ironies of her detachment. These, she presumed, had been unblunted by time, but Annabella grew conscious in the course of their interview of the still keener edge of her own experience. It was a pleasure, almost, to feel the weight of it bear.

'Now I won't ask you how you are,' Mary began. 'Everyone, I'm sure, is always asking you that, and I have long been determined, as you know, to be unlike everyone. I will call for more tea. I believe we still have a few cherry tarts.' She lifted from the recesses of her lap a little silver bell and gave it a tinkling shake. 'And I will try in the meantime to think what the devil I can ask you that isn't that.' After a pause: 'Have you seen the new dresses at Delacourt's?' There was a knock at the door, and one of the maids appeared, curtseying. 'Tea, please, Lizzy,' Mary said, 'and have we still any cherry tarts?'

'Yes, miss. Two or three, from dinner.'

'We'll have them all.' And then, when the girl had gone: 'Have you been lately to Vauxhall?'

'I have not,' Lady Byron answered, smiling, 'nor have I seen the dresses at Delacourt's. But I have not come to you, my dear Mary, to talk of nothing. I talk of nothing all day. Except with my mother: she talks to me of the law. But between Nothing and the Law, I trust, there is still enough room for a conversation.'

'May I ask you then anything?' Mary said. 'Shall I take your hand and kiss it and say, was it very terrible, the company of men?'

'If you do, I shall answer: it was a great deal like the company of women, only lonelier and less various.' She hesitated, to give her friend a minute to consider the possible scope of such consistency, and then, taking her courage in both hands, continued: 'Though as for that, there were women enough, I believe, in the house of my marriage. I am sure you have heard the rumours of one in particular. No, I have come, in fact, after too long an absence to ask something of *you*—a favour.'

Mary, in the pause, reached out for another stick of fir. These were stored in a basket beside the fire, and as she stooped towards it, a book fell out of the folds of her rug onto the floor between them. She pulled a branch from the cluster of branches and threw it on the flames; they watched it crackle and flare and turn black. Sparks flew up into the chimney, and the ash of the needles sighed and bent away from the wood. When it was quite burned out, Annabella glanced down at the book, which lay open at the spine. It was a copy of *Childe Harold*. Mary looked her frankly in the eye, with a twitch of amusement in her lips. Then, more soberly, she said, 'You asked me once before for my advice; I gave it. I don't believe it did you much good. I would willingly give you anything else you wanted of me, but I am rich, I believe, only in advice, which is a poor sort of thing to be rich in.'

Lady Byron stooped to retrieve the volume and spread it across her lap. She began quietly to read. Mary, somewhat ashamed for once, held her tongue. She had not supposed herself in a position to be 'caught out' and was annoyed at having to admit to the role. She watched her friend turn a page. Annabella might have been reciting a passage from it, when she said at last, 'I am told you are acquainted with a woman by the name of Thérèse de Villiers.'

'Yes, I know her. She has something to do with the court and is very silly: vain as a peacock, though perfectly featherless. Ugly, I mean. She is stupid, though fancies herself clever, because she says what others daren't—in which respect, I suppose, she is rather like me. Who told you I knew her? It isn't a thing one would generally like to be known.'

'She did. She said you would vouch for her character.'

Mary, after a moment, was equal to the highest good humour. 'Have I vouched?'

Annabella met it. 'As much, perhaps, as I require. We have begun a sort of correspondence—that is, she has been writing to me about her *very dear friend* Mrs Leigh. She believed that I had mistreated her. At least, she believed that my sister-in-law had suffered more in this affair than was generally admitted to, and that a word in season (I was the only one placed to make it) might have helped her to repair the damage to her character. I explained to her how reluctant I was, for reasons that I trusted were abundantly plain, to pay Augusta a visit.' Annabella stopped and seemed to reconsider; she had an air of beginning again. 'We were once, I confess, very close, sisters in affection as well as in name, which is why I believed that her striking resemblance to Lord Byron, and the still-living tenderness of our mutual relations, would have occasioned me in the aftermath of the separation a fresh pang. It was quite like a proposition in logic: if A, then B, and then C. But since the middle term had been proven, as I might safely put it, erroneous . . .'

She was spared, however, from completing her thought; Lizzy entered with a tray, which she set down on the table beside her mistress's chair. Mary dismissed her and began to pour the tea. That was the noise against which Annabella continued her little confession. 'I had decided in any case, for the sake of my own happiness, to detach myself from the affairs of that family. Rumours, of course, had begun to circulate about them, and I positively assured Mrs Villiers that not one of the reports now current had been sanctioned or encouraged by me, or by my family, or by my friends. I could not, in consequence, consider myself in any degree responsible for them.'

Miss Montgomery, with a quizzical look, offered a cup to her friend. 'I presume the matter rested there.'

Annabella lifted it to her face and blew against it. 'I have recently been given grounds for reconsidering my position. Lord Byron, I am told, once his household is established, intends for his sister to join him. It has always, I believe, been one of his fondest hopes to set up a home with her. I have been guilty, perhaps, in the past few months, of an occasional indifference to the plight of my sister; but I am not cruel. I should never like it to be said that I was cruel, and I am determined not to stand idly by while Augusta, in all the waywardness of her affectionate nature, consigns herself to ruin.' She collected her thoughts. Her voice had grown somewhat heated, and she more softly said, 'I have been searching lately for a suitable purpose. My time had been so busily occupied, in the year preceding, with being miserable. I was married to misery; that, as I like to think of it, was the marriage that failed. And the worst of my unhappiness was that it has made me selfish. I wish to devote myself—it is really a question of finding my feet again and looking around—for the space of a day, or a week together, to somebody other than poor Lady B. I believe I could devote myself to Augusta. I believe she needs it.' When Mary continued silent, Annabella added, 'You have not asked me about the nature of these reports.'

But Miss Montgomery still hesitated. 'What is she like?' she said at last.

'I owe her a great deal.'

It was not an answer to her question, and Mary let the silence

that followed give a point to the fact. Eventually, Lady Byron continued: 'I was very much in love with my husband. You have not,
from a tact, Mary, that is quite unlike you, questioned my feelings
about him. If in the reckoning of our married love we came up just
shy of the required sum, then the dearth lay all on his side. It is not
necessary to think ill of his heart in general, but to me it was hard
and impenetrable enough that my own must have broken before
his had been touched. As long as I live, my chief difficulty will
probably be *not* to remember him too kindly.' She bit into a cherry
tart and brushed the crumbs from her lips; her complacence was
just as formidable a display as the wildest courage. 'Augusta, who
was in so many ways his sister, failed just in that respect to live up
to the family character. There was something in her capacity as a
receiving vessel that was not quite passive. She is almost made for
love, and I am perfectly conscious of the implication carried by
that phrase and the extent to which my own poor feeling nature
might be said to fall short of such a description. The channel of
my affections, which had on the whole been thwarted by my husband's coldness, turned gratefully into her open heart; and there
were times when one of her kind words or touches made the difference for me between life and death.'

Annabella guessed that the credulity of her friend would never
stretch to such high drama. It was the taint of the Byrons, Mary
might easily suspect, to colour everything so richly; and Annabella
began, carefully, to defend herself against the charge of exaggeration. 'You know, my dear, how little I like to be dependent, and
you may well imagine that I was capable of loving her only upon
the condition of my own advantage. I had no doubt of my superiority in many respects, in virtue and understanding, though I
could not with confidence build upon my sister-in-law's stupid-
ity. You asked me what she is like. I will tell you. Gus, at least, is
pretty enough *not* to be counted at first glance among the clever.

(I am honest enough to admit that my own reputation proves on just which side of that equation my attractions lie.) There is an archness in her face and manner that suggests not so much self-consciousness as the ready wit of a shy, lovely girl who is used to attracting the good humour of men. Self-consciousness, in fact, is just the quantity in Augusta that baffles measurement. She possesses either a very great deal of it or none at all. As our friendship deepened, I inclined to the latter view. Her innocence was so delightful a phenomenon that it was a positive comfort to believe in it—especially since it might be supposed to allow to one the privilege of a guiding role. That, for her sake, is the privilege I intend to take up.'

'But why have you come to me?' Mary could not keep out of her voice a kind of distaste.

Annabella met it with her most charming smile. 'You may imagine that I have grown a little tired of acting on my own behalf.'

'I don't suppose you are asking me to act on anyone else's.' Lady Byron felt for the first time in her friend the sheer front of opposition. It gave her something to press against, and the effect of such a meeting was practically an embrace of just what was hardest, least loving, most truthful in each of them. They had both at that moment in their minds the last piece of advice Mary had given her, three years before. *I only wonder whether your sins stretch quite as far as you fear, whether loving-kindness and patience and charity are not predominant in you . . . I do believe you wish to be a little less perfect than you are.* Mary, after all this time, looked sufficiently answered. She said: 'What do you propose we should do?'

'She must be stopped,' Annabella broke out, with renewed heat. 'She must be made to confess.'

'To confess what?'

'My dear, have you really not heard?'

In the silence that followed, Lady Byron could almost trace in her friend the slow painful action of persuasion. The fire had sunk, but neither had the heart to build it up again; their tea had grown cold, but Annabella, at least, poured herself a fresh cold cup. Mary looked at her, and what emerged at last in her face was the strangest pity. It seemed to afflict her like a kind of pain. Lady Byron had opened again the book on her lap and held it out to Mary with her finger on the page. 'Augusta,' she said, while her friend read. She watched the murmur in Mary's lips and repeated the name: 'Augusta, Augusta, Augusta.'

'Has she never confessed to you?'

'We had a kind of understanding. But she never confessed, and now the understanding is gone; she plans to rejoin him. She must be stopped,' she repeated. And then: 'I will not be a party to her ruin. I will not stand idly by . . .' Against the echoes of her own shrill outburst, Annabella offered at last a quieter assurance: 'I could not be so cruel.'

There was a pause, the longest yet, and Mary closed her eyes against it. Perhaps she had aged. Annabella had been accustomed to treating her tiredness as a kind of ornament, the proper dress, as it were, to her character, in which the modesty of Mary's virtues, her patience, her curiosity, her capacity for amusement, showed to best effect. But she appeared now rather exposed in the light of fatigue, almost undressed by it. There was a comfort to be felt in her own superior energies, and Annabella was honest enough to admit to it. Her appetite for life was undiminished; she had the strength yet to satisfy it. Lizzy returned to remove their tea. She swept up into a little silver pan the crumbs that had scattered, and only when she was gone and the door had shut softly behind her did Miss Montgomery lift her head. 'But what can we do?' she said. 'What can Mrs Villiers and you and I hope to do?'

Lady Byron had her answer ready. 'We can work on her.'

Chapter Seven

—

MRS VILLIERS WAS THE FIRST to be 'worked on', and she gave way with such alacrity to their persuasion that they almost regretted employing, for the sake of their purpose, so unsteady a prop. She was a small plump bustling woman of forty years, with pretensions, as Mary had said, to a youth and beauty that she had never had claims to possessing. Thin red clumps of hair crept out from under her wig; her pockmarked face truly suggested nothing so much as the violence of plucked feathers. She made a great show at first of supporting her friend. Miss Montgomery had invited the pair of them to take tea in her room, and Wilmot Street became, by a kind of tradition, the scene of their councils. But a word in her ear was enough (it was Mary who uttered it, in an elaborate hush that proved to her friend she had managed to draw, from their distasteful secrecy, her usual dose of amusement) to turn her quite the other way; and she directed at Mrs Leigh's reform the energies she had prepared to use in her defence. Annabella, for a moment, felt something like pity for poor Augusta—to see her surrounded on all sides by such good intentions.

They had decided—it was really delightful to gather each week in Mary's pleasant room, with such confederate purpose and such good cakes—to approach Mrs Leigh, in her difficult position, with what Annabella had called the threat 'of withdrawing her favour'. Lord Byron himself lent his hand to their enterprise. In the first few months of his self-proclaimed exile, he produced a series of letters and poems that bore not only on 'the separation question' but also, more particularly, on the peculiar and tender offices of the sister who had stood, it seemed, so firmly beside them both. It mattered not in the slightest whether they were published or not, so great was the private appetite among fashionable circles for the least effusion of his pen. Annabella (and she suffered, in fact, no sharper pang) was forced to endure, as the London summer wore on, the general exposure of his own fine fanciful view of their relations; and the worst of it was, that no one emerged more beautifully loving and clear from the wreck of their marriage than Augusta herself. She was painted, it practically seemed, in the pink of dawn and seated on the ocean-borne shell of his bright muse. There were times, indeed, as Mrs Villiers read out, too loudly, perhaps, for the comfort of their little salon, the latest of his brotherly professions, that Annabella almost regretted her decision to share amid such company so delicate a duty. It surprised her to find that she had not yet moved beyond the reach of pain, that there was something in her pride as his wife that she yet clung to. Rumours, meanwhile, of every description were flying; and Lord Byron's pen had at least the effect of making Augusta utterly dependent, for her continued station in high society, on the sanction of her sister-in-law's friendship. That was the dependency they counted on; that was the sanction they threatened to withdraw.

Mrs Leigh, however, was pregnant, and Miss Montgomery considered it a matter of what she called, with a conscious smile, 'expedient decency' to suspend their 'assault' until the end of her confinement. This had the advantage of giving them (which was really the opportunity that Mrs Villiers and Lady Byron took up with greatest gusto) the leisure to consider just what the object of their attempt at persuasion should be. Every Tuesday, at about four o'clock, the three of them gathered in the cosy front room at Wilmot Street and discussed, with a distinction that flattered Mrs Villiers' sense of being 'in the know', their own more pressing version of the separation question. How could they be certain that Augusta was saved? This was the worry that drew from Annabella the richest, most selfless vein of her curiosity. How should her sin be expiated? Of just what miracles of reformation was the human heart capable? Or was there a taint so deep that nothing, short of death, could clear the blood of it? If Augusta denied her intention of joining Lord Byron abroad, Miss Montgomery suggested, then she for one was willing to let the matter rest. The past was awful enough; they might be allowed to confine their duties to the present and future. Lady Byron, however, contended that if any common avowal or casual intention could have kept them apart, it should have done so already; at which Mrs Villiers broke in, that Mrs Leigh would never be free of her sin and the desire it entailed unless she confessed to it. Confession, she continued, a full open unequivocal confession in the presence of witnesses, was the least of the assurances Augusta could give of her sincere remorse. Just, however, what the *most* might run to was the quantity that Lady Byron considered in the strong light of an intelligence not unacquainted with the frailty even of remorse.

Nothing would satisfy her, and, for a different reason, nothing would satisfy Miss Montgomery. In the course of their debate on the nature of the pledge or promise they might be persuaded to accept from Mrs Leigh, she remained, as Lady Byron was moved finally to describe it, 'stubbornly ironic'. And so they proceeded (when they did at last, in Mary's phrase, begin their 'assault') on a pale breezy afternoon in June, the scents of which blew into the opened windows of the parlour on Wilmot Street, with an object that remained to them as much in the dark as the means of attaining it were. Still, they contented themselves with the strength that one might, it was reasonable to suppose, accrue from 'first steps'. Augusta had so far given the key to the tone they would take by letting it be known publicly, on behalf of her brother, how greatly she resented the intermeddling of certain third parties in the conduct of his and his wife's affairs. She had in mind, one presumed, not only the active involving spirit of Lady Milbanke but also the zeal of her supernumeraries, men no less distinguished than Dr Lushington. It would have taken, however, in the three women, a sum of blind confidence far greater than that possessed by at least one of the little party at Wilmot Street not to see in Augusta's remarks the thrust of a personal allusion.

A letter was drafted, made up of their composite intentions. It showed in consequence, as Miss Montgomery put it (she contributed, in general, nothing so much as her hesitations), 'the awkwardness of walking on so many legs'. The line recalled to Annabella —she was at the time very sensitive to reminiscence—one of Lady Melbourne's sharper insights, uttered in the heat of a very different discussion, though it had also concerned the question of marriage and Lord Byron. Her niece, she had warned, had a tendency *to rise up on stilts*. Annabella was forced to concede to their hostess, who had got to her feet for once and stood staring out a window onto Wilmot Street, that they had been guilty of a certain stiffness in the style of their approach, which was inevitable, given the delicacy of the subject to be broached. But what she more privately reflected, as she moved to her friend's side, was only that, far from having the sense as she put pen to paper of 'rising up', she had never so painfully felt the constriction of crawling on all fours. 'Augusta had done nothing,' she said at last, to quiet the scruples of her friend, 'to wound her more hurtful in the long run than compelling her to adopt, in all their relations, so contorted a sense of being in the right, that it was almost impossible to *keep it up* for very long.' This little attempt at persuasion had perhaps a greater effect than she intended. Miss Montgomery was finally moved, not only to concede the point and to agree to the sending of the letter, but even to a brief faint show of tears, which she turned on her friend with an earnest-ness that suggested the force of self-reproach.

This was the letter Lady Byron sent her sister:

Before your confinement I would not risk agitating you. But having the satisfaction of knowing you are recovered, I will no longer conceal from yourself that there are reasons, founded on such circumstances in your conduct as I am most anxious to bury in silence, which indispensably impose on me the duty of limiting my intercourse with you. I should more deeply lament this restriction to a relation that has at times been the spring, not only of comfort, when I needed it most, but of pleasure, when the necessity of comfort, for once, had ceased to be the first of our considerations, if your feelings towards me could give me the power of doing you any good. But you have not disguised your resentment against those who have befriended me and have countenanced the arts that have been employed to injure me. Can I then longer believe those professions of affection and even of exclusive zeal for my welfare, which I have been most reluctant to mistrust? And on this ground my conduct, if known, would be amply and obviously justified to the world. I shall still not regret having loved and trusted you so entirely . . .

That last phrase was wonderfully the invention of Mrs Villiers, who believed that there was nothing Augusta's quick feelings responded to more vividly than the reproaches of love. She was a being formed, as she said, to shape itself to the affections of others, as a vine might be said to shape itself to the side of a wall; she was clever only in her ability to grasp, as it were, at the cracks one offered for a person to cling to. It was necessary, in consequence—and Mary, to do their new friend justice, could hardly refrain from a burst of applause—for Annabella to offer just such a crack for Mrs Leigh to reach for. To approach her, then, with a surface scored by the failures of love would act on Mrs Leigh as the clearest of invitations to stretch forth in the full cleaving tenderness of her affections.

They posted the letter after one of their Tuesday sessions and met again the next day to consider the reply, but no reply came. They had, in fact, an anxious quiet week of it, which only brought out the tensions in the ties that bound them. Really, the blustering vanities of Mrs Villiers almost made the two old friends doubt the sanctity of their mission. But on the following Monday, Annabella received her excuse to summon them to another council at Wilmot Street. Augusta, cornered, had revealed to everyone's surprise, perhaps, but Lady Byron's, the sharpness of her dignity. As a summer rain beat against the glass and conveyed what seemed to them the almost pleasant pressure of a world they were only just keeping at bay, it was Mary who read out, with a relish that suggested a renewed faith in the free harmless play of her ironies, the response of Mrs Leigh:

As I always mistrust the first impulses of my feelings and did not wish to write under the influence of such as your letter could not fail to produce, I would not answer it by return of post. I cannot say that I am wholly surprised at its contents. Your silence towards me during so long an interval, and when all obvious necessity for it must have ceased, formed so decided a contrast to your former kindness to me—and to what my conscience tells me my conduct towards you deserved from you—that it could not but require some explanation.

    To general accusations I must answer in general terms. No sister ever could have the claims upon me that you had. I felt it and acted up to the feeling to the best of my judgement. We are all perhaps too much inclined to magnify our trials, yet I think I may venture to pronounce my situation to have been and to be still one of extraordinary difficulty. I have been assured that the tide of public opinion has been so turned against my brother that the least appearance of coolness on your part towards me would injure me most seriously. I am therefore for the sake of my children compelled to accept from your compassion the 'limited intercourse' that is all you can grant to one whom you pronounce no longer worthy of your esteem or affection!

'Come.' It was Mary who broke the silence her own recitation had produced. 'It is almost as a good as a confession. It is, in fact, the clearest she could reasonably make. She says what we all know to be true in such a way that makes the plainest appeal to our decent sense of what she cannot say. I had not expected so much from her. This is discretion brought to such a pitch of subtlety it is practically a virtue in itself. It is almost noble; it is certainly humorous.'

    Mrs Villiers, however, was not so easily persuaded. 'My dear,' she began, 'it is easy for one who has not been practised upon as I have to believe her innocent affronted airs. But it is not a confession; I hope you will allow to me the privilege of frankly disagreeing. It is just the sort of thing she has always made. It is nothing. It is all hints and vagaries, which you trust in because you suppose her capable of dealing more plainly with her own private conscience.' Mrs Villiers, in the heat of her eloquence, had risen to take the letter from Mary's hands. She stood for a moment considering it in the light of a candle that burned on the mantelpiece. The windows were quite fogged up in the wet, and the room was as dark as dusk. 'The fact is, such hints and vagaries make up the only language she knows—it is entirely the style of her private thought. I for one should like to understand what she means by acting up to her sisterly feeling etc. to the best of her judgement etc. She should never have consented to come to Piccadilly. I remember the whole affair. She asked my advice at the time, in the coyest of terms, and wanted to know whether a sister could decently intrude upon a brother's marriage to soften for his wife the effect of his ill temper. But who was the cause of his ill temper? who continued to excite it? I don't wonder he didn't go mad; she did her best to drive him to it. I can't entirely deny her good intentions. She has the sickness of the Byrons: she is the fool of her own affections and never supposes for a minute that she does any harm by acting on her instinct, which is quite unnaturally developed, to be loved. She led me to believe at the time, it was only at Lady Byron's urgent request that she came to live with them in Piccadilly. Lady Byron has told me it was not; and I have been made, unwittingly, an accessory to her doing the very things she ought most to have avoided. What a pretty piece of indignation this is! A situation of extraordinary difficulty! Who put herself in the middle of it? The truth is, she cannot leave her brother alone. She hasn't the least sense of the extent of her crimes, and until she does, she is lost to us—she is lost to all decent society.'

'I don't suppose,' Mary countered, 'that I have either—I mean, a sense of her crimes. It isn't a thing one is used to measuring up. I shouldn't myself like to measure it. She has written just what a decent and sensible person *would* write in what she calls her situation. I don't think we can ignore our own part in pushing her into it. As for decent society, we all know that keeping her *out* of it is the one threat we have at our disposal. I should be sorry to make use of it.'

'It is,' Annabella was conscious of being, in her way, at the centre of their disagreement and strove quite beautifully to make herself agreeable to both the parties to it, 'perhaps the best letter she could have written. She shows herself sensible. She shows herself dutiful. She plays up, even, to what might be called—and I am perfectly willing to call it that—our *appetite* for the intricacy of her position. I am glad, too, of the little answering stiffness in her tone. She has seldom felt so sure of her ground.' Mary gave her a look of relief, which hardened into something else as Annabella continued. 'Her reply has such a fine clarity, it is almost brittle. We may be confident, at least, that it will be easily broken. Women like Augusta (there is no one here, I believe, who loves her or knows her better) are never lucid two days together. She has been extremely lucid, but her good sense has never been so durable as ours. It will give way beneath it. We have only to keep up the pressure.'

'Until she breaks, you mean,' Mary said.

'Until we are sure of her—of her soul.' And then, for she owed her friend that much, she added: 'I understand very well your aversion to *measuring up*, as you say, the extent of her crimes. You may believe me when I tell you that I share it, though I have not had, as you have, the luxury of closing my eyes. You suppose whatever it is to be unspeakable, but that does not in the least make it untrue. You wish to treat it as a thing quite apart, so that it may be left alone; but it runs through—through everything. He is her great love, I can put it no plainer than that. She is his. He is mine. There you have what might be called, in mathematical terms, the inequality, which I was forced in the end to admit my despair of solving. I *have* admitted it. I have relinquished my claims to him, but forgive me if I stop short, at last, of leaving to them the remainder. I suppose you will suspect me of something worse when I tell you, I love her too well for that.'

Mary, at such an appeal, contented herself with remarking: 'I do not suspect *you*.'

Lady Byron had promised to 'work on' Augusta, but it was Mrs Villiers in the weeks to come who assumed the real burden of their task. Even Mary could not help but admit what a talent she had for elucidating the possibilities of that strange little verb. There were times, however, after their friend had gone home again, when Annabella would turn to Mary and confess that there was something in Mrs Villiers' efficiency that she could not quite reconcile herself to making use of. Just what Thérèse (they were all, by the end of the summer, close if not cosy enough for such familiarity) hoped for herself to achieve by such 'good offices' was a question the two old friends were perfectly equal to discussing between themselves. 'Mrs Villiers' Revenge' is the name Mary gave their curious project—it had no clearer title.

Thérèse, who had a position at court, was perfectly placed to keep up such pressure as the three of them chose to bear, at least while Mrs Leigh was stationed in London, in attendance on the elderly Queen Charlotte. Annabella, once, confessed herself almost jealous of Mrs Villiers for her easy proximity to the poor Goose. It was a part of their project for her to deny to Mrs Leigh the sanction of her company, but she sometimes regretted, she said to Mary, 'just what the limit of our *limited intercourse* has entailed upon *me*.' To give up, she went on (it was a line whose repetition offered her a kind of comfort), both of the Byrons at once was something she hadn't the heart or the stomach for; and the only thing that might have persuaded her to desist from Mrs Villiers' Revenge was the consideration that it could cost her, in the end, the friendship of Mrs Leigh. 'She has been kind to you some-times, has she not?' was Mary's quiet reply. 'There were times, my dear,' Annabella said, with the dignity of her candour, 'in which she saved my life.' But before Miss Montgomery could interpose a word, she had continued: 'It seems the least I can do in return is to bother myself a little about her soul.'

It was Mrs Villiers, however, who took on much of the bother, and she had in recompense the pleasure of making, one day in September, to their little salon in Wilmot Street a first report of her progress. The leaves were turning, and several lay matted on the windowsill. Lady Byron, who expected the conversation to demand of her a certain variety of expression, took up a position at the card-table, staring out, to avoid the necessity of living up to it. Thérèse was determined to give a full account and began with the beginning: with what she called, with heavy emphasis, her first *subsequent* meeting with Mrs Leigh. Augusta had been summoned from Six Mile Bottom to London for the Regent's fete. 'It was, you may remember, in the very heat of July. She wrote to me to prepare a dress for her. When we first met—for the first time, I mean, since I had become intimate with her crimes; it was an interview I dreaded beyond measure—our whole conversation turned on gauzes and satins. But I was foolishly dissatisfied. I thought her looking quite stout and well, which by the bye she still does, and perfectly cool and easy. This rather provoked me, but I checked my tongue. You would, Miss Montgomery, have admired my for-bearance—I know quite well that's the side of the question *you* come down on. A thing may stand firm, I reasoned, to a sudden assault, which gives way easily to a steady quiet underhand sort of pushing. That was the sort of pushing I resolved upon, and it has had, as I can now tell you, its effect.'

She paused and refreshed herself for a minute with a cup of tea. Lady Byron wondered again just what could have driven an old friend of Augusta's to so sudden and enthusiastic a conversion to their cause. She was struck, then, for the first time—and the comparison was so unflattering that she gave herself a little credit for admitting to it—by the resemblance between their friendships with Mrs Leigh, who was not only prettier than either of them, but softer and more generally formed for the conveniences of love. A sort of resentment would grow over time in the hearts of her companions at repeated proofs of such a contrast. Lady Byron began, in the really admirable indifference of her self-reflection, to consider whether a virtuous act could ever derive its motive from such resentment.

Mrs Villiers, meanwhile, had continued with her narration. 'Well, you asked me to work on her, and I may say in all humility that I *have* worked. I have begun, at least, to be rewarded by the first results. Yesterday she dined at my house, and I declare that in all my life I never saw anything equal to her dejection, her absence. Her whole mind was evidently preoccupied and engrossed; she was apparently insensible of being in society. Mr V, who exerted himself much better than I expected to show her as much kindness as before (I have had, you may imagine, to let him in on our little secret), tells me that while I was called out of the room he could not extract an answer, even a monosyllable from her, except when he joked about the predicted destruction of the world today. You know, it has been in all the papers. He said, apropos to some arrangement our boys wanted to make: "We need not give ourselves any trouble about it, for the world will be at an end tomorrow and that will put an end to all our cares." At which she quite exclaimed before the children, the servants, etc. "I don't know what you may all be, but I'm sure I'm not prepared for the next world, so I hope this will last." That looks well for her mind. If the feeling can be steadily kept up, I have every expectation it will yield us whatever we want *in time*—but do not think me brutal or even unkind if I tell you the work is not done yet.'

Exactly what Mrs Villiers' method of 'working' Augusta had been, the two old friends devoted several afternoons by Mary's fire to speculating. Thérèse herself, when asked, only smiled and adjusted her wig, and mentioned the effect one might hope to achieve by creating a *tone*. They suspected it had something to do with God and Hell-fire, with what Annabella called 'all that Pye-House sort of talking'. That was the notion, at least, that inspired in Mary of all people a glimmer of the way forward. The closest to confession that Augusta had come was only to say that Lord Byron *had* invited her to join him for the winter on the continent. She had decided, she told Mrs Villiers, to decline him for reasons that—and this was the code she yet clung to in all such discussions—concerned what might be called, among some of their friends, the betrayal of Lady Byron that such a visit would suggest. By this time it was perfectly understood between them just what was meant by such a betrayal, but Mrs Villiers could not bring Mrs Leigh to attempt a cruder avowal. (It would strike them, they each supposed, when it came, as almost immodest.) She may have created a tone, but that was also the tone that Augusta kept to.

She did, on the other hand, show Mrs Villiers one of Lord Byron's letters. The poor woman could hardly, in relating the tenor of it to her two friends, keep out of her voice the short fierce breath of delight. She held up her first real piece of evidence as brightly as a flag and shook it out for everyone to see. 'It was practically a love-letter,' she all but sighed. By this point, the distaste aroused by her enthusiasms had become for Mary and Annabella the subject of frequent confidential exchanges. Thérèse, however, was by no means as stupid or insensitive as she appeared. She possessed the kind of cunning that sees nothing so sharply as intended slights. Lady Byron began to suspect that the term Mrs Villiers' Revenge should by no means be limited to the persecution of Augusta. It was a task that afforded Thérèse, along the way, the chance to strike out in a number of little directions.

'Lord Byron has practically declared,' Mrs Villiers insisted on reading out from Augusta's letter, which she had persuaded her to give up, the more scandalous bits, 'that he never loved anyone but Augusta, and that only Augusta could ever love *him*. He says: *Do not be uneasy, and do not hate yourself.* That is very striking, I think; almost an admission. He says: *If you hate either, let it be me.* And then he thinks better of such just remorse and adds: *But do not; it would kill me.* And so on. And then—here we come to it at last. *She, or rather the separation*, he says (a very significant distinction, I believe) *has broken my heart.* And then: *I feel as if an elephant had trodden on it.* Hardly the word of a gentleman, but that is not the line I meant. No, here it is: *I always loved you better*, he says, *than any earthly existence, and I always shall, unless I go mad.* That is very clear, I believe, quite unequivocal. You should see how poor Mrs Leigh hangs her head at that, hangs her head and says nothing. It is the saying, I suppose, we must bring her to at last. It will make all the difference.'

Annabella could scarcely, at such disclosures, refrain from considering their personal allusion, though the letter also inspired in her strange sympathies for Augusta. Her own correspondence with Lord Byron had been forcibly exposed to her mother's inspection and suspended. Nothing, in its way, had been more painful to her than the forfeit of her right to communicate with him. She had got, almost in spite of herself, into the habit of tenderness he had instilled in her; and to give up her dose of expressed affection had had the effect on her of breaking the habit. It struck her then that this was, in its way, just the effect they were seeking. There could be no clearer proof, she supposed, of the strength of her spirit than the willingness she showed to make use of the lesson in suffering she had had at their hands. That, at least, was the lesson she sought to apply; and she offered at last, to their little salon, a suitable object for the delicate difficult duty they had undertaken to fulfil. They must persuade Augusta to resign to herself the conduct of her correspondence with Lord Byron. Annabella was willing, she said, for the sake of Augusta's character, to accept a responsibility that would involve her so often in revisiting old wounds.

Just what would bring Augusta to give up her rights as his sister was still the question, and here it was that Mary herself proved, in answering it, unexpectedly resourceful. There had been, as she afterwards admitted to Annabella just before bed, over a cup of green tea, a not unselfish motive behind her little inspiration: she had wished to enlist in their cause a figure that might lend it the unimpeachable sanctity of his reputation. She was well aware, she said, of the resemblance they might suggest in the public eye to a 'coven of women'; there was nothing they could do to dispel it so simple as accepting the good offices of a man. The right man, indeed, almost instantly came to mind. No one was better placed to administer to the conscience of Mrs Leigh than their old friend and her vicar, Mr Eden. She had mentioned his name with a cautious sidelong glance, but Lady Byron met it with a bright generous measure of her own unblinking gaze. She was willing, she said (just mindful of the repetition), for the sake of Augusta, to expose to one who might be said to possess the most painful scrutiny the sad brief history of her marriage. She confessed that he was not unacquainted with certain details, and they might expect of him the really remarkable sympathies of his understanding. She supposed that he could, almost as a matter of professional pride, bring to bear upon Augusta a moral pressure that—

It was at this point that Mrs Villiers begged them to allow to her another day or two to 'work upon' her subject. She had yet to play what she called her *trump card*, which was only to impart to Augusta the not quite innocent truth that Lord Byron had betrayed her secret, several times over, and mostly to other women. She had great hopes of the effect of this little revelation. It might just push her, indignantly, into the open. Thérèse believed that Mrs Leigh was clinging to nothing so fiercely as to what she supposed to be her brother's honourable intentions. And it was decided at last, that they could do no better than 'work' in concert towards what they could now more clearly envisage as the end and object of all their designs: Augusta's confession and the conscious resignation of her affairs into Lady Byron's hands. Mrs Villiers finally took her leave with an almost grotesque expression of confederate eagerness, and Annabella retired to the room she had begun to keep in Wilmot Street—her disposition had become, as she put it, incorrigibly nomadic, and she had begun to draw on the full range of her acquaintance for her nightly bed—to write what they might easily imagine would prove a painful and difficult letter to Mr Eden.

Chapter Eight

—

AUTUMN HAD COME. Mrs Leigh had been summoned by her husband to Six Mile Bottom. He had got together a little shooting-party, and there was no one who could make everyone as comfortable as Augusta, who was, as her brother used to say, comfort itself. The colonel quite depended on her to see that 'things went off'. That was the news Mrs Villiers offered, at first, on a dark and dripping afternoon at the beginning of October. She had an air of suppressed high spirits. Mary was sure she had kept something back, and said so, at which Mrs Villiers allowed an awkward silence to grow (Lizzy was bringing the tea) before she declared: 'Well, I believe, at least, that *my* work is done.' And then, when no one replied, she continued: 'I suppose Mr Eden will find the ground prepared.'

Mr Eden, Lady Byron broke in, had only just written to say, that he had seen Mrs Leigh and proposed to wait on them at their earliest convenience in London. He intended, he said, to follow the mail into town; she had got the letter that morning and expected him any minute. He had wished particularly to see her. The impression he had received (it was his own odd phrase, Annabella remarked) could not be communicated but in person.

'Well,' Mrs Villiers replied, 'I suppose I know what he means. I had it myself, you see. You may say that I brought it out in her at last.' The tea arrived, and while it was being prepared, Thérèse said, 'If he's coming now, I guess I had better be quick. I had hoped to draw it out more. I wanted to do it justice.' She drank a little and set her cup down and closed her eyes briefly: to gather, as she said, her thoughts, before she began. She opened them again and drew a deep sharp breath. 'It had struck me suddenly, you know, the line I should take—that I really should have taken from the first. I had tried to make her sensible of her wrongs, of the harm she had done and the harm she continued to do by indulging (these were the phrases we confined ourselves to) her brother's *ideas*; and she resisted me, quite as you might say, with her head down.' She stopped to pick out a macaroon from the tray Lizzy had set between them. 'What I should have attempted is to impress upon her what she owed—to *you*, my dear. That, I fancied, might just be the thought that makes her look up.'

Mrs Villiers waited for any kind of a response. It was left to Mary to make it. 'I shouldn't like her,' she said, 'to look too closely'—a remark vague enough for Thérèse to ignore it. 'Last week,' she continued, 'just before she set off for Newmarket (I was watching her pack), I decided to act on this idea. I said to Augusta, there is nothing that could have saved you but your brother's marriage. Lady Byron might really be said to be the sacrifice he has made to your virtue.' Her voice fell to a whisper. 'It was all but obscenely plain, one might have reached out and touched it. To which she, bowing her head, could only reply, that she knew exactly what the cost of her virtue had been and who had paid it. My dear, I said, you were lucky to find in a sister anyone half so good as Lady Byron; she has been, I think I may say, your guardian angel. "I know it" was her only answer, but, believe me, she felt the shame of having contracted upon so virtuous a woman so grave an obligation.'

Annabella grew conscious, as her friend made a pause, of a strong wave of disgust. It was by no means confined to Mrs Villiers, as she bit into her macaroon. It took in Mary; it took in them all; it quite overwhelmed them. She had, practically, to keep it down, although it passed just as quickly as it had come. She might have forgotten the feeling entirely, though it left a sort of taste at the back of her throat, were it not for the fact of its recurrence. The nearest she could come to describing it (an attempt she once made in her diary, many years later) was to say, that if she had set out to eat her own hand, without, that is, being sensible of the pain, and if she had found that it disagreed with her, she might be supposed to have felt just such a strange revulsion. The best that could be said, perhaps, of these fits of nausea was that they left little enough behind for the conscience to dwell on. She owed, in fact, even the brief metaphorical flight of her analogy to Lord Byron himself, who had accustomed her to a number of ideas at which her imagination might once have stoped short.

'It was then I deemed the time ripe,' Mrs Villiers took up her story again, 'for a final thrust—I led trumps. It seems only fair, I said, to inform you that Lord Byron has betrayed your secret, several times over, to what can only be called a variety of women.' She paused for an effect, which turned out to be as much as she had to offer, though she brought out at last: 'I was made to feel just how far she still had to sink in her own estimation by the depths I witnessed her plunging to at that moment. But she fell too deep to make herself heard; she was sunk entirely. We must trust Mr Eden to bring her back *up* again.'

Mr Eden, however, kept them uncomfortably waiting, though Mrs Villiers showed no signs of turning homeward. The sun had set and a grey dry dusk had replaced a grey wet day before he was announced; the women were about to sit down to a light supper. Miss Montgomery had acquired the habit of dining in her own rooms, to keep out of the way of her father's company—she sometimes hadn't the heart for general conversation. Mr Eden, wigless, half-drenched, and stiff with the cold, accepted an invitation to join them, though what he most desired was a seat by the fire and a small strong drink. Thérèse pressed him for 'news' while his trousers steamed; he sat practically flat-footed on the hearthstone. 'Nothing like news,' he said. He spoke with a sort of economy that just shied short of effrontery and ate, when supper was served, with a steady unhurried appetite that was quite as good as a wall for keeping out their curiosity. Mary had said to Annabella that she shouldn't in the least bit mind the introduction of the masculine note. Whether she minded or not was impossible to say. The fact was, it quite drowned out all the others—and the noise that it made a great deal resembled General Conversation. He was at his most vicarly, as she afterwards put it, bidding Annabella goodnight, and she for one had fallen so completely in step that she had begun, privately, to rehearse her catechism.

After supper, when Lizzy had cleared the plates away, he said he should like a private word with Lady Byron. He wondered, was there a room to which they might quietly retire? Thérèse, undaunted, replied that 'They were all in the business, as far as that went, together.' Annabella, who felt the force of being singled out, admired her for it. Her friend continued: 'They kept no secrets from each other or rather, for she hated hiding behind generalities and preferred plain speaking, they kept *one secret* very much between themselves, and he needn't scruple to discuss it with them. He might easily suppose that it formed the cornerstone of their conversation. Nothing he could possibly add to it would surprise or shock them.' It was only when she added,

'Besides, whatever was said to any of them was bound to be discussed by them all,' that Annabella found cause to blush for her friend's self-assurance. Mary had for some time been quiet. She had retreated behind her pallor, as she sometimes did; it kept off a great deal of embarrassment.

'Thank you all the same,' Mr Eden said, 'I should like a private word with Lady Byron.'

This demanded from Miss Montgomery her only contribution. They might have her sitting room for the purpose. She herself was tired and ready to prepare for bed; and Mrs Villiers, she supposed, who had been so assiduous on Lady Byron's behalf (she could not resist pointing up a distinction), had her duties to return to at home. Mrs Villiers finally reddened; her face looked awkward enough under her wisps of red hair. 'I trust I might have the pleasure,' she said to Mr Eden, 'of finding you here in the morning?'

No, he was staying with a friend with whom he had a little business in town, and he planned to return at first light to Newmarket. He was not one of those clergymen who saw in a good living an excuse for continual holidays. He disliked leaving his parish; he had made a great exception. The quiet immodesty of his sense of duty recalled Annabella forcibly to just those considerations that had persuaded her to decline his offer of marriage some years before. She took a kind of strength from the reminder. She guessed from his tone that she might have need of it in the upcoming interview.

When the others had gone, she invited him to a seat. He said he preferred to stand—what he had to say should not take long. Only when Lady Byron herself, pleading fatigue, took up one of the armchairs by the fire, did he begin to feel a little foolish and, in a softer tone, accept its companion, where Miss Montgomery herself was wont to sit. His large stately head was an eloquent

register of age and what might best be called the scars of his professional sympathies. A little notch above his nose, no bigger
than a thumbprint, suggested the expression that had become to
him habitual. His face had fattened, too, and filled with lines,
though handsomely enough. And his eyes stood out with a practised openness: one sensed that he rarely enjoyed the luxury of
turning them away. Lady Byron, in fact, was unwilling to lead
the conversation, and she left it to him to make a breach into the
silence that had grown up between them.

'I have spoken to Mrs Leigh,' he said at last. If he had had any
hesitation in commencing upon so delicate a subject, it expressed
itself by adopting the straightest line—'as you requested me to do.
She is, as you may imagine, an indifferent churchgoer, but I made
a point, on seeing her one morning in town, of desiring her attendance the following Sunday. The sermon I preached,' he smiled
now at his cheap subtlety, 'was on Jonah and the whale, on sin and
secrets, and it had, at least, the desired result. She approached me
afterwards in the confessional.' This brought him up short again,
and he shifted in his seat and picked up a poker, which was leaning against the hearth, and weighed it in his hand and set it
down again, before resuming. 'Whatever was said to me *there* lies
between her and her God, but I believe I may venture on an
impression—that is the word I have chosen to use—and it is really
of that impression that I wish to speak to you now.' He paused
again and looked up at Lady Byron with his large clear eyes. 'She
was quite painfully overwrought. I mean, it was painful to me to
witness the state of her nerves, which had been stretched, almost
exquisitely, just to the—in fact, she broke down on several occasions in tears. I presume she is not unused to such shows, but they
had become habitual; she could only with a kind of violence break
out of them again. I don't mean to say that she was in the least
hysterical; she was quiet and steady and miserable. Left to herself,

she might have cried for days. It seemed such a terrible effort for her *not* to cry: it was quite like holding her breath. I held my breath, too. I had the sense—I had the sense that she had been practised upon. One saw upon her, as it were, the effect of several rough hands. I did not like—I do not like to think that one of them was yours.'

It was a charge so vague as to be almost unanswerable; Annabella, at least, did not attempt to answer it. Instead, she said, 'I suppose you know *who* she was crying for?' And when he kept silent at that, she added, with just a touch of rising pride: 'And did you give her, while holding your breath, absolution?'

This brought out in him a sharper note. 'It isn't only a question,' he all but cried, before stopping short. 'There is a kind of innocence,' he began again, with a gentleness that still better expressed how much he was keeping back, 'which is better left unblessed—by which I mean, unshriven. Which cannot survive what you might call a full confession. I believe Mrs Leigh has it and would not like to answer for the consequences—'

'Of what?' Annabella broke in, her temper just flashing. 'You speak, I have noticed, little enough of my own injured innocence.'

But his anger was equal to it; it was as bright almost as love. 'I did not believe that you possessed such an innocence, it's true, but a virtue infinitely higher, which could make, nor ever fear, the completest confession.'

It hung there, for a minute, between them (as palpable practically as the heat from the fire), the thought that she might confess to him now, she might empty her heart entirely; and in the silence that followed, she was almost tempted to give in to what was really his greater indignation. Just what she might have confessed to, however, was for several days the question that puzzled her. She had, as a quantity, after his visit, a strong sense of wrongdoing; it was only the terms that might make up its sum that eluded her. Instead, she said:

'For myself, I have little pretension just now to the virtue I used to consider my special pride. Lord Byron, you might say, has beaten it out of me—it was such a great weight. I used to care, I believe, less for the virtue of others' than for my own. Perhaps I may take some credit now for the fact that my concerns are all the other way.' She grew conscious, uncomfortably, of the name commonly given to such selflessness. It was very crude: hypocrisy was only a fraction of what she suffered from. 'No one is dearer to me,' she attempted a warmer explanation, 'than Augusta. She is all that remains to me—of his.' She had hesitated over the word, but the pronoun in the end seemed clear enough. 'I have done what I can to save her, and there is nothing quite so dangerous to her as what you are pleased to call her innocence. At least, that is what I, what all three of us, have set out to protect her from.'

He stood up at last. 'Well, I will not put my hand to it.'

She sat up for several hours after Mr Eden had gone, staring at the fire. She was trying to add up her sins: she wanted to see them as clearly as Mr Eden had seen them. All that she saw, however, was the fact that where she had been blind and weak, she was at least growing stronger. 'You must come again to Newmarket,' he had said, taking his leave in a tone of wonderful politeness. 'I'm sure that nothing would delight Mrs Leigh more than such a visit.' And then, with one of his heavy deliberate smiles, 'It would delight me, too.' Later, when she had retired to sleep, Mary surprised Annabella in her nightcap and sat at the foot of her bed. They talked companionably enough for a few minutes before she ventured to ask, what Mr Eden had said? 'Nothing to the point,' she answered; and then, 'I believe Mrs Leigh has quite taken him in.'

Mr Eden's contribution to the cause had had at least its effect. A few days later, when she was next in town, Mrs Leigh summoned the courage to pay Lady Byron a visit. Annabella smiled to think that one of the hands she sensed on Augusta's conscience was Mr Eden's own. She arrived at Wilmot Street under swift autumnal skies in a grey dimity gown and bonnet and grey gloves: she was dressed, as it were, from head to foot in self-effacement. They watched her from Mary's window. Mary said, 'How pretty she looks, not like a mother at all. She might be a girl still, just on the verge of her coming out.'

'You forget, Mary, that I am a mother, too. It is, I believe, no great sign of age.'

Mary smiled and stood up. 'I don't suppose you'll need me. I should prefer, in fact, to return to being useless. It's what I like best.'

Augusta showed none of Mr Eden's resentments when Lizzy ushered her in. Lady Byron rose to shake her hand, which she hardly dared touch: she curtseyed instead and thanked Lady Byron for condescending to see her. They sat down together on either side of the fire. The beginning was somewhat awkward; it was Annabella who made it. 'I believe we have sat by a fire together often enough to be not the least bit shy of keeping silent'—a line that produced, however, only a greater awkwardness, in the midst of which Lady Byron had her inspiration. If *his* opinion was to be the price of her degradation, she might as well enjoy the use of it. 'I presume you know,' she said, 'that Mr Eden has called on me? He was very much concerned for you. He says that you came to see him.'

'It's true; I have been very low.' And then, 'It means a great deal, I'm sure, that you receive me. Not just for my sake but for my children's, too. I feel'—she hesitated, and Annabella caught a glimpse, then, of the force of her pressure, which could produce in her poor friend so painful a quiver—'I have been left (I should say, I have resigned myself) to *his* protection, which has been no protection at all. Or rather, worse than none. When I might all along have resigned myself to yours—when I might have trusted in *you*.'

It was the clearest appeal, and Lady Byron met it beautifully, almost with tears. 'You really might, my dear. I have been waiting only for your complete confidence to act on your behalf. I hope I understand you as well as any human being can another. I think there is a similarity between our characters. We have certainly suffered enough at the same hands.'

Augusta was equal to her tears. 'Oh, you have suffered much, much more than I have any right to.'

'We all have a right to suffer, to suffer as much as we like; and there never was anyone so taken in by your brother as you.' She let it sink in a minute. It marked a change in tone, and she watched Augusta receive, visibly, its effect. 'He has been your worst friend, as you, I'm afraid, have been his.' Lady Byron leaned forward. She had tried to tune her voice to gentleness, but her manner suggested nothing so much as the enumeration of proofs. 'Our visit to Six Mile Bottom, even the very first night of it, will make you sensible of this. His feelings towards you have by no means been as invariably tender as it pleases his muse to declare. You have read, I am sure, his latest effusions: Lady Caroline has been showing them around. But to me, privately, he spoke of you sometimes with compassion, sometimes with bitter scorn, and sometimes with dispositions still more reprehensible.' She paused and, in the silence that followed, saw a way to bring her pressure to bear. 'The only time when I believe he was really on the brink of suicide was on an occasion relating to his remorse about *you*.'

At which, Augusta, blushing, for the first time demurred. 'It was not, quite, remorse.' But she ventured at last into this open ground: 'I don't suppose any two beings could have loved each other better than we did. It seemed a sort of nonsense—I was so wrong!—to deny him anything.' And then, for she knew quite well the penance she had come to make and, put to the test, could make it almost proudly: 'I denied him nothing at all.' Mrs Villiers had once complained that Augusta kept her head down; well, she was looking up now. Even Annabella was forced to admit that she had been sufficiently plain, but Augusta was determined to make herself plainer still. 'He was angry only because I had begun to refuse him what I had not, until your marriage, refused. It was only because I was determined to honour you. You must believe that.'

She had got what she wanted, what they had worked for; still, she saw in Augusta's confession a remnant of pride, a kind of insistence on her own point of view, which is just what Annabella had determined to stamp out. She had all but the sense, as she answered, of putting her foot down. 'As for that, I don't care for my honour as much as I used to do—it's yours that concerns me. Mrs Villiers has told me that you are in communication with your brother. Your refusal, as you put it, has not gone far enough. Until it does, no decent respectable woman can be seen with you; and I have, I believe, still ample claims to both of those qualities to lament the limits they will place upon our intercourse.'

'He is, regardless of anything else, my brother,' Augusta said simply, which brought out in Lady Byron a softer remonstrance.

'Forgive him, desire his welfare, but resign the pernicious hope of being his friend more nearly. Do not think me cruel. You will not be offended when I say that I think his mind too powerful for you. I could not feel secure that he would not bewilder you on any subject.' And then, with a smile of such calculated sweetness that she could almost congratulate herself on having measured it out, she added: 'Alas, my dear Augusta, you do not, I believe, *know* him.'

A shower fell slanting against the windows. The trees outside bent beneath it, and the pair looked up to watch the last of the daylight, enriched, engorged by dark cloud, cut against the line of rain. Then the cloud passed and Augusta's face emerged from the light into a clearer shadow. 'But what am I to do when he writes to me, such letters, too—you have never seen such letters—'

'All the more reason,' Annabella said, 'to give them to me.'

The price of her penance was plain enough, though Lady Byron could never quite make out the spirit in which Augusta paid it. She did not give way to tears. She did not bluster or blush, and her fine face, just as handsome as her brother's, though quieter—slower, that is, to express the play of her feelings—showed little but the blankness of duty as she reached into her purse and removed from it a neat bundle of letters. She had not yet perfectly recovered from her lying-in, and her hands had retained the plump awkwardness of her confinement; there was something childish in the way she offered up her prize. 'I suppose,' she said, 'you, who are so good, will find a suitable answer to make him. I never could.' It was only after Mrs Leigh had taken her leave, and Annabella had returned to her seat by Mary's fire and begun to read the letters, that she believed to taste in Augusta's innocent remark just the slightest bitterness of revenge.

This is what she read:

I have recently broken through my resolution of not speaking to you of Lady Byron, but do not on that account name her to me. It is a relief, a partial relief, to me to talk of her sometimes to you, but it would be none to hear of her. Of her you are to judge for yourself, but do not altogether forget that she has destroyed your brother. Whatever my faults might or have been, she was not the person marked out by providence to be their avenger. One day or another her conduct will recoil on her own head. She may talk, think, or act as she will, and by any process of cold reasoning and a jargon of 'duty and acting for the best' etc. impose upon her own feelings and those of others for a time—but woe unto her, the wretchedness she has brought upon the man to whom she has been everything evil will flow back into its fountain. I may thank the strength of my constitution that has enabled me to bear all this, but those who bear the longest and the most do not suffer the least.

What a fool I was to marry—and you not so very wise, my dear. We might have lived so single and so happy as old maids and bachelors. I shall never find any one like you, nor you (vain as it may seem) like me. We are just formed to pass our lives together, and therefore are we— at least I am, by a crowd of circumstances removed from the only being who could ever have loved me—the only being to whom I can feel unmixedly attached.

Had you been a nun, and I a monk—that we might have talked through a grate instead of across the sea. No matter. My voice and my heart are

> ever thine
> B

She had got what she wanted, the thought recurred to her, and Lady Byron was willing to admit, she had only herself to blame if she didn't like it. What if she threw the little bundle on the fire? Such a relief it might be to answer his eloquence, as it seemed to her, so completely. But something in the hurry of his penmanship, which sloped and dwindled across the page, made her stop short. They had loved each other well enough, she remembered, in their letters; and this was, in its way, the first from her husband that Annabella had been permitted to see in almost a year. The sun had set, and in the darkened room, her hands surprised her into the strangest gesture: she reached the letter to her lips and kissed it. It smelt of Augusta. Annabella could almost persuade herself that what most upset her was not the acrimony Lord Byron had showed towards her but the fact that she had never been granted so easy a relation as a sister: someone to whom she could feel 'unmixedly attached'. That she was jealous, not of her, but of *him*. She had always wanted a sister. And as the rains continued to fall (she watched a young gentleman with a stick in his hand wait under a tree for a gap in the weather), she considered the fact of her solitude—which could only grow deeper, if solitude deepened, or stronger with time, depending—until, with a smile, she acknowledged the comfort a stray thought reminded her of. *She* had Augusta now.

Chapter Nine

—

IF INVALIDISM HAD GIVEN her old friend Miss Montgomery a defence against change, Lady Byron in the years to come drew from her vigour a similar protection. Strangers approached her, again and again, to catch a glimpse of Lord Byron's wife; and she found consolation in the fact that the profile she turned to avoid their prurient stares had scarcely been touched by time. She had once, in her twentieth year, sat to have her miniature taken by a man named Hayter. He had asked her to lift her chin and look into the light, and the portrait had suggested almost too brightly an angel glancing wistfully back at heaven. The pose, at least, had hidden the fat of her chin and the length of her nose; it brought out what was really her best feature, her large clear eyes. She prided herself now on having kept up so faithfully such looks as she possessed. Her moon-face, as Lord Byron used to call it, had neither waxed nor waned, and her complexion was just as pale and pure as the image called up by such gentle teasing. She had retained, as she put it to herself, a sufficient moral vanity to make of the question of her looks a matter of curiosity: nothing that reflected, however dimly, her spiritual state could fail to interest her. Yet she was conscious, too, increasingly so, of the deeper change that her state of preservation only too crudely implied. She looked, as her mother now looked, all but unsexed; and the gossip that dimly reached her ears, from the strangers who recognized her, concerned mostly the wonder that so famous a libertine could ever have fallen in love with that face.

News of Lord Byron still reached her from time to time, through several channels. Augusta, of course, continued to send her his letters, and Annabella often smiled to see the lengths to which his restlessness could take him. It was almost always away from *her*. He wrote from Ostend, from Geneva, from Venice, from Ravenna and Greece. What struck her as especially humorous was the way her own restlessness humbly mirrored her husband's. She could never settle anywhere for long and shifted from Kirkby to Wilmot Street, from Seaham to a small house in Frognal, every few months. Ada accompanied her whenever there was space for the household entailed by a child; otherwise, she stayed at Kirkby with her grandmother. Lady Milbanke, to persuade her once into a longer visit home, accused Annabella of being 'an unnatural mother', a charge that had, predictably, the opposite of its intended effect. 'I have quarrelled with my mother for ever!' she declared to Miss Montgomery, on arriving at Wilmot Street one afternoon without Ada—a line that brought out, in her memory, an odd sort of echo. It was up to Mary, in the end, to remember its source: she had once overheard Lord Byron, many years before, making just that remark. Annabella blushed at the recollection, which chastened her into a kind of justification. 'Ada,' she said, 'loves me as well as I wish—and better than I had expected. I had a strange prepossession, you see, that she would never be fond of me. Well, she is fond enough, and grows old and wise without me. She is, after all, her father's daughter.'

The world, as it happens (at least, that portion of society whose opinions filled the papers and reviews), began over time to soften towards her husband's point of view. He expressed it publicly so often; he was very persuasive. In poem after poem, their marriage reappeared—dressed up, she once complained, giggling, in clothes no decent woman would dare to be seen in. In harems, on hilltops, in convents, and camps, they fought out their battles; and it was the peculiar trick of his eloquence to grant to the lady in the case each unhappy victory. The worst of it was, the feelings he showed himself capable of reviving, almost at will, in *her*. 'You must defend yourself,' her mother declared during one of their reconciliations, and added, unaware of the inconsistency, 'you must make them forget you.' *Manfred*, his latest publication, lay spread out between them on the lawn; they were sitting on a rug at Kirkby on a calm sunshiny late summer's day in 1817. Ada was picking daisies and laying them out carefully beside each other. 'How is it possible,' Annabella answered, 'when Lord Byron continually reminds them in a medium much more powerful than I can command? Surely this must appear to any dispassionate person. Besides,' she added (they had been eating currants and spitting the seeds in the grass), 'I am sick, quite sick, of taking my own part. The worst consequence to my feelings has been the opposition between my own views and those of some of my friends.' She was mindful, too, of keeping up the battles with her mother that other women had become used to contesting with their husbands. She was growing ageless, and she resisted, as much as anything, her childish dependence on Judy's good opinion.

Mrs Leigh, at least, allowed her to exert an influence of her own, though Lady Byron grew increasingly saddened by what appeared to be its continuing effect on her sister's character. Where Augusta had been playful, she had become shrill; where she had been shy, she had grown foolish; where she had been helpless, she had become absurd. There seemed to be no greater proof to Annabella of her own strength of will than the utter abjection of Augusta's, and she shrank, sometimes, from too strict a contemplation of what she had proved capable of. Even so, the threat, occasionally repeated, of Lord Byron's return to England, or of Augusta's escape to the continent, persuaded her against the possibility of, as she once put it to Mrs Villiers, 'relaxing her grip'. Annabella had suffered too much from the exclusion entailed by their sibling relations (just as *he* now suffered from the exclusion entailed by their own) to relinquish to Lord Byron again the right to resume them. She was honest enough to acknowledge that he had the better claim to her, but selfless enough, too, to maintain that Augusta suffered a little less under her own care than she had under her brother's.

Not that he had lost the power of harming her. The worst of each renewed 'assault', as he once called his poesies, 'on the public patience' was the effect that they palpably had on his sister's position. It was only Annabella's continued kindness that offered her any protection at all. There were people (Lady Byron was rather obliged to them) who would extend to Mrs Leigh an invitation only on the understanding that her sister-in-law agreed to accompany her. Another source of disagreement with her mother. 'If I know anything of human nature,' Lady Milbanke declared, 'then Augusta must hate you. People dislike those whom they have injured, especially when they have reason to be grateful to them.'

'On the contrary,' Annabella could never resist an argument with Judy when she knew herself to be in the right, 'she is, if anything, *too* grateful. It is her gratitude, as the saying goes, that leaves me to mourn. I should like to see her show, occasionally, a greater spirit of resistance. She is entirely too pliable.'

When Lord Byron threatened to publish a memoir of their marriage, Annabella informed his sister. She had been offered, she wrote, the privilege of contradicting whatever she wished to, but there were things she could neither decently admit to nor contradict. What should she do? Augusta appeared at Annabella's door—she was living in Frognal at the time—in so vivid a state that Lady Byron dismissed the servants and admitted her sister to her private dressing room. 'He cannot feel for me,' Augusta cried; her shrillness gave to the long Byron face a very shrewish appearance. 'He cannot feel for my children. God knows he might, at least for *one* of them.' Lady Byron always found her heavy hints distasteful. She had tried to cure Augusta of the habit. 'He must be mad,' his sister continued. And then, showing a little of that spirit of resistance which Annabella had found wanting in her, she cried: 'Let him publish. If *he* is not ashamed, then I, certainly, have nothing to fear.' It was left to Lady Byron to work against him with the chill of her formidable propriety. 'I received your letter of January 1st,' she wrote, 'offering to my perusal a memoir of part of your life. I decline to inspect it. I consider the publication or circulation of such a composition at any time as prejudicial to Augusta's future happiness. For my own sake I have no reason to shrink from publicity, but notwithstanding the injuries which I have suffered, I should lament some of the consequences.'

Afterwards, she admitted to Miss Montgomery her own reasons for deploring such a publication. There might be in time a kind of argument over whose account of their marriage should prevail: hers or Lord Byron's. She had as a resource nothing like his facility of expression, but she enjoyed, at least in private circles, the advantage of being 'on the spot'. She had high hopes that the quiet blamelessness of her life, and what she called 'the eloquence of her silence', would convince even her greatest detractors of her point of view. 'I have sacrificed,' she said, 'self-justification in a great measure to Augusta's salvation. It may be, however, that that sacrifice will on its own prove gently persuasive.' Mrs Leigh herself threatened to become more voluble, but she was, Annabella supposed, so conscious of being 'in her debt' (as a practical matter, she owed Lady Byron several hundreds of pounds) that even her confused sense of gratitude might be reliably appealed to, to effect her saviour.

Miss Montgomery was accustomed to letting her friend talk: there was no one else, after all, in whom Lady Byron allowed herself to confide. But she offered, for once, a contradiction. 'I used to admire your own eloquence when it was a little less serene and a little less silent. Your conversation, I believe, was generally considered an ornament to good society, and much sought after. You used to like to talk, and people liked to listen to you.'

'Now,' Annabella said, not in the least abashed by such praise, 'they only like to stare and gossip about me to my face. I have grown tired of all company but my own—and yours, my dear. Besides, it requires too much exertion to keep up the character of a saint. At least you, who know what a sinner I am, will think so.'

There was nothing Mary could add to this. Annabella's vision was large enough, and she showed, after another pause, just how far she *did* see. 'I have been touched, I can all but feel it, with posterity. It is just like walking through a sleeping house in the dark. It makes one quiet; it makes one careful. I want to be very sure, you see, of the noises I make. They are liable to sound rather loud. I can't pretend, however, that I'm not enjoying myself: one can say so much with so little. And Lord Byron made me feel rather painfully just how little, by comparison, I have to say. You needn't contradict me. I know perfectly well how great a difference there is between little and nothing.'

Occasionally, she received from her husband, without the mediation of Augusta, a personal letter. To prove what quantities he was capable of, she had only to add up the pages. It amused her after all those years to hear again the brisk discursive prattle of his daily life. 'I may as well,' he once said to her, 'if I write you at all, write much as little.' It was just, she confided in her diary, like reading the weather: it was all very colourful and real; it bore sometimes violently upon oneself; and yet there was nothing at all that one could do to . . . influence it. This was, she discovered at some cost to her vanity and still greater to her peace of mind, not quite the case. He offered once, amidst his rambling news, to attempt a reconciliation, if only for Ada's sake. The child was then four years old. He had sent Annabella a locket and asked her to return it with a clasp of his daughter's hair—and one of her own, too, if she still cared for him. For a week she hardly dared to get out of bed; she was nerveless with fear. At the end of it, she rose and sat down at her desk to write a single line, which she dispatched at once to him through one of their intermediaries (she never answered his letters directly): 'Lord Byron is well aware that my determination *ought not* to be changed.' By the time, however, that she confided the matter to Miss Montgomery, she was placid enough to make a joke of it. They had not, she believed, been terribly happy together. Besides, it rather irked her than otherwise, the idea that he might add to her memories of him. She had, she supposed, she said with a laugh, more than enough already.

After that, he fell quiet; even the stream of his letters to Augusta dried up. His verse continued to appear, but no matter how closely she read it, she struggled to find in it the least reference to herself. 'I'm afraid I shall at last,' she said to her mother, 'be suffered to drop into obscurity!' Thank God, was Judy's reply. It was one of their final reconciliations. Lady Milbanke died at Kirkby in the winter of 1822, and Annabella's inheritance, which was considerable, included not only her mother's name but a certain measure of her piety, too. She began to interest herself in the prison question; she began, the capitals were her own, to Do Good. Sir Ralph, who had, after the death of his wife, learned to number himself comfortably among his daughter's dependants (these included, to various degrees, Ada, Augusta and Augusta's children, and several of her mother's former servants), once said to her that for someone who had suffered so much, she had kept her wonderful air, he had always admired her for it, of being untouched—by time, he wanted to say, though time was not quite what he meant. They were playing chess in the kitchen of their house at Seaham, which went largely unoccupied for much of the year and was difficult to keep warm. She declared that he was attempting to distract her with flattery that was not quite flattery; but after placing her piece, she indulged her own appetite for self-reflection. 'My natural feelings,' she said, 'create a sort of scepticism as to my ever having been injured by anybody. I think that the harmlessness of my life is its chief, though not brilliant, quality.'

'My love,' he said, his large face reddening, 'you have many more brilliant qualities than that. There was never any clearer proof of what that man has done to you than to hear you parade such a nonsense of modesty.'

She had never known anyone, she answered, who had taken her own measure more precisely; he need have no fears for her vanity. But he would forgive her for adding, that she had been made too intensely aware (a fact for which she was not ungrateful) of the nature of true brilliance to keep much faith in her own. During their honeymoon at Halnaby, Lord Byron had permitted her to transcribe a number of his verses, fresh from the pen, as it were; and this insight into his genius had given her the sharpest context for her own. There was nothing, it turned out, that she understood better than herself. Her thoughts depended on a very narrow range of ideas. The most that she was guilty of, perhaps, was repetition. She tended to sacrifice liveliness for the sake of correctness. The quickness, or mobility as Lord Byron sometimes called it, that made his mind as various as the world, that enabled him to see, to express, to persuade, at a single stroke, had always been lacking in her. She had, however, other qualities, which she supposed were just as good. At least they had proved more durable than brilliance might have.

The following autumn, she received her first letter in many years from Lord Byron. He was about to set off for Greece, to whose liberation he had pledged to devote his life. The scenes in which he intended to make himself useful were more isolated than those he had become accustomed to living amongst. Could he persuade her, as a rare favour, to send him a portrait of Ada's mother, to soften the effects of his reclusion? He had been very sorry to hear (the news had only just reached him) of the demise of Lady Milbanke. She had had in her possession, he believed, a miniature of her daughter painted by Hayter at the time of her coming out. It captured perfectly just how she had looked when he met her; that is, just how she had looked before she met *him*. It was entirely like Lord Byron to conceal within the tenderest appeal a few subtle barbs, but Annabella, for once, was willing to disregard her own capacity for subtlety. Sir Ralph found it for her at the back of a chest of drawers, in which he had thrown together those relics of his wife that he hadn't the heart to throw out. Annabella, without so much as a line of commentary, sent it to Byron.

Chapter Ten

—

THE NEWS OF HIS DEATH REACHED HER, as a great deal of his news had done, through the press. She was staying in Beckenham with a friend of her mother's—she had lately begun to treat them quite as her own—and the papers were brought to her in bed with a pot of coffee and a pile of buttered toast. She sat up to read, aware that the woman who served her had lingered and stopped by the doorway. 'Yes, thank you,' she said, to dismiss her, when her eye alighted on the page. 'Lord Byron Dead', it declared in thick ink. 'Thank you,' she repeated to the maid, 'that will be all,' and waited till she was gone to read:

> The poet Lord Byron has died at Missolonghi, on the 19th of April, of a fever. He had been sent as an emissary of the government to expedite the liberation of the local tribes from Turkish rule. William Parry, who had served his Lordship in the capacity of firemaster, reports: 'At the very time Lord Byron died, there was one of the most awful thunderstorms I ever witnessed. The lightning was terrific. The Greeks, who are very superstitious and generally believe that such an event occurs whenever a

much superior, or as they say, a supreme man, dies, immediately exclaimed, "The great man is dead!"'

She lay in bed for an hour or two; the late spring day grew bright then hazy in her window. When she arose, slowly, at last, she sat down at her writing-table and composed a short note to Augusta: 'I have no right to be considered, but I have my feelings. I should wish to see any accounts that have come. Please pass on my interest to Hobhouse and anyone else with whom you are in contact. God bless you.'

These more personal reports began after a few days to arrive; by this time she had returned to Wilmot Street. She could not bear, she said to Miss Montgomery, the company of strangers, and Lord Byron's death had had the unaccountable effect upon her, with a few exceptions, of making even old and intimate friends appear indifferent and strange. Mary, she added, with a touching smile, was one of these exceptions: she had known them both together, after all. She should like to see Augusta again, when she was ready; she was not ready yet. In the meantime, she pored over everything that was sent to her, and though she never left the house (nor Mary's own parlour, very often), she dressed meticulously each morning in black and was careful to eat what she could. One of the first things she had done on arriving in Wilmot Street was to send for a tailor. The May weather was brilliant and blue. Day succeeded day cloudlessly, and the light fell through Mary's large windows and managed to make of Lady Byron's mourning weeds a positive colour. She looked at times, in a slant of dust, a very rich green; she looked almost verdant.

Lord Byron at least had died, as Augusta put it, 'in very good company'. It made his widow smile: she meant, Annabella joked to Miss Montgomery, that there had been no women present. Among the reports that Hobhouse passed on to her was an account by one of his old Italian friends, a man named Gamba. The poet, he testified, in his final delirium, had wandered continually between English and Italian. It seemed very strange, Annabella remarked, that he should rave in Italian, he had always raved so happily *at* the English; but then she remembered (they quietly counted it up) just how long he had been away. It was more than eight years since she had seen him, and almost as long since he had left England behind. Gamba, it seems, she added, reading on, was the brother of that woman the countess with whom Lord Byron had contracted a final liaison. There had been some talk, a few years before, of arranging for a divorce to accommodate in him a second marriage. Nothing had come of it. His first experiments in matrimony must have dissuaded him from attempting a second; but his Italian, at least, had sufficiently improved that Lady Byron was required to refer to a dictionary to puzzle out some of what she called 'his famous last words'. 'Io lascio cosa di caro nel mondo' she read out to her friend, taking, in spite of herself, a certain pleasure in the rich strange phrases. 'There are things,' she said slowly, 'which make the world dear to me.'

Mary, as the first week wore on, congratulated her friend on her decent and dignified reception of the news. 'I have had,' Annabella answered, 'a reasonable interval to accustom myself to his absence. Besides, a decent grief is all I feel that I have a claim to.' She was conscious, if anything, of just how little had changed. Indeed, she felt securer in what she called 'her knowledge of her husband'. His dying struck her almost as a gesture of intimacy; it had revived old impressions, which he himself was now unlikely to contradict. When Lizzy came in one morning to announce that a man named Fletcher, of a rough mechanical appearance, had called to see her and was waiting outside, Annabella told her to send him in: it was only Lord Byron's valet. Mary, with her fine sense of deference, excused herself and left Annabella to wait, with her hands folded on her lap and a real appetite for the news she supposed Fletcher would bring. It was almost as if, she reflected, someone had come to talk to her about *herself*. Her vanity seemed obscurely flattered by the continual private application of what was, after all, a very public piece of mourning.

Fletcher himself, however, struck a wrong note. He was not quite what she had remembered him to be, or rather, his appearance aroused in her other memories less flattering to her complacence. She had known him, it could only be said, at the worst, and his hanging arms and square stubborn face wore an aspect, it almost seemed to her, of her own former misery. Nevertheless, she rose bravely to greet him and said, as much perhaps to reassure herself as him, 'I have always thought of you with kindness.' To which he, with his head ducked to one side, from the back of his throat distinctly replied: 'For my part, I've always remembered you with pity.' She offered him a seat, which he refused; and she rang for tea, which he also refused. Lizzy stared at him and made Annabella feel the shame of being forced to interest herself in so undistinguished a guest. He had little enough to tell, he said, and he hoped to tell that little quickly. He had only just returned from Greece, where he had 'served' (his taste for what seemed to him a legal exactness was only sharpened by high company) 'as a witness' to Lord Byron's death. He was willing to answer all questions respecting that event: he had got used to curiosity.

Indeed, he seemed to expect it, for he continued almost unprompted and with a certain air of rehearsal. His lordship had at the beginning of April contracted a fever, for which, since it persisted unevenly for several weeks, his doctors had proposed to bleed him. His lordship was always very stubborn; he had refused. The doctors—there was a regular crowd of them, including the Italian, Bruno, who had come on from Genoa, and an Englishman, Millingen, sent by the committee; one of them was the Pasha's own attendant, a small grubby pale sort of fellow named Vaya; another, a German gentleman from the artillery corps, a Dr Treiber, very tall and weak-chested, who complained steadily of the heat—were allowed in to see him on the condition that they held their noise. It was Fletcher's job to throw them out if they didn't. Lord Byron's hands and feet by this time were cold as stone. The doctors gave him something for his thirst (he was very thirsty) and stuck two blisters against his thighs. He wouldn't let them near his feet—'as I believe you remember, miss,' he added. It struck Annabella for the first time just how miserable the poor man was, and that his refusal to sit or look down and his general air of delivering himself of a duty tediously prepared were his only defences against a complete and abject collapse.

On the morning of the 18th, Lord Byron began to give way to fits of delirium. In his calmer moments, when he could be heard, they just made out an expression that he was willing to be bled at last, and Dr Bruno applied the leeches. What they took out was two pounds of blood, but it was too late. He was talking a great deal, though not much to the point: a lot of Italian gibberish, as Fletcher put it, though some of it English. He thought he was leading a battle charge sometimes and cried out, 'Forwards—forwards. Courage—don't be afraid . . .' There was also an old witch, he imagined, in the neighbourhood, who was giving him the evil eye; he wanted her to be brought to him. He supposed, as he said, 'he would out-stare her yet'. Annabella could not help but reflect uncomfortably on the possibility of an allusion; Fletcher, however, distinguished his story with no sort of pause. Between bouts of bleeding, they offered him purgatives, and he was continually relieving himself: the air in the room was very sour, and thick with people besides. There were the doctors, Bruno, Millingen, Vaya and Treiber, and the young Greek gentleman with the long name, who was called the Prince. There were Gamba and Parry, the firemaster, and Tita, his manservant, and no women at all, only Luca, who was just 'one of his lordship's boys' and very bored. He had to be bribed by sweet things to stay by his master's bed, for Byron doted on him. But it was Easter Sunday, and he was wanting to see the parade. The Prince at one point left to lead the soldiers out into the hills; he didn't want the master to be disturbed by their salutes. Nobody slept; nobody ate. His lordship was talking steadily, most of it nonsense, but they all crowded round to hear, which is just, in a way, what he had come to see *her* about. His master, Fletcher said, during what he called 'one of his quieter ravings', had particularly wished him to say to Lady Byron—and at that point for the first time he stopped for breath.

'To say what?' she broke out at last, after an age in which she grew conscious of just how painfully she had been holding her own.

'Why, that's just it,' he answered, 'I couldn't be sure. He talked of Ada and wished me to send his blessing, and Mrs Leigh and her children. And he said, "You will go to Lady Byron, and say—tell her everything—you who are friends with her."' The personal application gave him a pause, and he continued, as if to excuse himself: 'Which is why I have come. I have done my duty.'

'But what did he say?' She was on her feet now, beseeching. 'What did he tell you to tell me?' It was as if, she suddenly felt, a veil had been wrenched, which had decently covered his death. He was there again, vividly before her, as he had not been in years; she had all but talked him away. But he had talked himself back again, as he always could: he had practically opened his mouth.

It was Fletcher who kept his own shut. 'What did he say?' she repeated. She was beginning to pace and sob, but the drop in her dignity had only the effect of making him stand upon his. He offered, in fact, a face as blank as a wall; she had almost the sense that she was throwing herself against it. The violence of her feelings suggested to her stretched memory nothing so sharply as the noise of soda bottles breaking underfoot. That, at least, was the appeal *he* had made to her; that, it almost seemed to her now, was just what her cries amounted to. 'What did he tell you to tell me? what did he say?' Her sobbing, at least, robbed her of breath, and breathlessness hushed her. In the pause, he offered at last: 'He was very far gone, very quiet and wild. Though not too far to practise his usual humour.' He was weeping himself, flat-faced and blinking. '*Fletcher*, he said, *if you do not execute every order I have given you, I will torment you hereafter if I can*. That was his way, you know: he was always tormenting me. He thought me humourless, because I took him at his word. I suppose he is tormenting me now. *You will go to Lady Byron*, he said—and I guess you'll allow that I've gone. But I did not hear him. About six o'clock, he got up to relieve himself. They had bled him another pound and given him Epsom salts. When he came back to bed, he said, *I want to sleep now*; and that was the last I heard.'

After Fletcher had gone, Annabella waited for Mary to come to her. She hadn't the strength for rising herself. The day grew only brighter and fell through the window in thick squares. She was careful to sit with her face turned away from the door and out of the light: she wanted her friend to come all the way to her, to draw out of her slowly just how much she had suffered for his news. It was an expression she found difficult to keep up in its first freshness, though it occurred to her, as the muscles of her misery tired and the bloom rubbed off it, that nothing could suggest more plainly the state of her feelings than a worn-out grief. What had he meant to tell her? This was the thought that recurred with the low irresistible insistence of a cricket's song. Fletcher's account had almost brought him to life again. He had stepped out from behind his own tombstone to address her, with his intimate grace and soft insinuating voice. She breathed with the vision; she all but spoke for him. *Do you think there is one person here who dares to look into himself?* It was the first thing he had said to her, at a dance in Hanover Square. And now, with an air almost of obedience, she looked.

She considered for the first time the fact that a period had been made in her own life; she could easily spend the rest of it gazing backwards. What she saw frightened her. Her marriage had been, she supposed, too unhappy a monument for even the staunchest mourner to kneel for a lifetime comfortably at the foot of it. Yet she was willing to admit (her gaze was remarkably clear) that nothing she could ever raise up without him would be quite so grand as that monument of grief. She had never had within her (he had forced her to feel it) the capacity to live up, publicly, to her own private sense of significance. She had all but conceded that fact to him; she had conceded so much. And the greatest of her concessions had been to make do without him again. The thought struck her as hard, practically, as a blow, that she needn't do without him any longer. There were others, perhaps, with a better right to his memory, but none of them had so strong a legal claim. She was his widow, after all; and he had bequeathed her the thing most precious to a poet, his name. It was up to her to honour it. She could make of his life the material for a tower of mourning.

Afterwards, she had no sense of how long she had sat there, waiting. The first thing she became sensible of was an appetite. The squares of light seemed to stretch with the sun to suppertime, but it was only her dinner that Mary came in, at last, to apprise her of—at which she turned on her friend the sweetest of suffering smiles.

The curiosity of visitors, as it happens, proved to be a new and not unwelcome addition to life on Wilmot Street. Friends were always stopping by with a piece of news or a rumour of Lord Byron's last days. Sometimes they came only to relieve a little of what Mary had called 'the tedium of staying mournful'. It was Mary who felt it most, and Annabella sensed in the joke, as she was no doubt intended to, the softest of reproaches: she had slipped, after all, so easily into her widow's weeds. But Lady Byron was almost beyond reproach now. She had taken a line, and it kept her from looking too much to either side.

She needed all of her strength of purpose when her husband's old friend, Tom Moore, stopped by to make his appeal. Mr Moore was a small bright officious ingratiating gentleman, who had been accustomed, as a matter almost of duty, to flirting with her in the days of her marriage. Whatever was lovely in her, she knew, had been stamped out since those days by something that looked in her face like the absence of doubt. Still, she was surprised to find just how little his manner suggested the attention it had once pleased him to show her. He had an air of great business, and the sympathy he attempted to awake drew on what he supposed to be their confederate grief. She resisted instinctively what seemed to her his claim to an equal right.

Lord Byron, he said, had left to him a memoir of his life, which had been written a few years before his death and described, among other subjects, it was useless to deny it, the period of their marriage. There had been since his death a movement afoot to destroy it: Hobhouse, Murray, Kinnaird were all against him. Mrs Leigh herself was wavering; she was too persuadable. Of course, he did have at stake a financial interest in its publication. He was also willing to admit that any posthumous association with so famous a poet might lend to a humble scribbler, such as himself, a few rays of Lord Byron's reflected glory. But he had never been taught—and Lady Byron, he guessed, would comprehend his plight—to shirk a sacred duty simply because it might tend to his advantage. And there could be no duty more sacred than the one he had been charged with. To preserve, for the sake of posterity as well as his dear dead friend's, what might properly be thought of, in a writer, as his real life's blood: the hard-wrung ink of his pen. He had read the memoir and was willing to attest, that it was frank, it was forceful, and that it was utterly in keeping with the genius of the man whom they had both, he supposed, once loved. It need scarcely be said, that Lord Byron had turned upon his own erring spirit as strong a light as any he had cast on the world. A word from his widow to sanction the publication would be almost unanswerable. It would be seen, moreover, as the largest, most generous gesture of selflessness from a woman who had always been held up as the standard of that difficult virtue.

If Fletcher's testimony had suggested to her the poet's opened mouth, she could not have imagined, at the time, that quite such volumes would threaten to pour out of it. She answered, to make a pause for thought, that she had learned to depend since their marriage on a different set of virtues than those she had been used to upholding. The old ones hadn't served her so very well. He smiled at that, without opening his lips: an expression that brought out nothing so clearly as the strain of his impatience. There was a great deal to be done, he seemed to feel, and the worst of his duties was the necessity of keeping up, for the sake of their execution, the customary exchange of sentiments. Well, she was perfectly willing to do without sentiments, too. The thought of her husband's memoir had haunted her, like a household ghost, for several years; it was almost a relief in the end to come upon it, as she had, in broad daylight. She had only to prove capable of staring it down. It struck her, suddenly, as the last of *his* ghosts that she would have to face.

He could not, she said at last, if he had read her husband's memoir—if it was anything like as frank and forceful as he described it—have remained in any doubt as to the true grounds for their separation, which had been the source at the time of so much painful gossip. There was no one, she believed, who stood to benefit so much from their disclosure as *she* did. This was exactly the reason that she could not, in all conscience, be seen publicly to support a publication. Mrs Leigh had remained a great friend of hers. Her brother's memoirs could only serve to damage irreparably her already precarious position in society. To give them the sanction of her blessing would be seen, in many circles, as little better than casting the first stone. He must appreciate the delicacy of her position; she was fenced in on all sides by scruples. The last thing she wished was to appear to preside over her husband's memory. Nothing was dearer to her than that memory, but she supposed it inevitable that a public by no means accustomed to taking her side would consider her least intervention as a proof of the worst.

Tom Moore blinked at her, like a man staring against the wind. The case was simple enough, he supposed; he could not entirely see his way into her sense of the complications. Lord Byron was the greatest poet of his age; he had written an account of his life; he had died. It was their duty to see that the memoir was published. Posterity would never forgive them if they failed to, and there were readers enough, he imagined, in the present day, with a sufficient interest in the honour of their country's literature, to condemn any attempt to suppress the posthumous glory of its brightest star. There was no one who stood to receive a greater share of that condemnation than the poet's widow. She had mentioned a concern for appearances. It struck him that she must, above all, from purely selfish motives (he had hoped, in her case, never to appeal to them) be *seen* to act on behalf of publication.

He must forgive her, Lady Byron replied, if she insisted on her own sense of the difficulties of her position, but she was willing to do this much for him. She would have a word with Mrs Leigh, who, having the most to suffer, had likewise the greatest occasion for what he called a gesture of selflessness. If Augusta was persuadable, Lady Byron promised to persuade her; she could offer no more.

Tom Moore bowed. There was a stiff dignity in his little formalities. He was exactly, as Annabella remarked to Mary afterwards, like a toy gentleman: one wanted to wind him up. Well, Lady Byron had managed to wind him. He had said to her, as he took his leave, that Lord Byron, shortly before his marriage, had dined with him one night in Piccadilly. The poet was suffering both from a violent hangover and the usual hesitations; and to cheer him up, he had joked that Miss Milbanke was sure to make a respectable gentleman out of him at last. To which Lord Byron replied, that he had understood the process to be exceedingly painful. He only hoped it wouldn't kill him in the end. Well, he was dead now, but the process, as he called it, was far from complete. Mr Moore supposed that it had gone far enough.

The next day, true to her word, Annabella sent a note to Mrs Leigh, who was staying in town at St. James's. That afternoon she called on her at Wilmot Street. The low grey summer's day was far from cool and brought out, in Augusta, an awkward sweat. She had always been a creature of appetites; it was terrible, in the end, to see which of them she had given in to. She was red as a beet on arrival, if only from mounting the stairs, and the small pale hairs of her skin stood out angrily, it seemed, against the blood of her face. Lady Byron congratulated herself on having preserved, if not the softness, then the shape of her girlish figure. Augusta had grown, as she expressed it herself, as fat as a hen.

This put her in mind, curiously enough, of little Ada; and Mrs Leigh inquired, how Lord Byron's daughter had received the news of her father's death. They had been staying, Annabella said, at Beckenham with friends of her mother's. Somebody had asked her (it must have been one of the servants) if she had wept at all since her father had died—at which the poor dear child, who was hardly eight, had wept indeed and cried out that no one had told her he was dead. She was meant to be staying with him next week at her home in Kirkby. It came out, of course, that she meant Sir Ralph. Annabella explained to her that Sir Ralph was her own father, which made him Ada's grandfather. Did she have a father, too? she asked. Yes, Annabella said. His name is Lord Byron. And is he dead? Ada asked. Yes, she answered; he died of a fever in Greece. At which the girl stopped to consider. 'Why have you a father,' she said at last, 'when I have none? Have you given me yours?' It seemed the least I could do, after all this time, was to tell her, yes.

Lady Byron concluded this little story with a look that seemed to her unequivocally sweet, but Mrs Leigh received it blankly. She had had by contrast, she said, to console those among her own children who had known their uncle. It was quite a point of contention between them, who had loved him best and suffered now the most for news of his death. This was the first sign she had given in several years of an act of resistance, which is what it amounted to; Annabella, in her sister's tone, could all but feel a kind of resentful bristle. You might have supposed, Augusta continued, that they had forgotten him, and perhaps they had. But they had watched their mother weep and liked to claim a share of anything she felt herself. It was almost the worst of motherhood to feel your despair reflected and multiplied in the eyes of your children. It had quite, she said, put her on her guard against too violent an expression of grief; she was thankful, indeed, to let it down now.

Lady Byron, in these remarks, felt the challenge implicit to her own claims and rose to meet it. 'Whoever has once in life,' she said, 'seen a desert spread before him will recognize the feeling in another mind. It may be lived through, but how much of faith is required to believe this! and we seldom take the right way. Ever since his death, I have had the sensation of passing through the dark alone. What a comfort it is (only you can guess how great) to communicate these feelings to another soul condemned to share them.'

'I don't understand,' Augusta said. She was determined, it seemed, to stop short at her sister's subtleties; and her next remark, when it came, was painfully clear. 'I thought you hated him.'

Annabella all but stared. She had seldom felt so vividly the obligation of speaking plainly, but there was nothing, she believed, that could do less justice to her case than the simplest account of it. She paused, as it were, to rummage around and was rewarded at last by the discovery, it seemed little less, of a sentiment that might really answer all of the demands that had been placed upon it. It was practically a relief to utter it—it tasted so richly of the truth. The low grey clouds had given way to the softest of rains, which fell, wetly and silently, against Mary's windows. She waited a moment, and when the shower had passed, she said: 'I feel I have been reaching towards him all my life, without the warmth of his affection, the cold hand of love.'

Augusta, for once, was equal to her lucidity, which had had its effect. Her bristles were all, it seemed to Annabella, smoothed down. Her plump red face looked grey in the shadow of the rain and her eyes rather bulged; they brimmed for the first time with tears. 'I fear,' she said (her tone was beautiful), 'you may have rested it too long on me.'

There was a sense, Annabella had it wonderfully, of something lived up to, and they both for a moment shared the comfort of a perfect equilibrium. But as the mood, inevitably, began to slip, she determined *not* to fall with it and struggled to reclaim the higher ground. 'Tom Moore has approached me,' she said. 'I have little doubt that he has already made his appeal to you. His motives are plain enough. There is no one who stands to gain more from publication than himself, and in the crudest terms: Lord Byron has bequeathed to him the value of the copyright. Unless you consider, after all these years, the degree to which the baldest statement of the facts (I suppose your brother has made it) would contribute to my own justification. Nothing, however, would pain me more than to see you suffer on my own behalf. We have both suffered, I believe, long enough on *his*. Of course, what might be called the peculiar state of our relations at the time of my husband's death prevents me from involving myself in the question of his posterity. I can myself give no appearance of approval to any kind of suppression. On the part of a wife, it would suggest to an unfeeling heart (and who can have felt what we have?) only the bitterness of revenge.' She paused on that note to consider just how explicit she needed to make herself; it struck her at last that she had still stopped short. 'I can trust, I believe, to your own self-interest to see that the memoirs are burned?'

'Well,' Augusta said, 'he is dead now. I don't care what becomes of me, or the rest of us.'

A few days later, Lady Byron received her assurances—though at some cost to her reputation, as her husband had once expressed it, for being 'Truth itself'. Augusta had not been present at what she referred to as 'the ceremony', though Mr Moore had called on her both before and after the fateful event. He had begged her in the morning to lend her voice to his cause. It was not too late; it would be like watching him die again to see his memoir destroyed by those with only the narrowest concern for his reputation. They were acting, he said, out of the very prejudice that had driven Lord Byron into exile, and which he had spent the best part of his literary life in resisting. Had Lady Byron done nothing to persuade her to take their part? Lady Byron, Augusta had been forced to confess, had expressed her conviction quite the other way. At which Mr Moore, succumbing at last to the general will, remarked only, that it seemed a terrible pity that a great man's remains must be left to the care of his envious friends. A few hours later, he had returned from Murray's office on Albemarle Street to report that the memoir was burned. They had torn it up a few pages at a time and fed it to the fire. How they crowded round! while he kept up, to the last scribbled leaf, a steady stream of protest. 'Well,' he had said to her, stopping just long enough for a cup of tea, and liking his own wit, 'the moth has quenched the flame.' The phrase seemed to offer him a little comfort, for he continued to repeat it, she said, until he took his leave, without the least attempt at explanation.

Annabella was almost glad to note, in her sister, the return of what she judiciously thought of as a sting in her tail, although the words carried for Lady Byron no offence. They seemed rather a testament to those qualities she did possess, of perseverance, of single-mindedness. Without her husband's grace or eloquence— she was, after all this time, perfectly equal to the admission—she had nevertheless managed to get what she wanted in the course of ten difficult years. A period of her life (and there was consolation in the thought) that had at least this merit: she would never, thank God, have to live through such years again. A reflection that brought home to her just what it was, in the long years ahead, she still intended to take from him. He had really, in his own way, offered himself to her, however reluctantly, once more. His side of the story had gone up in smoke. What was left was *hers*, and she felt, not unlovingly, the duty this imposed on her. She reached for the album in which she kept her husband's memorabilia. It was almost as if, she thought, slipping Augusta's letter inside it, they had been married again.